THE *Link*

THE *Link*

PENNY LOU LYONS

ARCHWAY
PUBLISHING

This is a work of fiction. All of the characters, names, incidents, organizations, and dialogue in this novel are either the products of the author's imagination or are used fictitiously.

Archway Publishing books may be ordered through booksellers or by contacting:

Archway Publishing
1663 Liberty Drive
Bloomington, IN 47403
www.archwaypublishing.com
1 (888) 242-5904

Original artwork done by Sharon Langford.

ISBN: 978-1-4808-8016-0 (sc)
ISBN: 978-1-4808-8017-7 (hc)
ISBN: 978-1-4808-8018-4 (e)

Library of Congress Control Number: 2019910674

Print information available on the last page.

Archway Publishing rev. date: 8/19/2019

Dedicated to:

My loving husband Martin who has always
encouraged me to reach higher.

My amazing son Jared who has always inspired
me to live life to the fullest.

To my brother Steven who has the heart of a knight

To my talented sister Debbie who has taught me courage.

To my sister Linda who embodies nurturing.

To my great-grandmother Babe who taught me
unconditional love and devotion.

And to my trusted tribe who always proves that
blood does not make you family.

I love you all.

Contents

The Reale Family:

Ailbe – Eldest of the Reale family. Retired as head of the family
Ailill – Ailbe's husband. Died a year ago

Ailbe and Ailill have 8 children:
Ruth – leader of the entire family Married to Se'ighin - USA
Faela'n (Fwaylawn) - Brazil
Ide (EEdeh) - Australia
Ro'nnad - Mongolia
Aengus - India
Buach - Greece
Deaglan - Norway
Caoimhim (Quee-veen) - Angola

Ruth and Se'ighin have 4 children:
Arden married to Bina (3 children: Michael, Rach-El, Amani)
Olivia married to Antonio (4 children Jonathan, Ace, Steven, Lindsey)
Aharon married to Isabelle (4 children Mark, Hayden. Linda, Debbie)
Elijah married to Chaya (3 children Malachi, Benjamin, Amelia)

CHAPTER 1

The sun was burning. The soft lapping sound of waves onto the wood woke her up. She felt the pain throughout her body. No clothing to shelter her from the scorching sun. She felt a sense of urgency thinking, "I have to get there. I have to warn them… but who? What did I have to tell them?" She shouted, "Oh come on! You had it!" The pain was relenting. "Just let me die already. I can't do this! I failed!" She cried into her sunburn hands and realized she had no tears. She put her hand in the water hoping it would cool her off and knowing that would probably make it worse. She screamed as loud as she could, "Help me! Please help me. I have to get there!" As she started giving into her death, she felt a soft splash and her hand being pushed up out of the water. She struggled to sit up and look around for the first time. But she saw nothing. No land. No ships. No nothing. She heard a noise and tried to focus her eyes into the water. There was a pod of dolphins swimming around her. One large one with scars all over its face was right under her hand. In desperation, she asked, "Can you guys give a girl a break and help me get to land? Either that or flip me over and drown me?"

Sitting up made her dizzy and nauseous, so she slid back down into a fetal position. Trying to keep as little skin exposed as possible and barely conscious, she started to dry heave. She tried to get more comfortable and stretch, but her feet touched the back of the boat. "What, I couldn't find anything smaller to escape in?" It was all too much and she closed her eyes.

She didn't know how long she had been unconscious, but when she woke, it was dark. She sat up and patted the water in hopes to see some form of life. The dolphins were a glimpse of hope. To her surprise, the dolphins surfaced immediately like they had never left.

At that point, she didn't expect to survive. She was more talking to herself when she asked, "Anyone have an extra meal for the starving girl in the boat? Maybe some basics, ya know, food, water, shelter? Anything ya got would be appreciated." With that, the large scar faced dolphin lifted itself almost totally out of the water and dropped a fish in the boat. "I must be hallucinating, Did you...?" She was too weak to finish her thought. She lifted the fish to her mouth and took several small bites until she lost consciousness again.

It was still dark when she felt cool wet strips of.... "What is that... seaweed?" being thrown into the boat. She looked around and there was enough to cover her skin with. She called out to whoever was listening, "Thank you, but unless I get there soon, I might as well die here. No one will ever know that I survived." She curled up into a ball feeling helpless. She felt the boat being pushed. "Pushed? Who is pushing me?" She heard whales singing in the distance. She thought, "Whales singing. I'm going to choose to enjoy this." She stayed focused on the whales and the slight breeze. She tried sitting up but the seaweed dried onto her skin and the salt was stinging her where the blisters had opened up. She put her hand over the side of the boat into the water again to feel the coolness on her finger tips. She felt the large scarred dolphin's head. She said, "Oh there you are my old friend of two days. Would you happen to have another fish? Some fresh water? Oh and a nice comfortable bed would be grand." As if the dolphin understood, another fish was dropped into the boat. "Thank you" she yelled up to the sky.

Not a cloud in sight, she cried out for rain, for some fresh water. She ate more of the fish than before and felt she could keep it down if she just fell back to sleep. It worked. She woke to mists of salt water cooling her off. She heard large splashes which seemed very close. She sat up quickly. "Oh no! They found me!" She was relieved to see that it was just the whales. "Have you come to drown me? Have you come to mock me? Either help me or let me be. But don't dangle life in my face then laugh at my prolonged suffering!" A younger whale started to push the boat as she was desperately trying to remember why she escaped. But the longer she stayed in this boat, the foggier her minimal memories were becoming. "Remember, you have to warn them. You have to get there quickly before...before what?" She balled up her fists and tapped her head yelling out to the empty ocean around her. "Come on stupid. You have to do this!" She looked at her body. It was bright red and covered in blood and blisters. Even the bottoms of her feet were swollen and bleeding. "I give up. They win. I choose to die." She started throwing the seaweed into the ocean. The large scarred dolphin came up along the side of the boat. She looked into its eyes. She thought how beautiful it was. They kept eye contact for a few minutes. She said, "I wish I could understand what you must be thinking of all this. Maybe I will understand from the other side. You have been a dear friend, my only friend." She closed her eyes and wished for death to come. She heard a distant voice. "Fight Princess. Just one more day." She knew that was coming from her subconscious, so she ignored it. She had no more fight left.

The whales were furious at the dolphins for not going faster. The mother whale of the calf pushed the young calf out of the way and went below the boat and as gently as she could, lifted the boat and swam toward land. She gave orders to the other members of her pod to go deep and make sure they were not being followed. The dolphins swam and jumped around her to draw as much attention as they could. They were in prime fishing lanes now. The scar faced dolphin thought, "They have to be here. There are always fishing boats around here." The dolphins and whales have always avoided the fishing boats for a list of reasons, but now they were heading right for them. The large scar faced dolphin jumped high to see inside the boat. It hadn't seen her move for hours and questioned, "Could she have gone to her ancestors?" It asked the whale to lower the boat into the water so it could see if she was still alive. The whale agreed and lowered the boat. The large dolphin looked over the side. It was glad to see her breathing but terrified that she was not breathing like she was when they first found her. She was breathing slowly and bubbles of blood were coming out of her mouth and nose. It motioned for the whale to hurry. It called for any loyal creatures of the ocean to come and help them get her to land, to her people. The deep water sharks came up and raced into the fishing lanes. Several swordfish worked together and jumped so high that anyone within twenty miles could see them. The dolphins tested their speed against three shortfin mako sharks. A small pod of killer whales joined in. The large whale carrying the small boat feared the worse. "If this doesn't get their attention, what will?" she asked to her pod.

One of the killer whales announced. "Boat! I hear a fishing boat straight ahead." The large female whale gently lowered the boat back into the water. The large scar faced dolphin began to push it again. The small boat began to crack and take on some more water, but the girl didn't move. They were desperate. The sun was setting and how were the humans going to see her in the dark. The birds offered to join in. One screeched, "If we can't make enough of a ruckus to get their attention, then nothing will." A killer whale saw a fishing boat turn and head for shore. A great white shark broke the water with lighting speed. It must have jumped twenty-five feet in the air. Still, it seemed that no human on the boat noticed the frenzy of activity just a few miles behind them. With a dolphin on each side trying to hold the boat together, the large scar faced one hit the back of the boat hard to get it moving quicker. It was breaking apart more and more with each push. The mother whale could not go much farther into the shallower waters. The whale pup was frantic and wanted to help, but the mother whale stopped him. The mako sharks where catching up to the fishing boat. They jumped in front of it several times before they finally saw a human. It felt like the entire ocean was in a panic.

Tom yelled, "Hey Rick, stop the engines. You have to come out here and look at this." Rick stopped the engines and hurried to the side of the boat to where Tom had one hand on his hip and the other scratching his head. "What do you make of that?" Rick looked out further to see a flock of birds making a ruckus and sharks jumping out of the water. Rick looked confused. "Looks like dolphins are chasing something." He squinted, "Or are they pushing something? Something must be dead out there. Maybe whale pup or something. Let's go. We've had a long day and we're already late getting in." Tom kept looking at the strange activity as Rick turned and walked away. It seemed like all the commotion was coming right at them. He couldn't stop staring at the chaotic scene. "What is that? Is that a dinghy? What the...." He called back to Rick. "Hey partner, you better get back here now! I think that's a dinghy and it looks like there is something in it!" Rick said to himself "He's a crazy old goat." But he walked back to the side of the boat. "Now what are you looking at?" Tom said, "Get the binoculars. I don't think it's a dead whale pup." Rick reached into a compartment next to the door to go below deck and pulled out a pair of old binoculars and handed them to Tom. Tom quickly adjusted them and looked out toward the commotion. Rick said, "Dead whale right?" Tom turned back toward him pale as a ghost and said, "No! It's a half sunk boat with someone in it!" Tom ran to start the engines. He turned the wheel sharply and gunned the engine.

The mother whale took a long deep breath and blew water fifty feet in the air. She motioned for her pod to dive and dive deep. The sharks all scattered without allowing a thank you. The large dolphin told everyone else to leave and that it would stay until she was out of the water.

As Tom steered the boat along side the dinghy, Rick threw a small grappling hook into the dinghy and pulled it close. He called out, "Call the police! There's a girl in there!" Tom got on the radio "MAYDAY MAYDAY MAYDAY!!! Is anyone out there? This is Tom. MAYDAY MAYDAY MAYDAY!!!" Rick yelled out, "She looks half dead and she's bleeding pretty bad!" Tom heard the radio come to life. "Tom, it's Curtis. What's going on?" Tom's hands were shaking and he dropped the microphone several times. When he finally got a grip on it he yelled into the microphone. "Curtis, we were comin' in and the sharks were all over, and and and, there's a girl in there!" Curtis took a second to try and understand what Tom was trying to say. "Hey Tom, could you repeat that, and a little slower this time." Tom grabbed the radio with both hands and tried not to yell. "Rick and me, we were comin' in. And we seen some sharks. Then we seen a dolphin doing something. Rick said it was something dead cause of all the birds going crazy. Then I looked hard and saw it was a half sunk little boat. Kinda like an old dinghy. So Rick caught it with his grappling hook and he looked in. It's a girl in there and she don't look good. We're comin' in slow so we don't sink that little boat. You copy all that?" Curtis asked, "Tom, you found a girl in a dinghy?" Tom wanted to knock some sense into Curtis. He took a deep breath. "YES!" Rick screamed so Curtis could hear him. "And she is all cut up and bleeding real bad!" Curtis, "How far out are you? How long will it take you to get back to the marina? Can you get her into your boat?" Tom "We'll be there in about ten minutes. We can't go too fast." Rick yelled, "I'm afraid to touch her. She's full of blisters and she ain't moving. Geez Curtis, this is bad! This is real bad!" Curtis "Get here as fast and safely as you can. I'll meet you at the marina with an ambulance. Curtis out"

Curtis called over the police radio. "Assistance Chief Cappola calling all available units and first responders to the Reale Marina. Fishing vessel towing a small boat with unresponsive female. All available units respond code 3. I'm calling the hospital now. Cappola out."

Curtis called the hospital to update them. "Hey Charlotte, it's Curtis. Your dad is bringing in a girl that they found out in the ocean. Call a 'code trauma.' Get everyone in. This is looking like something really bad happened out there." Charlotte made a confirming sound and hung up. Charlotte loved working in the emergency room but no one likes a trauma. She made the appropriate calls to the on-call trauma team and over the PA system of the hospital. Within minutes, the ER was bustling with preparations to assemble the trauma team and have everything ready when she came in.

Rick kept a tight grip on the grappling hook rope. "Oh dear Lord, Oh dear Lord. Please lady, wake up. Oh dear Lord don't die lady. Lady, we're almost there. I can see the police lights. Come on lady, please wake up." It took over thirty minutes before Tom limped the boat into the marina. Three officers saw that the dinghy was falling apart and sinking quickly. The naked woman inside was not moving and the water was almost covering her mouth. They flipped off their shoes and unclipped their gun belts, which fell onto the wooded dock with a thud. They grabbed a cervical collar and jumped in the water. Curtis grabbed a blanket and laid it down across the dock. One officer gently put on the neck brace and the two officers lifted her up out of the water and onto the blanket. No one noticed the large dolphin a few inches away. Once the girl was out of the water, the dolphin swam back out to sea. Curtis felt a wave of nausea at the sight of her. He muttered to himself, "Who could have done something like this!" He reached down and touched her shoulder. He felt it. He felt that feeling when he greets a family member. He tried to think of who she might be. He half mumbled, "Impossible." He shook it off thinking, "I know my family. She is not a Reale....is she? Oh stop it. There couldn't be a Reale that I don't know about."

The paramedics tried to start an IV, but there was no place that they could touch her. One paramedic called out, "Let's just get her to the hospital. They can put in a central line. She's too dehydrated. I'd just be adding to her pain. LET'S GET MOVING GENTLEMEN!" They lifted the four corners of the blanket, placed her onto the stretcher, and into the ambulance. Without another word, they were speeding down the street lights and sirens toward the hospital.

Arden was up and sitting out on the second floor deck when he saw flashing lights in the distance. He thought, "Wonder what happened at the marina?" He was mildly curious but had plenty of other things to do, when Curtis linked to him. "Call me." Arden called him on his phone. "Good evening cousin. I saw the lights down at the marina. Are you involved with that?" Curtis always loved talking to Arden. He got right to the point. "Listen, Tom and Rick found a girl out in the water and she's pretty bad. Um, I think...." Arden cut him off and said, "I will call the hospital. Whatever she needs, she will get without question. Have a good evening." and was about to hang up when Curtis quickly added, "No Arden wait, I don't mean she needs money help. I think she is a Reale." Arden blurted out, "WHAT? That's impossible. I'm the head of the protectors, I would know if any family member needed help. What would make you think she is a Reale?" Curtis "Listen Arden, I thought the same thing. But when I touched her... I mean I felt it. She could link, but when I tried, I got nothing. Maybe if she was conscious, I don't know. I think you need to get down to the hospital right now." Arden rubbed his face hard. "I don't know what to say. I'll talk to Mother and we'll be there shortly." He hung up the phone without pleasantries.

Arden linked to his mother Ruth. "I'm coming up. Be dressed. We leave in ten minutes." He then linked with all the protectors. "Michael, Jonathan, Mark, Malachi, we leave for the hospital in ten minutes. Everyone else… we are on alert. Have teams of four parked every five miles from here to the hospital and wait my orders. I want to know everything, about everyone, in and around the hospital. Monitor but do not get involved." Arden broke the link and knocked on his mother's door. It was partially open, so he walked in. His mother was assigned as the leader of the entire family almost a year ago, and she is perfect for position. He stood in the doorway watching his mother calmly get ready. She turned to him, "Fill me in." Arden shrugged his shoulders and said, "I don't know much. I spoke to Curtis, Tom and Rick found a girl out at sea. In pretty bad shape from what I gather. He doesn't know her, but when he touched her, he felt that he could link to her." Ruth stopped dead in her tracks. "Impossible! Get James Kelly on the phone. I will talk to him in the car." Ruth was out the door before he could pull out his phone. He oddly loved the sound of her shoes of the marble floor. He took a deep breath and turned to follow.

Everyone in the Reale family had a job to do. The protectors start their training from a very young age. By the age of twenty-one, they were proficient in controlling most situations quickly and efficiently by whatever means necessary. Great-Grandmother Ailbe, who is the last of her generation and just abdicated her position as the leader of the entire family, just turned 104 years old. Ailbe had a soft spot in her heart for the protectors. Not only was she a protector in her younger years, she also, up until recently, still taught several of the classes. She even enjoyed participating in a few of them now and then. Countless young protectors underestimated her ability and have the scars to prove that she is not one to be trifled with. She had been visiting all the clanns to say her good-byes. She had chosen her time to go be with her ancestors. The July 4th party here at the compound was always her favorite, so she decided to stay here until she isn't anymore.

Ruth linked to Ailbe to wake up. "We have an issue. I'm getting in the elevator now." Ailbe was at her door by the time the elevator opened. Ailbe hugged her daughter tightly. (Too tight for Ruth's liking) Ailbe said,

"Tell me what has happened that you wake me up at this ungodly hour." Ruth and Arden stood there for a second before Ailbe said, "Oh come on children. I'm not getting any younger." She took Ruth's hand and Ruth linked the information. Ailbe laughed under her breath. "I think Curtis has been living with the De'nola for too long. There is no way a member of my family is missing, has been missing, or ever will be missing. It is impossible. But just to error on the side of caution. Let me ask to the clann." She closed her eye and opened a link to her children. Linking a lifetime can take a few minutes. So it only took a few moments to link about this girl and for her children to link to their children and so on, until everyone was accounted for. Ailbe smiled and reassured Ruth and Arden. "This unfortunate girl will have the best medical care possible, but she is clearly not a family member." Ruth "I'm going to the hospital to see for myself. The official story will be that a distant family member was on a yacht with some girlfriend, they met with some harsh weather, and the yacht went down. We are hopeful that this woman is our niece, but seeing we have never met her, she will have to be properly identified by her father who will be arriving from Norway in a few days. Is there a rejection of this?" Ailbe and Arden both nodded no. Ruth kissed her mother on the cheek. Ailbe said, "I have chosen very wisely." and closed her door.

Jonathan was the only one who could transport his grandmother Ruth anywhere. It was a huge honor, and he took pride in the fact that he could pilot any vehicle. Ruth and Arden stepped out the front door and into the waiting car. Jonathan and Michael in the lead car and two other cars followed closely behind them. Mark driving one, and Malachi driving the other.

As they arrived at the hospital, they were keenly aware of the utter chaos that was going on behind the Emergency Room doors. The Reale family owns almost half of the island, and has been here long before any records were kept. The family has intimate ties to just about everything. So when the hospital heard from the police department that this could be a Reale family member, then a call from Ruth Reale to the CEO, they called in every doctor that was available. Every test was being done. Everything was by the book.

Ruth stepped into the hospital first and was immediately greeted by the CEO Mr. Kelly and his wife Piper. They looked disheveled as they both walked towards her with out stretched hands. Mr. Kelly "Mrs. Reale, so nice to see you, but I hate under these circumstances. How can I help make this better for you and your family?" Michael loved watching his grandmother at work. There was no one better at making people perform at high standards, and putting them at ease at the same time.

Ruth smiled and took Piper by the hand and said. "Oh dear Piper, I'm sorry to hear about your grandmother. Did you get the flowers I sent?" Piper was shocked that at a time like this that she would remember her family. "Yes I did. Thank you, but I'm here for you, not the other way around." Mr. Kelly chimed in, "Mrs. Reale, we don't know very much just yet. The doctors are in with her now. She is getting the best care possible. She only arrived a short time ago. I can't pull anyone away for fear of delaying her care. I hope you can understand that." Ruth nodded in agreement.

Arden spoke up. "How long do you think before we can get an update or even see her?" Mr. Kelly looked down at his hands and started to respond slowly. "Well, you see… in a trauma, our staff can do everything perfectly and… um… you see. Sometimes a patient's condition…um… or… injuries are so severe that… um… let me put it this way…when she came in, she is severely sunburn, over her entire body… That is the least of her health issues. Her kidneys have failed. We are giving her a fluid challenge now. The Nephrologist, Dr. Kara Cronin is here as well…" Michael was bursting at the seams and cut in saying, "Mr. Kelly, please just tell us. We don't have time to beat around the bush like this." Mr. Kelly looked embarrassed and said, "This is difficult for me to say. Our families are much more than professional acquaintances. Ruth, you and my mother are good friends. So it pains me to say that her injuries are severe. Her condition is grave. If she has any family that would like to come and say their final good-byes, now is the time." Everyone stood there in shock. Ruth finally broke the silence. "Well, allow me to elaborate on what I know. My brother Deaglan from Norway allowed his granddaughter to go off on a yacht with several girlfriends. They apparently met with bad weather, and a search party ensued. Not knowing where they were, the family set out a

broad net to search. We were informed that they might have been heading
to us for the July 4th festivities. So by that account, we can only assume
that this young woman is part of that group. Her father Elias is scheduled
to arrive in a few days. In the mean time, I am her health care proxy and
Michael will be the secondary until we have further information. Now I
must insist on seeing my grandniece. Even for a second, but I must insist."

Michael watched how she carried herself and chose her words. He was
always impressed by her grace and charm. Mr. Kelly held up his hand. "I
understand. Let me check for you and I will be right back. Piper can show
you to my office." Ruth pushed back her shoulders. "No thank you. I will
wait right here." He hesitated before he turned and walked through the
large double doors. Michael could see inside, it reminded him of a swarming hornet's nest.

About ten minutes later, Mr. Kelly walked back out with Dr. Kevin
Scott, who has been a long time family friend and had stitched up every protector more than once. Behind them was Charlotte. Charlotte
and Michael have been dating for more than five years. Michael had
plans to propose to her at the July 4th party. He had already spoken to his
great-grandmother, his grandparents, and both his parents. Grandmother
did not forbid anyone from marrying a De'nola, a human, but she felt that it
took a very special De'nola to marry into this family. She needed him to be
positive about her loyalty. Michael's only hesitation was when he saw his
aunts and uncles, their bonds were so strong. They had no secrets because
they had nothing to hide from anyone in the family. He wondered if he
could ever have that with her. But Charlotte was everything he wanted.
She was kind, generous, smart, funny, and was good friends with a lot of
his cousins. He knew that his sister Rach-El and Charlotte were already
knee deep in planning the wedding. Michael had about two months to
plan the perfect proposal. It would have to be spectacular. He was the heir
to the line of leaders of the entire family. He had to live up to everyone's
expectations.

Michael smiled when he saw Charlotte but she didn't even look up
at him. He knew that the girl must be in worse shape than he thought.
Dr. Scott started by saying, "Ruth, I am so sorry to see you under such

circumstances. I will let you and Arden come in, BUT strictly for one minute. Let me tell you what I know so far. Her kidneys have failed, she has 2cd degree burns over her entire body, she has fluid in her lungs, she has lost a lot of blood, her blood pressure is critically low, she is running a high fever, but most disturbing are the scars. Now this is important. What do you know of those scars?" Ruth rarely looked flustered. She held back tears. "What scars?" Michael thought of all the stitches he had received that left scars, no one blinks. But a girl gets a scar and the government is called for child abuse. Dr. Scott continued, "She has scars over most of her body. Some were crudely sutured but many seem to have been left unattended. I've never seen anything like it. Her x-rays are coming back slowly, but the radiologist called me to tell me that it looks like almost every bone has been broken, if not once, then several times. Ruth, this girl has been tortured for years. This is not a girl that has been missing for a week. This is a girl that was kept alive just to cause as much pain as possible."

Ruth's knees buckled and with lighting speed, Arden and Jonathan grabbed her. Her tears could not be held back. With all the strength she could muster, she said, "My brother told me she ran away in her early teens and has just recently been reunited. I didn't want to share such untidy family business. It makes no difference who she is. I will take full financial responsibility for her medical bills. Now I ask for the last time. May I please see her?" Dr. Scott looked down. "Ruth, I'm so very sorry." Ruth pulled her shoulders back and said, "Thank you my old friend. We will see to it that justice is granted to this child." She turned to Michael. "You and I will go in. Thankfully Charlotte is here." She looked at Jonathan, "Please have the car ready. We will leave soon."

Ruth took Michael's hand. Michael felt an odd twinge of fear, which was a foreign feeling for him. He had been trained all over the world in martial arts, weapons and survival. A sick girl is not going to get to him. He prepared himself for what Dr. Scott told his grandmother. He would be strong for her. They were lead into the large trauma room. The room was shoulder to shoulder medical staff. Michael saw blood on every surface. Charlotte called into the room before they walked in, "Cover her NOW! Her family is here." They followed Charlotte to her side. Michael was taking in every detail of the room, the people, names on IV bags, bottles of injectable medications, monitors, and counting how many tubes where going under that sheet. He wondered if the blood on the ceiling was her's, and how it could have gotten there. He held onto Ruth with a firm grip. It reminded her of how her mother would hold her when she was terrified. Ruth stepped to the head of the hospital gurney and leaned down to kiss her forehead. As if she was hit by lighting, she sprang up and ran out of the room. The room became eerily quiet. Michael didn't know if he should follow her. He tried to link with her, but all he heard was her linking with Ailbe, so he turned to see Charlotte. Her face was tearstained. He looked at everyone's faces for the first time and took note that everyone in the room had tears streaming down their faces. He nodded at Charlotte and followed his grandmother out of the hospital.

Once outside, he noticed his grandmother was out of breath, Jonathan was at her side. She looked at Michael as if she was angry with him. She struggled to lift her shaking hand, pointed at him and firmly said, "You are now charged as her protector. You have no other duties until this is resolved. Do not let her know another second of pain or fear! The protectors are under your command." She turned toward Jonathan, "He will need your support. I partially release you from your duties to me, but not right now. Take me back to the compound." Arden patted Michael on the back. "Congratulations, you have passed your training. I now give you my position as head of the protectors." He turned without a word, got in the car and they were gone.

Ruth linked with Ailbe. "Mother, she is Azili. Be ready in thirty minutes. I want you to leave tonight." Ailbe "There are a few things I need to do first. I won't be thrown into disorder. That is how mistakes are made. We will be methodical in moving forward." Ruth knew she was right. She linked to Bina. "Call each elder on the phone. Do not link this. Update them. Tell them we must figure out who she is and fast. She is Azili. Someone must know her." Ruth linked to Curtis. "You were right of course. She is a Reale. I'm sure you took a crime scene photo of her face, use the De'nola methods to see if you can find out who she is." Ruth linked to Rach-El. "In a few hours, text Charlotte for an update. Get the gossip.

You know the family line." Ruth linked to the protectors. "Take your orders from Michael. Stay linked with him."

Michael stayed linked to the protectors. "Ok guys. She's one of ours. Let's do this family proud and catch the son of bitch who did this." He started assigning four members to a team. "Team 1, when you get here, two outside the doors and two check parameters. Switch out every 4 hours. No one gets in or out without me knowing every detail." They knew exactly what to do. Michael was confident that this was now the second safest place on the planet.

Michael walked back into the hospital with Mark and Malachi. They split up and checked every corner of the hospital and hospital grounds before anyone knew what was going on. Michael went to Mr. Kelly's office. The door was open so he walked in and started to call out, "Mr. Kelly, it's me. Michael Reale." Mr. Kelly came around the corner. "Michael, what can I help you with?" Michael "I need regular updates on my cousin." Mr. Kelly "Well the problem is that we still don't have a proper identification on her. We have her as 'Jane Doe' right now." Michael "My grandmother is on the phone with her father now to arrange photo ID and proper signatures. The police officer at the marina took her photo and we emailed it to her father. He has positively identified her as his daughter. As Grandmother said, I will be her health care proxy until her father arrives. And make no mistake sir, she is my cousin and I am not leaving her side."

Mr. Kelly was well aware of how close-knit the Reale family was. He asked, "What's her name? I'll update the computer. But I don't want you to worry about her here. We have a fantastic security team. We have never had a violent incident here." Michael was caught off guard. He never even thought of a name. "Her name? Um her name is Anastasia. Yes, Anastasia Reale." Michael heard a quick 'uck' in the distance. He ignored it. The two men finished some financial paperwork to insure payment. Once completed, Michael asked, "When can I see Anastasia?" Mr. Kelly "Lets walk down together and see if we have any news." The two men walked in silence back to the ER waiting room.

Michael felt like an eternity had passed before he saw Dr. Scott and Charlotte walk through the doors. They both had a slight smile. Michael stood up and could not contain himself. "When can I see my cousin?" Dr. Scott "Listen son, I know this is difficult, but I need to speak to the legal next of kin immediately. She is in tough shape. I don't think she can hold on until her father gets here." Michael "I'm her health care proxy, does that make me the person to speak to?" Dr. Scott "Michael, don't play the tough guy with me. I pulled more crap out of that nose of yours and told more lies to your parents to protect you and Jonathan from getting your asses beat. I need that poor girl's father to know that she is dying. I want him to know, father to father, that I'm trying my best, but he needs to hurry up and get here. Now I will take you back to her, but you better drop this macho bullshit!" Michael had never been talked to like that before. He didn't know if he should stand up and be the head of the protectors or crawl under a rock. Dr. Scott was waving him to follow and Charlotte was standing off to the side. Michael caught up to Dr. Scott and whispered in his ear. "Your son is the one that held me down and pushed those peas up my nose." The two men laughed as the walked down the hall and disappeared through the double doors.

Ruth was on the phone with a family lawyer regarding proper signatures on legal forms and proper identification. Aharon's daughter Debbie took the photo that Curtis had taken, photo shopped out the sunburn and blisters, then de-aged her fifteen years, added a scenic background, and just like that, they had an old photo of Anastasia Reale. Ruth then sent it to the family lawyer. The lawyer said, "I trust you Mrs. Reale, but I'm putting my neck on the line." Ruth "I understand, but you know that neither I, nor anyone else in my family has ever lied to you. I have positively identified her as my niece. All I need for the hospital is for her to be identified legally, that is the only reason why I woke you up at 3a.m." The lawyer responded, "Ok, I understand the urgency. It will be faxed over in a few minutes." Ruth was pleased that something was finally going right tonight.

Michael followed Dr. Scott into the trauma room. There were still a crowd of people around her. Michael felt overwhelmed. He was now her protector. He knew his job and he would perform it flawlessly. He took in every detail about her. Her face was swollen and severely sunburn, his eyes unwillingly filled with tears. "Where can I touch her?" he asked to anyone listening. But no one answered. He reached down and touched her hair and then the top of her head. He felt her try to link. Linking was a skill that needed to be taught, practiced, and mastered. Parents and children could link easily, siblings took some practice but usually was mastered quickly. It was part of their daily chores. The older and more experience someone was, the better they were at it. The elders were the only ones who could link long distances, and absorb much more information.

For protectors, linking was there first priority. They needed to work as one unit, and this is exactly why he was forced to master it with the other protectors. They were all very physically and mentally close. They lived together, trained together, and vacationed together. Without that intensity, they could put their lives and the lives of the family at risk. Michael opened his mind the best he could and asked, "Who are you?" She responded in the link, "I don't know." Michael linked to his grandmother. "She linked with me. She doesn't know who she is." Ruth was surprised that being a young woman who no one has ever met and in her current condition could link. Ruth responded, "Keep your link with her as best as you can. Update me with the smallest detail. I want to know everything."

Michael linked the information to the other protectors. "Updates every five minutes. Her name is now Anastasia Reale." ('uck') For the public who would find men taking orders without talking to each other would seem suspicious to say the least, they wore earpieces and microphone clipped onto their collars. But Michael always hated the earpieces.

Charlotte hated this side of Michael. She thought he took this whole, 'Gotta protect my family' and 'My family comes first' and 'Oh I can't see you tonight, I have to go camping with my cousins' was like an armchair football players… 'My team can't win if I'm not at the game' bullshit. But she loved him and knew in her head that once they were married and started their own family that he wouldn't be so attached to them. She would be his priority, she would see to that.

Michael refused to leave to trauma room, he wished Jonathan was with him but he was grateful for Malachi. They each stood on opposite sides of the door taking in every detail. Hours of intense organized chaos was finally starting to slow down. Michael continuously tried to communicate with her. He felt her open in the link but no further responses. Michael was running on fumes. He was tired, and the fatigue was getting the better of him.

Charlotte was on the phone giving report to the ICU nurse. Michael sent a team of four protectors to scour every inch of the ICU and the floors above and below. Mr. Kelly came into the ER. Michael thought he looked proud of himself as he walked toward him. "Well, it took some work but I managed to move all the patients in the ICU to one side of the unit and made two rooms into one large room so you all will have plenty of space and privacy." Michael was grateful. "Thank you, my grandmother will hear of your kindness during this distressing time." Mr. Kelly smiled widely, "Anything, anything you all need, I will be available 24/7. But one thing... I know this is a delicate subject. I have arrangedned extra hospital security, so I see no need for all of this." as he pointed to Malachi and Mark as they were standing by the main double doors. Michael knew this was going to be a battle. "Mr. Kelly, I understand your concerns. You are responsible for this entire hospital. All the staff, patients and visitors. I can assure you that my teams will be indiscernible and respectful at all times. This is your hospital, but I feel like I have to remind you of the loyalty that my family has shown you over the years. I will do nothing that you are not full aware of in advance. But regardless, I will protect my family either here, where my grandmother wants her to be, or I will have her transferred to another facility to where I will also transfer our very generous donations. Do I recall correctly that the new ICU wing is called 'The Alley' after my great-grandfather Ailill Reale?"

Mr. Kelly was slightly ashamed that he even mentioned the family security, but lifted his head high. "Now Michael, I'm not saying your security is not welcome. I, of all people, am grateful for all you boys. When my own twins were missing during that Girl Scout hike, your father came with dozens of your security staff to help, and may I remind you that it was your father who found them. Piper and I are grateful beyond words. All I'm saying is that we are well equipped to handle things." Michael meant to protest but he put up his hand to continue "But as you say. Your teams will be discreet, so I will allow it, but if I hear otherwise... Well then, we will cross that bridge if we need to." Michael paused for a pinch of drama and to watch him squirm just a little. "Good, we are in agreement. I will update my grandparents. Now on a personal note, can you arrange to have a cot in Anastasia's ('uck') room for me to sleep on? And have Charlotte transferred up to the Alley?" Mr. Kelly was prepared for Michael's requests. "Yes on the bed. I've already arranged it, it's not much, but it's better than the cots we have. On transferring Charlotte up stairs, I'm afraid not. She is not ICU certified, so that is more of a legal issue. I could have her transferred as a nurse's assistant, but I don't think either of you will appreciate her in that capacity." Michael thought and replied. "You are right of course. I wasn't thinking." Mr. Kelly was convinced he was still in very good graces with the family. "You just take care of yourself. You look utterly exhausted my boy. They will be taking her upstairs any minute now. You call me if you need me. Give my love to your great-grandmother. I hope to see her soon. She is a remarkable woman." and he walked off.

Ruth and Se'ighin linked to all their immediate family in the area. Most of them lived in or near the compound. At one time, the whole family lived on, and owned the entire island. It's over 42 miles long and 26 miles at its widest point. The family has been protecting it since they fled. In the past two hundred years, they had begun donating parcels of land for the hospital, schools and parks. Some were even sold to developers. But fifteen years ago, someone threatened to sue them to sell off more land just outside their compound walls, so the family released a map from their archives that made world wide news. The headlines read, 'Vikings discovered America' and 'Viking map is authentic' and 'Vikings settled off coast of Virginia'. The Viking village was coincidently the same land that was being sought after by some high power land developers. The extremely well preserved Viking village was excavated and donated under the provision that it will be used as a living museum.

The southern end of the island is the compound that they live on. It's just over 11 miles long and the full width of 26 miles. They allow the road along the beach to the marina, to be open to the public. It has ample parking, showers, and bathrooms for beach goers, but it remains Reale property. Any family member and their families are welcome and even encouraged to live in the compound. There is the main house, which is enormous even by The Antilia in Mumbai's standards. Most rooms are more like apartments. But the elder's wings are breathtaking. Each elder makes it there own by personalizing their private residence, offices, and libraries. A private elevator with bio-entry level security features makes it impossible for any unwelcome visitors. Not that anyone had concerns regarding a family member. The Reale can go anywhere in the house, but no De'nola had ever, nor will ever walk those floors.

The main house easily houses two hundred family members very comfortably. But for those who want a bit more privacy or their 'own home', there is an entire small city on the property to choose from. Ranging from a small one bedroom bungalow with zero lot-lines, up to a large house with up to five bedrooms and a fenced in yard with a pool. There is a gym, a community pool, a nine hole golf course, a grocery store, a spa, a horse stable with endless trail for riding and a show ring (which is open to the public, but you have to be voted in and the application processes and waiting list is lengthy), a movie theater, a private beach with lifeguards, several parks, maid service if needed, restaurants, and mail service. The elders are always thinking of ways to improve everyday life on the compound.

So when a family meeting is called, it's like poking an ant hill. There are not many De'nola in this local clann, but there are a few. When a family meeting is called, it's not forbidden for them to come, but most are not included. When Ruth and Se'ighin linked and called for a family meeting, 'Everyone is to make themselves available', everyone stopped what they were doing and heading to the main house.

Once they were satisfied that everyone was present, except for the protectors. Ruth and Se'ighin walked up to the balcony that overlooked the great room. She raised her hands and began speaking. She kept the link open and spoke so the De'nola could take part. "Good morning family. We have had some disturbing events that I need to make you all aware of from last night. Several of you all ready know, but last night a young woman was found at sea. We think by her condition that she was in a small dinghy for approx four days. She is in grave condition and is not expected to survive, but she is strong and trained (to link). She has no memory of who she is or who trained her, and she is unknown to any other family member. Michael was able to (link) communicate with her for a very brief moment. The official versions of events are as follows: She was a bit of a rebellious child and ran away from home at thirteen, and believed to be with a rather shady boyfriend. She has been estranged from her parents and the family for approximately ten years but recently reconciled under privacy to avoid family embarrassment. She was on a yacht with a group of girlfriends coming here for the July 4th festivities when the yacht met with foul weather, and apparently went down sometime last week. A frantic family search ensued, but sadly, not knowing where they were when the yacht sank, all hope had been lost of finding any survivors. Our family is indebted to Tom Calhoun and Rick Bailey for their heroism in finding her and bringing her into the marina where Assistant Chief of Police Curtis Cappola, was prepared with first responders on scene to render medical attention. We will forever be in his debt for alerting us. Her name is Anastasia. On hearing the news of her rescue, her father Elias was making arrangements from Norway to get here to be at his daughter's side when he suffered a heart attack. We are not going to allow Anastasia to be told this information for concerns that she will be devastated, and in her current condition will cause her unnecessary burden.

Now this is your charge. Go out into the community, but not off the island. This is already on every news channels. I want to get our story out locally first and quickly. Talk to everyone you know. Start the conversation. Allow all the questions to be asked. Olivia, go to your Priest and ask for a prayer chain. Those women are better than a team of reporters getting information out. Antonio, go to the public golf course and have lunch with your friends, invite their wives. I'm sure they will jump at the chance to get the story first hand. Aharon, go to the college campus and ask to see any new students grades for the scholarship program. Isabelle and Bina, go to the diner. You will draw a huge crowd there. They have great food but the staff is not known to gossip and we need them talking. Elijah and Chaya, take Amelia to the Synagogue and the park. The parade will be meeting from their parking lot, use that. Everyone else, go out and be seen, make phone calls, ask your friends to light candles, and make it known that we are not hiding from this. Any questions that you can't answer or any information you get. Come to me immediately. Keep all (links) calls to a minimum. Michael is to stay in constant (link) communication with Anastasia (Michael heard 'uck'). Make no mistakes, she IS a Reale. The compound is now on lockdown, only family and previously cleared De'nola. Are there any rejections? (She was not expecting any response but she waited regardless) Good. Now you all know your duties. Be available and visible." Without a moment's hesitation, the family began their tasks.

Bina asked Rach-El to bring Michael breakfast and to talk to Charlotte. Rach-El quickly packed all of her brother's favorite foods from the kitchen and arranged to pick up a set of his favorite sheets to sleep on. She was very close with her brother and had always felt overly protective of him even though she was younger. She arrived at the hospital and walked right passed security. She mumbled, "Pfft, that's what they call security? No wonder why Michael has this place surrounded." She knew exactly where to go. She had been here every day when her great-grandfather was here last year. He commented on how he had no rest or privacy. It was too busy and noisy and it sounded like a bowling ally.

She walked right through the large double doors where the hospital security guard was sleeping in a chair and two protectors on either side of him so he wouldn't fall over. She waved at her cousins and walked in. Michael was sitting on the small bed that Mr. Kelly had provided for him. She stared at him for a few minutes before he noticed the smell of food. He stood up and took a deep breathe, he smiled when he saw it was his little sister holding a bag. "Oh thank God! I'm starving. I think I'll keep you around for another day or two." She laughed as she put the bag on the small bed. He gave her a bear hug and cracked her back. She made a 'oh ugg' sound as he put her down. "Thanks big bro. I needed that." She looked over at the girl in the bed, she knew from what everyone said that she didn't want to look too closely. Rach-El had a bit of a weak stomach. "How is she doing?" Michael rubbed his eyes and yawned like a feral cat. "No changes. Grandmother arranged for an anesthesiologist, that weird guy, Doctor I'm God's gift to women Connard, to sit and monitor all of her vital signs and the tube down her throat." Rach-El looked around the room and took in every detail of all the machinery, the beeping, flashing lights, IV bags, and tubes running under the covers. "Why are her arms tied down!? That's horrible!" Michael rolled his eyes slightly. "I asked the same thing. The nurse told me that when someone is on a ventilator, they have to keep them from reaching up and grabbing the tube. I don't know. All this is out of my element. This is Charlotte's gig, not mine." Rach-El said, "Speaking of Charlotte, is she going to be transferred up her to take care of her? You know Grandmother will insist on it." Michael "I spoke to Mr. Kelly about it, but he said no, it's a legal thing and she isn't certified or trained for up here. So I guess I have to accept that. The nurses up here all check out and so far seem nice.

The charge nurse Barbara is coming in this morning. She's going to be the primary nurse. Malachi had her checked. Except for a crazy x-husband, a son that likes monster trucks and a few parking tickets, she's fine. Well, all but that monster truck thing." They laughed as he started to pull food out of the bag and eat. Rach-El said softly, "Michael, I have to admit. This is really freaking me out. Who is she really? I mean. I'm not touching her and I can feel her. Super freaky right?" Michael whispered back. "I wish I knew what to tell you. When I saw her last night, I could feel her too. I knew she was able to link, she was open to anyone. I even heard her for a second, but I had a real hard time focusing after I saw some of the scars. I heard they are all over her body... Almost all of her bones have been broken, more than once. I mean like ten lifetimes of real torture. I can't imagine what she's been through, but I can tell you this. No one will ever hurt her again... EVER." Rach-El "Well not with you as her protector. I hope she can feel that she is safe now."

Charlotte gave report to the oncoming ER staff and she clocked out. She went up stairs to see Michael. As she was coming through the ICU double doors she could smell the food. She walked pass the men sitting outside of Anastasia's room and saw Michael and Rach-El eating breakfast and talking. She was glad that Rach-El was here. "Good morning. Well that was an intense night. How is everyone holding up? Any word on when her father can get here?" Rach-El lowered her voice. "I'll talk to you about that later." Charlotte was a little confused. "What's wrong?" Rach-El turned her head toward Anastasia. Charlotte "Pfft, she can't hear us. Dr. Connard has her under general anesthesia."

Michael felt a wave of anger. He was too tired to address the comment now, but he took a mental note. Rach-El turned to Michael. "So... did you get much sleep last night?" Michael pointed to his eyes. "These bags don't lie." Charlotte chimed in, "Why don't we go to my place and get some rest. Rach-El or someone can sit with her. You'll feel better after some sleep." Michael was about to say no when Rach-El spoke up. "That is actually a great idea. Dr. Scott said that all these specialists are coming in today to do a billion dollar work up. You would have to stay outside anyway. I'll stay right here. I promise. Grandmother gave jobs to everyone but me. So when Mom told me to come over, I thought I was staying anyway. So go. Get some sleep. You look almost as bad as you smell." She laughed and punched him in the arm. Michael did feel drained, but he needed Grandmother's ok. He linked to Ruth. "Rach-El is here. Is it acceptable if I take a few hours and go to Charlotte's apartment for a shower and nap?" He updated the details in the link. Ruth knew he needed sleep to be proficient. "Have Rach-El link me every detail as it happens. There are a lot of specialists coming in this morning and I need to know everything." Michael "Rach-El has been training with me, she will do you proud. I will be back in a few hours. I will update the teams. Thank you." Rach-El knew he was linking to Grandmother, so she kept talking to Charlotte.

Michael linked to the protectors with updates on Anastasia and his plans with Charlotte. "You all know where she lives. If anything happens, come get me. I'll be back in a few hours." He received a collected "Go, we got this." in response. Michael was thankful that Rach-El knew him so well. He was too tired to even try to explain how he was all of a sudden ok with leaving. "Ok, I'm tired. Rach-El, thank you. You are the best. Call Grandmother with every detail. I mean it. Names, tests, results, what shoes who is wearing...everything. Got it?" Rach-El look annoyed. "Control freak much??? I got it, now go before I change my mind and go get a mani-pedi instead." They laughed slightly, hugged and Charlotte pulled her keys out of her pocket. "Aaannnd we are off. Ba-Bye everybody." As she waved and walked out. Michael was wondering if this was the right thing to do. Rach-El thought, "Poor Charlotte."

The drive to Charlotte's apartment was less than two miles away. As he sat in the car, he realized how badly his feet where throbbing and thought, "This is nothing compared to what she went through." Charlotte broke his deep thought when she put the care in park and pulled up the emergency brake. "We're here." He got out of the car without saying or thinking anything. She opened her apartment door and he plopped down, face first onto the couch. Charlotte pulled him up. "No, you're not going to sleep like that. Let me help you get these smelly clothes off." Michael asked, "Do I really smell bad?" as he lifted his arms and took a deep breath. "Oh don't answer that!" He pulled off his shirt, flipped off his shoes and undid his pants, allowing them to fall to the floor. He stepped out of them and onto the toes of his socks so he wouldn't have to bend over. He did his famous (in his head) Halloween zombie walk into the bathroom and started the water.

He put his head on the wall and felt himself drifting off to sleep. He pulled himself into the warm water, rubbed the half wet bar of soap across his chest and thought. "I wonder if she got to take showers." He had to clear his head. He had to stop feeling. He needed to do his job. He turned off the water, stepped out of the shower, wrapped a towel around his waist, and walked into Charlotte's bedroom. He sat on the side of the bed with the knot of the towel coming loose. He had spent many nights at her apartment and she had been spending more and more time at the compound. The past several months, they talked about moving in together. He would arrange to have one of the homes outside the main house. That way he could still be close enough to link with the other protectors and be an active participant in family matters. Charlotte wasn't as thrilled with the idea of being that close, but she would have to adjust. This is exactly what Grandmother had warned him about. He needed to be 100% sure of her loyalty to him and the family. Besides that snarky comment she made at the hospital that he was going to talk to her about later. He seemed satisfied.

He had clothes and pajamas here for times he spent the night, so he pulled a pair of sweat pants out of a drawer and started to put his feet in when he felt her kissing his neck. He turned around to kiss her back. She said, "It's May and it's hot out. Just sleep naked." He managed to nod his head in agreement as his head hit the pillow. His eyes were closed and he felt the cool breeze of the fan on his naked body. He allowed himself to finally relax. His thoughts went to Anastasia. "I wonder if she is comfortable." He linked to Rach-El. "Update." Rach-El knew if she didn't immediately have information for him that he would shoot himself out of a cannon to get here. "Seeing you just left, there are no updates. Dr. snooty Brent Connard is here. The protectors just changed shifts. Mr. Kelly wants to make sure Grandmother knows how much he is sucking up. Dr. Scott came up to check on her. That is about it. Oh, the charge nurse Barbara has a new purse. And that is all Captain Sleepy Pants. Now get some sleep. Link me when you wake up. Little perfect sister signing off now." and she broke the link. Michael couldn't help but laugh out loud. Charlotte hated when he did that. "What? What is always so funny in that head of yours?" Michael "Nothing, just something I remembered Rach-El said." As he air kissed her, he started dozing off to sleep.

Charlotte rolled over closer to him and started kissing his neck. He loved when she kissed him. He never questioned his feelings for her when they were intimate. She completely gave herself to him. He had been tempted several times to ask her to marry him when they were in a moment of passion. But today was not the time for romance. His family has never had a situation like this in their entire history and Grandmother charged him (HIM) with an enormous responsibility.

He didn't feel right doing this now. He needed sleep and to get back to the hospital. He thought, 'I should have stayed with her. I shouldn't have left. I could have slept there.' Charlotte moved down and began kissing his chest. In his head he was telling her to stop and that the timing is inappropriate, but no words, only sounds came out of his mouth. He was laying there enjoying her as she moved down to his stomach. The sounds of pleasure where louder then he meant for them to be. He really did want her to stop, but his body was responding. She always knew how to take his mind off stress. He touched her hair with both hands as she reached his bellybutton. He was ticklish and pulled her up to kiss her. She came willingly. He loved being with her, he loved getting lost in her. She was the one for him. Her hands lightly scratched their way down his chest to his groin. He moaned with pleasure. She felt him ready for her. She sat up and straddled his body. He opened his eye and looked at how beautiful she was. He reached up to hold her, she was about to put him inside her when he pulled away. "Stop. I don't have a condom." She sounded irritated. "I have told you for years… I'm on the pill. We don't need a condom. I hate those things."

Michael was having a difficult time focusing. "I just don't want to take any chances. My family would kill me if…" Charlotte whispered, "Don't you trust me?" as she started to kiss his neck again. Michael "Yes, I trust you. But ultimately it's my responsibility." Charlotte "We are going to be married soon. No one cares, but besides… I am on the PILL. I'm not getting pregnant." She started to nibble gently on his nipples. He moaned. She kissed down his chest. He moaned again. She purred, "Do you like this?" He could only moan. He was exhausted and couldn't think anymore. She put her mouth near his genitals and breathed slow hot air on him. He stroked her hair. She softly asked, "Do you really want me to stop?" He didn't answer. She teased him for a few minutes then she straddled him again, and put him inside her. He arched with pleasure. He made a weak attempt to push her away but failed. She put both hands on his chest and whispered, "You just lay there. I'll do all the work." She made love to him just the way he needed her to.

He reached up and pulled her close to him. "I can't hold out any more." She moaned and kissed his earlobe. "Don't hold back. Give it to me." He moaned and squeezed her tight. She felt him tense up, then his entire body relaxed with a slow exhale. "I love you." He whispered as he drifted off to sleep. Charlotte thought, 'I wonder what the ring looks like?' as she snuggled up underneath his arm and was fast asleep.

Ruth told Jonathan he was on partial protector duties until further notice. He couldn't stand doing nothing while everyone else was so busy. He asked to speak to her after the family meeting. She told him to meet her in her private office. He knew she had nothing to eat all night, so he stopped by the kitchen and made her a small breakfast sandwich and her favorite peppermint mocha latte and headed up to her office. She heard the elevator and smelled the latte, and as the door opened she called out. "This is the sole reason I chose you as my transporter!" He laughed as he made his way down the hall into her office. "Bribery will get you everywhere with me young man. Now what can I do for you?" as she took a long deep slow whiff of the brew. Jonathan put the small plate with the sandwich down on her desk. "Are we going somewhere or can I resume my duties to the protectors?" She sat back in her chair. "I will need you and Mark well rested soon, but I admire your commitment to Michael. He does need you more than I do. Go to him, but not as a protector, but as his close confidant. I warn you, he will fight you on this." Jonathan was confused. "Fight me? On what?" Ruth "He will not like that you are taking care of him. He has always been a stubborn child. Now he is a stubborn man." Jonathan "Oh, yeah. You have him nailed, but if anyone can take his abuse, it's my sister Lindsey." Ruth laughed and shooed him away.

Jonathan was glad that she didn't need him right away. But he would stay well rested for when she did. He knew Michael was at Charlotte's apartment getting some rest and Rach-El was at Anastasia's bedside, so he went to his room, packed a bag for whatever his grandmother would need him for. Took a shower he linked to the protectors, except for Michael and asked for an update. Quickly all the responses were, "Nothing new." So he laid down for a few minutes to clear his head.

Ruth and Ailbe were in a heated discussion regarding arrangements for the very risky move. To have all the elders meet in person... Not since the attack on Atlantis has an elder risked such a meeting. Ailbe was getting frustrated with Ruth. "Daughter, It MUST be done. If we all physically link, one of us has to remember something to explain this. She didn't just fall out of the sky!" Ruth was just as frustrated. "Mother, I am responsible for every member of this family. If I am reckless, then they (she pointed to nothing particular) can be reckless, and if they are reckless then we die. I will not allow that to happen. I will not allow this to be our end. You cannot ask me to do this!"

Ailbe "I'm not asking you, I'm telling you! This is the only way to be 100% sure. Do you think that I would risk the life of even one Azili!?"

Ruth "No. I know you would never, but this is too dangerous. Too risky! I just can't put anyone's life in danger. Why can't you understand that?"

Ailbe "If we don't do this, and do it quickly, then you are putting ALL of our lives in danger!"

Ruth sat down in her desk chair. She felt backed into a corner. She looked out the window out at the ocean. She heard the whales in the distance and saw the dolphins close to the shore. She finally spoke. "We have no choice do we?"

Ailbe "No. No we don't."

Ruth put both hands on her desk. She took a defeated sounding deep breath and struggled to her feet. "Make the necessary arrangements, but not for today, I just sent Jonathan to be with Michael."

Ailbe "Done." Both women went their separate ways to prepare for the meeting. Each not feeling the excitement that they normally would when planning to see family.

Michael woke up startled and felt something was wrong, "What!?" he called out. Charlotte stirred a bit and mumbled, "You're dreaming, go back to sleep." He linked to Rach-El. "Update." She responded, "Get here! Benjamin is outside to pick you up." Michael was dressed and out the door by the time Benjamin put the car in park. He jumped in the passenger seat and responded. "Rach-El, I need Jonathan." Rach-El "Already on his way." He asked Benjamin, "What happened?" Benjamin "I'm really not sure. The building and property are all secure. Rach-El told me to come get you and I heard some commotion but my job was to get you." Michael knew the answer before he even asked the question. He had to calm down. His job is to be the calm in the storm, not add to the storm. It took less than five minutes to get to the hospital, but it felt like an eternity. As Benjamin pulled up to the main entrance, Michael opened the door and was gone before Benjamin could actually stop the car. Benjamin felt the urgency, parked the car, and went inside ready for war.

Michael stormed into the ICU unit. He was met by Rach-El holding her hands out and putting them on his chest to stop his momentum. "Michael stop! The neurologist is in with her now. You can't go in just yet."

Michael demanded an update. "What happened?" Rach-El quickly said, "I think she had a seizure. She is running a really high fever. The doctor changed her antibiotics and gave her something to stop the seizure. They are putting bags of ice around her to cool her off really quick."

Michael "What medication did they give her?"

Rach-El "I don't know. They said it was to break the seizure."

Michael "You don't know! What kind of an answer is 'I don't know'? You told me that you would get every detail! Oh forget it. Why did I trust you?" He tried to push pass her but she stood firm. Rach-El "Listen Michael. We are all stressed out. Do not take this out on me. I am not your enemy." Michael didn't hear much of what she said, but he did hear how she said it. He hugged her tight as he looked over her into the room. He kissed the top of her head and side stepped her to get into the room. He was standing at the foot of the hospital bed. The tears in his eyes welled up and flowed down his face. This was the first time he saw her entire body. Her skin was different patches of bright red sunburn, deep brown pealing areas and raised blisters. Several of the blisters ruptured during the seizure and oozed a foul smelling thick yellow fluid. But what took him to his knees were the scars.

When Jonathan arrived at the hospital, the first person he saw was Rach-El standing outside of the building with her back up against the wall. She looked dazed and confused. She didn't notice as he walked up beside her. "Hey, where is Michael?" Rach-El turned to him and he saw the look of shock and fear in her eyes. He asked again, "Where is Michael!?" Rach-El couldn't talk. She just pointed to the doors. Jonathan took the stairs two at a time, he couldn't wait for the elevator. He was ready for whatever he found, but he was not ready for what he saw. He came up behind Michael as nurses were rushing in and out. He looked into the bed. He put his hand on Michael's shoulder and tried to say something strong and super-hero(ish), but nothing came out. There were no words to be said.

Jonathan guided Michael over to the bed that Mr. Kelly provided. The Two cousins sat there, trying to stay out of the way. They both felt numb as they watched in horror. Dr. Jacqui McKay stepped in front of them and broke their stare. "Which one of you is Michael?" Michael half lifted his hand as if he were a child being scolded. Dr. McKay asked, "May I speak to you for a moment? Outside please." Michael stood to follow but his legs failed him. Jonathan helped him to his feet and they followed the doctor. They walked into the doctor's lounge and sat down. She started, "This is difficult for me, so I will just get on with it. Your cousin has a critically high fever and consequently had a Tonic-Clonic, or what they used to call a grand mal seizure. We gave her Lorazepam to break the seizure activity without positive effect. She went into what we call 'Status epilepticus'. It is when we cannot break a seizure or when a seizure continues. I gave her as much medication as I could and we packed her in ice. That seems to have broken the seizure for now, but I have some serious concerns. I have ordered additional tests, but my main concern is she might have brain damage or worse, she might be brain dead. Dr. Connard has stabilized her vital signs for the moment." She sat quietly while Michael and Jonathan processed the information. Michael finally broke the silence. "What can I do?" "Pray" was her only response. Jonathan thought that she was being insensitive until he saw her face. She just had nothing else to offer. She stood to leave and said, "I will be here the rest of the day if I can help in anyway. I will know more after the tests are completed." Michael couldn't speak to say thank you but she was gone before he tried.

Rach-El and Lindsey have always been close. They were born two weeks apart and learned to link to each other by two years old. It was quite a shock to the adults, who wondered how many lies that had gotten away with over the years. They were the main reason that Ruth had opened the stables to the public. They were the little cowgirls in the family. Always had dirt under their nails, hay in their hair, and boots that smelled like a bad night of beans. But they made a lot of friends outside of the family and a De'nola here and there had horses and the girls all liked to trail ride together. Once while trail riding outside the compound, Rach-El fell and broke her wrist and a few ribs. But she was too stoic to link to her parents, and Lindsey would have teased her till the end of time. So she got back on and rode home. By the time they got back to the compound, her wrist was so swollen and she couldn't breathe, that she had to go to the hospital and spend a week in the infirmary. After that, Ruth felt it would be easier to have their friends be on their trails inside the compound then have protectors try following them.

Rach-El linked to Lindsey, Great-Grandmother and Grandmother with the update and the obligatory, "Lindsey, I need you". Ruth knew that they had run out of time. Ailbe was in the car with Mark before Ruth and Lindsey got down stairs. With all three women in the car, Mark wished he would have suggested taking the helicopter to the hospital. Once there, Mr. Kelly saw them getting out of the car from his office window. He clenched his fists and called out to his secretary, "Why doesn't anyone ever listen to me? I am to be notified BEFORE they get here!" He tucked in his shirt, threw on his blazer, and stormed out of his office toward the ICU.

Ailbe walked straight pass everyone without any pleasantries and motioned for Dr. Connard to leave the room. When he did not immediately move, she hip checked him right out of his chair. "Oh dear, my apologies sir. May I have a brief moment alone with my niece?" Dr. Connard quickly corrected her. "It's Dr. Connard Mrs. Reale. We have met before. I would…" Ailbe had no time for kiss-assess at the moment and she cut him off mid sentence. "I'm sure you are dear. Now be a lamb and get me a soda, in a glass, with clear ice." Dr. Connard did not like to be disrespected, even if it was just in his head. But he would never dream of correcting her any further. He left the room in search of a soda thinking, "Clear ice? What the hell is that?"

Ailbe placed her hands on both sides of Anastasia's head and touched her forehead to hers. She was going to link as deeply as she could. That is if she was not brain dead. She felt Anastasia accept the link. But Ailbe saw nothing, she felt nothing before the moment she woke up in the dinghy. Ailbe dug deeper. Anastasia allowed it. Ailbe asked in the link, "Do you remember anything, anything at all?" She heard a faint, "Nothing." Ailbe "Please child, I don't want to go too deep and harm you." Anastasia was weak and far away, but Ailbe heard, "Please help me. I can't remember what I need to do. I just know I need to do it." She sounded desperate. Ailbe forced herself to go deeper than she should have, but still nothing… Ailbe and Anastasia were both exhausted. Ailbe heard her ask, "Please try again." Ailbe responded, "No. I will do what I can from out here, but your memories are too deep, and I will not risk harming you. They will come back when they are supposed to or they will remain buried. We will love and protect you regardless. But for now, you have to fight. You are in a bad way sweet child." Anastasia felt loved. "I will. I promise". Ailbe closed the link and looked at Ruth. "She is a fighter our new little princess. It's time to go. Get Jonathan." Anastasia thought, 'What... what did she just say?' Then she allowed her mind to succumb to the effects of the medication. She was finally resting.

Michael and Jonathan were walking back to the room when they saw them. Ruth looked at Jonathan. "Good, you look rested. Time to go." Jonathan wanted to protest (badly), but he looked at Michael and said, "I'll be back as soon as I can. Stay strong." They hugged and Jonathan ran after Ruth. Ailbe was still standing by Anastasia's side. As Michael came closer, in a low tone she said. "Your girl is a fighter." Michael knew she had more to say but he blurted out. "Is she ok? She isn't brain dead? I've been trying to link with her but I get nothing. Is she in there? What did she say? Is she in any pain? Did she ask about me?" he quickly thought... "What a stupid question." But he hoped his eagle-eye all knowing 104 year old great-grandmother didn't catch that...pffft! Ailbe put her hand up to his mouth. "Shh... she is still with us, but she is weak. Stay by her side. No matter what! I have my suspicions and there are a few things that I need to check into. Keep your link open to her as best as you can, and remind her to fight. I will see you soon." She did not allow Michael to ask anymore questions. Probably a good idea. She turned and left. A moment later Dr. Connard walked into the room with a coke can, a glass full of ice, and a strange look on his face. "Where did they go?" Michael looked around, "Where did who go?" Michael heard a faint laugh. He looked at Lindsey sitting on the bed with Rach-El. The girls were holding hands, wide eyed, and smiling.

Ailbe got into the car directly behind Mark as Jonathan opened the back passenger door for Ruth, and then he got into the front passenger seat. Ailbe said out loud, "Poor Charlotte." The other three nodded in agreement and left.

Charlotte woke up to an empty bed. "Ugh. I hate when he does that.

Why can't I ever wake up to my boyfriend!?" She looked at the time and knew she had to get ready for work. "I'm already sick of this. After we're married, I'm gonna put a bell around his neck." She got up and ready, packed a quick dinner and headed off to work. She thought of calling ahead to see who she was working with tonight, but was already in a foul mood. "I'll find out soon enough."

She was pleasantly surprised when she arrived, it was nice and quiet. Not one patient in the waiting room and the only one in the treatment room was being discharged. She could easily talk to Mr. Kelly and sneak off to see Michael. She clocked in and got the easiest report of her life and settled in for a quiet night.

Michael sat down on the bed in-between Rach-El and Lindsey and slapped his hands down on each of their knees. They both yelled, "Ouch, What was that for?" at the same time. He had a smile on his face since he spoke to his great-grandmother. "Just to let you girls know how much I love and appreciate you both." Rach-El rolled her eyes in a very over dramatic way. "Ut oh, what do you want now?" Michael "Nothing. I have everything I have ever wanted right here." Lindsey followed Rach-El's lead and rolled her eyes. "That usually means that I'm going to do something that I know I shouldn't do, but I do it anyway and I get in trouble." Michael belly laughed. "Normally I would agree, but tonight I just want you to know that I love you." Rach-El "I think he bumped his head." Lindsey "Me too."

Michael felt Anastasia listening. Dr. Connard sat up in his chair and looked closer at the monitors. "Barbara, could you come in here?" A nurse came in. "Barbara left for the day. I'm the night charge nurse Jessica." Dr. Connard "Whatever, that's fine. Just write down the time and these vitals. She looks like she is coming around a bit. Oh and call Dr. McKay. She'll be interested in this." Michael felt content and leaned back on his bed. "I really hate this bed." Rach-El took the opportunity to link to her younger sister Amani with a few minor instructions.

The three were still talking when Dr. McKay walked in. "Well, I see you guys got the good news even before I did. It must be nice to be rich, powerful, and connected." Michael pretended to be confused, but he already knew from Ailbe's link that she wasn't brain dead. Dr. McKay continued. "So I can give you the official report and my current assessment, but I will need just a moment with her." Michael asked, "Dr. McKay can we please stay? If you have to uncover her, then I'm outta here. But otherwise…(he gave her his best puppy eyes) can we pleaseeeee stay?" Dr. McKay could not hold back her spontaneous laugh. "Ok, but I warn you. I talk a lot during an exam. So no interruptions." "Deal!" Rach-El yelled out louder than she expected to.

Dr. McKay began her assessment. "Anastasia, honey, my name is Jacqui. I'm the Neurologist that was called when you had your seizure. Your fever came down nicely after we changed the antibiotic. I have called in a Pulmonologist Dr. Roger Herzog. You will love him, he has the warmest hands you will ever feel. (Michael laughed and knew there must be a story behind that statement.) Your vital signs are getting stronger by the hour, but I would like for him to keep the tube in your throat for a few more days. That also means keeping you heavily sedated. I'm going to take a pin, it is NOT going to hurt you, it will just poke you. If you can, try to move the body part that I poke. I'm going to start now."

Michael, Rach-El and Lindsey all sat there with their mouths open. They had never seen a doctor work with so much compassion. The three of them watched her closely. When she was done she looked at the three of them. "Ok, who has questions?" They just sat there. She continued, "Well, I wish I would have waited to speak to you earlier Michael. I'm afraid I put you through a terrible experience for nothing. She is responding very well. I recommend that we continue what we are doing now, and I will recheck her tomorrow." Michael collected his thoughts and stood up. "Thank you. I mean, really thank you. You were great with her. I'll be sure to update my family." As she was leaving she smiled. "You all need to get a good night sleep. Even though she has improved, it doesn't mean that she isn't in for a long road ahead. See you in the morning."

Mark pulled out of the hospital parking lot going in the opposite direction of the compound. Jonathan knew better than to ask questions. Ruth "Jonathan, have you been working on blocking links like I showed you?" Jonathan "Absolutely, I did exactly what you told me to do." Ruth

"Good. Block every link, that isn't from me, until I tell you differently." If he knew anything, he knew that the elders choose their words carefully. So he didn't question it, he just did what he was told. Mark drove to the small local airport. As Mark parked the car, Jonathan noticed one of their helicopters being fueled on the helipad and wondered why they didn't use the helipad from the compound. He opened the door for Ruth and then Ailbe. They walked to the back of the car as Mark was pulling out suitcases. Jonathan laughed as Ruth was lining them up. Jonathan didn't want Ruth to think that he was laughing at her so he said, "Good thing I packed this morning or I'd be a stinky travel companion." Ruth looked surprised. "Didn't I tell you to be ready?" as she walked away. Mark walked by him and slapped him on the chest. "Ya got to learn to take what they say literally or you'd be flying duck taped to the wing." He laughed as he walked to the helicopter. Mark and Jonathan completed their pre-flight check and they were off the ground in fifteen minutes. As they flew over the hospital, Jonathan wished he could let Michael know that he didn't desert him, but he was sure he already knew that.

Jonathan tried to guess at where they were headed but he already knew they were heading to the inland airport. They landed and stepped out of the helicopter to a line of four cars waiting. Mark assisted Ailbe into the seat directly behind the driver and Jonathan followed suit and opened up the back passenger door for Ruth. The driver got into the second car and they drove over to the terminal for needed paperwork and itinerary. In record speed, they were back in the cars headed to a small hanger where their private jet was being towed out and onto a taxi way. The three other cars all stopped next to theirs. Two men got out of each car and walked directly into the jet. Mark did not move, so Jonathan did not move. They watched the door to the jet until one of the men motioned for them to come aboard. Mark sat in the pilot seat and Jonathan sat in the co-pilot seat. They completed their pre-flight check with the tower and were cleared for takeoff. Mark wasted no time in taxing down the runway.

Once in the air, Ailbe stood up to stretch her legs. "Oh where are my manners? Mark and Jonathan, I'm sure you remember these Azili from your Great Uncle Deaglan's clann in Norway. Bjorn, Leif, Olav, Rolf, Hans, and Erik." Mark put the jet on the auto-pilot and stood up with Jonathan to reconnect with their cousins. They all exchanged hardy handshakes and pats on the back. Ruth said, "Ok, that is enough chit-chat. I need my beauty sleep. No need to scare you boys so early in the trip." She stood up and went to a bedroom at the back of the jet. She turned to Ailbe "Mother, are you going to play poker with these boys or are you off to bed? We have a long few days ahead of us." Ruth didn't wait for a response as she closed the door to the bedroom. Ailbe stood up. "As if you boys would stand a chance with this old dog. I'd clean with floor with your money." And without allowing any time for a reply, she walked to the back of the jet and disappeared behind the second bedroom door. Jonathan liked this side of his elders.

Just as he was about to suggest they start flying the jet again, Bjorn spoke up. "I'm not here to step on your toes. My suggestion is four hours shifts. Leif and I. Then Olav and Rolf. Then Hans and Erik? And then you two of course." Mark did not hesitate. "Absolutely. I would have suggested the same." They landed only to refuel and back up in the air. Things were going smoothly, almost too smoothly for everyone's liking.

Arden wanted an update regarding what was being talked about in the community. It's almost three days since Anastasia's rescue and the media seemed to be everywhere. Linking was to be for emergencies only, so he did it the De'nola way. He spread the word that he is calling a family meeting in the main house. If anyone had any information regarding the talk on the street, meet at 6p.m for dinner. The dining room filled quickly. He wondered how De'nola communicated that way and maybe he made a mistake. But the feedback was just what he had hoped for. The family had gone about their daily lives and were not hiding from talking about what was happening. Several news agencies had taking up camping outside the compound's main gates. Ruth's statements of, "Please respect our privacy." and "No comment." and "This is a family matter." hard lines worked to only fuel them to dig deeper, but Ruth strategically being video taped in the community and times at the hospital while being surrounded by family and hugging hospital staff was clearly turning public opinion against the overly aggressive reporters.

The reporters were like cut-throat pirates in their attempts to get an exclusive. They talked to everyone that would stop, they even tried offering money, trips, and TV air-time to local islanders, but the locals were loyal to the Reale family. There will always be a handful that have something to say, but they only came off as bitter. Arden encouraged the family to continue updating the community. Aharon's wife Isabelle asked, "What about July 4th? That is the question that I get asked most. The hotels are all booked, the food is all ordered, it's just not us that plan this for months, it's the entire island." The family agreed. Arden spoke over everyone. "We are NOT cancelling the July 4th activities. Come rain or shine, no matter what happens with Anastasia, no family or local issue will cause us to cancel. But that gives me a great idea. Tomorrow morning Bina and I, along with Olivia and Antonio, Aharon and Isabelle, and Elijah and Chaya, we will walk out together and make the announcement that we are humbled by the outpouring of love and support that has been shown to our family. That this will be the biggest July 4th weekend we have ever had, and this year will be dedicated to the heath care community. We will provide more information as details are finalized. Do I hear any rejections?" The room fell silent. "Fantastic. I will start working on additional services." Arden and Bina finished dinner and went up to Ruth's office to start working.

Michael started feeling hungry. "Ladies, can I tempt you to a fine dinner of vending machine potato chips and flat soda?" Rach-El looked up from her phone. "I really thought someone would send us over food. Is this the life of a protector?" Hayden called out from outside the room. "Yuppp." Lindsey stretched, "I'll fly if you buy." Michael did his puppy confused look. "If you bring me food that doesn't have an expiration date of two months ago on it, I'll buy you that purple pony that I promised you on your 10th birthday." She threw a pillow at him. He heard a faint giggle in his link with Anastasia. They all discussed what they wanted while Hayden asked the other protectors.

With list in hand, Lindsey was walking out the door when Charlotte walked in. She seemed to ignore Michael until she talked to everyone else first. He thought it was odd and wondered if he made her mad somehow. They had an incredibility intimate morning together, and he was careful not to wake her up, what could he have done? The thought didn't last long as he thought, "I don't have time for crap like this!" When she made her way over to him she kissed him on the cheek and said, "Oh Michael, there you are. I thought you must have fallen off the face of the earth. No call. No text. No I'm here at the hospital, let me run down to say hello to my girlfriend. Nothing, just a good old romp in the sack and out the door." She stood there with one foot slightly cocked out, one hand on her hip, and the other one looking at her nail polish. He was blown away by how inconsiderate her words and actions were. He walked around her and snatched the list out of Lindsey's hand and walked out.

Charlotte looked genuinely shocked. She always got the rise out of him that way in the past. She would ignore him, then he would come and chase her for a bit, she would pout, he would feel bad, and buy her something pretty or pay more attention to her. She looked at Rach-El and asked, "What is wrong with him?" Rach-El shook her head, blinked a few times and stared at her. "Seriously Charlotte?! What was that little show about?" Charlotte threw both hands up in the air. "What? I came up to say hello and I'm getting the crooked looks? I think you guys need some sleep. Come on, I brought snacks." Lindsey and Rach-El truly didn't know what to say. Lindsey finally spoke up. "Charlotte, we appreciate everything that you have done for Anastasia, but I think it is time for you to go back to work." Charlotte dropped her arms. "Guys, come on, you know me. You know I was joking! You guys tease each other all the time." Lindsey gave Rach-El the courage she needed. She took a few steps to stand shoulder to shoulder with Lindsey. "Charlotte, you and Lindsey are right. We all need to relax, so I would prefer if you left my cousin's room before I say something that I will regret later. I will tell Michael that you feel misunderstood, and that you were only attempting to lighten the mood when he returns. Have I properly worded your defense?" Charlotte took a few steps toward Rach-El with her arms out as if she was going to hug her. Rach-El took a step back. "Charlotte I will not ask you politely again... Please leave my cousin's room." Charlotte did not move, taking an almost defiant stance. Rach-El calmly said one word, just one. "Protector."

Before Charlotte could open her mouth, Hayden and Steven were on each side, and Malachi was standing toe to toe in front of her. Malachi's lip was twitching with restraint. He calmly but firmly said, "Ma'am, please follow me." Lindsey had already sent a text to Mr. Kelly asking him to come immediately. Charlotte stared back at Malachi and said daringly, "I'm not afraid of you Malachi!" as she turned to plead her case again to Lindsey and Rach-El. "Seriously guys, come on. It was a joke. I was just playing. I love you guys. I love Michael. Ok, maybe it came out wrong, but I would never hurt any of you on purpose. I'm gonna wait here for Michael. I'll apologize and you'll see it's fine."

Rach-El and Lindsey turned their backs as Malachi turned and started to walk. Hayden and Steven each took her by an elbow and followed Malachi. She kicked and screamed as they carried her out of the ICU as Mr. Kelly stepped out of the elevator. "What is going on? Take your hands off of her!" Charlotte broke free of their grip and ran to him. She stood behind him and began crying and telling him what had happened.

As he was trying to make sense of it, his cell phone began to ring and the PA system crackled to life. "Mr. Kelly, please call the operator. Mr. Kelly, please call the operator." He looked at Charlotte. "Ms Calhoun why are you away from the ER? Get back to work. I will sort this out." He looked at the three angry looking men and said "Gentlemen, please return to the ICU. I will be in shortly." His cell phone continued ringing, he hit the answer button, but before he could say hello, there was a very upset sounding Se'ighin already talking, "I'm on my way over there now." and hung up. He picked up the nearest hospital phone and called the hospital operator who nervously said, "I'm sorry to bother you, but I have Mrs. Ailbe Reale on the phone for you. She says it's urgent. I'll patch her through." Before he could say no, he heard, "Hello James? I'm holding for Mr. Kelly." Mr. Kelly was nervous, "Yes. Hello Mrs. Reale, It's James. How can I help you?" Ailbe "James, I'm not feeling well or I would come talk to you in person. My Michael has asked that Anastasia be transferred immediately. I think that is a terrible idea, but what is going on down there?" Mr. Kelly "I'm sorry that you were disturbed Mrs. Reale. I'm handling the situation. I hope you feel better. I must run now. Good night." And he hung up hoping that she would forget about this later.

Rach-El was so angry that her hands were shaking. Lindsey sat next to her with her eyes closed trying to calm down. Dr. Connard had taken a few hours to go get some sleep in the doctor's lounge. None of them noticed that the foley catheter collection bag was filling up with blood. Jessica the night nurse, and one of the aids Amy, had seen and heard the entire situation and were writing everything down while it was still fresh in their memory. Jessica was known to make lists for everything. Her co-workers couldn't figure out if she was brilliant for doing it or pre-dementia. Either way, if it was on her list, it got done.

No one was paying attention to the monitors. No one noticed the color draining from Anastasia's face, and still no one noticed the blood in the bag. Michael was still in the hospital parking lot. He had called his father to help him calm down and was still on the phone with him as Arden and Se'ighin pulled into the parking lot. They sat outside talking for a bit. Arden had never seen his son this angry before, and by the sound of things, Rach-El and Lindsey were pretty hot too. Se'ighin went inside to find Mr. Kelly and once Arden felt that Michael had regained his composure, they walked in and passed the emergency room. Arden could here Charlotte yelling and telling co-workers her version of events. Arden tried to drown out her voice but he knew Michael heard every word. They went up the elevator and as the doors open, Malachi was waiting.

Malachi knew to answer the questions asked and not try to elaborate on the event. Arden said what all three men were thinking, "How do the De'nola get any real information this way!?" Michael said, "I really need to get back to Anastasia. I don't want to get too far away and break the link. I just hope she didn't hear any of that." As Michael walked into the ICU unit, he knew something was wrong. There was a flood of information that stopped him. He looked around and nothing seemed out of place. Then he walked into the room. "I need a nurse in here! WHERE is the doctor? I need a doctor in here NOW!"

Rach-El and Lindsey had no idea what was going on. They looked around the room, just a few feet away, almost eye level, was the bag that normally has urine in it, was filled with blood. They wanted to be anywhere else than there. They had not done their job. Arden and the protectors felt useless. All they could do was watch the chaos. Michael went to the head of Anastasia's bed. That was going to be the best place for him to stay out of the way.

He held her head in his hands. He put his forehead onto hers. He felt the link but she wasn't responding. He screamed at her in the link. He wasn't sure if she could respond. He begged her, "Please, please, please fight Anastasia. (He heard 'uck' in their link) Is that you?" She responded, "Who's there? Who are you!?" Michael tried to stay calm. "It's me, it's Michael. Your protector. Great-Grandmother told you to fight, she told me to remind you to fight this." He didn't hear a response. "You are bleeding. I need you to focus and try to heal." He heard a weak response. "Where are you?" Michael felt a flash of hope. "I'm right here. Just follow my voice. Promise me that you will follow my voice."

Arden knew they were in a link. He tried to keep anyone from touching Michael. Rach-El and Lindsey could not justify their actions. No punishment could be worse that what they were doing to themselves. Lindsey said, "Michael will never forgive us." Rach-El said, "I will never forgive us." The two girls curled up together on the bed watching the pain they caused.

Jessica called the urologist Dr. Joel Sweetsir, the nephrologist Dr. Kara Cronin, and the emergency room to see if Dr. Scott was working. She was thankful that he was and asked his to come up STAT. Dr. Connard woke with all the loud PA system calls. He opened the door to find hospital staff running into the ICU. He followed as he recalled his contract with the hospital and the family. "I'm just here to monitor her vital signs and keep her sedated just enough that she doesn't pull on her ventilator tubing, that's it. I can take meal brakes and get sleep as long as there is a family member in there with her... I did nothing wrong. Oh I just hope nothing went wrong." As he walked into the room, he stood off to the side and observed.

Dr. Scott from the ER was on the phone with the laboratory. "I don't care what your protocol says. I'm standing here with girl who is bleeding out. You did a type and cross three days ago! I know because I ordered it. Send me four units of 0 negative blood stat! I will sign off on it and take FULL responsibility. Yes yes yes. The health care proxy is right here and he is talking to his lawyer as we speak. (He was standing next to Arden.

Arden was hanging on every word. He motioned to Arden, who knew exactly what he was asking him to do. Arden pulled out his phone and called his lawyer) Yes Mr. Kelly is right here too. Don't waste another second of my time. Just get me that blood!" Dr. Sweetsir called for a cystoscope, which was already next to him. "I need a sterile field and clear this room." Rach-El and Lindsey could not move quickly enough. They were looking for an opening to slither out. Michael was not going to be moved this time or any other time. He was solely focused on keeping Anastasia talking to him in the link. Jessica read his body language and was not going to choose that battle so she left him there. Arden took just a few steps back as a nurse closed the sliding glass doors.

When the ICU, aka The Alley, was reconstructed last year after his great-grandfather died here. The staff has a lot of input on what they wanted and needed in the unit. The number one issue was access to the rooms. So the architects designed a brilliant proposal. The rooms would have walls that could be opened to create large rooms. They would all face the nurse's station and would be made of thick (bullet proof) shatter proof glass of four panels that could be closed and sealed (isolation precautions, fire, terrorist attack, zombie apocalypse, the list was endless) or opened completely and sits flush against the wall. A large thick curtain could be drawn for visual privacy. The design allowed for countless staff and equipment to be at the patient's bedside.

Jessica called labor and delivery for one of the privacy shields that they use in Cesarean Section (C-section). They put is across the mother's upper chest and keep the father up by her head so no one has to witness what is going on. It was there in seconds. The labor and delivery nurses set it up for her and before they left, one asked, "Is there anything else we can do before we leave?" When no one answered, they gladly left to get out of the way. Once Jessica knew that the room was cleared of family except for Michael who was safely behind the curtain, she flung the lower half of the Anastasia's sheet up around her chest. She took a pair of scissors out of her pocket and cut the balloon that was holding the catheter in place and pulled the foley out and threw the entire thing into the trash can. Michael kept his focus on calling out to Anastasia.

She was weak and her responses were faint but she was responding. "Who were you fighting with?" Michael wasn't expecting the questions but he was glad she was responding. "A nurse. Now focus on my voice and let's get you back here. (My love)" He quickly asked himself if he really just said that, but he wasn't going to dwell on a slip of the tongue right now. Jessica asked Mr. Kelly for two of the float nurses to come and help, which he did without hesitation. And their arrival was welcomed, but no time for lengthy instructions. Jessica told them "Each of you grab a leg and lift her bottom up off the bed." As they did she placed a thick hard orange half board under her hips to give the doctor support as he started the procedure.

Dr. Sweetsir poured Bedadine directly over her pelvic area, a surgical team heard the multiple calls over the PA system to the ICU and were on standy-by. Some of the surgical team wondered upstairs to the ICU to offer assistance. But it was really to get the scoop first hand on what was going on. The entire hospital was aware of the news stories and gossip about the Reale girl lost and sea and found half dead. But Jessica didn't care about any of that, she was glad they were there and asked them to prepare the sterile field. Dr. Sweetsir was scrubbed up and waiting impatiently to proceed. Dr. Scott yelled out to the nurses' station. "Call the lab again. Where is my blood?"

The lab arrived with the blood, Jessica called out, "Can anyone check and handle that for me?" No one responded. Dr. Cronin jumped in. "I got it." She took several empty viles and drew blood off the central line. Dr. Cronin was a paramedic before going to nursing school. During her time as a nurse she hated how some doctors were disconnected from the hands on part of medicine. So she decided to do something about it and went back to school and graduated top of her class in med school.

She followed hospital protocol of verifying patient ID and blood ordered. She hung the unit of blood and opened the IV pump to allow the blood to run in as fast as it could. Dr. Sweetsir inserted the cysto-scope into Anastasia's bladder and found the source of the bleeding and cauterized the area. He inserted a CBI (continuous bladder irrigation) catheter. He looked around that room for the first time. He took a mental note of everyone who jumped in to help. He took a few deep breaths. Everyone was frozen where they stood. He finally said, "Nice job everyone." Jessica quickly started to clean up the room and cover Anastasia. She knew that at least six family members were standing just a few feet away. She opened up the curtain and saw the family standing there consoling each other. She opened up the sliding glass doors and put them flush against the wall.

Dr. Sweetsir was double checking the CBI. He told the two float nurses. "Vital signs every five minutes. Email me each result." He turned his attention to Arden. He put out his hand but Arden stepped in for a hug. "Hello my old friend. I know you are here in a profession manner, but on a personal note, boy am I glad to see you." The two men hugged for a few moments. Dr. Sweetsir looked around, "Well that went south quick. You owe me a stiff drink." Arden felt exhausted, "Joel, I owe you much more than that." Rach-El thought that clearly there was an inside story in there somewhere but she didn't dare say a word. She and Lindsey were terrified of what Michael was going to do once he wasn't focused on Anastasia.

Michael "Anastasia can you hear me?" He felt himself being pulled deeper in the link. She was so far away again. He needed to pull her back.

Michael "The doctor is done. He did a procedure. You had some bleeding in your bladder. Are you in any pain?"

Anastasia "No."

Michael "You have to fight to come back."

Anastasia "I think I want to go back to my friend."

Michael "I will bring your friend here. Just tell me a name."

Anastasia "I don't think I know its names."

Michael "Can you describe them? I will find anyone you need me to find."

Anastasia "It tried to help me. They all tried to help. One called me Princess before it swam away. Why did it say that?"

Michael "Who tried to help you? Did you put it in the link? I can find anyone. Give me something to go on."

Anastasia "I don't know. Why don't I know?!"

He felt her mind foggy from the heavy medications. "Sleep my

Princess. I will not leave your side again. You are safe." Michael kept the
link open as best he could as he felt her drift off.

Ruth and Ailbe woke from a few hours of sleep. Jonathan and Mark
were getting to know their cousins better the De'nola way. They were
talking and exchanging funny stories. Ruth and Ailbe loved seeing family.
They talked about ancient family history and speculated on the future.
The conversation was all light hearted and uplifting. The Norway cousins
were very excited to have been chosen by their clann elder Deaglan to
come on this adventure. They were to make sure the family had all the
help they needed.

Bjorn was their head protector but had no difficulty taking directions
from Mark. Even though Mark trained with their group a few years ago, he
also had additional training by Ailbe since he was 16 years old. He always
hoped that he would never have to use any of her skills but he was glad
he learned them. After two days of travel, Jonathan asked jokingly, "Are
we there yet?" Mark knew he was joking, "Actually, we start our descent
soon." He pretended to get on a radio. "Good morning folks. Our local
time is 7:32a.m. We have started our descent so please buckle up. Keep all
hands and feet inside the aircraft until we have come to a complete stop.
Thank you for flying Air Reale. I'm Captain Marvel Mark and my co-pilot
today is Jerk-face Jonathan. Welcome to Kathmandu and don't forget to
tip your waiter." Ailbe "Oh now stop that and just fly the darn plane. You
know I get nervous flying into this God forsaken place." Only Mark knew
their final destination, although most had figured it out by now. They
packed up their belongings and prepared for landing.

Mark and Jonathan landed the jet with perfect precision. Mark knew
exactly where he was going. He taxied to a private hanger. This airport
was one of the most dangerous in the world and could only be attempted
by the most experienced pilots. The crosswinds, mountains and short
runways have cost many people their lives. Ailbe was glad to be on solid
ground and in one piece.

Jonathan saw four black SUVs parked in front of the hanger. They
pulled up being guided by a man holding two bright orange flashlights.
Once fully stopped, Hans and Erik opened the door. Two men stepped out

of the first car and walked to the plane and stood near the rolling stairs. Then two men stepped out of the second car and walked around the plane and stood towards the rear. Then two other men stepped out of the third car and walked around the plane and stood near the front of the plane. No one moved for a few moments. Then the first two men rolled the steps to the plane and locked the stairs into place. Hans and Erik guided Ruth and Ailbe to the steps and watched them till they were at the bottom. Mark and Jonathan followed close behind but passed them and walked directly to the first SUV. It was already running with the heat on. Mark sat in the driver seat. Jonathan got into the passenger front seat. Olav and Rolf followed next. Olav opened the back driver side door and Ailbe got in and he closed the door. Rolf opened the back passenger side door and Ruth got in and he closed the door and tapped on the roof of the SUV as Mark drove off. Bjorn and Leif remained in the plane. They closed the door and Bjorn finished bringing the plane into the hanger. Olav drove one SUV into the hanger. Hans and Erik got into the third SUV and Olav and Rolf got into the fourth SUV. Hans knew where he was going, so he was in no rush. He knew very well that everyone has a job to do, and he was going to do his very well.

Mark drove about an hour into the Solu Khumbu region. They arrived at a small Inn. Jonathan looked at the exterior. It was an old brick two story structure. The old wood door had seen better days. It had rotted away a bottom, the top was chipped and it didn't latch any longer. It swung slightly in the breeze. The handle didn't fit right into place and was tied on with twine. Jonathan thought. "This is every protector's worst nightmare."

Jonathan heard the back door open. He turned his head quickly to see Ailbe getting out and closed the door. He looked at Mark, who was not moving nor did he look concerned. He looked back at Ruth, who also did not seem to have a care in the world, but now he had to say something. "Grandmother, are you comfortable? Can I get you anything?" Ruth smiled graciously and shook her head no as she looked around him to watch the door. The other two SUVs pulled in and parked beside them. They sat in their vehicles. Jonathan thought. "This has to be a test. Am I the only one who doesn't know what the Hell is going on?"

Ailbe pushed the door open with ease and walked in. There were a few men sitting around at various tables and at the bar. They we shocked to see any visitors to their village. Most tourists are hikers and they want to hike Mt Everest. And this was an elderly woman wearing a modest skirt and 1 inch heels. One man leaned over to his drinking buddy at the bar and asked, "Is that Queen Elizabeth? Of England? I saw pictures of her last year. I think that's her." Ailbe heard the comment but did not acknowledge it. She had business to attend to first. She pulled back a tattered old sheet and stepped into the kitchen. A young thin woman saw her and took a gasping breath. She stood up with her arms outstretched and shouted. "AILBE!!!" and hugged her tightly around her neck. "I did not hear you were coming back so soon." She didn't wait for a response. She turned her head and starting calling, "Geetu... GEETU! Come now. Geetu!" as she turned back to Ailbe. "I am so honored to have you back." A sleepy looking small child turned the corner and through a gap in a doorway covered by a piece of plywood. He was rubbing his eyes when he saw his mother hugging Ailbe. He perked up and started yelling (almost screaming) at the top of his lungs. "Mamma Ailbe, mamma Ailbe!" Geetu was so excited he ran away still yelling, "Mamma Ailbe!" Ailbe laughed at his excitement and turned her attention back to the young woman. "Pia-Jiun, how wonderful to see you. How is the family?" Before Pia-Jiun would reply, Geetu came screaming back into the room pulling and fragile looking elderly man. "See Gaya, see! I told you. Mamma Ailbe is back!"

Geetu dropped his hand and ran to Ailbe. She bent down to greet him and he ran straight into her so fast and hard that he knocked her to the floor. Her skirt pushed up above her knees and her shoes went flying half way across the kitchen floor and her small pillbox hat was tilted sideways. Pia-Jiun grabbed him by the shoulder to pull him off and help Ailbe up, but she was not surprised when Ailbe was laughing and tickling the boy. She rolled him over onto his back, lifted his shirt slightly and raspberried his stomach. The old man stood there with bowed legs and cloudy eyes listening to the sounds of laughter. Ailbe looked over at him. His smile was so welcoming. She just looked at him for a few moments to take in every detail of the moment. Finally the old man clapped his hands together. "Ok, now that you have broken every bone in that old lady's body, go get Imay." Geetu jumped up, kissed Ailbe on the cheek, gave her one more big hug, and ran out the door.

Pia-Jiun was giggling as she helped Ailbe up off the floor. "You do realize he is getting bigger and stronger by the day. You really shouldn't allow him to be so rough with you." Ailbe was going to need some Advil tonight, but she gave Pia-Jiun her hands to help her up. "I know, I know, but for right now. I still think I could take him in a fair fight." The old man laughed. "Yes you could, but he is a feisty child and doesn't fight fair." Ailbe lowered her voice. "Shhhh neither do I. But don't tell anyone." The old man laughed, "I never have and I never will."

The old man put out his hand. Ailbe took it and the long embrace gave Pia-Jiun enough time to stir the rice she had been cooking. She muttered to inform them but not to disturb them, "Go sit down, I will bring you food. How many are with you this time?" Ailbe held up eight fingers. She didn't want to talk. She wanted to enjoy and take in the moment. Pia-Jiun covered the rice and went out front to bring in their guests in from the cold. As she pulled open the front door, a cold blast of air hit her in the face. She just put her arm out to wave the other guests in.

Ruth took a deep breath and opened her door, got out, kicked it closed and ran inside. Mark moved quickly opening and closing his door and running inside. Jonathan looked over at the other cars to see both cousins in both cars get out and run into the building. Jonathan said out loud, "This has to be some kind of a test." He opened his door and as he stepped out, the cold air felt like it went right through him. The twenty feet to get into the building seemed like twenty miles. He was out of breath, his cheeks were bright red, his fingers were blue and he couldn't feel his toes. His cousins were already huddled around the fireplace.

A beautiful young woman was putting more wood into the fireplace. Jonathan wondered, "Where is Grandmother?" As he squeezed right into the middle of the pack. Ruth had gone straight into the kitchen. She saw Ailbe and the old man still in their long embrace. But they had come here for a reason and had to get to. "Mother" she said firmly. "Has Imay been notified?" Ailbe pulled away from the old man. Ruth saw they both had tears in their eyes. Ruth turned and walked back into the dining area. About ten minutes later, all the boys were warm and cozy.

Jonathan was still complaining. "Seriously people. Why am I the last one to be told? I was told to block all links. Are you guys linking? You guys are linking right?" They were laughing but not giving him any satisfaction. Ruth walked up behind him and ruffled his hair. They had pulled three tables together and they saved her the spot closest to the fireplace, but she pulled out the chair next to Jonathan and sat down. Jonathan smirked, "Eat it up gentleman. She likes me best." Ruth leaned back in her chair looking at the group and shook her head and mouthed 'no'. Then she leaned forward again and put her arms around Jonathan, "You know you are my favorite. That is why I picked you as my transporter." Saying it through pursed lips as if she was talking to an infant. The boys all laughed and Jonathan stuck out his tongue.

Pia-Jiun was shaking her head and enjoying the sounds of big laughter and family teasing. She missed these times in her own family since her uncle died. He was a Sherpa. The best Sherpa within a thousand miles of here. He had been up and down Mt. Everest hundreds of times, and saved more lives of stupid rich hikers than anyone could imagine. Nine months ago he was sent to look for a hiker that had gone missing. The hiker strolled back into base camp two days later without a scratch on him, but Juddha wasn't with him. The hiker said he never saw him, but something didn't add up. The search went on for a week without finding a trace of him. The entire village was devastated. Her family has not been the same since.

Pia-Jiun was the best cook in the village. Good thing too, because this was the only place for miles to get food, liquor, and a nice clean warm bed to sleep in. Mark thought, "This is the perfect retreat." As Pia-Jiun put clean plates and silverware on the table, Mark watched and thought she moved with perfect precision. Ruth could smell the food and realized that she was very hungry. To everyone's appreciation, the food came out in quantity and quality. Ailbe and the old man stayed in the kitchen. Ailbe pulled up a wooden crate and fixed him a plate. His hands were old and calloused. He was missing all of his fingers on both hands. She fed him before she would take a bite. She was so tender that an on-looker might think it was a romantic gesture. They sat on the crate eating in silence when the old man giggled. Ailbe waited for him to explain the joke that she was missing. He said, "You know the food is good when six grown men are quiet." Ailbe laughed in agreement. There was no denying that he was right. The food was fantastic. This was her favorite food on the planet.

When Ailbe and the old man were done eating, she took the plates, washed them and put them away. She tidied up and sat down next to him again. She took his hand. "How are you holding up?" He didn't want to talk, he wanted to just sit with her. She pressed a little harder, but knew his level of pain was intense. "How is the village doing?" He didn't want to be rude to Ailbe of all people. He knew she had his best interest at heart. He turned towards her. His eyes were filling with tears. She brushed the tears away. "That's all I needed to know. Now let's show these kids how to make a day of it in Nepal." He motioned her toward the door and said, "You go, I need to get something. I'll be right there." Ailbe kissed his hand and she went and sat down with her family.

Rolf noticed her first and smiled, "Please tell me there is more of..." he realized he had NO idea what he just ate. "Of...um....this." as he pointed to his plate. Pia-Jiun smiled as she began to collect the plates but was embarrassed that she didn't have any more. She lowered her head and said quietly. "No, I didn't know you were coming. Geetu ran to the market. I will have plenty for dinner, breakfast will be a little late, but it will be fresh." Ailbe shot Rolf a glare that he could have sworn pierced his soul. They were literally licking their plate as Ailbe said. "Oh no my sweet baby girl, we won't be staying for breakfast." As she was about to continue her conversation, the old man shuffled out from the kitchen.

He had on an old pair of blue 'Zoot-suit' trousers with suspenders, a Hawaiian shirt that was faded but clearly was once brightly colored, white sock and a pair brown dress shoes that looked way to big on him. He had an apron around his neck with a pocket in the front. There was a large jar in the pocket. Pia-Jiun rushed to his side to help him, she took out the jar and set in on the bar. The protectors all noticed that he had no fingers on either hand. Then their attention went to the contents of the jar.

It looked thick and brown, almost like mud. Ailbe's eyes got wide, her smile was almost electric. She took a deep breath that felt like she sucked the air out of the entire room. Her hand flew up to her mouth. "Is THAT what I think it is!?" He smiled like a coy teenage. "Yes it is." She looked at the table for a glass. She was closest in proximity to Mark. She grabbed his glass and threw the liquid content in the fireplace and sashayed up to the bar. "I thought I would never see or taste it again!" The old man was so proud of himself. "I have been saving it for the right occasion, and if you are back this soon, then it is the right occasion."

Mark suddenly understood what Jonathan meant by being confused about what is going on. Mark had been here once before. Last year when one of the old man's sons had died, but he was sworn never to talk about it and Ailbe made him stay at a hotel in Kathmandu. Pia-Jiun pulled out fresh glasses from behind the bar. The men who were in there when the family arrived had been long gone. Jonathan looked at Mark and said. "Am I the only one who's Spidy-sense is tingling?" Mark shrugged his shoulder. "I have never understood her (Ailbe) and this place. Stay sharp. I feel eyes on me."

Ruth was taking it all in. Every detail of every nook and cranny. She never understood her mother's connection to this place. She had only been here three times but was always told to stay in a hotel back in Kathmandu. This is only her second time even seeing the old man. And the first time was only a wave at the door when she picked her up from a month long vacation. Heck, she still didn't even know his name. Her mother never allowed it in a link, never talked about it. It's like this place doesn't exists. Ruth knows her mother is the most powerful Azili alive right now, and she was resolved not to make her angry.

Michael lifted his head and saw his father and Dr. Sweetsir talking. Michael had known Dr. Sweetsir for most of his life. He felt relief for his father that he had a friend here to talk to. He felt betrayed by Charlotte and did not want to deal with anymore drama for today. He felt intense fear in the room. He leaned back down and touched his forehead to Anastasia's. He called out in the link, "Don't be afraid, I'm right here. You have protectors now, you're safe." He heard a faint response. He wasn't trained to go deep, he knew he could hurt them both. He felt she understood but the fear was growing. "Please Anastasia, please don't be afraid." She mustered up enough energy. "Not me, them."

Michael felt the powerful medications in her system. "Sleep well." He kissed her forehead and looked up. He hadn't even notice Rach-El and Lindsey holding each other so close they could be considered merged. They both felt the blood run out of their faces when he looked at them. He walked around the hospital bed and as he passed his father and Dr. Sweetsir, he put a hand on his father's shoulder and gave an exhausted nod. He took a few more steps toward his sister and cousin.

Michael had never hit anyone in anger. He was 6'4" about 195lbs of muscle and broad shoulders. It takes a lot of work to get him angry, but when he reaches that point, mountains move out of his way. They didn't know what to do and their options to choose from were getting smaller by the second. Michael had his head down when he took the last step. He was in striking distance. Lindsey loosened her grip on Rach-El as if she was about to run. Michael reached his arms out and around the two girls. He hugged them so tight that they both lost their breath. Neither knew what was happening. Was he killing them? Rach-El felt she was about to loose consciousness when he loosened his hold just enough so they could breath again. They each took a deep breath expecting the second wave of fury.

He finally collected himself enough to kiss each of them on the head. He released his grip and walked silently back into the room. Rach-El looked around and took notice of all the extra staff that was still in the ICU. Some were documenting, some were cleaning, some were on the phone to other departments, and it was all a blur. In a low whisper she said, "I have never felt more useless and terrified in my life." Lindsey couldn't remember what just happened. She was frozen and replied, "I can't feel my face. Tell me the truth. Did he just rip my face off?"

Dr. Cronin was at the computer checking results. She printed several pages and walked back in the room. Michael was standing back at the head of the bed with both hands on either side of Anastasia's head. She started talking to Michael but he put his hand up to stop her. "Please Dr. Cronin, With all due respect… I can't, I just can't anymore today. Please speak to my father." And he lowered his hand. She felt an overwhelming urge to give him a hug. She thought, "He is so young to be taking on so much responsibility. He must love her very much." She didn't disturb him further.

She stepped out and interrupted Arden and Dr. Sweetsir. "What a night… but I do have some test results. Who wants the good news and who wants the bad news?" Arden said, "I could use some good news and you two can talk over there about the bad news. I can't hear it right now." Dr. Cronin nodded, "I can understand why. Well, the good news is that her lab work has improved slightly. You know that medicine is a practice and we try this, and if it doesn't work, then we try that, and so on. I think what we are doing now is working, but her body has been through an unimaginable trauma and needs time to heal. I will leave you two alone. I will see her in the morning." She noticed Rach-El and Lindsey still clinging to each other. She smiled and left.

Bina wanted desperately to go to the hospital with Arden. Two of her children were in emotional pain and she wanted to be there. Arden left her with a list of things to do that would help. First she had food prepared and sent over. She almost considered calling Curtis to go lights and sirens, but thought better of asking. Second she had cleared it with James Kelly to order a bed for Michael to sleep on. She also arranged to have two hospital rooms up on the top floor for protectors to get some rest.

There are currently two hundred and three fully trained protectors, four classes of twenty who are about to graduate, two classes of teenagers who are too young now, but are in training. And for the first time, they have an all female special unit that has been training at multiple compounds and are here for the July 4th party. Also, most of the men in her generation were trained as protectors. There are so many coming and going from the hospital that everyone is a bit frayed and tired. But right now Anastasia is the priority and all hands on deck. "We all have a job to do, and I'm going to do mine very well." She thought. Third thing was to have Rach-El more involved as a protector. She has been training with Michael and needs to be more involved. Her new instructor would be contacting her shortly. Fourth is to get things moving along for the July 4th festivities. "We have less than two month to go and we are behind schedule."

Mr. Kelly sat down in his office chair hard. He looked out the window at the sky. "Thank God she made it." Now he had to call in Charlotte to find out what in the Hell was she doing. He called down to the emergency room and asked for her to be sent up. She was walking through his door before he could organize his thoughts. She had already started talking before she even got into his office and at a high rate of speed. His head was spinning. He put up both hands in hopes that she would shut up but not have to say the actual words. Thankfully she did because he was about to loose his patience.

She watched him take a few breathes and then she started talking again. "You and everyone else here knows that Michael and I have been together for over five years, I'm not some one night stand following him around. You even told me to make sure that they have everything they need right! You remember that right? Well, I just went up to say hi and his bitchy cousin was whining about no food around here so I offered them my dinner. Mine! That I brought from home. And she flipped out on me! Michael always takes his family's side on everything, so he flipped out on me too. Then his sister, who by the way is my best friend. Well...she WAS my best friend, and then she called her other cousin to have me taken out! And for what??? Because I tried to protect the hospital from them complaining about how much money they give this place and they have to eat from a vending machine! I'm so pissed right now and you should be too. They badmouth all the nurses and the doctors aren't smart enough. It's just rich people bullshit. I'm not going to get in trouble for trying to bring them food am I? You can talk to Dr. Scott, It was super slow and I asked him if I could go up and he said 'sure'. And what is up with them pushing me like that! Did you see them have their hands on me? It is a federal law that you can't hurt a nurse when she is at work. You know that right? I should press charges. My arms are still hurting. If I have bruises tomorrow, I'm gonna call the cops on them and you are my witness that they grabbed and dragged me down the hall. You are my witness. They are not even supposed to be here. You are liable for anything they do ya know. You are letting them walk all over this place. I'd put a stop to that before they hurt another nurse!"

He didn't even hear much of what she actually said. All he heard was high pitched screeching. He had to jump in while she paused to take a breath. "Listen. Calm down. (she started to interrupt) Take a few days off. (She started to talk over the top of him but he just kept talking) Obviously it will be paid. Think of it as a mini vacation. I will get your shifts covered and I will approve it with payroll that this is a paid time off. Go and relax. Make up with Michael. (She started to pace and talk, but he ignored it) And when you come back, this will all be a distance memory for everyone." She thought for a moment, "Fine. As long as I'm not in any trouble." He would have givin her is car to get her out of his office. "No no no. No one is in any trouble. You have to understand that Michael is under tremendous stress right now. You two love birds will be married with kids and laugh about your first fight. Now I have a lot of work to do. So have a good rest of the night, and start your vacation at 7:01a.m."

She wanted to vent some more but was satisfied with a week paid time off. So she agreed and left. When her shift was over, she gave report to the incoming nurses and she left. Now that she was off work and alone in her car she replayed the scene over and over in her head. She liked what Mr. Kelly said about this was their first real fight in five years. He was right and she knew in her heart that she would text Michael a good apology and he would forgive her. After all, she believed that she knew him better than anyone else.

The room which was so warm and cozy had a sudden breeze and chill. The protectors and Ruth turned toward the door expecting all their enemies to storm the room. Nope, it was just a deluge of villagers. All making their way to see Ailbe. Mark and Jonathan stepped into a corner so they could be prepared for anything. The other protectors had the same reaction. Jonathan was curious to see his grandmother also positioned herself near the rear door. Pia-Jiun was grabbing every container she could find to use as shot glasses. She even took beer bottles out of the trash and rinsed them out. She started lining containers up on the bar.

Pia-Jiun opened the jar and took a sniff. Mark noticed her and thought it must have tickled. He wondered if he felt it tickle her nose as he scratched his own. He wanted to help her as he watched her stir up the contents of the jar and dip the glasses in to fill them. Ailbe was in her glory. It felt like the entire village had come to see her. She was hugging and kissing and slapping people on their arms. Mark had never seen her like this. Ailbe passed out the containers until everyone had one. She lifted her glass and bellowed, "I would like to make a toast." The old man shuffled close to her. Mark thought, "This is it. Shit gonna get real any second." The other protectors felt his tension and got ready. They each starting picking out who they needed to take out first. They were trained to go for the big ones first. They all made eye contact and a knowing nod.

The old man said. "I will give my toast first." Ailbe lowered her container and bowed slightly and took a half a step backward. Someone in the crowd yelled "Hey, they don't have a glass." The entire bar turned to look at the protectors. But Jonathan was going to do his job. But Ailbe looked like she was the only real threat in the room. The men each took a container and wondered where they could pour it out. The old man stood up straight, regardless of the pain that Ailbe knew he was in. He cleared his throat. "To my friend, my confidant, my heart, and my protector. I have kept all your secrets close and your love closer. My home is the home of you and your people. My family and our village will continue to fight for the Azili. (Mark almost passed out thinking 'WHAT DID HE JUST SAY?') We pray for you all everyday until the time you go to dine with your ancestor. May you all give your bond wisely and find peace!" He drank the liquid, and then everyone else drank. The cheer that followed was deafening. The protectors all looked at Ruth for guidance if they should drink or not. She was gone. They leaned into a run when they heard Ailbe's voice. "Now boys! A lady does not need six men to escort her to the restroom! Now did you miss the toast?" They all looked at the drink in their hand. Jonathan said, "Oh, what the hell." And he downed the shot. The other five followed and all six felt like they just swallowed a live hand grenade. The cheer that followed was explosive.

Pia-Jiun collected the containers and started filling them again. The protectors started to make their way toward each other. Once they were all shoulder to shoulder they started to compare notes. Erik said, "I'm looking forward to the next one." They all looked at him. He laughed loudly, "Cause it will kill me and put me out of my misery." Ailbe was satisfied that everyone had a full glass, she raised her glass. Ruth appeared at Jonathan's side. Everyone was startled. Jonathan jumped and shouted, "Where the frig did you come from!?" Ruth laughed a little bit harder than she expected to. "I wouldn't drink that if I were you." They were all thinking it, but Jonathan had to be the one to ask. "Why not?" Jonathan started giggling uncontrollably as he watched Ruth's face turn colors and slide onto the floor. She looked at the other protectors and pointed. "That's why." She turned to walk back into the kitchen again when she heard them all start laughing.

Ailbe started her toast. "Old man, your family has protected us, sheltered us and fed us for thousands of years. Now your village has shown us the same love. I raise my glass in respect and vow that all Azili will know of your heroism. I love you and I love my village. So a toast to my village!!!" she drank and raised her glass and everyone else drank. This time the six newest male members of the village cheered too. Several of the villagers brought musical instruments and the debauchery began. The singing, dancing, and hugging their new friends, was all a bit much for Ruth to partake in. But she loved to watch anyone having fun. She did feel bad that the meeting was going to begin soon.

Geetu came running in through the back door and made his way to Ailbe. He was so proud of himself that he completed what she had needed him to do. She hugged him and said, "I charge you with caring for the old man." He threw back his shoulders and said, "Just like your protectors, I'm his protector." Ruth nodded to Ailbe that it was time to go. Ailbe leaned over to Pia-Jiun, "Keep your eye on Mark, Watch him very closely. Make sure that they can't follow us." She laughed widely, "Who? Those boys?" she nodded in their direction. "The ones trying to teach the village (in air quotes) 'walk like Davy Jones…hey hey we're the monkeys.' You mean those boys? They won't be following you." The two women shook their heads.

Ruth and Ailbe walked outside and up a small hill. The amount of noise coming from the Inn would drown out any sound of the approaching helicopters. Ruth looked at her mother, who was swaying a bit. "Mother, are you ok to do this?" Ailbe just looked at her and winked. Two helicopters were approaching quickly. One landed while the other made small circles above it, a man jumped out and opened the side door for the women. They got in without hesitation. The man jumped in behind them, slammed the door and jumped back into the co-pilot seat. And without a word, the helicopters were gone.

Michael stood and the head of Anastasia's bed for over twelve hours without moving. Dr. Connard had positioned a seat in that corner so he could be comfortable and monitor her vitals, but with Michael standing there, he was forced to come in and out of the room. There was a slight commotion but Michael did not move. He was linked with her and was continuously singing every song he could remember and reassuring her. He heard familiar voices but he was NOT going to leave her.

"No, first you have to take that."

"Oh dear God, could you be any louder?"

"No, put it here! No! Not there. HERE!"

"Just give it to me. You can go. I feel sorry for your bond! I bet she irons your underwear!" Michael opened his eyes and looked up. Rach-El and Lindsey had the small bed that the hospital provided him out and another small bed brought in. Michael felt fatigued but he appreciated the gesture. The girls were trying so hard to be quiet. He watched them fumble, trip and drop things for a few minutes. But when he saw Rach-El trying to make the bed, he laughed. They both turned around. Rach-El said very softly. "Mom sent over a new bed and we (she pointed at herself and Lindsey) went across the bridge to that store that Grandmother gets all her sheets from. We want you to be as comfortable as you can." She took a cautious step towards him. "Michael, I (Lindsey whispered "we" into her ear) um…. We are so sorry. We don't know what to say. I…. um, I meant WE hate ourselves. But could you ever not hate us?" Michael smiled and rubbed his eyes. "I don't hate you. How could I ever hate you? I'm just tired and freaking out. I'm her protector. Twice I left my duty, and twice something bad happened. You guys should be mad at me, not the other way around."

Lindsey burst into tears. She loved her cousin very much. She hated to see him hurting like this. "What can we do? Really, anything, just name it!" Michael tried to smile but it was half hearted. "Naw. I think I'll feel better after I talk to Charlotte. I was super tired and super hungry. I was wrong to snap at her like that." Lindsey sat down on the half made bed. Rach-El bit her bottom lip. They didn't say anything. Michael didn't like this at all. "What? Why are you acting like that? Did something happen?"

He pulled out his phone to check messages. He scrolled through normal family group text and voicemails. Then he saw a few from Charlotte and pages from some of her friends. He looked up and tossed his phone to Rach-El. "Please delete anything that is going to piss me off." Rach-El started deleting pages and pages of text messages. "Um... Can we tell you what happened?" Michael didn't want to talk anymore. He needed to make sure Anastasia was ok. Lindsey sent a text message to her dad Antonio asking for his advice. "Father, I really messed things up here for Michael. I need help." Antonio texted back, "I'm in the car with Se'ighin. He wants to visit with Anastasia." Lindsey tucked her phone away and sat on the bed quietly.

Antonio is married to Olivia, Ruth's second child. Olivia and Antonio have four children. Jonathan, Ace, Steven, and Lindsey. Lindsey is the youngest and only girl. With three brothers, she was more of a tom-boy than she was a pigtail and cute clothes girl. So she fit in perfectly. Antonio is from the Andalusia region in Spain and looks every inch the part of an imposing Flamenco dancer. He is tall and thin, with pitch black hair that he slicks back. When he walks, his shoulders move in an almost poetic motion. When he stands still, his back is slightly arched and shoulders back. His bum looks tucked in and with indents on each side. If you ever see him with his shirt off you would swear than no man could have stomach muscles like that naturally. He speaks with a thick old-world sounding Spaniard accent but most people don't listen to what he says, they just want to hear him talk. Not many people have ever heard him raise his voice. As a matter of fact, when he is angry, he lowers his voice. But the most striking feature for Michael was that he could smell him before he entered a room. It wasn't a heavy fragrance that came from a bottle...no, it was his natural ambient air about him.

Michael loves him deeply and considers him his favorite uncle, but would never say it out loud. Michael remembers countless times when their fathers would take them on a 'boys only' trip. Those were the best! Their dads would let them fish, climb trees, stay up all night, eat junk food, burp, and fart without sayings 'excuse me'. Good times....

Michael was overjoyed when he smelled him walk into the room. Michael opened his eyes, his grandfather Se'ighin and favorite uncle were standing there. He told Anastasia in the link that they had come to visit. He saw her foot move and heard her in the link. "What is that beautiful smell? It seems so familiar to me." Michael "That would be Uncle Antonio. You are going to adore him." he smiled and walked around the bed to greet them both. Se'ighin realized immediately why Michael has been exhausted and maybe a bit irritable. Se'ighin was not here in an official 'Reale family elder' manner, he was just a grandfather very worried about his grandson. He would leave the business end of this to his very capable wife. He motioned to Rach-El and Lindsey. "You ladies look like you need some fresh air." And before he could turn his attention back to Michael *poof* they were out of the room.

Antonio grabbed Michael's face firmly with both hands and kissed his cheeks three times. (Right side, left side and right side again) Then stepped back to allow Se'ighin to greet him. Se'ighin said, "Come, let's sit for a minute." The two men sat on the bed and Antonio pulled over a chair and sat down facing them. Se'ighin held Michael's hand and sat quietly for a moment. Michael noticed how amazing he was feeling sitting with the two men. Se'ighin smiled, "Do you feel better now?" Michael thought the question was odd, but responded, "Having you both here is a real shot in the arm." Antonio laughed and patted his leg. "Yes, but how does your body feel?"

Michael had been taught from infancy that he will be continuously learning things about 'us'. As he masters one skill, another skill will be taught. It takes time and maturity and a dedication. Many give up in their teens and then gradually start training again in their twenties or so. He was keenly aware that his parents are far more powerful than he was, and grandmothers' generation is where they were the most powerful. His great-grandmother Ailbe is the most powerful woman on the planet. One of her endless talents is that she is the only one who can speak directly to the ancestors. Another is she is the only one at the moment allowed to ask for a blessing. So with that in mind, Michael knew he was about to learn something...

Michael "Actually, I do feel less fatigued."

Se'ighin "Michael, when we touch someone, even the De'nola, we give a little of ourselves. The person we are touching takes that energy and feels uplifted. That is why we teach you from a very young age about who and when to touch someone. The family is big on hugging because we freely exchange with each other. But we set firm boundaries to protect ourselves. Do you understand?"

Michael felt an epiphany. "Ohhh, wait. So when we link while we are touching...what does that do?"

Antonio smiled at Se'ighin as he replied. "Now it usually takes two to exchange energy. One giving and one receiving. Both are aware and one only gives a little and one only take a little. You follow?" Michael nodded yes.

Se'ighin continued, "What is happening here is, she is as close to death without going to the ancestors that I have ever felt. She does not want to die and is fighting with her failing body. Are you still following me?" Michael was taking in every word and nodded yes. "I don't think either one of you know what you are doing to the other one. But you are freely giving her your Chi and she is freely feeding hers for the purpose of healing her body."

Michael put his hands up to his head and made a motion that his head exploded. "Well that is a piece of 'need to know' information. WOW. I feel better just knowing that. We should really put that in the Kindergarten manual."

Antonio laughed, "So now that you have a new skill to work on, how are we going to proceed? This is uncharted territory. May I suggest that we start to have healthy family members come for a visit, take the skill that Noah mastered, and have them come two by two and give her small amounts of their energy. Then no one person is drained."

Se'ighin smiled. "Brilliant idea. And I will see you every few days to make sure that I give you some of mine."

Michael questioned, "So is some peoples' energy better or worse than others?" Antonio was beaming with pride and slapped his own hands together. "See Se'ighin, I told you! He has Ailill's spirit guiding him."

Se'ighin did look very proud. "Excellent, you are going to master this skill very quickly... Yes and no. You can be out camping with your favorite uncle, cutting firewood, setting up camp and you feel energized. Then there is verbal argument with your girlfriend and you feel drained." Michael sat there taking in every word. He realized that Se'ighin's left hand was on his shoulder and Antonio was leaning forward so his right hand was on his lower leg. "Wait... you guys are doing it now. Right? I mean that I feel like I could take on a small country all by myself."

Se'ighin smiled at Antonio and tried to mimic his accent "Bueno mi amigo, Nuestro trabajo aqui' ha terminado." (Well my friend, our work here is done.) Then he continued "My counsel to you is, 1. If she is communicating with you, let her know what's happening. I can't imagine her doing this to you on purpose. 2. Set limits on how long you touch her for. Several light touches instead of camping on her forehead. 3. Most importantly, take care of yourself first. I've given you a lot of information in a small amount of time. Don't get overwhelmed and DO NOT OVER THINK IT." Michael smiled. "How did the ancestors choose me to have you two in my life I will never know, but I'm so glad they did." Se'ighin stood up "Now let me say a proper hello to my new niece." He walked to her side.

He opened a link but did not expect much. He reached under the sheet and touched the palm of her hand. He could feel that she was very powerful. In the link he said, "I'm Se'ighin. Michael, your protector, is my grandson. We are all praying for you. Fight this and come back to us." He was pleasantly surprised when she responded. "I heard you. Is it true that I hurt Michael?" Michael knew they had linked and hoped they were communicating. Se'ighin smiled and Michael knew they were. "You drained him, you didn't hurt him." She felt ashamed. "I don't understand, but I promise I won't talk with him anymore if it hurts him." Se'ighin didn't know how to explain it to her. How can she be this powerful but not know anything about the power she has? He had been tremendously skeptical of this entire situation, but in the link he 100% knew she was telling the truth. "Now that would truly hurt him. He is your protector. Keep your link with him open. Your memories will come back in time." He broke the link and asked for Michael to step out of the room with them for a moment. Michael was full of energy and sprang up from the bed and was on the other side of the curtain like a kid. Se'ighin and Antonio shrugged their shoulders and followed him.

Michael "What's up?"

Antonio "What happen with Charlotte?"

Se'ighin "Lindsey and Rach-El are very upset. Neither of them has ever felt the need to call a protector into a situation before."

Michael "What??? For who? For Charlotte? Why?"

Antonio "Michael you tell us. We didn't want to have any information from anyone but you. You are the one who needs to find out what happened. If you are considering giving your bond to Charlotte, may I suggest that you get some rest and figure out how you feel."

Michael "It all happened kind of fast. Lindsey was going to get us something to eat. I didn't realize about being drained." He was recalling the conversation. "Wow, I snapped pretty hard. I felt like she disrespected the family…and I left…. Yeah, thinking about it, maybe calling my elders was childish. I guess I have some apologies to hand out and some crow to eat."

Se'ighin "One of the most difficult things for us to do is dating or bonding with a De'nola. We just don't understand the head games and drama that they seem to enjoy. Before you do any apologizing, link with Rach-El and Lindsey. Find out what happened and how they felt and why they did what they did. If you still want to apologize, then I will support your choice."

Michael "I will. I'm so sorry for all this chaos. I really felt I was ready to do this job."

Antonio "You are doing a fantastic job. In all our history, we have never had something like this. No one could have taught you how to prepare for this. We don't even know what THIS is. We are breaking new ground here. You and Anastasia will be in our history links forever." As he swung his hands up over his head in overly dramatic gesture.

Se'ighin "I will see you in a day or two. We have lots to do back at the house. I will start having family visits start tomorrow."

The men hugged Michael and they left. Michael felt very satisfied, like after eating a large Thanksgiving dinner. He mumbled, "Note to self: my family rocks!" He went back and stood at Anastasia's side.

Dr. Connard had taken the opportunity to sit back in his chair when he saw Michael was out of the room talking to some family and the girls were taking a walk. Michael didn't mind, he would take what he has learned and master this skill. He looked at her laying there. He would give his life to protect her and he still knew nothing about her, but that was just details. He knew all he needed to know. She was the strongest woman that he had ever met. "Where have you been? I would have saved you if I knew.... (He reached under the sheet and took her hand.) But nothing else matters right now except you healing." He heard a quiet but stronger response. "I will." Michael smiled and sat down on the bed. It felt just like his bed at home. He laid down and thought, "You should be here with me." He didn't think he said it in the link, but he felt her move closer to him.

Antonio and Se'ighin walked out of the hospital toward their car. Rach-El and Lindsey were standing there waiting. Both girls chewing on their finger nails and kicking pebbles. Antonio thought the girls looked so pitiful. Normally he would take an opportunity to tease them, but this was not the time. Before they could speak, Se'ighin explained to them. "Michael has not heard anything about the words you had with Charlotte after he left, nor does he want to revisit the situation. He wants to speak to you both but he is not angry with anyone. He feels responsible for what happened. I expect you girls to say your peace about it and then come back to the compound for a good night sleep." Lindsey didn't say a word, she just hugged her father and started crying again.

Antonio felt his daughter feeling deeply distraught. He kissed her on the top of the head. "Go talk to him. You will feel much better." All she could do was nod yes. Rach-El had nothing to say either. She put her arm around Lindsey's shoulders and the two girls walked back into the hospital. Antonio's heart was breaking for his daughter, he wanted to fix it. Se'ighin tapped the car hood to get his attention. "Let them handle this by themselves. It will bring them all closer. Michael will reassure them. Let's get home. I have a family schedule to make. Ruth is so much better at all of this than I am. Did Jonathan happen to mention how long they would be gone?" Both men knew that a transporter would never discuss anything of travel plans. Antonio shook his head no and got into the driver seat with Se'ighin in the passenger seat and the drove off.

The girls walked back into the hospital and into Anastasia's room. Michael heard the curtain open. He sat up smiling and patted the bed for them to come and sit down. Michael whispered so Dr. Connard would not hear them. "We are going link what happened and then that is the last of it. I was the one who was overtired and irritable. All you two did was protect me and Anastasia, and when you felt a threat, you called a protector. That is exactly why I love you guys. You did your jobs very well. I am so proud!" The two girls dissolved into each side of his chest. The three of them opened a link together. They exchanged information and closed the link. Michael put his finger to his mouth and said. "I have nothing to add except that I am sorry that I put either of you in that position. I am responsible. Period. Not another word. Now go home and get some rest. I think the staff here has everything under control." Rach-El opened her mouth to speak, but Michael stood up, "So Dr. Connard, how is my cousin doing?" Dr. Connard started to update him on her vital signs while the girls stood up and wiped the tears from their eyes and they left. No one saw the tears running down Anastasia's face.

CHAPTER 2

*A*ilbe looked out at the mountains as they flew towards their destination. "I will never get tired of this view." They flew for about thirty minutes. Imay motioned for them to put on their oxygen masks, which they did. Another ten minutes and they flew over a small cabin. Ruth looked down to see seven other helicopters in a small clearing a few yards away. Two men with bright orange flashlights where giving Imay visual assistance to land. Once on the ground, Imay stayed in the helicopter as the other man took off his seatbelt and climbed into the back and opened the door. The two men with the flashlights assisted the ladies out, and then he shut the door with himself inside. The four walked to the small cabin. One man opened the door and the two ladies went inside, followed by the second man with the flashlight. He locked the door from the inside and stayed at the door. The cabin was Ailbe's great-great-grandfather's. He built it strong enough to withstand any natural or unnatural storm. From the outside it was rather unassuming, but the inside was warm and cozy. Family photos dotted the walls, a substantial library lined the staircase, there were deep tunnels that ran for miles, and bomb shelters to comfortably sleep fifty people for months if needed. Thankfully, they had never needed it and it fell into a distant memory. So this was the perfect place to meet.

All seven other elders stood and embraced Ailbe and Ruth. Ailbe looked into each of their faces. "My children! All eight of you here together is the best gift I could ever receive." Then her expression and tone went into business. "Ruth is the head of the family, but I called this meeting. We must figure out who this girl is. I don't want to risk linking until we have to. Let's talk this through. The questions that must be answered are:

1. Who is she?
2. Is she a threat?
3. Where did she come from?
4. Who has had her?
5. And finally, how many protectors, healers and fighters can you spare and keep your clann safe?

Now, has everyone spoken to their family? Does anyone have any new information?"

They all talked for another two hours. The elders were more frustrated than ever. No one had any information. Ailbe put her hands up to quiet the room. "I had high hopes that we missed something, one piece that would put this whole puzzle together. I was mistaken. We cannot allow what happened in Atlantis to happen again. It still haunts me as our most devastating loss since our escape. We will say our good-byes now, then link. I will not risk the Eile sensing us." They all hugged tightly and said their peace and promised to be in touch soon. Ruth promised daily updates and her siblings promised to send protectors to help immediately. Ailbe instructed the man at the door to tell the pilots to be ready for immediate take off in ten minutes. He unlocked the door and left.

Ailbe stood in the center of the room. Her eight children formed a circle around her. They held hands and stepped in until they were shoulder to shoulder. They lifted their hands to touch Ailbe. She opened the link strictly to her children. The link was strong.

They exchanged every detail of everything that they knew, everything that their children knew, and everything that their grandchildren and great grandchildren knew. With such a strong link, they also exchanged the feelings, smells and sounds of all their memories. Ailbe closed the link satisfied that everyone had done their job to try to figure out who Anastasia was, but the impossible truth was that no one knew. Ailbe smiled and said "One small toast to my children before we leave." She went into the kitchen and took out nine shot glasses that all had a variety of Disney characters on them. She pulled open a cabinet and in the back was a brown bottle with a cork half pushed in. She gripped it with her teeth and pulled it out. The smell brought her back to beautiful memories on the mountain.

She poured the nine shots and put them on a tray and returned to the living room. Buach was the first to see the shot glasses and roared with laughter "Are those the glasses from out Disney trip!?" Ailbe nodded yes and the group started all talking at the same time about what a great trip it was and all the beautiful memories they had together before they had to separate. They each took a glass. Ailbe lifted her's, "To the family." They all drank, put their glasses down and left. They were all back in the helicopters that they had arrived in and up off the ground in minutes.

Ailbe and Ruth were sad to leave. Ruth hasn't seen her siblings in four years since Ailbe announced her plans that she would be stepping down as head of the family in the next few years. Ruth had hoped that she would not be chosen as her successor, but when she was, she accepted her duties as an honor. Ruth visited each of her siblings individually to receive their recognition. But it was too risky for more than two elders to be in the same place. She loved that all of her children lived on the compound but hated that one day her family would have to be separated too. They flew back in silence.

Ailbe and Ruth landed and headed back the inn. They could hear the music and singing long before they entered through the kitchen door. Ailbe shouted over the noise to Ruth. "I LOVE THIS SONG!" and she kicked up her heels and was off to make her way to the middle of the dance floor. Ruth watched as her mother sang and danced for the next few hours. She could have watched that ruckus crowd the rest of her life, but her mind focused on the war that was coming. She rounded up her boys and motioned to Ailbe that she had fifteen minutes until sunrise.

She had a difficult time convincing the protectors that it was time to go. Mark suddenly realized "Ut oh. I've been driving, I can't drink! We shh would just sway whitt here." The last few words were not real clear but Ruth understood the message. She loaded three protectors in each car. Two in the back seat and one in the passenger seat. Both helicopters had landed and the four men arrived at the inn to give Ruth a hand. Two of the men got into the driver's seat of the two cars loaded with the very inebriated protectors and left.

Ruth looked at her watch, "Two more minutes and then I have to go get her. What has my life become that I have to drag my 104 year old mother out of a bar?" But Ailbe was in the car in 1 minute 58 seconds. "Right on time Mother." Ailbe just rolled her eyes and tried to smile. Imay and the other man from their helicopter got into the front seats and they drove out heading for the airport.

Dr. Connard finished giving Michael the update on Anastasia's health status for the past twenty four hours. Michael sat back down on the new comfortable bed. He wished it had been here the entire time. His back was stiff and cracked every time he stretched. He was going to have a good night sleep. He thought it must be well past 7p.m. because it was dark out. He didn't have a watch on and was too tired to get up and look at the clock in the nurses' station. He thought of what he was going to say to Charlotte. He didn't want to fight, he usually just gets her a card, some flowers and has the family jeweler make her something blingy and apologizes. He doesn't think of those as fights. Those little things don't even happen very often, but they have had disagreements in the past, nothing big. Just sometimes she says things that she considers joking, but that he just couldn't understand. But this time he knew that it was his fault. He needs to own this one.

He thought for a few more minutes and called down to the emergency room. When he asked for Charlotte the ER tech said, "Hey Michael, it's Kirsten. Charlotte is off the rest of the week. Roberta is covering for her. Do you want to talk to her?" Michael knew she was supposed to be working tonight and thought he needs to find out more of what happened. "No, that's fine. I'll try her later." He hung up his phone and noticed it was almost midnight. He thought, "Wow, it's that late? I'll call her tomorrow."

Charlotte tossed and turned but finally fell asleep. When she woke up she grabbed her phone to see if she missed any calls from Michael. When there were no missed calls or text messages, she was furious. "I hope he's miserable!" but Charlotte was not one to sit around and do nothing. She got up, took a shower, and got dressed up. She called a few friends to go out with. She was going to be seen all around town having a great time and looking fabulous. "I'll make him SO jealous. I might even start seeing one of his cousins. That'll piss him off!" She giggled at her plan, took out her license and a credit card and put them in her bra, grabbed her phone and keys and left her apartment.

She met up with a few friends at the one and only hot spot in town. Kat, Andi, Emily and Charlotte have been friends for as long as they could remember. But since Charlotte started dating Michael, she has been more interested in getting in good with his family than hanging out with her old friends. But not tonight, she was going to reconnect with her good old party years. The girls screamed and hugged when they meet at the door. They walked in hand-in-hand and made their way straight to the bar. It was still a bit early for the place to be in full swing, but that gave the girls plenty of room on the dance floor. They wanted to be noticed and they got noticed.

Almost everyone in the bar knew either Charlotte or Michael or both. Charlotte was not holding back in telling everyone her version of events. Charlotte could play the victim better than anyone and she felt she was finally getting the sympathy that she deserved. Men were buying them drinks and asking them to dance, and as the night went on, the drunk texts began.

Kat was the selfie queen in the group. She documented her life down to the decision of which spoon to stir her coffee with. Michael enjoyed being around her because he felt that she was the most loyal out of Charlotte's group of friends. Michael had even asked her out on a date when they were teenagers. They stayed in contact for awhile but Michael was traveling to train and didn't have much time for a girlfriend. Andi was the sweet one in the group. Always making sure everyone was having a good time. And Emily was the muscle. She made sure that no one got too friendly with any of her drunken friends or she would start a verbal shaming that could make anyone go hide under a rock. Tonight was no different. As Charlotte continued to embellish her story a little more each time she repeated it, the text and photo messages to Michael became more and more aggressive. And Charlotte was becoming more and more angry when there were no responses. She started to think of her next strategic action. But Ain't Your Mama by Jennifer Lopez started playing and she forgot all about being angry, tonight they would party till the sun came up.

The next few days were quiet. Anastasia was improving. Multiple doctors had been in and out several times a day. Se'ighin felt her progress was to the point that Dr. Connard no longer needed to be at Anastasia's bedside, but he agreed to continue to be at the hospital and available 24/7. He was in about once an hour, but didn't stay long. Anastasia was still intubated and heavily sedated but she was communicating much stronger in the link.

Family members were stopping by on a regular basis to give her small amounts of their energy at a time, and to go through Michael's phone to delete anything that would upset him. Bina sent regular meals for Michael and the protectors, and notes updating him on the July 4th festivities. The protectors had their routine down to an exact science. Most of the hospital staff had even forgotten that they were even there. Michael felt he could finally breathe easy. He thought, "The only thing that could make this easier for me is to have Jonathan here." As he looked at his phone, he thought of calling him, but knew he would be here if he could.

He took a deep breath and said out loud, "Ok. I guess I have no more excuses. I should call Charlotte." He heard Anastasia in the link. "Tell me about your Charlotte. I heard the harsh words the other night but I didn't understand most of what happened." Michael felt embarrassed. "You've met her, she works here…" Anastasia cut him off. "I understand all of that. I want to know your Charlotte. Who she is to you?" Michael almost wondered that himself, but he was confident that he could make it right with her soon. "She is my girlfriend. I plan to bond with her." As he heard his own words, he felt some hesitation.

Anastasia's choices of words were telling. "Why do you make excuses to speak to her?" He had no answer. He leaned over and kissed her forehead. "You focus on healing. That is a direct order." Even though she was still heavily sedated, she smiled slightly, "Who is so bold as to order me around?" (In her best impersonation of Antonio voice) Michael followed suit. "It is I, Sir Michael of the Azili." He heard her gasp. He stopped and asked, "Are you ok?" She hesitated, "Yeah, I'm fine. Just a sharp pain, but it's gone. Go and call your Charlotte. I'm sure she is... I'm sure she would... She is a lucky girl to have you as her protector." and she closed the link. Michael spoke into her ear. "A protector can only have one charge. I am your protector. Please keep a link open with me, don't shut me out. You are more than my charge, you are my family." He kissed her forehead and thought 'I love you', which he quickly followed that up with 'like a sister'.

He sat down hard on his bed and flipped off his shoes and put his feet up. He started to call but thought a text to Charlotte would be safer. "Good morning babe, I'm sorry about the other day. It was all my fault. I was tired, hungry, and irritable. That gave me no right to snap at you. I hope you can forgive me. I love you." He knew Charlotte very well and did not expect a response for a few hours. He wasn't sure if he always caught her at a bad time or if she wanted to make him wait. She picked up her phone and saw the text. She smiled and thought of a response, but she would have to think of the perfect message and she was getting her nails done. So he would have to wait. She thought, 'He just added another carat onto my engagement ring.'

They arrived back at the airport in Kathmandu. Imay and the other men drove to the private hanger. The jet was ready for immediate take off. The weather was turning bad and Ailbe did not want to wait. Imay and the other men assisted the passed out protectors onto the plane, laughing loudly the entire time. Imay turned to Ailbe. "You should have brought smaller protectors with you." Ailbe "These are the small ones." Imay smiled and shrugged his shoulders as Ruth pointed to the back bedrooms of the plane. "Just make sure they are on their sides and give each one a bucket if they get sick!" Imay did as he was asked.

When everyone was on board, Imay hugged Ailbe good-bye and turned to leave without another word. The last man looked at Ruth, "I'm sorry, but I don't have instructions on what to do with the cars and helicopter." Ruth nodded toward Imay and said, "Ask him. They're his now." The man looked confused but turned and left. The door was closed and the plane began to taxi toward the runway. Ruth was looking out the widow as the man walked up to Imay. A few seconds later Imay threw his hands up in the air and mouthed, "Come on. I can't accept this! You know the old man will be angry." Ruth turned her head. Ailbe had a scowled look on her face but didn't say a word. Bjorn and Leif were laughing at the scene but had work to do. They had the jet up in the air in a matter of minutes.

Jonathan woke up with Mark and Erik in a bed. He was disoriented and tried to jump up out of the pile of men. But he could only move his eyelids. His head was pounding and his stomach felt like he ate rocks. He looked over and saw Olav, Rolf, and Hans in the other bedroom. They looked as bad as he felt. He tried to make a noise and hoped that someone would come to his rescue. It worked, but he regretted it. Bjorn popped his head into the small rooms and with a loud booming Viking voice Bjorn said, "Good morning ladies. How are you all feeling? We thought you all died back here." He shook Olav, who repaid the gesture with vomiting on his shoes. Ruth called out. "Leave them alone. Let them sleep it off. We will be home before they can remember how to walk." Ailbe called out to the hung-over men, "My own grandfather Adison, used to say 'take a bite out of the dog that bit you'. Would you like another shot?" She heard several of them vomiting. She laughed, "AMATURES!" Ruth slapped her arm "Mother! Be nice." But she was smiling and laughing too. The flight home was thankfully uneventful. They landed only for fuel, food and to allow Bjorn and Leif to rest.

On the last leg of their journey home, Ruth looked at Ailbe very sheepishly, "Mother, I have a small confession." Ailbe was momentarily frozen with fear. "Pia-Jiun made me promise not to show you until we were far enough away that you could not return it. But she made meals for all of us for our trip home." Ailbe turned toward the window. "You should have never made that promise." Ruth was confused, "Why? I thought that Bjorn and Leif could eat it. They stayed back and didn't get a chance to try it." Ruth waited for an answer but Ailbe just stared out the window. Ruth could not understand why she seemed so odd this entire trip and had just about enough of it.

Then Ailbe turned back to face her. Her cheeks were stained with tears running down to her chin. She pulled a tissue out of her pocket and said "What we ate...was their food for the entire month. And then we took more?" Ailbe could not contain her sadness. She suddenly felt weak and ashamed. She walked to the back of the plane and sat in the last seat. She closed her eyes and buried her face in her hands. Ruth sat there for a few minutes trying to imagine watching any of her children go hungry while other people ate their food. She never felt like such a failure before. But she vowed to make it right. The heaviness lasted the rest of the way home. Ruth made sure that the boys kept drinking water but called ahead to the compound to have them taken into the infirmary and given some IV hydration. Once landed, the boys were helped off the jet and into awaiting helicopters. They needed to get back to the compound as quickly as possible. They all needed a hot shower and fresh clothes….and sleep.

No one in the house disturbed any of them for an entire day. The compound was feeling the weight of whatever events must have happened. Ruth and Se'ighin have a very strong bond and even he had never felt her so distant. So he respected her need to be alone and gave her the time she needed to process whatever information or event that happened.

Michael woke up the next morning feeling strong and well rested. He knew that today was going to be a great day. He still had not linked with Anastasia since yesterday. But she closed their link. He knew she needed time to heal and think. Bonded families don't keep links open all the time. There is no reason he knew of to keep a link open like this except, if Anastasia remembered anything, even the smallest detail, then he would know instantly. But she must be so scared and frustrated to have no memory. How could a person have zero memories?

His phone beeped to alert him of a text message. It was Charlotte. "You hurt me." He took a deep breath and text back. "I know and I'm sorry. What can I do to make it up to you?" She waited a few minutes and text back "Tell Rach-El and Lindsey that you knew I was just joking. I know it was bad timing. But you know me better than that. I can't stop crying." She hit send but then remembered all the photos of them at the bar. She quickly sent another text. "My friends had to drag me out of the house and pose me for pics so everyone would think I'm ok, but I'm not." Michael hated the thought of her sitting home crying. He sent a text. "Can you come here for a visit? I need to see you. I love you." Charlotte didn't know how much he knew, or what she said to Mr. Kelly. "Your family must hate me. I took some time off. I can't even look my co-workers in the eyes." Michael felt horrible and text. "Just come over. My family LOVES you. Everyone is just really stressed. I promise. Just come over." She texted back, "You come here. I look a mess." and then sent him a selfie of her with mascara running down her face and messy hair. He thought of how upset she must be and he would fix it. "You are more beautiful than ever. I can't leave. Just come over." She smiled, "Ok, but please talk to your family. I want an apology from your sister!" He smiled. "I promise."

He sent a text message to Rach-El and Lindsey asking them if they were coming over and that he needed to talk to them about Charlotte before they came. Rach-El called him the second she got the text. "Good morning big bro. Lindsey is waiting for Jonathan to wake up. They just got back yesterday." Michael was glad to hear that they were back. "Listen, Charlotte is coming over. I really need for everyone to just calm down. This whole thing is really nothing. Charlotte teases me all the time. I shouldn't have snapped at anyone. Please please please let's just forget it and move on. I'm going to marry this girl and I can't have her scared that my family doesn't approve of her."

Michael knew what he was asking his sister to do and he didn't like it, but he did love Charlotte enough to ask. "I will not reject her. You know I would do anything for you, but I have to say my peace, I think she is behaving badly, very badly." Michael didn't take what she said to heart. They have been good friends for a long time. "Great. Could you kind of spread it to whoever knows what happened? Thanks sis. I love you." He hung up without a response.

Rach-El was true to her word and sent a text to Charlotte "I just spoke to M. I'm sorry about the other night. drinks later? I'm buying. XOXO" Charlotte looked at the message and yelled at her phone, "Damn right you're sorry! Bitch! Good thing you are his sister or I would have slapped you for talking to me that way!" but she sent a text back, "Would love to hang with my BFF tonight. Going to see M then I'll tx you. XOXO" Rach-El got the text and went in to see her mother.

Bina was in the library and had two phones, one in each hand. She was

coordinating a list of things that Ruth had added onto the July 4th festivities. Bina mouthed, "Add beach torches and no swimming signs to be the
unforeseen hitch of the day." Rach-El waited impatiently for her mother to
get off the phones. Bina finally looked at her daughter. "Rach-El, I'm sorry,
what can I help you with?"

Bina was Arden's childhood love. Arden was visiting his Uncle Faela'n
in Brazil. He was used to being on the compound where everyone is family.
Kids could run and play and never be far from a family member. But he
found himself wondering too far and got lost. He was too young to link to
anyone but his parents. Just as he was about to panic, a little girl noticed
him and took him by the hand to her parents. Thankfully she was a distinct
cousin and he was reunited with his uncle quickly. Even though they were
just kids, he promised her his bond and she promised him hers, he left the
next day to go back to America. He practiced linking for hours a day until
he was strong enough to find her. He went back to Brazil to study when he
was seventeen, but it was really to be with her. They married at eighteen
and have been inseparable ever since. Rach-El always admired her parents
and hoped she would have a strong bond like theirs.

Rach-El said, "Mother. I need some advice."

Bina "If this has anything to do with Michael and Charlotte, I suggest
you stay out of it."

Rach-El "How did you know that?"

Bina "If Michael has chosen to bond with a De'nola, he has to figure
out for himself if she can be loyal to this family. If you or I try to interfere,
then he will be pushed into 'listening' to her instead of 'knowing' her. Does
that make sense to you?"

Oddly Rach-El felt better. "Yea, I think it does." She smiled and turned
around. Bina cleared her throat. "We have visitors from the Norway family.
There is one that your grandmother is anxious for you to meet." Rach-El
took a deep breath. "Oh dear God mother! How desperate do you think I
am that I need my grandmother to set me up!" she turned and walked off.
Bina called out, "But he's cute!!!"

Lindsey was waiting for Jonathan to wake up. She heard him shuffling
around in his room so she knocked and walked in without waiting for an

invitation. She took one look at him. "Oh my God! What happened to you? You look horrible! Did you run into trouble? Are you ok?" He laughed but wanted to vomit again. "No, the trip was great from what I can remember, but it was really weird. Great-Grandmother said she wants to talk to me about it tonight. We went to the old mountain in Nepal. But I got drunk and I think I gave my bond to Olav, or was it Erik. Either way, I woke up back on the trip home. Oh, and I sold you for a goat."

She laughed and they hugged. "You need to go see Michael. He has been taking all the responsibility for Anastasia. He is stretched too thin. And then there was this thing with Charlotte…" Jonathan shook his head. "What thing?" He asked a bit too quickly. He always had a bit of a crush on her. But when Michael started to date her, he backed off. Lindsey linked the information to him. Jonathan was confused. "Why is she acting like a jealous teenager? I don't understand De'nola when they don't understand OUR responsibilities. They should be just as loyal to their families. But Michael clearly doesn't want you guys in it, so stay out of it." He kissed her on the top of the head and went in the bathroom to start getting dressed. "Hey, did you meet the Norway cousins yet?"

Lindsey "No but I heard they are here to help."

Jonathan "Yeah, and more are coming within the week."

Lindsey "How many are coming?"

Jonathan "I'm not sure. I just heard Great-Grandmother talking to Ace about wiring one of the big houses near the beach and to have all the bungalows ready by July 4th."

Lindsey "Do you think Anastasia will be home by then?"

Jonathan "She should be. That is plenty of time for her to heal."

Lindsey "I don't know about that. Dad saw her the other day and said that he has never seen or felt someone so close to death and she might not be able to fight her way back."

Jonathan "Well if anyone can talk her into fighting, it's Michael. Let me see if anyone needs me and I'm going to run over there."

He left her alone in his room as he walked around the house saying his hellos and catching up. Then he spoke to his parents about Anastasia's condition and what happened at the hospital with Charlotte. "Wow, I'm shocked that Charlotte would act that way, but she has a jealous side. If Michael wants to talk about it, then I better get there." Jonathan arrived at the hospital still feeling the effects of the brown liquid he drank in Nepal. He asked Malachi to quickly link what the protectors have been doing and on a personal note about the incident with the girls.

Malachi is the oldest son of Elijah, Ruth's youngest son. His mother Chaya is a brilliant engineer. Her family has been instrumental in the construction of all Seven Wonders of the World. He has a brother Benjamin and a sister Amelia. His brother Benjamin is also a protector. Amelia is the youngest of the cousins and hasn't found her niche yet, but she is still young.

He walked into Anastasia's room and when Michael looked up and saw him, his face lit up. "Hey there! Boy have I missed you. Tell me everything about your trip. I hear someone puked on one of this new guy's shoes. You gotta tell me every detail." Jonathan grabbed his head. "Dude, It was insane. Great-Grandmother is a beast! She was cutting up the floor. Dancing, cursing and drinking like a sailor!" Michael felt like he forgot how to laugh before Jonathan got here. "NO WAY! I'm sorry. I can't picture that! I've only seen her take ONE sip of champagne once when she heard Linda was pregnant." Jonathan shook his head. "Dude… she was doing shots! And I mean a lot of them. I did one and almost died, but she was doing them like it was her mother's milk." The two men laughed about the trip and Jonathan tried to remember words to songs that the villagers taught them.

Jonathan asked, "Hey, do you know anything about the old mountain in Nepal?" Michael had never been there. "No, I know Great-Grandmother loves it there but it has never been someplace that she has ever talked much about. I know that Grandmother has asked her but she only said she will open that up in her final link before she goes to the ancestors. My guess is that it isn't family business so she hasn't made it a part of our business yet." Jonathan leaned in and whispered. "You should have seen this place… it was amazing, but really bad."

He stood up and walked to Anastasia's side. "And how is our beautiful girl doing today?" As Charlotte walked into the room. She heard

Jonathan and knew he was talking to Anastasia but she answered. "Well aren't you sweet. I'm doing much better now, thank you for asking." She gave Jonathan a quick hug and then went to Michael and gave him a long inappropriate kiss. "You could learn a lot from him (Jonathan) on how to talk to a lady." Michael smiled, "I'm so glad you're here. Please just say that you can forgive me and I never want to talk about it again."

Charlotte pretended to think for a second and she said, "Done. All nasty business in the past." He hugged her tight. Charlotte said, "Good, if Jonathan is here, why don't we go out to dinner?" Michael was firmly planted in this room. He had made everyone aware that he is never going to leave Anastasia's side again. "No babe. I'm not leaving. But we can have dinner brought in. Please understand." She was irritated that she got all dressed up to go out, but they just made up and she didn't want to push it. "No. I understand. I just wanted to see you and let you know how much I love you. I'll let you spend time with your family. I know how important they are to you and you know I would never ask you to leave her like this." She nodded in Anastasia's direction.

Michael was convinced that he was more in love with her right now than he had ever been. "That is exactly why I love you and want to spend the rest of my life with you." They kissed and she turned to leave. "I'll swing by in the morning to see if you need me for anything." And she left. Jonathan sat down on his bed and watched Michael watch her leave. "Boy she could charm the brains out of me any day." Michael shot back, "Hey that is your future in-law." Jonathan didn't know if it was the right timing but he said, "You know I'm in your corner about her, but maybe take another look at what happened." Michael did not want to talk about it. "Grandfather and your dad explained to me what happened. I didn't know I was giving all my energy to her (he looked at Anastasia) and she didn't know that she was draining me. I'm the one who snapped and started the whole thing. So can we please just drop it? I can only fight one battle at a time and right now, I choose Anastasia." Jonathan opened his eyes wide. "You choose Anastasia?" and thought, "Poor Charlotte." Michael leaned his head back. "You know what I meant. Now let's talk about anything else." So they did.

Several nurses were in and out and glad to see Michael in a better mood. They talked well into the night. Michael was yawning. "It's getting late, you should get home." Jonathan "Nope, I'm staying right here with you." Michael always felt at his best when he was with Jonathan. He closed his eyes and quickly fell asleep. Jonathan sat in the reclining chair that Dr. Connard had put in there, and fell asleep hoping to feel better in the morning.

Anastasia stayed awake all night. She wanted to like Charlotte but every time she heard her speak to Michael she wanted to rip the tube out of her throat and tell her off. She wanted to link with Michael. She missed the feeling of being safe and loved when he spoke to her. But she was afraid that she would tell him what she thought of his girlfriend. "He wants to bond with her? I don't understand how he can't see it." She would get no sleep tonight.

The next morning, Mr. Kelly came into the room and woke Michael, which also had Jonathan on his feet. "Good morning gentleman. I have a request from the nursing staff. Since Anastasia has been improving so nicely, it would free up the staff if we had a nursing student come in and help with morning cares." Michael "I need her name first. I will have (He didn't know who was on this shift. Benjamin was standing outside the room and heard the conversation and linked to Michael, "Benjamin and Hayden") Benjamin and Hayden run a check on her." Mr. Kelly put up his hands. "Not necessary, I have known Lucy and her family for years. Lucy will be graduating at the end of this fall and she has been a volunteer here since she was sixteen." Benjamin linked, "Got it. Hayden is checking her out now." Michael smiled, "Well, if you trust her then I'm sure my family will trust her as well." Benjamin linked back, "She's cleared." Mr. Kelly "Good. I just know that she will do a great job. Thank you boys. She will be here in about a hour."

The mornings were always busy with doctors coming in and out and ordering more test and nurses checking bags of IVs and tubing. Michael usually just gets out of the way and watched. Today was no different except he had Jonathan, his rock, by his side. Dr. Sweetsir was the first doctor in. He looked satisfied that the bleeding in her bladder was resolved. "Well

Michael, I think this is a step in the right direction. I'm going to stop the bladder irrigation. Her blood counts have been holding steady and the lab says there is no blood in her urine. So for right now we're going to watch carefully, but I think we have one problem fixed." Next came the Nephrologist Dr. Cronin. She looked like she had been up all night when she came in. "Well Michael, I can say that her kidney functions are almost normal. She is still in critical condition but I can say we might upgrade her soon. She's a fighter!" She touched Anastasia's toe, "You keep fighting young lady. We want to see you at the July 4th party."

Jonathan took a deep breath through his nose. He smelled bacon. He looked passed the curtain to see Rach-El and Lindsey bringing food into the nurses' station. Lindsey put two large bags down and Rach-El held a large bag, two small bags and a coffee holder with four large cups in it. He looked at Michael. "Please let the coffee be for us." Michael laughed as Rach-El and Lindsey stopped to give Benjamin and Hayden a small bag and a coffee each then stepped into the room. They put down the food and went to the head of the bed. Each girl put their hands on either side of Anastasia's head and leaned over. To anyone walking by it looked as though the girls were praying for her, but they were giving her small amounts of their energy.

Jonathan had the bag unpacked and set it up on a tray table as if it were a proper sit-down meal. Jonathan was too hungry to wait too long. "Ding ding ding, Breakfast is served." They sat down and ate together. The girls didn't take their eyes off Anastasia for more than a second at a time. Michael could not take it another second. "Come on you guys. I don't want this to be weird. Please. Everything is fine. Can we just relax and enjoy being together?" Lindsey straightened up her back. "You're right. It's days in the past and Rach-El has a date tonight." Rach-El almost pushed her out of her seat. "You snitch! It's not a date. I'm just showing Bjorn around the compound later tonight." Michael, Jonathan with Benjamin and Hayden sitting outside of the room, all made an "OOOooooooo" sound. Michael raised the pitch of his voice. "Details, I want every detail." Rach-El shoved food in her mouth and pretended to try and speak. They laughed and ate and joked for a few minutes.

Lindsey had an odd feeling, she couldn't put her finger on it, but it was just odd. They finished their breakfast as Dr. Connard came into the room. "Good morning. Glad to see everyone in a good mood. Dr. Herzog the pulmonologist will be in this morning. We are going to discuss extubating her. I'm sure she will feel better once we get that tube out of her throat. She will be more alert and maybe we can talk to her soon." Rach-El and Lindsey cleaned up their mess. Lindsey hugged Michael and whispered, "Watch her close. I just have a weird feeling." Michael kissed her cheek "I will."

As the girls were getting ready to leave, the ICU nurse Barbara walked in with a woman. "This is Lucy, she is one of our nursing student. She'll be helping us out this morning." Lucy was in blue scrubs and a white lab coat that read 'STUDENT NURSE' on the front and back. "I will leave you to it. Come get me if you have any questions." Lucy introduced herself and then turned her attention to Anastasia. "Good morning Ms Reale. My name is Lucy. I'm going to help get you washed up." She took a look at her hair and without judgment said. "Oh dear, you have such pretty long hair but what happened?"

All Lucy really knew is what she saw on the news and what Mr. Kelly had told her. She was the only survivor of a boating accident and she was out at sea in a dinghy for days. It is a miracle that she survived at all. The girls politely excused themselves, "We were just leaving." Lucy smiled as the girls left. She turned towards Michael and Jonathan and asked, "If you two are going to stay, can you stay over there? I'm not going to expose her, but she still deserves privacy."

Michael and Jonathan were impressed by her compassion. They did as she asked and moved the bed farther away and sat talking as Lucy worked. She hummed and talked to Anastasia the entire time. Dr. Connard seemed unimpressed as he sat in his chair reading a book. Jonathan whispered, "WOW, now that is a De'nola that I could listen to all day." Michael agreed but couldn't shake what Lindsey had said. He hadn't linked with Anastasia in two days. And when he tried, he felt her but she didn't communicate. So now he was going to try again. He was thrilled when she responded.

Michael "Are you ok?"

Anastasia "Yes, I'm sorry if I worried you.'

Michael "Please keep our link open. I need to know you are ok."

Anastasia "I'm ok. I feel stronger."

Michael "Why did you close our link?'

Anastasia "I don't want to feel when you get hurt and she hurts you all the time."

Michael "You mean Charlotte? Let's not talk about her. Let's talk about family. Maybe that will help you with your memories."

Anastasia "I'll keep our link open. I'm sorry that I closed it. I'm going to rest. I'm having hard time breathing but nothing to worry about."

Jonathan knew Michael was in the link with her. He watched Lucy getting warm water in a bucket and took some shampoo out of her pocket. She said, "I brought this from home today. The shampoo they have here isn't very good." Michael was not comfortable with what she said in the link. Did she not like Charlotte? Lucy told Anastasia that she was going to wash her hair. She tried not to disturb Dr. Connard as he sat there taking up most of the room at the head of her bed. Lucy put her hair into the bucket as far up to her head as possible. She moved her hair around to loosen the sand and seaweed that had dried in it.

She looked in the bucket and Jonathan saw her face. "What? What's wrong?" now Michael was asking, "What happened?" Lucy quickly reassured him. "Nothing is wrong and don't scare her like that. She just has a TON of sand in her hair. Poor thing, it must itch so bad." Michael hadn't thought of that. He asked Anastasia, "Did you hear that? Do you feel all the sand in your hair?" Anastasia hated to complain and responded, "It's fine." Michael walked over to her and took her hand. "Please be 100% open with me. I promised to take care of you, but if you don't tell me things, then I failed, and I can't live with myself if you have one more second of pain or are uncomfortable." Anastasia laughed in the link, "Ok. It has been driving me crazy."

Michael asked Dr. Connard, "Can you give her a small amount of pain medication so Lucy could scrub her hair without hurting her?" He nodded, "I'll give her just a little bit but Dr. Herzog is coming in soon and I don't want her overly sedated." Lucy rinsed her hair two more times just to get the debris out and then washed her scalp three times just to get all the sand out. Then she put some leave-in conditioner in. She was talking out loud, so not only Anastasia, but also her two cousins, who were literally sitting on the edge of the bed watching her every move, could hear and see what she was doing.

It took her almost an hour to comb out all of the knots in her hair, then she braided it off to the side. Anastasia was grateful for the gentle touch. "Michael, I love her voice." Michael smiled, "Jonathan does too." Lucy looked up and asked, "Can one of you strong men help me turn her so I can wash her back?" Jonathan jumped up to help. Michael was grateful and leaned back. He didn't want to see more of her scars nor could he shake what Lindsey had said. Lucy told Dr. Connard that she was going to roll her to clean her back. He just nodded with the approval. She told Anastasia, "Your cousin Jonathan is here with me. He will not let you fall. I'm going to keep you covered and roll you towards him on the count of three." She looked at Jonathan, who hung on her every word. "Are you ready?" He smiled and tried to think of a witty response but when he opened his mouth all he could think of was, "a hua." Anastasia laughed, "What was he trying to say to her?" Michael "I have no idea, but do you think I should help him?" Anastasia "Don't you dare embarrass him."

Lucy counted to three and rolled Anastasia toward Jonathan. He did exactly what he was told to do. He kept her covered and kept his eyes only on Lucy, who was working quickly to wash, dry and lotion her back. Michael kept all his attention on her and every detail. He felt something wasn't right. "Are you uncomfortable?" Anastasia felt on the verge of panic but she tried to control it. "No, but it's still hard to breath." Michael spoke to Lucy. "I think she might have had enough for one day." Lucy agreed, "Perfect timing, I'm all done. Let me just clean up my mess and I will be out of your way." Jonathan was trying to delay her. "Well, can I thank you by taking you to lunch?" Lucy smiled, "Thank you, but no thank you. I have a few other patients to do and then I have to get home to study." Jonathan stumbled over his words, "Mr. Kelly told us that you are graduating this fall. I was a great student, I could help you study." As soon as he said it, he knew it sounded ridiculous. Michal heard Anastasia laugh.

Lucy "Did you study medicine?"

Jonathan "No, I'm sorry, I don't know why I thought I could help. I mean.... Hey Michael, um..."

Michael laughed out loud, "I can't help you out of that one."

Jonathan looked at Lucy. "Can I start over?"

Lucy continued to clean up her mess. Jonathan asked, "How can I thank you?"

Lucy "You just did. It was a pleasure meeting you. I hope to see you all again." She turned to say good-bye to Anastasia, but something didn't feel right. She looked up at Dr. Connard. "Excuse me sir." Dr. Connard did not like being called sir. He corrected her "Dr. Connard." Lucy corrected herself. "Yes, Dr. Connard, how are her vitals?" Michael asked her in the link. "How are you feeling?' Anastasia "I feel weird. But I think it's the pain medication." Michael was on his feet. "How is your breathing?" Anastasia took a moment to respond. "It's a little hard to breath." Michael asked, "Dr. Connard, you said that the pulmonologist Dr. Herzog was coming in this morning. Do you know what time?"

Dr. Connard "He should be here soon."

Michael "I don't like the way she's breathing."

Dr. Connard "The machine is breathing for her. We are going to deicide if the tube can come out today. She's doing very well. It can be nerve wracking, but she is fine."

Michael began to feel Anastasia's panic. "Something is wrong. Lucy can see it too." Dr. Connard shot Lucy an angry look. Lucy put her hands up and said. "I'm just a nursing student. I can't say for sure, but she 'looks' different." Dr. Connard looked at his equipment. "Everything is fine." And he looked back to his book. Jonathan saw Lucy look annoyed, "Dr. Connard, I may be just a student but please prove me wrong and listen to her lungs. This is a great opportunity for you to teach a student a..." Michael was leaning over Anastasia and interrupted. "Dr. Connard, I don't think she is breathing." He felt Anastasia panic. "It's hard to breath. I can't breath! Michael I can't..."

Michael called out to the nurses' station "Please get Dr. Herzog in here now!" Dr. Connard was on his feet checking his equipment. "Everything looks fine." Lucy said, "But SHE doesn't!" She took a stethoscope off a table that was there and started to listen to her lungs. Dr. Connard, "What do you think you are doing!?" as he took his own stethoscope and started to listen to her lungs. He called out, "Call Dr. Herzog and see how long until he gets here!" Dr. Connard looked back at Michael. "Everything seems fine, the tube just might need to be adjusted." Michael thought he sounded like he was trying to convince himself more than he was trying to convey information to him. Several nurses came rushing in. Jonathan took Lucy by the shoulders and pulled them both out of the way.

Michael yelled to Anastasia, "Help is here. You are going to be fine." Anastasia tried to open her eyes. Michael saw and felt her panic. "MICHAEL! HELP!" Michael looked at Lucy for reassurance. Lucy pointed at her own throat as if to tell Michael it is a problem with the tube. She whispered into Jonathan's ear, "It sounded like the tube is clogged." Jonathan linked the information to Michael. Michael shouted. "Get the tube out. Get it out now!" He was desperate for Anastasia to communicate anything. He felt her in full blown terror. The protectors were surrounding the entire ICU. Dr. Herzog walked into the chaos and quickly went to her bedside to listen to her lungs. He turned to Michael. "I have no time to explain, if I pull the tube out, she might not be able to breath on her own yet. If I leave the tube in, if it is clogged, she will die." Michael was already talking, "Get the tube out. Get it out now!"

Dr. Herzog cut a small tube that was holding air into the balloon that held the tube in place. He said to no one, "Please dear God, she has been through enough already." as he pulled the tube out. Lucy watched as everyone was just standing there waiting for something to happen. She pulled away from Jonathan and grabbed the sheet that she placed under Anastasia during her bed bath, and flipped her toward her. She started firmly pounding on her back with cupped hands. Starting from her low back and working her way up. Dr. Herzog called out. "I need suction!" The ICU nurse Barbara plugged in the suction machine to the wall and stepped in. Lucy stood firmly in place until Barbara put a small tube into Anastasia's mouth. A large blood clot was sucked out. Lucy backed into Jonathan, as he stood there in awe of her quick thinking.

Michael held his breath. "Come on. Breathe Anastasia, breathe." It felt like an eternity when he finally heard her in the link. "Thank Lucy for me." Dr. Herzog took a deep breath of his own. "Thank God." He patted Michael on the shoulder and walked into the nurses' station barking out orders with a list of lab work and chest x-ray. Barbara had a team of nurses in the room making sure her airway was clear and she was breathing on her own. Michael felt a wave of relief and he stepped away toward Jonathan. Michael looked at Lucy's eyes, they were darting around the room, taking in every detail of every person, what they were doing and saying and every action and reaction that was taking place. It takes moving a mountain to truly impress Michael, but he was impressed.

Mr. Kelly had giving strict instruction from day one that he is to be notified immediately if there was any issues regarding Anastasia. He knew this hospital would never be what it was without the Reale family. They have generously funded all their projects for generations. He did not like that there have been several calls from the family with concerns for her care. So when he got yet another text to come immediately, he was going to resolve whatever new issue quickly. He was standing outside the room observing the entire situation but did not interfere.

Michael felt Anastasia getting stronger by the second. She was breathing on her own. Her color went from blue back to a pink natural color. Dr. Herzog came back into the room and took a deep cleansing breath and let it out. "Great catch Brent. You caught that just in time. Anastasia, you are one lucky lucky girl." He turned to Michael "Well, let's get a cup of coffee and let the nurses get her cleaned up a bit."

Michael looked at Anastasia, "You look much better." She tried to open her eyes, "I feel much better. You go with the doctor, but I need Lucy to stay." Michael looked at Jonathan. "You two stay put. I'll be right back." Lucy went to step out, "I have to go finish my clinical. I have to get to my other patients." "NO!" Michael said louder than he wanted. Lucy froze. She knew she had stepped way out of her scope of practice as a nursing student. If anyone reported her, she could be kicked out of school.

Mr. Kelly caught her eye and he motioned for her to step out with him. Jonathan saw the exchange and linked it to Michael. Dr. Herzog and

Michael stepped outside the room and stood next to Mr. Kelly. Michael turned to him and with his best family businesses voice said, "Mr. Kelly, when you informed me that Ms. Vans was hand picked by you today to come in, I was unaware of her talents and outstanding professionalism. My Great-Grandmother always speaks so highly of your uncanny ability to choose the staff that best fits the patients' needs. She will be here later this afternoon and I'm sure she, and my Grandmother, will want to thank you personally." Mr. Kelly looked very proud. "Our staff is the best in the world, even our nursing students have to be superior. I look forward to seeing them when they come in. Now can I be of any further assistance to you?" Michael was relieved that he was leaving. "Can we expect Ms. Vans back anytime soon? She was outstanding today and I feel comfortable having her here." Mr. Kelly "She is just a student and cannot perform in any capacity outside of observing. It is a legal issue that is uncompromising." Michael heard Anastasia, "I trust her." Michael replied, "So do I." Dr. Herzog added, "James, she did jump into help and got out of the way when she couldn't. I like that in a new nurse. I'd keep her around after she graduates. But Michael, I do want to give you a quick update on what I think happened. I'm going to run some tests to make sure she is ok. You know she had a terrible pneumonia. I think when the student turned her, that got the junk in her lungs moving around and it collected into the tube. I was going to extubate her today anyway. This just moved up my time frame about an hour. She is breathing on her own now and we will slowly bring her out of the sedation. She will hopefully be talking in a day or two." Michael was thrilled, he hugged Dr. Herzog. "That is all fantastic news. I'll update my family right away. Everyone has been waiting for some good news for a change." Dr. Herzog patted him on the back, nodded to Mr. Kelly and walked into the nurses' station to document.

Lucy was looking for her time to escape. Jonathan said, "So... how about dinner tonight." Lucy laughed. "You don't have to buy me dinner for doing my job."

Jonathan "No, I just want to thank you for your help."

Lucy "Repeat after me...Thank you."

Jonathan smiled, "Thank you."

Lucy "See that wasn't so hard. Now your debt is paid in full."

Jonathan "Well, that doesn't seem enough." Lucy was desperate to get out of there before someone yelled at her. "When are you coming back?'

Lucy "My ICU rotation is already done. I needed a few hours of clinical to make up some time. I won't be coming back here."

Jonathan "Seriously? Well can we hire you? I know we are looking for a nurse in our family infirmary. It's just for the compound."

Lucy laughed, "I'm not a nurse yet. Besides, I'm a full time student and have a job, well two jobs, and I take care of my parents. I'm kinda all booked up."

Jonathan linked to Michael, "Help me."

Michael was watching this play out but added, "Lucy, listen. I hear that you are busy, very busy, but I'll let you in on a small secret. Our July 4th party will be honoring all health care workers in honor of what everyone has done for Anastasia. My grandmother will be furious when she finds out about today and that we have not locked you into coming."

Lucy "I have always wanted to go to one of your parties. I hear they are amazing. But I have two disabled parents and I can't leave them alone and I can't manage both of them by myself."

Michael "That's an easy fix. I can arrange...." Lucy cut him off

Lucy "No. I don't take handouts. I'm not a charity case. Thank you. I don't mean to be rude, but I can't make it. I will try to see if my instructor will allow me to come back. It was a pleasure meeting you all. (She looked at Anastasia) And Anastasia, I hope you feel better soon. I will light a candle at temple for you tonight." She left quicker than she expected. She didn't want anyone to see the tears she was holding back. She went straight to her car and sent a text massage to her instructor that she was not feeling well and had to leave the hospital early. Jonathan and Michael were speechless as they both tried to figure out what just happened. Michael linked the information to Ailbe and Ruth.

Since Ailbe arrived home from Nepal, she has spent most of her time in the Thinking Room. It was her sanctuary that she handed down to Ruth when she became head of the entire family. Ailbe felt closes to her roots in that room. She spent hours looking out the windows that were floor to ceiling, watching the dolphins as they swam the coastline, and listening to the whales far off shore singing to each other. She loved the smell of the saltwater on the breeze. She was deep in thought about the past few days and wished so badly to return. She thought of how insensitive Ruth had been taking the food and giving them gifts. The old man would never forgive her for leaving him cars and helicopters, even though the entire village would benefit. She just let the tears run down her face.

Ruth linked back her excitement of Anastasia's improvement and wanted to be there later that afternoon, but she had loads of details to attend to. Michael went to the head of her bed and touched both sides of her face and touched his forehead to hers. "Take whatever you need from me. You will have more visitors soon. Everyone wants to come and see you, but I'm holding them to just a few minutes at a time." Anastasia "I'm truly feeling stronger. Once I get these drugs out of my system, can I eat? I want to try bacon! It smelled so good." Michael "You can have anything you want."

Michael went back to Jonathan and sat on the bed. "So cuz, how far do you want me to go?" Jonathan knew exactly what he was talking about. "Everything. I need to know everything." As they were about to call Benjamin and Hayden into the room, Charlotte came in. She kissed Michael and turned to hug Jonathan. "I heard you guys just had some more excitement in here?" Anastasia thought, "I have to learn to like her, she will be my protector's bond soon." She tried to lift her hand toward Charlotte. Michael noticed the movement, "Charlotte, I think she's trying to hold your hand." Charlotte reached over and held her hand. "Well hello. I'm glad you are waking up. I was with you when they first brought you in." But before Anastasia could respond, she turned her attention back to Michael. "So what are my two favorite boys up to? Hungry yet? How about I take you both to a late lunch or early dinner?" Michael felt happier than he had in weeks. Jonathan wondered if he was happy that Charlotte was in a good mood or that Anastasia was more alert. "I'm staying here. If you and Jonathan want to go, can you bring me back something?"

Charlotte looked disappointed but turned to Jonathan to accept her offer. Jonathan said, "I feel like I just got here, but I could use some fresh air. I'm not good with blood and medical stuff." Michael knew that wasn't the truth, but he needed time to dig into Lucy's situation. Charlotte let go of Anastasia's hand and put her arms around Michael's waist and they talked for a few minutes. She asked, "What do you want us to bring you back?" Michael blurted out, "Bacon." Charlotte waited for him to elaborate, but he didn't so she looked at Jonathan, "He is so weird, but he is my weird. Let's go." She kissed him and left. Jonathan reached down and kissed Anastasia on the cheek and whispered, "You smell so much better now." Michael heard her laugh in the link, and he left to follow Charlotte.

Michael linked to Benjamin and Hayden with instructions on what to do. They did a quick safety check on Lucy before she arrived but seeing they were long over their shift, they knew they could go upstairs and get some rest before they started their task. Michael went out to the nurses' station. He noticed all of them stiffed up when they saw him coming towards them. He lowered his shoulders and sat down in a chair backwards. He wanted to look as casual as possible. "Wow ladies, I could never do your job! The way you all work as a team, it's like you just know what to do. Can you read each other's minds or something? I am so impressed!" The Reale family is well known for gifting very generously to people in the community. So it was no surprise that they all wanted to talk to him so casually like this. Barbara "It's all in our training. It takes a special nurse to be an ICU nurse." All the nurses nodded in agreement. Michael "Well, I applaud you all. Hey, are you guys coming to the July 4th party? I want you all there." Barbara answered first. "The hospital has a few travel nurses to cover for most of us. We all want to go." Michael slapped the counter top. "Good, I want to see all of you there. It is going to be the biggest ever. I want to be on each of your dance cards." Another nurse made an "ooooo" sound. Michael stood up and leaned into Barbara, "So, what is up with that student Lucy?"

Well that was the trigger that Michael had hoped for. Out of the five nurses and two aides, all but one of them huddled around him like a flock of seagulls.

Barbara "Well, you didn't hear this from me, but I heard that she failed out of nursing school and begged to get back in. So they put her in the night classes."

Nurse #2 "I heard she was caring for an old guy, and she was caught stealing, right out of his pocket in broad daylight."

Nurse #3 "I heard her parents are in wheelchairs and they are so difficult to get along with that they can't keep a home health aid. They all keep quitting.

Nurse #4 "Now ladies, stop being so hard on her." Michael was glad to hear at least one person would stick up for her. "You know she isn't very smart. So be nice." She turned to Michael, "She could never work up here with us."

Aid #1 "I can't stand working with her. She is just a student and she thinks she is better than everyone else. I've been working here for six years. I know more than she does, and she keeps telling me what to do."

Aid #2 "I think she is just here to get her 'MRS' degree. If you know what I mean?" She winked at Michael and continued, "So are any of your cute security staff looking for a date for the party?"

Michael had a lot of information, almost too much information. He stood up and put his hands in his pockets. Mainly so he wouldn't have the urge to flip them off. "Well thank you ladies. I'm afraid my cousin Jonathan was starting to get a crush on her. I'll be sure to steer him clear of that train wreck." Barbara flipped her hair back slightly, "Hey, if your cousin is looking for a date. I'm available." The other girls laughed, but Michael knew she was very serious. "I'll let him know." as he walked back into the room. Anastasia heard every word and in the link, "Snarky aren't they." Michael rubbed his eyes, "Sounds like a lot of jealousy to me." He linked the information and further instructions to Benjamin and Hayden.

A few hours later Jonathan came back in alone. "Where is Charlotte?" Jonathan handed Michael a small bag. "As we were walking in she saw Malachi doing a parameter check, she said she won't step foot back in here if he is here until she get an apology from him. I have never heard Malachi apologize for doing his job." Michael shook his head, "It's done and over. I'm not going to ask him to apologize for what happened. It just got out of hand. I've talked to Charlotte and she agreed that it just got out of hand and we just need to drop it and move on. Why is she still holding on to this?"

Jonathan "I don't want to pile on to it, but all she talked about was what happened. And I gotta tell ya, her story gets more elaborate every time I hear it."

Michael "Do you think I'm making the right choice? Sometimes I'm 100% sure that I want to give her my bond, but then when I think of the family, I'm not so sure."

Jonathan "You know that I think she is an awesome girl. But you are the grandson of the head of the entire family. If she chooses your dad, which she has made it clear that she will, and if he chooses you… You could possibly be the head of the entire family one day. You need to think of that. Could she handle that? The answer might be no… If THAT dust up got her panties in a twist, what happens if you give her your bond and in a few years she is fed up with the traveling, and all the secrets, and how tight-knit we all are…? What if she wants a divorce? What if she can't get along with the family? You just really need to think of everything." Michael had thought about it in passing, but he never really thought it through to the point that he could realistically be responsible for every member of the family some day. "That puts a spotlight on it. I have a lot to thing about before July 4th." Jonathan "Think fast, its coming up quick."

The next few days were filled with vast improvements. Anastasia was starting to speak, Just a word or two in a whisper, but her voice was getting stronger. The physical therapist Brett was in several times a day working to get her joints moving again. The doctors continued to come and go rather quickly, but all pleased and amazed at how quickly she was recovering. She could eat small amounts of soft moist foods. Swallowing was still tricky, but the nurses were there ready with the suction machine if she started to choke. Jonathan rarely left Michael's side. He checked in frequently with Ruth to see if she needed him, but was happy when she always replied "Michael needs you. Stay with him." Family members were coming regularly and staying a little bit longer. Anastasia was happy and thriving.

Mr. Kelly had come down and said the doctors all feel that she could be moved out of the ICU within a another day or two and then maybe home with round the clock nursing staff. Michael had wanted to get her out of the hospital and back to the compound where he knows she would get better care and security, but for right now, he felt that everything was going to be fine. Charlotte was still icy to his family but now that she was back to work she was thawing out. Mr. Kelly was convinced that he had solved the problem by giving Charlotte the week off. And the preparations for the July 4th party were on track and going smoothly. Ailbe was even coming out of the Thinking Room more and more.

Michael and Anastasia had learned to easily keep their link open. It was a safe place for both of them. Anastasia kept her feeling about Charlotte out of her mind and when she came in for a visit, it was always short. Charlotte had now firmly attached herself to Michael and he was more convinced than ever to bond with her. He was working out the details of how he was going to propose. But for now, his energy was to Anastasia and getting her to a complete recovery.

Jonathan watched the two of them talk about anything and everything. Michael's face would light up when she learned something new or tasted something for the first time. Jonathan couldn't understand how everything she ate seemed like it was for the first time. He watched them for hours and thought, "How does he not see this? I wonder if I should tell him?" All in all, he was just thankful that she was with family and was safe. Ruth had sent Rach-El and Lindsey shopping for some loose clothes for her to wear instead of the hospital gowns. Michael was glad that she didn't have to look down and see the scars all the time.

Jonathan was here for his cousin and did not want to ask him about Lucy, but things were relaxed and Anastasia was with the physical therapist. She could walk half way around the nurses' station with a walker now. The subclavian access line in her neck was still in but not hooked up to anything. The doctor said that he will keep it in for the next few days 'just in case', but he would take it out soon. Jonathan thought it was a good time to ask, "Hey, I know you have your hands full, but have you found out anything more about Lucy?" but the look on his face, he knew Michael had.

Michael "You know, I've been meaning to talk to you."

Jonathan "I don't care what you found out. I can't stop thinking about her. There is something about that girl that I have to know her better."

Michael "She was impressive, but it's been a few days now. Don't you think you should be over a crush by now?" Michael said in a very juvenile teasing voice.

Jonathan "I don't think she is a crush. I really think she is the one for me. I can't shake the feeling. I just know she is the one."

Michael "I guess I shouldn't tease you about it. Anastasia and I felt it too."

Jonathan "It was weird right. It's almost like she just fit in, like family, but not family. But I could feel something." He put his head in his hands, "Oh geese, I've lost my mind."

Michael "No, you haven't lost your mind. I can tell you this, she's not Azili. But she is a great girl. She didn't fail out of school. Her parents were in a car accident. They can walk, but they need wheelchairs to really get around. They lost everything. Her dad was a college professor of Ancient religions and her mother was a paralegal, but they can't work and they had to sell everything for medical bills. Lucy works hard to keep the bills paid. If you were gonna fall for a De'nola, she's the one to fall for."

Jonathan "Is she gonna to come to the party?"

Michael "Grandmother is working on it. I don't know yet."

Jonathan "Should I call her or would it be creepy? Maybe I should swing by her house or would that be even creepier?"

Michael "Yeah, I think that would creep her out. Hayden said she never has time for herself. She is always on the run and ten minutes late for everything. He arranged for a study buddy, but it sounds like she studies in between other things. I feel for the girl. She is a hard worker."

Jonathan "Wow, I had no idea that she is going through all that. Now I think I love her more." "Love who more?" Anastasia asked as she walked back into the room with the physical therapist. "Who loves who more?" Charlotte asked as she walked in behind Anastasia. Jonathan and Michael grabbed hands. Jonathan said, "Ladies, we have something to confess." Anastasia laughed and Charlotte said, "I'm sure you can't fuck him the way I can." Anastasia looked at her and thought, "Way to keep it classy."

Michael heard it in the link and stood up talking over her as if he didn't hear it. "So Charlotte what brings you by at this time?" Jonathan and Anastasia locked eyes. Jonathan shook his head, 'no.' when he saw Anastasia's lip move like she was about to say something. So she kept walking with Brett. They both clearly heard what Charlotte said Brett asked, "Ok then, the bed or the chair? Have I worn you out the day?" Anastasia was glad for the momentary distraction. "The chair please. I'm meeting my cousin Linda in a little while. She is pregnant and can't wait! I want to look my best for the baby."

Michael whispered in Charlotte's ear. "Please watch your language. That was really unnecessary!" Charlotte snapped back, "You take shit way to seriously when you are around your family! He can joke but I can't. When can we have some alone time? You haven't left this room in weeks." Michael kissed her cheek. "Soon I promise." He turned back to Jonathan with a forced smile. "So lovah…" as he slid next to him and nuzzled his neck. Charlotte rolled her eyes. "I need to get back downstairs. Call me later." She kissed him hard on the lips to let him know she was irritated and she left.

Jonathan didn't even say good-bye and Anastasia muttered. "bye-bye" as she gave a sarcastic Queen's wave. Michael was embarrassed. "I'm sorry about that." Anastasia thanked the physical therapist, he turned around and looked confused. "I'm out of my lane saying this, but why do you put up with her? That was so disrespectful. I'm embarrassed for you." He kept walking out of the room shaking his head. Michael was not used to people outside his family being brutally honest with him. He knew most people would tell him anything they thought he wanted to hear. "Brett, please wait a second, how well do you know her (Charlotte)?" Brett wasn't sure what Michael wanted to hear, so he just answered the questions. "Well enough to only talk to her when I need to." Michael pushed the issues. "Why is that?" He looked Michael right in the eyes and boldly said. "She is rude, and since she found out that you are planning to propose to her. That is all she is talking about. Like all of a sudden no one can disagree with her and that her opinion is the only one that counts. And only because she is going to marry a Reale. I don't care who you are. I'm going to do my job and do it to the best of my ability. I don't have VIP patients. They are all very important to me." He left without waiting for a response. Half because he was afraid of getting told off and half because he knew he was wrong by spewing off about a co-worker. Michael sat there with his mouth open. Jonathan and Anastasia sat there very uncomfortable until Linda walked in with her younger sister Debbie.

Anastasia's face was beaming with excitement. Jonathan stood up as they walked in and introduced them. They reached down and hugged Anastasia. Debbie had been by with her parents Aharon and Isabelle earlier in the week, but Anastasia was sleeping. Michael told her later that they stopped by.

They talked for a few moments until Anastasia couldn't wait another second to ask, "Linda, may I say hello to your child?" Linda had spoken to Ailbe and Ruth before she came to visit. She wanted to know if it was safe for the baby. No one knew anything about this girl. But both Ailbe and Ruth reassured her that Anastasia was no threat to anyone in the family. She was the victim.

Linda was slightly hesitant but stepped forward into Anastasia's outstretched arms. Anastasia felt the hesitation and pulled her arms back. "I am so sorry. I have made you feel uncomfortable. I should have never asked such a personal thing." Michael felt how deeply hurt and sorry she felt. Before he could intervene, Linda took both her hands and placed them firmly on her belly. "NONSENCE! Don't you ever apologize for wanted to say hello to our Cheri!" Anastasia felt loved and accepted. She relaxed her hands and smiled. The baby girl jumped at Anastasia's touch. Linda said, "Oh, she is an active little one today." Anastasia closed her eyes. Linda could feel them communicating. Linda was about to pull away, but she felt her baby girl was happy and was in no danger.

Anastasia laughed and looked up to Linda, "She really does not like the name Cheri." Linda "She told you that? I have just started to be able to link with her, but only her emotions." Anastasia pulled her hands away and looked at Michael. "I'm sorry, did I do something wrong?" Linda saw the tears welling up in Anastasia's eyes. "Anastasia look at me. No, you did nothing wrong. I should not have reacted like that." Anastasia relaxed.

Michael was comparing how his family reacts to situations and how Charlotte always reacts with anger. He really needed to talk to her about that, but for now he re-focused on what Linda was saying. "Here, let's try again." She took Anastasia's shaking hands and placed them back on her belly. The baby jumped and kicked. Linda said, "She is happy. She isn't afraid of you." Anastasia smiled and closed her eyes again. Linda felt them communicating and said to the room in general. "What can a six month old be talking about?" Everyone laughed but knew that parents can link with their unborn children, and the elders can but they have to be close or even touching the mother at the time.

Michael linked the information to his grandmother who immediately responded "interesting" and closed the link. Anastasia took her hands off Linda's belly. "Now you be nice to your mother while you're in there." And looked up smiling. Linda laughed, "So she doesn't like the name Cheri? Does she like any of the names we liked?" Anastasia loved the feeling of being accepted. "Stephanie. She also likes Starling." No one said anything. Debbie poked Linda in the side "See, I told you Starling is a cool name." They all laughed nervously.

Michael finally spoke up "How do you know how you can link with someone else's child? Do you remember being trained" She shook her head. "No, I don't remember being trained, it just seemed natural." Linda smiled and asked "What else did she say?" Anastasia "Nothing really. She feels happy. She knows she is loved. She is curious about the world. She told me about the names and asked for a blessing." Michael lifted up a hand for everyone to be quiet. He linked to Ruth "Grandmother, the baby asked Anastasia for a blessing." Ruth responded immediately and probably harsher than she meant to. "Get everyone out of there. Do not leave her side. No one is to touch her. I'm on my way."

Anastasia knew she did or said something wrong. "I never meant to hurt anyone. I would never hurt anyone." Michael raised his voice. "Leave. Everyone leave now." Linda took Debbie by the hand. She saw the terror in Anastasia's eyes and said "You did nothing wrong. Remember that." As Michael was ushering everyone out of the room. The nurses noticed the commotion. Michael asked, "Can you help me close the glass doors." The nurses where in motion as he was almost done closing them. "You can keep the curtain open but we need privacy to discuss family issues." The nurses moved slightly slower knowing that it was not a medical problem, it was just a rich family person problem. Jonathan felt Michael's anxiety and called the protectors to do a parameter sweep.

Ruth linked Ailbe, Se'ighin and Arden the information. They met at the front door and were in a car leaving for the hospital within minutes. Jonathan positioned himself inside the door and two protectors were on full alert on the outside of the door. No one was getting in or out except family. Michael bent down in front of Anastasia. He saw the panic on her face and felt it in their link. He tried to calm his emotions before he spoke. "Anastasia... Only the highest elder can be asked for a blessing. And not like old age. Anyone can pray, but a blessing? No... never. Not even in our ancient history has anyone even asked anyone but the highest elder or a royal family member. Even an unborn Azili knows that." She knew he was trying to reassure her, but she was confused and terrified. "So a child misspoke. Is that a reason to scare the life out of me? I thought I hurt someone!" Michael still looked confused himself. "I didn't mean to scare you. But that has to be in your memory. How could an unborn Azili even think to ask you? She had to sense a memory in you. Great-Grandmother will be here soon to link. If the baby found a memory, then Ailbe will too. Are you ready for this?"

She was excited to think that her memories could be coming back. She tried to stand up on her own but fell backwards. She put out her hand. The nurses saw that she was trying to get up and they came to the door, Michael linked to the protectors to let them in. The protectors moved aside and they came in. Anastasia was grabbing at anyone to help. One nurse asked, "Are you ok? What happened?" They saw she was crying. They were about to ask for Michael and Jonathan to leave when she said, "I'm sorry, I insisted that they tell me why my father has not come to see me yet, and they just told me that he had a heart attack and can't come. My aunt is on her way here now to give me a letter she received from him." The nurses tried to console her as they helped her back into bed. Still wiping tears from her eyes. "Thank you ladies. You are always so kind to me. Now I need to be with my family." The two nurses saw the look of pain in her eyes. They closed the curtain half way so they could still see her, but to give them as much privacy as possible.

Michael and Jonathan knew that no one had told her of the line they had conjured up if anyone questioned why her family had not arrived from Norway. Anastasia looked at Jonathan. "Please help me get ready." Michael lowered his shoulders. "Wait, just slow down, relax. They will be here in a few minutes. I don't want you to think anyone is mad at you or going to hurt you."

Anastasia refused to look at him. "If my memories are coming back, then I don't want to waste any time in getting to them."

Michael wished he said things differently. He hated himself for hurting her. He stepped toward her. "Please stop! Let's not get worked up. If your memories are coming back, being upset might suppress them again. You need to relax you have nothing to be afraid of." Anastasia felt like she wanted to run. The tears were streaming down her face. "Don't you get it? I can't relax! I have been terrified ever since I woke up in that boat! I know my memories are right there! (She pointed to her head) I'm so close. I keep replaying the feeling that I had to get here, I had to warn you...You don't understand that I'm... I'm so scared. What if I had to warn you about ME! What if I'm some sort of weapon! What if I'm some evil person sent to kill you all?!"

Michael "You are not a weapon."

Anastasia "How can you be sure of that!?"

Michael "I would have felt it. You don't want to hurt anything."

Anastasia "I don't think I want to! But what if that is the plan? How can I not remember anything?" She pulled up her pant legs and pointed at her scars. "How could I not remember getting cut and cut and cut!? I heard the doctors. I heard them say my bones have been broken and some of these cuts are old but some are within weeks. How do I not remember!? I'm terrified that I might be dangerous. I feel you holding back, I know you are scared of me too!" She buried her face in her hands.

Jonathan was trying to hold back tears, he would have done anything to take her pain away. Michael had no response, he couldn't think of anything to say. "You're right." Jonathan turned to him slowly. He could not imagine how he could say something so cruel. Michael continued with a monotone voice. "We don't know who or what you are. We don't know who or what did this to you. We assume the Eile are responsible, but you do not even exist." Jonathan was livid that he was emotionless and cold. Anastasia slowed down her crying slightly. The nursing staff was glued on their every move. They could only imagine what was happening. They loved watching drama unfold.

Michael waited for her to respond and when she didn't, he continued in the same heartless tone. "We have not rejected you, but we are cautious of you. The elders have met and it is my charge to find out who, and what you really are." Anastasia felt her emotions going numb. "So that is what I am to you? A charge? A duty to perform?" Michael looked straight into her eyes. "Yes." Jonathan had never seen him like this, never heard him talk like this to anyone. He trusted Michael with his life, but right now, he felt as if he had no idea who he was.

Anastasia stopped crying and wiped her face. She stiffened her shoulders and said. "Well then, let's get this over with shall we." She fixed her pant legs and laid back on the bed and got into a comfortable position. He was surprised that she didn't close their link. Michael turned his back to her and stood there... stone faced until Ailbe arrived with Ruth close behind. Ruth walked passed the two protectors and barked at Jonathan. "Se'ighin and Arden are right behind us. No one is to disturb us." He closed the curtain and stood facing the closed glass door next to Michael. He wanted to say something to break the tension, but thought better of it.

Se'ighin and Arden walked to Mr. Kelly's office and told his secretary that it is an urgent matter. Mr. Kelly came out even before his secretary picked up the phone to call him. "Gentlemen, what seems to be the problem?" Se'ighin "May we go you're your office? We need complete privacy." Mr. Kelly "Absolutely." He looked at his secretary. "Please hold all calls." He motioned for Se'ighin and Arden to come into his office and he closed the door. Arden began speaking before any of them sat down. "Anastasia overheard some family members discussing her father's health issues and is very upset." Mr. Kelly was truly understanding. "Yes, and I'm very sorry.

One of the nurses called me a few minutes ago and told me about it. I can assure you that your family will have complete privacy." Se'ighin took his hand and shook it firmly. "Thank you. We appreciate you and your staff being sensitive in his troubling time." They left without further pleasantries as Mr. Kelly called to the ICU nurses station to update them and to give the family privacy.

Jonathan was focused on his job, but had difficulty understanding Michael's demeanor. He wanted an explanation and if Michael didn't offer it very soon, he was going to demand it. Ailbe took Anastasia by the hand. "Are you ready dear?" she said in a compassionate tone. Anastasia was in no mood for compassion. She wanted her memories back. "Go as deep as you can. Pull out everything."

Ailbe "I don't want to hurt you. Let's go slow and see what we can see." Anastasia "I don't care what happens to me. Just get the information that you need."

Ailbe "We don't need anything at your expense. It will come in time."

Anastasia "I'm not planning on staying here very much longer. Get what you need and leave me alone."

Ruth trusted Ailbe above and beyond anything else, but she could not understand why she was not addressing Anastasia's harsh tone and words. Ailbe went to the head of her bed and opened a link. Ailbe immediately knew that Anastasia was completely open and wanted her to look everywhere and anywhere in her mind that Ailbe wanted to explore. Anastasia first showed her what happened with Linda and the baby. Michael could feel Anastasia pulling Ailbe in deeper and deeper into their link. Michael saw nothing, heard nothing, felt nothing except the two women. Ruth added her energy to their link to allow Ailbe to go even deeper.

Michael was too young to go that deep. His head started to hurt. Ailbe was aware that he was there but ignored him. If it was ok with Anastasia, then it was ok with her. Ruth did not feel the same way but there was nothing she could or would do to change it now. Ailbe was as deep as she felt comfortable going. She knew Anastasia was in pain but she asked, "Do you want me to continue?" They had already been in the link for over twenty minutes. Michael thought of the intense pain she must be in as he heard her struggling. He turned around, opened his eyes and was horrified. Anastasia was arched in the bed. Her hands were gripping the sheets so hard she tore small holes in them. Her lip was bleeding and she was drenched in sweat.

He looked over at Jonathan who had his back to him, but his body language was stiff as if he wanted to stop whatever was going on behind him. Michael blocked out everything except for his job. Anastasia yelled out in pain, but said out loud, "Keep going." Ailbe swallowed hard. Ruth stepped in and placed her hands over Ailbe's hands. Ruth was never one for watching pain. She may seem insensitive but inside she was a loving mother to everyone. This….this was pure torture.

The link went on for another ten minutes until Michael felt her go unconscious. He wanted to run to her side, but he just closed his eyes and stood his post. Ailbe and Ruth were exhausted Ailbe stood there to catch her breath. Ruth put her arm around her shoulder. "Mother, you tried. You can't risk your own life." Ailbe was breathing heavy. "I should have crossed the veil to the ancestors a long time ago. What happens to me is of no consequence. She is our concern." She tried to straighten up but was too weak. Ruth called out to Se'ighin and Arden "I need some help in here." The two men stepped inside and Jonathan stepped out and asked for a wheelchair. The nurses who had been trying to hear what going on in the room, jumped and grabbed a wheelchair that was right next to the nurses' station. Arden took it to Ailbe and sat her down.

Ruth pulled back her shoulders and walked out with Arden pushing the wheelchair and Se'ighin brining up the rear. Michael looked out into the nurses' station. "You can open the doors, she is sleeping for now." Two nurses opened the panels and put them flush against the wall and opened the curtain. The room was in full view of anyone in the ICU.

The nurses came into the room. One looked at Jonathan. "What happened in here!?" The sheets were wet and blood near her hands and face. She was bright red, like when she first came in with terrible sunburn. Her hair was undone from the braid and a mess. Jonathan did not answer. Michael said in a low voice "She did not take the news about her father very well, but she is asleep now. Please don't wake her. The nurses took vital signs and cleaned up the room. Jonathan just stood there. He looked at Anastasia's body. She looked peaceful now. He wanted to rip into Michael but the look on his face seemed punishment enough. Jonathan linked to the protectors. "Update."

Rach-El was more nervous to spend time with Bjorn than she realized. She kept putting on makeup and taking it off and then putting it back on. She finally yelled at herself "Girl, you are a strong woman with her own set of rules. Relax!" She walked out of her room and down to the dinning room where they had planned to meet. Bjorn stood up when she walked into the room. They exchanged pleasantries and she asked, "So are you ready to see our sleepy little town?" He was nervous too, but she was so relaxed and causal that he instantly felt very comfortable around her. "If you have the time, I would enjoy that." Rach-El smiled, "Great. I thought it would be fun if we took a golf cart. It's not as risky as stealing Jonathan's Jaguar, but it is a lot more fun to see everything." Bjorn laughed and said, "I will follow you." They walked out the front door where she had asked that one of the small golf carts be left, they got in and started to drive down the coast line. It was a perfect evening. They watched the dolphins as they swam near the shoreline. "Listen, you can hear the whales singing. I always feel so peaceful when I hear them." Bjorn had an overwhelming desire to be with her forever.

They drove the entire parade route and she pointed out to him where the protectors would all be stationed. When they got to the end of the parade route, they got out of the cart and walked around. Bjorn "Your protectors seem to have thought of everything." She was very proud of her family. She wondered what his compound looked like. She thought "Yeah, I could see myself liking him… a lot." She asked, "Do you want to see our stables?" She loved the look on his face. "You have horses here? We have the most splendid horses back home." He jumped back in the cart and sat a little closer to her than he did before. He laughed and said, "What is your American saying? The Flintstones…CHARGE!!!" She laughed, "Not even close." But she floored the gas pedal and they headed to the stables.

Once home, Ruth and Ailbe went directly to the Thinking Room. Ailbe sat near the window and finally said, "What are you thinking?"

Ruth "I'm not thinking anything. I don't know what to think."

Ailbe "Could she really be her?"

Ruth "I can't imagine how she could be after all this time."

Ailbe "I have no real proof, but it's all I can think of."

Ruth "Well, you better have solid proof before you mention it to anyone."

Ailbe "That is the only thing that makes any sense."

Ruth "Wrong! It makes no sense. I won't have you put this family into an all out panic." Ruth left the room and slammed the door. Ailbe looked up at the sky, "Please let me be wrong. But it would be wonderful if I'm right."

Michael got up the courage to go stand by her bedside. From outside he heard a cheerful voice. "Hello boys, what's up?" It was Charlotte, she didn't wait nor really want a reply. She walked in and kissed Michael on the cheek. Oblivious to the heaviness in the room, she started talking about her day. "The emergency room is dead tonight so I asked for the rest of the night off so I could come up here and stay with you. Ya know, give Jonathan the night off." Jonathan looked at Michael who still wouldn't look at him. "Good idea Charlotte. Why don't you take Michael for a long walk... He seems to need some fresh air... I'll let Uncle Arden know that I'll do your job tonight." Michael walked out without a word or a glance or a link. Charlotte smiled and clapped her hands. "Yea! Now I'm glad I came up here. Thanks Jonathan. I'll take good care of him." She stepped closer to hug him but he turned and stood by Anastasia.

Charlotte stopped and looked at Anastasia, then back at Jonathan. "Ooooooo, what is going on here? Do I smell puppy-love brewing?" She rolled her eyes and ran after Michael. He was already at the elevator when she ran out into the hall. "So what do you want to do tonight? Dinner, dancing, bar hopping?" Michael put his hands deep in his pockets. "I just want to go home." Charlotte grinned, "Ohhhhh I like the way you think. My place or yours?" Michael mumbled, "I need to sleep in my bed." She ran her fingers up and down his arm and whispered, "Sounds perfect. Can we order breakfast in bed in the morning?" He just wanted to leave. "Whatever you want."

The ride to the compound felt endless. He heard Charlotte's voice but he had no idea what she was saying. He needed to stop thinking. He needed to stop feeling. He needed to sleep. Charlotte drove up to the main gates, but didn't even roll down the window. She just smiled and waved as they motioned her through. She was still unphased by Michael's silence and just kept on talking.

She pulled up to the main house and parked near the front doors. Michael opened his door even before the car was stopped and started to walk inside. Charlotte hollered, "Michael, don't be rude. Are you going to help me with this stuff?" He turned around and she handed him piles of color swatches, fabric samples, and wedding magazines. She was still talking when she opened the front door and went inside. "Oh, can you put them down there? (She pointed to a side table) I'm dying to show Rach-El what I'm thinking of and getting her opinion." He had no response. He walked upstairs and into his room. The familiar sounds and smells of his room loosen his apathy slightly. He started to feel, but he didn't want to feel anything. He tightened his lips as she walked in behind him... Still talking.

He was about to explode. "Taking a shower." were all the words he could form. He realized his last shower was at Charlotte's and thought, "God how long ago was that?" He took a quick rinse off shower in the doctor's lounge and he took a washcloth and soap to his face and armpits, he even managed to brush his teeth once a day, but nothing could have felt better right then, a long hot relaxing shower. When he was done, he got dressed in the bathroom and looked in the mirror, but as soon as he saw his reflection he turned away. He came out of the bathroom and sat on the edge of the bed.

Charlotte was lying in the bed but sat up beside him. "So what do you think?" He had not heard a word she said but he was not going to fight. "Think about what?" She playfully slapped his shoulder. "Haven't you been listening silly? Our theme and the colors? I know men usually don't care about wedding details and stuff, but I don't want you to hate it." He turned his head to kiss her. "Sure babe, I will love whatever you pick. It's your day." He took the papers out of her hands and started kissing her with more passion than she had felt from him since her dad found Anastasia in the dinghy. They made love all night and all over the room.

Michael couldn't sleep. He told himself over and over that he had a renewed sense of love for... Charlotte. He took another shower but still could not look at himself in the mirror, got dressed and went downstairs. He hoped he could leave without seeing anyone. "5a.m... Everyone should still be asleep." He passed the dining room heading for the kitchen. He looked in to see Rach-El and Bjorn talking as if they had been up all night. "Lucky man." he said more to himself than anyone around him. He left instructions to have breakfast sent up to his room as soon as Charlotte woke up, made Jonathan's weird latte that he liked and headed for the hospital.

The entire way there, he tried to think of a way to explain his unexplainable behavior. He couldn't understand it himself. He started talking to himself, well more like yelling at himself. "The fact is, I was told to do a job and I'm going to do that job! Feeling sorry for her or trying to protect her from getting to the truth is just slowing me down. You can't fall in lo... You are NOT in love with her! You feel sorry for her, nothing more. You love Charlotte. I need to separate my life from my job. Charlotte is my life and Anastasia is my job! Is that clear? Now go and talk to Jonathan and explain that to him." He didn't feel any better, but at least he had the latte as a peace offering.

Jonathan had pulled Michael's bed closer to Anastasia's. He didn't know how long she needed to recover or how long she would be asleep, so he held her hand and gave her small amounts of his energy. He started feeling drained as she stirred, "Michael?" Jonathan did not want to explain Michael's action or that he left. "No. It's Jonathan. I'm going to stay here with you tonight." She didn't need to say anything else. The tears rolled down the sides of her face, and she rolled over way from him. She knew he would protect her and she felt safe, but she felt alone without her protector. He touched her arm. "I'm right here if you want to talk about him." He saw her shoulders moving and he knew she was crying. He linked the information to Arden. Arden could feel Jonathan's emotions flying all over the spectrum. He linked back, "That is unfortunate. But don't judge him too harshly. You know his heart." Jonathan wanted to think of happier times with Michael. Then he started to daydream about Lucy.

Michael was nervous walking into the hospital. He was more critical of himself that he should have been. He walked passed the protectors, who gave him a disagreeable glance. He walked into the ICU. It was usually dark and quiet to encourage everyone to sleep. He smiled at the two protectors sitting outside her room. They looked at him and nodded but didn't smile back. He thought, "I have a job to do." He took a deep breath and silently walked into the room. He saw that Jonathan had pulled the bed close enough that he could touch her if she needed him. He was sound asleep with his foot through the side rails of her bed. She had rolled toward him and her arm reaching through the side rails as if she was reaching for him. Michael stood there taking in every detail of the room and the positions that the two were in. He put down the coffee and went to the bathroom near the nurses' station.

He looked at himself in the mirror for a long time. He finally said softly. "I hate you." He splashed water on his face and put his shoulders back and walked out. The night nurse was standing there waiting to use the bathroom. "I was getting worried that you fell in." She tried to giggle but he had a stern look on his face. He walked passed her without saying anything. He walked back into the room and found his book that he left there. He sat in the chair that Dr. Connard usually parks himself in and tried to read. He sat mouse quiet for hours before the normal daily activities aroused Jonathan.

Jonathan stretched wildly and made some indecent sounding noises. He sat up and looked at Anastasia. He immediately noticed Michael. "How long have you been sitting there?' Michael didn't look up from his book but gave a half smile. "Long enough to hear you fart and call for your mommy." Jonathan looked on the bedside table at the container. "Is that my latte?" Michael was not good at faking emotions but he tried anyway. "Yep, but I made it at 5a.m. It's ice cold by now. I'll go heat it up for you." Jonathan stood up and slipped on his shoes. "Naw, I'll go. I need to stretch and you need to talk to her." He nodded towards the bed and left before Michael could think of a valid reason for him to stay.

Michael sat staring at her. His heart was broken. He would call his grandmother and his father and tell them that he has failed at his job. He will resign immediately as the head of the Protectors and as her protector. He wondered who would be assigned to her or if he could choose someone. Mark is clearly the best choice as head Protector and Jonathan would be his first choice as her protector. Clearly Grandmother could find another transporter if Jonathan was reassigned. He thought, "Fine, it's settled then. I'll ask that Jonathan be her new protector." She instantly responded, "I will refuse a new protector, and if Ailbe or Ruth insists, then I will refuse further links." With her eyes still closed with a loud, clear, and firm voice.

Michael smiled and leaned toward her to whisper in her ear. "Have I been so cavalier as to forget to close our link? I didn't even feel you there. I fear that we are too familiar, too informal with each other. I can't do my job and be burdened about what happens to you at the same time." Her voice cracked. "But you're my protector." He thought for a moment. "The safety of my family is now, and will always be my first priority. I was charged with protecting you to find out what you know… (He paused so she would not hear his voice crack) You don't know anything. My job is done. The rest is up to the elders. Good-bye Princess."

He kissed her on the forehead. She felt a teardrop on her cheek. She opened her eyes to meet his. She almost didn't recognize him. He looked empty. She reached up to grab his face but he stood up and left without turning back. Jonathan was walking back in the room when Michael accidently bumped into him and spilled his hot latte. "Hey. You owe me a new one." Michael didn't hear him. All he wanted to do was link his resignation and drive. Jonathan looked at Anastasia's face. "What just happened?" She had no more fight left in her… "He quit." Jonathan felt a wave of shock and anger. "What? Michael doesn't quit anything. I think I'm missing something here." Anastasia struggled to sit up. "Please call Ruth and tell her I'm feeling better and would like to finish my rehab in a different location."

Five more feet until Michael was out the door. He was determined to never set foot back here again. Mr. Kelly stopped him. "Oh good Michael, I'm glad I caught you. I have planned a meeting this morning at 9 a.m. with all of Anastasia's doctors and members of her interdisciplinary team. She is doing remarkable well and I need to make sure that everyone is on the same page." Michael was anxious to leave. "I am not available today. My grandmother Ruth is her health care proxy. I was only secondary. If you call her she will make herself available. I can't say she will be here at 9a.m. but..." Mr. Kelly cut him off. "I just got off the phone with her, she said to tell you to attend the meeting and give her an update. Then you can take the time you need. Those are her exact words. She told me to write them down...see." He pulled out a piece of paper from his pocket.

Ruth linked. "I have told the other protectors to give you space. I have called Jonathan home for the day." Michael closed his eyes and said, "Thank you, I will meet you in your office at 9.a.m." Mr. Kelly shoved the note back in his pocket. "Excellent. I'll see you then." Michael gave him a half hearted nod then went to his car and took out his laptop. He had more than an hour before the meeting. He went onto the family's intranet page and started looking at satellite photos of the day Anastasia was found and tried to work his way backward looking for a needle in a haystack.

CHAPTER 3

9 a.m. came quickly. He closed his computer, walked back into the hospital and straight to Mr. Kelly's office. He could still sense Anastasia but he would not allow himself to feel her pain. He knew the farther he got away from her, the less he would be able to connect to her. He told himself over and over. "My duty and loyalty is to my family, not to her. Who knows who or what she could be. She even said it. She could be being used as a weapon." The door opened and Mr. Kelly motioned him inside. He entered the room where there was a large oval table with several people sitting around. Michael knew most of them and had seen all but two in and out of the ICU several times. Mr. Kelly started by saying, "I've called this meeting so we can all be aware of what the other disciplines are doing and to make sure we are all on the same page. I have many of you ordering the same tests and repeating what the other doctor just did. Can we go around the room, introduce your selves, and give a brief update. Who would like to start?"

Michael looked around the room and was thankful to hear a friendly voice. Dr. Scott said, "Michael, we have known each other for a long time, but I'm Dr. Kevin Scott. I am the ER doctor who was on the night she was brought in." Then another man sitting to his left started to speak. "Michael, we have not met yet. My Name is Dr. Ezriel Ziv. I am a trauma surgeon that has been called in to review her x-rays and scans. I must say that I called in my colleague Dr. Jeff Besler. I will let him introduce himself, but I have never in my life seen such trauma to one human body. I have seen bodies go through construction accident, car accidents, heck, even explosion, and I have never seen anything like this before. I am a mandated reporter and due to your high profile family name, I thought it best to call in the FBI. I have a close friend who works there, and he has assured me that this will be handled very discreetly. They have assigned an agent who was supposed to be attending this meeting but he has been slightly delayed." Another man began to speak. "Hello Michael, as Dr. Ziv started to explain, I'm Dr. Jeff Besler. I am a Trauma therapist. I deal with patients, like your cousin, who have traumatic amnesia. (Michael, I'm scared) In your cousin's case, (He's coming...) it is a clear case of..." (Michael.... He's here!!!! Protector! ***SCREAMS***)

Michael slammed both hands on the table and shouted, "Anastasia!" as he shot up out of his chair and ran out of the room. Everyone in the room sat there very confused about what just happened. The halls were full of people, who Michael violently pushed out of his way. He linked to all protectors. "Who is with Anastasia!" No one answered. Arden finally responded, "They were all told to give you space. Most are upstairs or back here at the compound." Michael shouted in the link, "I need everyone here now!" He didn't wait for the elevator, he ran up the stairs two at a time. He heard over the PA system, "CODE TRAUMA ICU, CODE TRAUMA ICU" He screamed in the link, "Anastasia answer me!" He felt intense pain in his leg, which almost buckled him to the floor. He heard screams and people running. He called out to Anastasia again. "ANSWER ME!!!" He felt her fading away. He burst into the ICU. He saw the nurses huddled in the nurses' station and people running, but he could not see what or who they were running from. He stepped into her room and slipped to the floor. He pulled himself up using the bed. "ANASTASIA talk to me!" Her face was pale and her eyes were open. He tried to step forward to the side of her bed, but he slipped and almost went down to the floor again. He was irritated that someone would leave something wet on the floor and not clean it up. Then he noticed his hands looked weird. "Why are my hands... red?"

Dr. Besler was the first to speak. "What was that about? Is he normally prone to sudden rage? I'll go talk to him." He stood to follow him when they heard the PA system ring to life and announce the code trauma in the ICU. The entire group jumped and ran for the door.

Jonathan had stopped to get a latte and was sitting outside the small café less than a mile from the hospital when he got the link. He dropped his drink and was in his car racing back to the hospital before he realized he should have responded that he was on his way. The protectors that were still in the hospital, sprung into action and arrived less than a minute behind Michael. Arden had every available family member, with even one day of training, in a line of cars racing to the hospital. Ruth linked to Ailbe, "I have made a grave mistake."

Michael looked a second time at Anastasia's body. She was on her stomach with her face to one side. Her left leg was... Michael struggled to understand what he was looking at. He thought, "Is that a... a bone?" Then the reality sunk in. Her leg from just below her knee, almost down to her ankle was sliced wide open and it looked like a bone was broken and both ends were sticking out. Blood had been spurting out but now seemed like it was oozing. Michael grabbed her leg to apply direct pressure.

Dr. Ziv was the first doctor to enter the room. He started shouting out orders. "Call the OR. Tell them we are coming in hot!" He pushed Michael out of the way. The nurses seemed to have snapped out of their shock and started moving quickly around the room. Michael was screaming at her, "Answer me. Just answer me. Please dear God. Take me. Take me!" Arden could feel his son's anguish. He was desperate to get there. Two nurses flipped Anastasia onto her back. One yelled "NO PULSE. NO RESPIRATIONS. Starting CPR." Dr. Ziv was calling out more orders.

The pulmonologist Dr. Herzog was a second behind and went immediately to her head, tilting it back and putting a metal hook shaped instrument in her mouth. He put a long tube in her throat and attached a bag. He started pumping the bag and called out. "We have an airway." A nurse had climbed up onto the bed, straddled Anastasia and started compressions on her chest. Counting out loud, "1-2-3-4 breath 1-2-3-4 breath." Another nurse ran in with an IV bag of clear fluid. "Ringers wide open." Dr. Ziv yelled, "I'm not waiting. We go now!" as several doctors wheeled the entire bed out of the room and through the double doors. Michael could still hear them yelling for a few minutes. Arden had linked to the protectors, "Do not leave her side."

Michael was suddenly alone. He was standing in a pool of her blood, covered in it. He stood there looking at his hands, in the room that he just abandoned her in. He felt her slipping further away. He begged her, "Please forgive me. I'm so sorry I was so cruel. Please don't leave me." He remembered his last words to her were, *Good-bye Princess.* Michael despised himself even more.

Ailbe linked to Mark that she needed to get to the safe house. He linked he would have a car waiting as soon as she could get downstairs. Ailbe and Ruth were downstairs in seconds. Mark pulled up to the front of the house and didn't even get out the help them in. When he heard the doors close, he was already speeding toward the helipad on the compound. Once there, he immediately jumped in the pilot seat, Ruth and Ailbe were close behind. They got in and the preflight check was forgone and they were up in the air and headed to the safe house at an undisclosed location.

Jonathan arrived to a sea of police cars and four large black SUVs with flashing red and blue lights coming from everywhere on the car. He got out and tried to get into the hospital. He was stopped by the hospital security team. One said, "Sorry, no one in or out." Jonathan was in no mood to reason with anyone. "I'm on the Reale security team. I have to get in there!" The man looked sympathetic but said, "Sorry sir, our orders from the FBI, nobody in and nobody out. You are going to have to wait." Jonathan screamed to no one but linked with Arden, "I can't get in to the hospital." Arden linked, "We are on our way, just a few more minutes."

Michael was numb, he sat on the edge of the bed. He relived his cruelty over and over and over in his head. He tried to feel her, he tried to communicate with her. "Hold on Princess. You are in surgery now. Fight. You have to fight with everything you have." He didn't get a response but he felt her and that would have to be enough for right now.

Dr. Ziv pushed through the OR doors. He knew there was always an OR room available for traumas. His trauma nurses knew his every move and could predict what he needed before he even asked. They scrubbed his hands and put him in a sterile gown and gloves as he was calling out check list questions. "Blood?" A nurse responded. "Blood bank has four units of O negative in the elevator now and six more units will be ready in five minutes." Dr. Ziv, "Cardio surgeon?" A nurse called out "One minute out. Start without him and he will catch up." Dr. Ziv yelled, "Brent, is she under yet?" The anesthesiologist called out. "3-2-1... and she is under. You can start now." The nurse doing chest compressions called out. "Seven minutes with no pulse. Continuing CPR." The cardiac surgeon Dr. Gabriel Lester pushed through the doors. "Chest scrubbed?" A nurse called out. "Stop chest compressions. Scrubbing chest." A moment later she called out. "Chest scrubbed." And with that the surgeon cut open her chest, cracked open her rib cage, put his hand inside her chest and started to manually massage her heart. "Get that blood in her!" Michael grabbed his chest. He felt pressure, pain, and couldn't breathe. He pulled his shoulders up and leaned back. "Anastasia, please fight."

Charlotte woke up and looked over for Michael. "Another morning and he's gone. I need to put a bell around his neck. Well, I'm gonna call down to the kitchen for my breakfast in bed anyway." She rolled over and picked up the house phone and called the kitchen but there was no answer. She looked at the clock. "9:45a.m. and everyone is gone already? I need to complain to Michael that the kitchen help needs to stay a little longer." She rolled over and went back to sleep.

Arden pulled into the hospital with a line of cars behind him that seemed a mile long. He walked with a purpose to the hospital main doors where the two security guards were standing. Arden had planned to just walk through them but decided that more blood shed would not be prudent. The two men knew Arden and did not want to have to tell him no. Arden approached the two me and put his hand out to shake theirs. "Hello Sam, Hello Dean, Please announce to Mr. Kelly that we are here. Dean got on his walkie-talkie and said, "I know I'm not supposed to let anyone in, but it's Mr. Reale." Very quickly Mr. Kelly responded. "Yes yes! Let him in. I'm on my way down to you." Arden tried to smile. "Thank you gentlemen for following orders. You are both to be commended." A man wearing a jacket that read 'FBI' on the back came and unlocked the door. "Mr. Reale?" Arden remained calm. "Yes." The man asked, "Arden Reale?"

Arden was getting irritated. "Yes, I am Arden Reale." The man turned, "Please follow me. We need help with your son."

The line of protectors was a long one. Once through the hospital doors they spread out in a search pattern. Arden had given instruction prior to them arriving and to them, this was more than personal. When they reached the ICU double doors, the man stopped. "Mr. Reale, I understand your son has been through a distressing ordeal, but he is in the victim's room and refuses to let anyone enter. There is a trauma therapist, Dr. Besler in there, and he is afraid for his safety. I'm hoping you can reason with him." Arden was concerned. Michael was conflicted and now he must be blaming himself for everything. "My son and I are very close. I will speak to him." Arden linked to Jonathan. "Stay at Michael's side. No matter what he says or does." Jonathan prepared himself for a verbal nightmare. They entered the ICU unit. Arden went straight to Michael. Jonathan scanned the unit and took in every detail of everyone and everything. The nurses were nervous having FBI agents and protectors all fully armed. But they were attending to patients and families in an effort to reassure everyone of their safety. Jonathan was ready for anything, except what he saw...

They stepped into Anastasia's room. Michael was sitting on his bed covered in blood. His hands and face were stained red. He was staring at his hands with a look of confusion and bridled rage. A towel was on the floor in what looked like an attempt to soak up some blood, it seemed abandoned there and saturated. Arden moved around the pool of blood and sat down next to Michael. "Michael." Arden waited for a few minutes without any response. He tried again. "Michael. Are you linked with her?" Michael whispered in a bloodcurdling tone, "Shhhh I can hear her heart beating again but it's weak." The PA system rang to life. "LABORATORY TO OR STAT. LABORATORY TO OR STAT." Jonathan walked around to stand behind Michael. Arden tried again, "Has she told you anything? Who did this?" Michael "I did." Arden felt his son truly blamed himself. "No, I meant the person who physically did this. Did she say who hurt her?" With dried tears on his face he turned and faced his father. "She said she was scared. She called for me and I ignored her. I did nothing to save her. Her blood is solely on my hands." Arden had pushed far enough.

"Jonathan is going to stay here with you." He stood up and walked away. Jonathan was about to say something but Michael put his hand up. "Shh! I need to hear her heartbeat." Jonathan sat down next to him where Arden was sitting, and they sat there in silence.

Arden's head was pounding and he looked imposing as he walked upstairs to where the protectors had been sleeping. He swept the room for anything out of place. He opened up a link to the protectors. "UPDATES! I want to know down to the last fraction of a second what happened. How did no one see this guy?" Within moments all the protectors had linked what they knew, what they felt and every detail of what they saw. Everyone's time line was perfectly synched with everyone else's. Arden shook his head, "What are we missing? Start from the beginning and search this place top to bottom. Widen the parameter to two miles." Arden was confused. He knew it was right in front of him. He went back down to the ICU and found one of the FBI agents. "Who is in command here?" "That would be Agent Kal Palmer." He got on his radio and located where he was in the hospital. The agent said, "Sir, I will take you there." The two men walked down long halls and made several turns before they came to a small door marked 'Security'.

Arden waited a few moments for Agent Palmer to appear. The door opened, "Mr. Arden Reale?" Arden thought about getting a name tag. "Yes, are you Agent Palmer? If so, I need an update. How close are we to identifying the person?" Agent Palmer hesitated. "Well, I think I need you to see something. This is raw video and it is not for a weak stomach. Do you think you can watch it?" Arden stood firm. "Absolutely." Agent Palmer moved out of the doorway so Arden could pass by and come in. Arden felt slightly claustrophobic in the small room.

Agent Palmer started to explain the security system. "There are ten cameras on each floor. They all record 24 hours a day. Certain departments and units have camera that are recording and show on these monitors while others just have motion sensor that trigger the monitors. The ICU is one of those units that have cameras on every room and one that covers the doors, and two that cover the nurses' station. I'm just going to follow our man as he walks in." Arden stood up straight "You caught him on video?!"

Agent Palmer nodded his head. "Oh yeah, the entire attack." Arden started to speak again but the agent stopped him. "Just watch. I'll stop it before it gets graphic." Arden said, "Wait. Should we have Michael involved? He was assigned to protect her. He is pretty shook up."

Agent Palmer tilted his head and wondered if that was a good idea. "Listen, I'm only showing you this because you have friends in some high places that are ordering me to keep you in the loop on every detail. So all I can say is that he is your boy, it's up to you. I heard he is taking it hard. This might not be what you want him to see." Arden thought and said. "That should be up to him." Arden linked to Jonathan but pretended to text him. Jonathan bent down to Michael and talked in a low voice. "Hey, your dad says they have video of the attack down in the security office. Do you want to watch it with them?" Michael stood up in a flash, linked with Arden to find out where he is. "I'm on my way." He looked back at Jonathan. "Stay here. Don't let them touch her blood. Don't let them touch anything. Do you promise?!" Jonathan nodded, "No one will touch a thing, but I'm coming with you." Michael took of in a sprint, Jonathan called out to a nurse, "DO NOT touch that room!" and he was out the door chasing Michael.

They got to the security office. Everyone tried not to stare at Michael. They understood that he was emotionally very raw right now. Michael showed no emotion and said, "Play it. I want to see the son of a bitch that I'm going to kill." Arden was standing next to the light switch. "Michael, are you sure?" Michael just stared at the screen. Arden turned off the lights and the video started. It showed two security officers at the 'Welcome desk', a man dressed in all black with black gloves and a black hoodie with it up over his face. He waved to the security guards and walked pass. Michael was furious. "Wait, you guys don't stop people?" The FBI agent stopped the video. One of the security guards sheepishly said, "There are so many of you guys coming in and out and he was dressed like one of you." Michael leaned in and saw the red strips around each arm and lower leg. "No uniform has that! We did that so we could see each other in a crowd. No one except our guys know that!" He turned to Arden. "Dad, it's one of us!" Arden went toe to toe with Michael. "Just keep watching. It isn't one of us." The video started again.

The man had an unusual walk, almost like a child's, a little clumsy, and he kept fixing his gloves like they were falling off. He turned the corner and hit the button to open the thick glass double doors. Michael thought it was strange because when you put any pressure on the doors, they open automatically or you can hit the button and is does the same thing. The man stopped at the nurses' station for a moment, waved at them and walked into Anastasia's room. The agent stopped the video again. "Listen Michael, I can't stop you from watching this, but I highly recommend that you don't. It is graphic and it turned my stomach."

Michael's voice was ice cold. "Play the video."

Jonathan "Hey Michael, why don't we just take his word about the rest."

Michael "Play the video."

Arden "Maybe another time. Let's go check on Anastasia."

Michael "Play the video."

The room was silent. Agent Palmer finally said. "Fine." They watched as Anastasia was sleeping on her back. The man stood watching her sleep for three seconds when she opened her eyes. He suddenly grabbed her left leg with his left hand and flipped her onto her stomach like she was a rag doll. He looked back at the camera, pulled out a knife with a jagged edge and a hook shape on the end. With his right hand and in one motion he put the knife in her pant leg and cut the cloth up to her knee, she tried to kick him but it happened so fast. He plunged the knife into her leg and sliced her all the way down to her ankle. He took the knife and stabbed her again about mid calf, twisted the knife and pulled up hard. Then he turned toward the camera, waved and left. The cameras recorded him calmly walking out the doors and down a hall. He turned the corner and the other camera never picked him up.

Arden turned on the light. Michael was pale and staring at a blank screen. Jonathan looked at Arden and back to Michael. "We need to sit you down." Michael "Play it again." Arden "No Michael. You saw it already!" Michael looked like a caged tiger. "Play it again." Jonathan was not going to say another word. He looked at Arden as he took a step backward. Arden had no idea how to help his son's rage. "Michael! You have an eidetic memory! You do NOT need to watch it again!" Michael did not blink, he did not move or twitch a muscle. "Play it again." Arden shook his head. "Just give me one good reason!" Michael looked at Agent Palmer. "Play.... it....again." Arden turned the lights off and closed his eyes. He could not bear to watch it again. He linked the information to Ruth. Ruth and Ailbe were almost to the safe house. Ailbe linked to the entire family. Anastasia has been attacked. Get to dry high ground and surround yourselves with your protectors. I will keep you all informed.

Charlotte woke up feeling refreshed, but hungry. She tried calling the kitchen again but still no answer. She got up and took a long hot shower. She has spent many nights here and had been leaving clothes for occasions just like this. She put on something casual and headed downstairs. She thought she could get used to living in the main house, but for privacy, she would settle for one of the houses with a pool. She expected the house to be a bee hive of activity in preparation for July 4th, but it was quiet, very quiet. She went into the kitchen and made herself a sandwich and said out loud, "Michael still owes me a nice breakfast in bed. I was looking forward to my lobster eggs benedict." She put her food on a plate and walked back up stairs. She made herself comfortable and turned on the TV.

There was a breaking special news report. There was an attack at the hospital. The reporter was saying. "It's a chaotic scene. We are waiting for an official statement from the CEO Mr. James Kelly regarding the victim, but the reports we have been hearing is that Anastasia Reale has been attacked inside the hospital and by the amount of family members that have been arriving, it appears that something has indeed happened to Anastasia Reale who was found at sea several weeks ago." Charlotte watched as the reporter attempted to interview several people but it seemed everyone was still shocked and no one knew what happened. Charlotte sat up in bed, grabbed her phone and started calling the hospital. No one would pick up their phones. She sent text message to Michael and any of his family that she knew their numbers. She shook her phone and screamed, "Someone call me back!" She repeated calling and texting until she decided she would just go to the hospital.

Michael watched the video again. Taking in every pixel of detail. The man hid his face well, but Michael wanted to remember everything about him. He was going to kill him…slowly. When the video ended the second time. Arden was already ordering Michael that he was not to watch it again, but by the time he started his sentence, Jonathan caught Michael as he was going down to his knees. His voice was weak and distant. "He sliced her… like a …and he broke her leg. He is the one that has tortured her all these years. That's how he breaks her bones." He started to vomit.

The realization hit everyone. Even a seasoned FBI agent like Kal Palmer was not immune to something like this. Kal took his phone out of his pocket and quietly spoke. "Sir… We need more agents. We have a sick fuck on our hands." and hung up without hearing a response. He tapped the security guard on the shoulder. "Make ten copies. I get the original and nine copies. Leave one sitting around. (He looked eye to eye with Arden) If one happens to disappear, I have no knowledge of it." He left the small room, walked around a corner and vomited into a potted palm tree.

Arden asked Jonathan to take Michael upstairs to the OR waiting room. And he would get an update on Anastasia. Michael snapped his fingers and mumbled, "Ace! I need Ace! He ran the wiring when we donated the upgraded security system. He would know how someone could tamper with it." Arden called Ace, who came to meet them immediately. Michael had a burst of energy. They walked the route that the man took over and over again. Michael kept saying, "I'm missing something! What am I missing?" Ace talked them through inch by inch of the install procedure. "There is NO way anyone could tamper with this. But where there is a will, there is a way. Let's call in three experts to see if they can actually hack into it." Arden agreed and set the arrangements in motion.

Michael felt lightheaded and went down to his knees again. Jonathan saw the blood drain from his face. "Anastasia? Dad, something is wrong. I can't feel her…" Jonathan tried to help him up as the PA system crackled, "CODE BLUE OR, CODE BLUE OR" Michael started to scream out loud and in the link. "Anastasia! Fight… Please fight!" Arden and Jonathan helped him to his feet. Ace felt helpless. Michael fought to take a breath. "Dad, you have to take me to her. I need to get closer." Michael tried to run, but his legs wouldn't hold him. Arden and Jonathan were practically carrying him with Ace only inches away.

Dr. Ziv yelled out. "Come on where is this last bleeder? She is cut so deep, the bastard almost cut her fuckin leg off! Get more blood from the lab!"

Dr. Lester yelled out. "She has a strong heart but if she has no blood it's just a paperweight!"

The men found their way down the hallway lined with hundreds of family members. Michael was overwhelmed with all the links at the same time and everyone talking and touching him. His mother Bina, Aunt Olivia, Aunt Isabelle, Aunt Chaya, Rach-El with Bjorn, Lindsey and Linda all wanted to protect him. The room was packed with family. Michael lifted up his hands and started to talk over everyone. "Please listen! I can't feel her. If she's here, then she's too deep for me to do this alone. Please everyone, help me reach her." Linda was the first one to start to form a circle. He said, "No, I will not risk Cheri." Linda stood firm rubbing her belly. "Stephanie is the one who is insisting."

He smiled for the first time today. Everyone formed a circle around him. They all held hands tightly, they moved in closer to where they were all tight and shoulder to shoulder. Michael was in the center of the circle focused only on Anastasia. Linda laughed and said, "Stephanie says she found her. She is at the veil." Michael was in the link. He dove deep. His head was pounding, his nose started to bleed and his heart was slowing down. He called out, "Anastasia... We are all here. Fight! Find your way back." He heard a faint sound. He wasn't sure if it was an outside noise, so he pushed deeper. He felt his heart slowing down even more. He couldn't stay here for long.

Then he heard her. "Michael? You can't be here, you'll die! Leave me to cross the veil in peace." Michael focused harder and felt his mind starting to give up his own life, but he wasn't going to leave without her. "Please fight." Anastasia sounded so far away. "I'm tired. I have nothing left to fight for. I was never supposed to survive. My time here is up. Good-bye my protector." Michael felt her move away. "No, please wait." Anastasia "Why? You're afraid of me. I'm afraid of me. Please, just let me go to my ancestors." Michael asked Linda to talk to her. Linda smiled, "Anastasia, if you can hear me, it's Linda and Stephanie. You were right. She didn't like the name Cheri. You taught me how to listen to her. And now our little Stephanie wants to grow up with her auntie Anastasia. Please come home to us." Baby Stephanie starting singing. Michael felt Anastasia stop.

Dr. Lester yelled out. "We have a beating heart again people." Dr. Ziv yelled. "I found it! I got the last bleeder!" The two doctors finished their separate procedures and the secondary surgeons were going to close up the wounds. Dr. Ziv called out to the OR nurses station to go tell the family that the surgery went as planned and we will be out to speak to the family soon.

Michael was exhausted and could no longer stay that deep in the link. He desperately wanted to hear her voice, but his body gave out and he lost consciousness. Jonathan grabbed him under both arms from the back and carried him over to a couch. After a few moments, he opened his eyes. The first person he saw was a smiling Jonathan. "Dude, if I'm going to carry you all over this hospital, then you need to loose some weight." Michael was in too much pain to smile but he tried none the less. Bina was at his side. "What were you thinking!? You could have killed yourself going that deep!" She was afraid that this might be all he had left. He would save her but kill himself? Michael looked at her. "Mom, I had to try. I love her." Bina smiled. "I know you do. We all know you do. How are men always the last ones to know?" Michael drifted off to sleep. The family gathered around him again and everyone gave him a little bit of their energy. With his eyes still closed he said. "Mother, I saw the ancestors." Bina held him tight, very tight. "Sleep now. Mommy has you."

The phone in the waiting room rang. Lindsey answered it. "Thank you." was all she said and she hung up. "Anastasia made it though surgery and the doctors will be out to talk to us as soon as they can." Michael heard what she said but he needed to rest for as long as her could. He was still covered in Anastasia's blood and now added some of his own. Jonathan was torn between wanting to stay with Michael and helping find the attacker. It had been hours since the attack and it seemed that they were no closer to figuring it out.

More than an hour later, the doors to the OR opened and Dr. Lester and Dr. Ziv walked out. They were smiling but careful not to give false hope. Michael stood up quickly and tried to look presentable. "How is she? When can I see her? Is she talking? Where is she? You need to take me to her." Bina had her hands on one shoulder and Rach-El held him by the hand. Bjorn was standing behind Rach-El taking a protective stance. Ruth ordered everyone who could help Michael to stay at the hospital and everyone else back to the compound to higher ground.

The vast amount of property of the compound had a small mountain with a large indoor structure that over-looked the ocean. It was built for this reason, but to the public, it was the perfect wedding venue. The walls were large hurricane glass panels. A fire strip that ran in between the glass panels could be adjusted from eight inch flames to sixteen foot tall flames. White curtains could be lowered or raised depending on the level of privacy the couple wanted. The basement was stocked with table, chairs, cots, blankets, pillows, food and water for hundreds of people.

Dr. Ziv looked around the room and was shocked by the amount of people, but he focused on Michael. "Michael, she made it out of surgery but she had lost a lot of blood. Her heart stopped for almost eight minutes." He paused a moment to see if Michael could comprehend what he was saying. "We are expecting a long road to recovery here. She will most likely have some degree of neuro-deficits." Michael quit listening to him and just wanted to hear her in the link. "Come on. Please Anastasia. Please. Just one word to let me know you hear me. One word." Anastasia "My chest hurts." Michael felt a wave of relief. "What's wrong with her chest?" Dr. Lester spoke up. "Well, that would be my part. She was not responding to CPR because she had lost a tremendous amount of blood. I had to manually massage her heart." Michael was slowly connecting the dots. "Manually? Like you... What? You opened up her chest?"

Dr. Lester was ready with some handout information. He has dealt with large families in trauma cases before and found that having the information written down that they could read and re-read was helpful. "Yes, it was a last resort. We could not get the blood in her fast enough and she wasn't responding to any of our efforts. I did not like the alternative of allowing her to die, so I did what I had to do." Bina said, "Dr. Lester, we are not questioning what you did or why you did it. We are all tired and scared. None of us has had a four hour stretch of sleep at a time in weeks. Our family has been shattered." Michael felt like he was a toddler safe in his mother's arm. The world was right in that second.

Dr. Ziv spoke up, "It has been a long and horrible day. I will come and get Michael when she is stable in the recovery room." The two doctors turned and left. Michael sat back down in his mother's arms and closed his eyes. Jonathan knew he was trying to communicate with Anastasia. The room stayed relatively quiet considering the amount of people that were in there. Michael could have been in the middle of a Rugby game and he wouldn't have heard anyone else. He focused only on hearing her voice. He kept repeating,"I'm here. I hear your heart beating. Focus on my voice."

He tried humming the song that Linda's child was singing in the link. It sounded so familiar but he didn't know it. He asked Linda to link with her daughter and asked her to hum it. The infant girl did and Linda started to hum along with her daughter and soon Michael was humming it correctly. Bjorn smiled and said, "I know that lullaby. My mother used to sing it for me. It's the Hurrian Hymn, from home. He taught everyone the words and the entire group sang it. Anastasia heard them in the link and started humming along. "I can feel her!" Michael shouted. No one responded, they were enjoying the calmness that they so desperately needed. Sitting there, surrounded by family singing an old lullaby from their old home.

Michael must have fallen asleep again. He woke up to his father tapping him on the shoulder. "Michael, the doctor said that you can go see her in the recovery room." He stood up quickly, too quickly, and felt light headed and dizzy and almost passed out again. Arden grabbed him, "Easy son. Slow down. Your girl seems to have mastered the skill of surprising us all." Michael was confused and looked around the room. "What happened?" Dr. McKay was standing there. She had examined Anastasia when she had the seizure. She was also there this morning at the meeting. Michael asked, "Did she have another seizure?" Dr. McKay touched Michael's arm gently. "No, Ezriel, I mean Dr. Ziv asked me to check her for signs of brain damage, and I have to say that I am amazed that as of right now… She is showing no signs of brain damage or swelling in the brain. She was even fighting the intubation tube so Dr. Herzog is taking it out now. She is heavily sedated but I think she is asking for you."

Michael's face lit up like an exploding firework. "Please, can I see her?" He was already starting to walk toward the OR doors before she could answer. Dr. McKay said, "I don't think I could stop you even if I said no." She laughed and asked, "Do you want a few minutes alone with her or would you like a family member to come along?" He looked at Jonathan. "Please come with me." Jonathan was humbled and ashamed of himself that he could ever think that Michael could be cold or heartless. Michael took him by the hand and held on tight as they began to follow Dr. McKay into the recovery room.

Dr. Ziv was standing a few feet from Anastasia as they walked in. He took a long deep breath and said, "This is going to look ugly and scary. That said, we want you to have as much privacy as possible. Be aware that there are other patients within ear-shot. Now, one of the bones in her leg was badly broken so I had to put an interior rod through it and an exterior fixation device. Her leg is going to be very swollen and bruised for awhile. Her chest will heal fine and you probably won't even notice the scar in a few months. Dr. Lester is a master of surgical glue and it helps the incision look better after it heals." He knew Michael was anxious to see her, so he quit talking. "Keep is short, sweet and simple."

Michael turned to Jonathan as they stepped to her bedside. He was frozen with fear and failing to hold back his tears. "I can't look. Just tell me she is ok." Jonathan looked at Anastasia, then back at Michael and smiled. "She is your Anastasia. She is beautiful. And she is smiling at you." Michael swung around to see for himself. Her face was a little swollen, her eyes were slightly opened and she was trying to smile. Her voice was course and it was painful to talk but she said. "You look horrible." Michael laughed through his tears. "I know. I'll shower soon." He touched her face so gently that she felt time slow down. She closed her eyes and moved her face into the palm of his hand. He sat down in a chair that Jonathan pushed over to him.

He leaned forward to whisper through his tears. "I was never afraid of you, I was afraid of my connection with you. I fell in love with you the moment I first laid eyes on you. Your strength is only matched by the heaviness of my heart. The ocean might have called you Princess but I will make you my Queen. I will honor you above all else, and elevate you to heights that you could never imagine. I freely give you my bond. I don't even need you to take it. I leave it at your feet to walk on or embrace it. That is your choice. Just don't ever leave me. You are not my charge, nor my duty. You are my heart and soul. I am now and forever yours."

Anastasia struggled to open her eyes. Her chest and leg hurt but she didn't care. Her eyes were soft and her tears filled the palm of his hand. She wanted her words to be clear. She opened her mouth to speak. "I Princess A'Llwyn, accept your bond and I present mine to you, as my promise to never leave your side." Jonathan gasped. Michael didn't care what her name was. He was now and forever bonded to her. He kissed her forehead "My love. (kiss) My Queen. (kiss) My forever bond. (kiss). Anastasia smiled.

They heard a loud noise. Michael and Jonathan both jumped toward the sound. They were ready to take on an army. There stood Charlotte standing in the doorway. Her mouth opened, her fists clenched and she looked like she was trying to speak but she was just making inaudible sounds. Jonathan stepped towards her but she hit the wall and ran out. Michael was suddenly aware that everyone in the recovery room had heard their entire conversation. No one moved. Not even the machines dared to make any noise. Dr. Ziv cleared his throat. "I guess I can be the first to congratulate you two." He was only a few steps away. He shook Michael's hand and wiped his own tears with his lab coat. "Now that is what I call a proposal!"

By the time Jonathan got to the door, Charlotte was nowhere to be seen and he wasn't going to go looking for her. He walked back to the OR waiting room where all eyes were on him. He was completely disheveled and scratching his head looking down at his feet. He didn't know where to start. Arden was on his feet. "Out with it! How is she?" Jonathan faced the crowd with a huge grin on his face. "She who? Your new daughter in law?" The room was silent. Everyone asked themselves 'what did he just say???' Lindsey was the first one to jump up. "THEY BONDED???" The room exploded with excitement. Jonathan made his way to Arden. "Um, her name...She remembers her name."

Charlotte heard the cheering and became more enraged. Michael and Anastasia heard it too. They smiled and stayed forehead to forehead, enjoying the moment. Dr. Ziv put his hand on Michael's shoulder. "That is about all my old heart can take for now and I'm sure she needs to rest." Michael didn't want to leave, but he knew Dr. Ziv was right. "Rest my love. We have protectors searching everywhere. The entire family is also sending us reinforcements to protect you. I need to speak to my parents. You are safe and deeply loved." She smiled, "You smell." He didn't have a response but as he stood to leave. He smelled down his own shirt. Dr. Ziv openly laughed out loud. "You might be the most romantic man in the world, but you are not the best looking right now. Go and talk to your parents. It sounds like a party out there and then come back into the doctor's lounge. There's a shower and I'll get you a pair of scrubs." Michael was thankful and gave a nodding yes. "I'll be right back." and he headed the waiting room.

Charlotte stormed out of the hospital hysterical. She got into her car talking to herself. "What just happened? What the fuck just happened!? He had to be just telling her that bullshit to give her hope or something!" She recalled after she heard the news reports and not being able to reach anyone, she headed to the hospital. It took her hours in traffic just to get there and then over an hour just to gain access into the hospital. She had to be cleared by the FBI, even after she told them that she worked there and that she was Michael Reale's fiancé. Then when they finally let her in, she had to get checked out on every floor. Then being insulted to have to call a co-worker to let her into the recovery room. She just wanted to show Michael that she supported him and his family. She called her friend Kat and invited her out for a drink. She told her she would explain when they met up.

Michael walked back into the OR waiting room. He was met with a swarm of hugs and congratulation. Arden and Bina were holding hands.

Bina had tears of joy. Arden spoke up. "Son, you broke with some traditions here." Arden didn't really care, he was thrilled. But there were
more questions now than the day she was found. Arden took his son by
the shoulders. "Just a few questions. What did she say her name was?"
Jonathan answered as he walked up behind Michael. "A'Llwyn, Princess
A'Llwyn." Arden said confidently. "Well, we KNOW that she can't be
THE Princess A'Llwyn...right?" Michael remembered where he knew
that name. "I'll link it to Grandmother. But she believes that's her name.
We know she can't be THE Princess, but when she was at the veil of the
ancestors, I could have sworn that is what they called her." Bina looked
at Arden. "That's impossible right?. Princess A'Llwyn died over 15,000
years ago." Michael laughed, "Mom, do you think you are the only woman
named Bina in 15,000 years?" Michael linked to Ruth the events of the
past hour. Ruth looked at Ailbe, "Maybe we should just rent a room at the
hospital..."

Michael felt loved like he had never felt before. The world was perfect
right now. He realized the reason he didn't want to wash off her blood was
because if she died, that is all he would have left of her. The protectors, the
local police, and the FBI were swarming the entire hospital. There were
two protectors and two FBI agents at her bedside in the recovery room.
He could take a shower in peace. He enjoyed watching the water turn from
red to clear. He scrubbed his hair so hard that he thought he might have a
bald spot. He toweled off and sat down. He allowed himself to remember
that past twenty-four hours. In less than a day he went from angry, confused and willing to marry Charlotte... to bonded. His thoughts focused
on Charlotte. He hated that she was hurting right now. He was lying to
himself about his feelings for her. He started to remember what he didn't
like and how he sacrificed his family to make her happy. He would take
a few days and then talk to her. He dressed in the scrubs that Dr. Ziv had
set out for him. He started singing the lullaby the helped bring Anastasia
back to him. Yep, Michael felt that the world was perfect.

Charlotte sat in a bar with her friend Kat. Charlotte picked this bar
and restaurant because it was attached to a hotel with a large parking
lot. All the hotels in the area were booked solid but for a price they were

allowing the news media to park campers and RV's on the property. And for an additional price, they even allowed large power cables to be plugged in. Anastasia's rescue was the biggest news story in the world for the past few weeks and now with her being attacked at the hospital earlier today, it had reached a whole new level of frenzy. Their sleepy little island was saturated with reporters all trying to get a scoop. The locals were all very loyal to the Reale family and the reporters were getting frustrated that they weren't getting the juicy gossip stuff.

When Charlotte and Kat were over heard having a bitch fest of anti-Reale rants, several reporters were delighted to loosen their lips with more alcohol and well timed compliments. Charlotte told them her embellished stories of wild sex and the sorted family stories and how her dad was the one who saved the Reale girl in the boat. Charlotte was painfully aware of HIPPA laws. But she felt justified that she was talking as a woman scorned and not as a nurse. The loose lips and drinking lasted well into the night as she continued to write the headline for morning papers and news channels. 'Michael Reale is dumped by fiancé after found in bed with cousin.'

Ailbe and Ruth discussed going back to Nepal, but they feared that this attack was a direct result of that meeting. If that was the case, then this was a declaration of war. They linked with the elders to update them and for their feedback. No one believed that this girl was a 15,000 year old princess, but Princess A'Llwyn was the only member of the Royal family whose body was never found. Ailbe felt very frustrated and said in the link, "So again, we have created more questions and still have no answers. I am on my way to see her. Michael says he went deep trying to bring her out and that he was almost at the veil. He heard them call her A'Llwyn." One elder suggested, "Could she have drugged him?" Another suggested, "Could she have hypnotized him?" And even another suggested, "If she is so powerful, could she have implanted the memory in him?" The theories were endless. Ruth and Ailbe had their fill and promised to update everyone soon, then closed the link. Ailbe was tired and turned to Ruth. "Can we give them one day to enjoy their bond before we go digging around in her head again? I do have a theory... You might not like it though." Ruth agreed, "I see no reason to keep everyone one on high ground. I think I know what you are thinking but I want to discuss this in the Thinking Room." The two women agreed and told Mark to take them home. Ailbe linked to the entire family. "Be vigilant. No one is to be left alone. Groups of two or more, more being best. Go back to your July 4th preparations. We have a shindig to throw soon."

Michael was allowed to sit with Anastasia until she was stable enough to return to the ICU. But she was terrified. Every time she closed her eyes, she saw the man and would start screaming. Arden wanted to take her back to the compound immediately. Dr. Ziv protested. "You have the resources to do it, but you do not have a surgical suite. She is healing at a remarkable rate, but what if she starts bleeding again? What if the hardware on her legs dislodges? The variables are endless! I cannot allow her to leave in this condition. Give me a few days. Let her chest start to heal. We have the freakin FBI inside and out. This is the safest place for her to be. No one can get in or out without going passed four security checkpoints to get to where we are standing. Then add your team on top of that! Nothing is going to happen. That man getting to her was a case of freakish dumb luck on his part." Arden hated to admit it, "You're right of course." He turned as Mr. Kelly was joining them. Arden looked at Mr. Kelly, "But the second she is stable enough to move her, we go up the VIP suite. And I will not indulge either of you at that point." Mr. Kelly and Dr. Ziv agreed.

Anastasia was exhausted, but could not rest. Jonathan was never more than ten feet away from Michael, and Michael never stopped touching his wife. Anastasia heard a familiar voice and popped up in bed. "Lucy!" she called out in her raspy voice. Michael laughed, "You and your bat like hearing, I didn't hear anyone." Two FBI agents walked into the ICU to find Michael. "Mr. Reale, we have a woman with no credentials..." Jonathan was already out the door. He saw Lucy and gave her a big hug. "Wow, great to see you. I didn't think you had another ICU rotation." Lucy was awkwardly flattered that he even remembered her name. "No, I don't. I just had some free time. I heard what happened and called Mr. Kelly to see if could help. You didn't know I was coming?" Jonathan said, "No, but I'm glad you are here." Lucy looked confused, "Oh, because when he called me back he said that he spoke to Michael's dad and that Anastasia wanted to see me. I would never want to impose." Lucy felt embarrassed and wanted to leave. Jonathan extended his elbow and bowed slightly. Lucy giggled and took his elbow and they walked in.

It had been several days since Anastasia was attacked. Her chest was sore and bruised but she was healing quickly and feeling better by the hour. Her left leg had countless stitches in the back and pins and rods coming out of both sides of her leg. Yesterday it was bruised and swollen, but today it looks a little better. You would never know the amount of pain she was in by listening to her. She never once complained. When she saw Lucy come into the room with Jonathan, she propped up on her elbows and gave Lucy a big smile. Lucy "WOW, you look fantastic! I was prepared with tissues and everything." She reached in her pocket and took out a huge wade of McDonald's napkins. Jonathan wanted to make sure that he memorized every detail of what she was saying. "Well, I'm not sure if I can be of any help to you. I'm so happy that you look so great. The news said your heart stopped and the doctor had to open you up to manually massage it. Ugh... ... What did that guy always talk about 'fake news'." Michael linked to Arden "Father, check the news and get Mr. Kelly on it!" Arden was furious.

Anastasia asked Lucy if she would help her get cleaned up and dressed. Lucy was thrilled to help. When Lucy was going to expose her chest, she asked to boys to give her some privacy. Anastasia's look took a serious tone. "Lucy I know we are going to be the greatest of friends, can I trust you with something?" Lucy felt a connection with her when she first saw her, but she never thought that they would ever become friends. "That depends on what you want to tell me. I will not keep a secret if it will cause pain or harm. Nor will I keep a secret if it will hide a crime. So please think about what you tell me."

Michael turned to Jonathan, "Bond with her! Bond with her right now!" The two men laughed. Anastasia bowed her head slightly. "I need that type of honesty. But what you heard on the news is accurate." She showed Lucy her chest. "My heart did stop." Michael was shocked that she was telling Lucy this, but he respected her to choose her friends and who to trust and who to avoid. But what Michael was impressed with was how she said it. Michael was more in love with her today than he was yesterday. She was kind and graceful. Her voice was comforting Lucy, who was clearly upset. Michael didn't pick up on all the clues that Lucy was sharing. All Michael knew was that this girl had NO spare time between school, work, and her parents. And here she is with a pocket of napkins offering to give a bed bath to a woman that she doesn't know, forty miles away from her home. And there is his wife, sharing intimate details to validate Lucy's feelings.

Jonathan leaned into Michael's shoulder, "I could listen to her talk all day." Michael agreed but then said, "Who?" Jonathan grinned, "Lucy. Her voice is….." Michael laughed. "Are all men as pitiful as us when they are in love?" Neither one of them wanted to talk. They just watched the two women talk and laugh. Anastasia asked her a million questions. Lucy asked, "So why type of music due you like?" As soon as the words came out of her mouth she apologized. "Anastasia, I am SO sorry. It was a stupid question. Please, I hope you can forgive me." Michael was moving to intervene, but Anastasia smiled. "No Lucy, you said nothing wrong. I don't remember any thing about music except one lullaby. But you can ask me anything and I will do my best." Lucy was embarrassed for herself and also for Anastasia. "No, I think it is getting late, and I have over-stayed my welcome." Anastasia asked, "What else did the news say?" Michael jumped in. "Whoa. I'm sorry, but I don't want to know and I really don't want you upset." Lucy nodded as Jonathan called her over.

Anastasia and Michael had started a conversation that Lucy wanted no part of. Jonathan asked, "Can I walk you out to your car?" She wanted to see Jonathan again but she was afraid he would press her to come to the July 4th party. She even tried to hire some help, but every agency was booked. The two walked out and down to the main entrance. Jonathan stopped at the FBI mobile command station and saw Agent Palmer. "Agent Palmer, I want to introduce you to Lucy Vans. She is a good friend of mine and Anastasia's only friend. We would like to have her on the 'access list' if possible."

Agent Palmer smiled and shook her hand. "Nice to meet you Ms. Vans. Do you mind if I ask you a few questions?" Jonathan kissed her hand and said, "I hope to see you soon, but if not, I will see you July 4th." He crossed his fingers in the air and left. Agent Palmer asked some simple questions regarding her name, address, and "How long have you known the Reale family?" Lucy felt very uncomfortable. "Well, Jonathan was slightly misleading on his statement. I just met a few of them the other day when I gave Anastasia a bed bath. I'm a nursing student. Mr. Kelly asked me to come in and help with personal cares because the staff was overworked. I think Jonathan is nice to anyone who is nice to him. He asked me to the July 4th parade."

Agent Palmer "Oh, so you don't know the family well?"

Lucy "I don't know them at all. Today was the first time I really even spoke to them." Agent Palmer "And what are your impressions?"

Lucy "I think they are very open, honest and respectful people. I mean I only met Michael, Jonathan, and Anastasia."

Agent Palmer "Thank you Ms Vans, you have been very helpful. Oh and one more question. Have you been watching the news about her?" Lucy felt that this was going to get bad but she was not going to lie about anything. "Yes sir, I watched the late news and this morning's news." He was glad that she was open and he didn't have to pull responses out of her. "And do you have any thoughts that you would like to share?" Lucy thought for a second and said, "I think it was disgusting." Agent Palmer "Disgusting? Can you elaborate?" Lucy "This is a girl that has been through Hell, and someone has to go and tell the world about what they 'think'. Give the viewers their opinion. This is Anastasia's story to tell."

Agent Palmer "Her story? Do you think it is a story? Do you have any thoughts or theories on who would want to tell her story?"

Lucy "I don't know and I don't care to know. The three of them seem like very sweet people, I don't understand how someone could hurt them. I just know I wasn't one of the nurses."

Agent Palmer "How do you know that?"

Lucy "The nurses up there have seen that family living a nightmare. None of them would want to add to their pain."

Agent Palmer "What about the story of them being caught in bed together? Do you find that disgusting too?"

Lucy "Sir, I respect the duty that you perform, But to drag me into gossip is beneath you and insulting to me. But I will get it off my chest. Michael has been by her side day and night. That man is devoted to her. I could give a rat's ass if they are distant cousins or not. I hope to God that everyone could find that kind of love."

Agent Palmer "Ms Vans, I'm sorry if I made you upset. We are investigating an attempted murder. Please, one more quick question. Why do you think that Jonathan called you his 'good friend'? You said you only met him one other time. Have you slept with him?" Lucy was outraged. "Agent Palmer! I have told you everything that I know. If I had romantic feelings for him, I would have shared that as well. I will not dignify that with an answer. I hope you have a very good reason to attempt to humiliate me in a parking lot. I will say good-bye and be safe!" She stormed off in a huff. Agent Palmer watched her for a moment and spoke to anyone inside the FBI mobile command station, "Please put Ms Lucy Vans on the 'access list', she checks out."

Ruth and Ailbe arrived back at the compound. The house was alive with nervous activity. People talking, phones ringing, music playing, and the general sounds of the stress of organizing a large party. Ruth and Ailbe went up to the Thinking Room. The room was Ailbe's connection to home. No one enter this room that the room itself did not invite in. Ruth and Ailbe sat quietly and asked the ancestors for guidance in trying to figure this out. Ailbe said, "Ok. We have two scenarios." and started writing it down.

"1. She is Princess A'Llwyn.

a. How has she survived 15,000 years?

b. Where has she been?

2. She is not the Princess.

a. How do we figure out how an unknown Azili suddenly shows up?

b. Is she a threat to the family?"

The two women talked well into the night. Ruth finally said, "I give up. We need to go see her and try again. Have you ever heard of information not being in the link? (She waited a moment and then added.) Don't answer that. We link with her again tomorrow. PERIOD. I'm tired, I'm going to bed." Ailbe stayed in the Thinking Room the rest of the night.

Jonathan came back upstairs. Michael and Anastasia were still talking about the news reports. Michael was ending their conversation. "You can watch it, that's fine. But I'm not going to and I'm not leaving your side." Jonathan "You can watch it on my phone." Anastasia's face lit up. "I can do that? That's great. How?" Jonathan pulled out his phone, looked up 'current news' and handed it to her. "Just hit that arrow." Michael looked at him. "Thanks buddy... Why throw gasoline on a fire?" Jonathan stood closer to Anastasia so Michael couldn't hit him. "She has a right to know if someone is talking about her. She's not our... (He regretted that!) She is your wife, not your child. I just think she can decide for herself." Michael snapped back. "I am her protector! I can't see how this will do anything but cause her pain." Both men understood both points of view and could have disagreed all night, but as they were arguing, Anastasia sat and watched several news reports. The latest one that was plastered all over every station was a picture of her in the recovery room. Her chest was fully exposed showing the new nine inch incision. Anastasia asked, "Who could be so cruel to take a picture like that?" Michael could not bear to see the photo. "My father is looking into it. I have to make rounds. Jonathan, you are here right?" Jonathan "I'm not leaving her side." Michael "Good, Ace had three computer experts competing for $10.000 to anyone who could hack his system. He wants to go over the results." He turned and left.

Michael must have walked the route that the man took thousands of times. It HAD to be a camera malfunction or a tape on repeat... he was missing something. "Think!" He yelled to himself. "There is an explanation and it is right in front of me. Come on Michael, You're better than this!" Ace arrived and they went over the results. Everything that the three separate experts tried, had failed. Michael said, "Ask three thieves." Ace was very proud of himself. "I did! I was wiring one of the houses on the compound and had the idea. I'd wire the exact system and build an exact replica of the route. They couldn't do it either. I'm telling you, it is NOT the security system." Michael was discouraged and went back to the ICU and told Jonathan to go home and get some sleep.

The rest of the night was the same. Anastasia screamed herself awake every few minutes. She was getting stronger by the day as evidence by Michael's shining new black eye. He went to grab her right foot as it was coming at his face but forgot to watch her hands.

The next morning Anastasia woke up to a beautiful day. She had no pain. Her chest looked almost fully healed. She was waiting for the trauma surgeon. Arden was busy training the reinforcement protectors from Spain, Brazil, Australia, Greenland, Italy, China and Greece. Six from Norway had already returned with Ruth and Ailbe from Nepal. Jonathan had a good night sleep in his own bed. Michael was still replaying how she got him with that solid left hook, but he was in high spirits.

The FBI was convinced that no staff member, in-patient, or hospital visitor was the attacker. They were also convinced that the attacker was no longer in or around the hospital. Agent Palmer was in constant contact with Arden. Mainly because two high ranking FBI officials were his close friends, and his direct supervisor was a distant third cousin. Kal's phone rang constantly and most of the time it was one of those three asking for an update. The July 4th plans were in over-drive with only two more days until the big party. Everything was going smoothly. The only lingering stressor for Michael was that he had not had the chance to speak to Charlotte. Michael heard several reports that she still needed some time to herself and to cool off. He wanted to be respectful and give her the space she needed.

Mr. Kelly was excited that he woke up in his own bed for the first time in months. He had been at the hospital 24/7 since Anastasia was found. His wife Piper had brought him fresh clothes daily and was volunteering with the city planners regarding their activities in the parade. Their daughters Nikki and Lisa both made the junior varsity cheerleading squad and were going to be marching this year for the first time. He was satisfied that the Reale family knew that the hospital was doing everything medically possible for their niece. The horrible attack was still a sticky pickle, but Ruth herself called and reassured him that she alone has taken the responsibility for lowering her security staff, which was the only reason that anyone could have gotten within 100 yards of the ICU doors, let alone near enough to touch her. The FBI had told him that his security staff for the hospital is otherwise outstanding. So today he was going to sit back and relax until he had to be at the hospital at noon for some quick paper-work and then he was off for the long July 4th weekend.

CHAPTER 4

Thursday July 2nd. Most of Anastasia's doctors had been in and out by 10a.m. Everyone was commenting that her recovery was nothing short of a miracle. Dr. Jacqui McKay was even writing a paper for the 'American Medical Journal'. The entire team of doctors had been contacted to present a case study in Washington DC. The hospital has been contacted by every talk show and news organization in the world to interview, what is now being called, 'The M (miracle) Team'. They have rejected all offers for now. Their work was not done and Anastasia would be recovering for months from the attack. Dr. Ziv and Dr. Lester arrived. Dr. Lester "Good morning and happy TGIF jr.! How are you feeling today our miracle girl?"

Anastasia smiled wide. Her voice was coming back strong and clear. "TGIF jr.?"

Dr. Lester smiled, "Why do I keep forgetting about your amnesia? It means 'Thank God it's Friday' and... forget it. Are you ready for the big party this weekend?"

Anastasia was hoping she would be able to go if only for a few minutes. "Do you think I can go?"

Dr. Lester took her hand and patted it gently. "I don't know what vitamins, herbs or magic potion you've been taking, but you are the fastest healer I have ever met. You have to remember your secret and bottle it. Or better yet, tell me and let me bottle it. I could retire in Tahiti in one of those houses over the water." Everyone laughed. "But in all seriousness, you are doing fabulous. I don't see any reason that you have to stay here in the ICU. I know it's upsetting to you and your family." He turned to Michael, "And to your fiancé over here." Michael stepped closer and gave him a hug. Michael was firm but emotional. "I have many thanks to give around here, but you had my heart in your hands when you were holding hers. I will never be able to repay you."

Dr. Lester teared up and tried to bring some humor in or he was going to start crying like a teenage girl. "Well son, you did hear me mention Tahiti right?" Jonathan leaned around to see Dr. Lester's face. "I'm on it doc." Dr. Ziv was laughing as he leaned over to Jonathan. "Hey, you do know that we are a team? So make that two houses. Our families have been friends for twenty years, so if you could swing it…make it side by side. Just not TOO close." There were laughs in and out of the room and two of the protectors shouted, "Don't forget us in that deal." Michael asked, "So Dr. Ziv, are you on board with us taking her home?" He bit his lip, cocked his head and said, "I think she is right on the verge of me saying yes….. BUT, and there is a but…..How about if we take her upstairs for the rest of the day and tonight. Your Grandfather and I spoke last night and he has upgraded your infirmary at home with the equipment I think she needs. I'm going to go over there this afternoon and check it out for myself. IF he did what I asked him to do, which I'm sure he has. Then I say she can go home tomorrow afternoon. Let's see how a night upstairs feels." Anastasia squealed with excitement. Dr. Ziv continued "The twist in my knickers… now listen carefully. This is either going to go great or be a disaster if I am not crystal clear. I have two residences and Dr. Lester has one. They are doctors BUT they are right out of school. Your Grandfather has agreed that the three of them and four nurses will be moving into some of the apartments on your property. The residents will be supervised by Dr. Lester and myself. Are we clear so far?" Jonathan had taken Anastasia by the hand and he was literally bouncing up and down and squealing along with her.

Michael was soaking it all in. In that moment he was the happiest he had been in a very long time. Michael wanted to join in the jumping and squealing, but he had to keep his composure for now. "I understand, and despite my cousin and my wife, sorry, soon to be wife, acting like kindergarten children, I swear on my soul that we will follow your direction to the letter." Dr. Ziv clapped his hands together once and said, "Excellent. I know you will. There is just one more thing. In the meeting, Dr. Besler was speaking to you when... um... Well, he never got to tell you that he is a 'Trauma Therapist'. We, her medical team feel that his services and expertise will be a valuable tool and addition to our treatment plan. I believe he rescheduled himself for today."

Michael did not want a therapist asking her loads of questions. What if she said to him that she is a 15,000 year old lost Princess? That would be something that a therapist might question deeper. Michael "I applaud the entire team for looking at her as a whole person, but I think she just needs to be around family and friends. Once she knows she is safe and loved, then I'm hopeful her memories will come back." Dr. Lester "I'm sorry son. But this is a deal breaker. Forget my house in Tahiti. The facts are that she has been through trauma. Real trauma, like I have never seen before and hope to God that I never see again. She needs this. And to be honest with you...You need it too."

Michael rubbed his hands together. "I don't know." Dr. Ziv "Give it one session. Just ONE. (He looked at Anastasia) If you hate it, or hate him. Then fine. I won't argue. Do we have a deal?" Anastasia reached for Michael. "I would love to meet him and speak to him. Anything that could help. My vote is for yes." Michael smiled. "She is the boss." Dr. Lester "You are a wise young man and already found the key to a long happy and successful marriage." Dr. Lester left to go to the nurses' station and document as Dr. Ziv examined her leg. "The swelling looks FANTASTIC. I need to tighten these pins and screws. You truly are like Wonder Woman aren't you? Maybe that's it. (He took the sterile instruments out of his pocket. Cleaned the pins and screws with alcohol. Scrubbed the area with Bedadine. A nurse came in and put a sterile chux under her leg and put sterile gloves on his hands and opened the bag for him.) Maybe you are Princess Diana of Themyscira and come here to save all mankind." (He said in an announcer type voice) Without thinking she said. "No, I am

Princess A'Llwyn of Uanza here to save my kind." Dr. Ziv had finished what he was doing. "You guys crack me up. I'll finish coordinating with Dr. Lester. You should be upstairs after we run some routine and simple tests. Just to be on the safe side." He waved and stepped out.

Michael and Jonathan stood there with their mouths open. Jonathan blinked a few times. "Um…I'd a… link that to Grandmother…" Michael "Done. She's on her way." Anastasia looked at them like they were crazy. "What?" Michael stared at her for a few moments. "Did you just hear what you said?" Anastasia crinkled her nose. "Stop staring at me like that. Michael I told you I think I remembered my name. Right? I think it's A'Llwyn. Why is that so strange?" They just stared… Michael finally took her hand. "I know what you said, but that was not English." Jonathan "Or anything else from here."

She lowered her shoulders. "Ha ha ha…. Pick on the girl with no memory. Here, eat this cherry but it's really a hot pepper." She was really hoping that they were kidding, but by the expressions on their faces, she knew they weren't. "Come on guys, you're scaring me really bad!" Michael stepped to her and held her face. "Don't be scared. It's great that your memories are coming back. Do you remember anything else?" She started to tear up. "No, just when he said about a Wonder Woman, it just came out. I wasn't even thinking. It just 'boop' and rolled out." Michael kept eye contact with her as her face was in his hands. They were nose to nose and kissed her. "I promised you that you will never be afraid again. And if you are THE Princess A'Llwyn of Uanza, then we have a lot more to do than plan a wedding."

Charlotte was getting ready to have a meeting with a reporter. She had to drive off the island for over an hour. She didn't want anyone to know that she was the 'anonymous family source' that the news channels were all quoting. But now it wasn't just her. Someone else at the hospital was texting her pictures of Anastasia from a restricted number. Charlotte was in full blown scorned woman mode and was arrogant in her belief that nothing could be traced back to her. She remembered stories that reporters would go to jail when they were pressured to reveal their sources of information.

As she was grabbing her car keys there was a knock on the door. "It better be Michael coming to grovel at my feet!" As she swung the door open, there stood two men in business suits holding badges in their hands that read 'FBI' on them. She wanted to faint as all the blood ran out of her face. One of them said, "Ms Charlotte Calhoun?"

She stuttered "Yeah...Um Yes, I'm Charlotte Calhoun. Can I help you?"

Agent Palmer "Yes you can. I'm Agent Kal Palmer, This is my partner agent J. We need to ask you a few questions."

Charlotte "I was just leaving. I could call you when I get back."

Agent Palmer "Where are you going?"

Charlotte "Um... To meet a friend for lunch."

Agent Palmer "Good, then we have plenty of time before lunch. May we come in?"

Charlotte "Um...I really should get going. I have a long drive."

Agent Palmer "I'll make you a deal. If I make you late for your lunch date, then I will take you there lights and sirens. This shouldn't take long. Just some routine questions. Deal?"

Charlotte laughed nervously, "Ok."

She stepped aside and let the men in. Charlotte's mouth felt like she had cotton balls in her cheeks. "Please have a seat." as she went into the kitchen. "Can I get either of you something to drink?" She poured herself some water. Agent Palmer "No thank you, we don't want to waste your time." She thought to herself, "Calm down, they just want to ask about the day she came into the ER. Just stay calm. There is no way they could know that I talked to the news. And it's not a crime!" She walked back into the living room and sat down. "Well, what questions do you have for me?" Agent Palmer started with routine name, address, phone number, place of employment, how long employed there, family names, friend names, and a few other benign questions. Charlotte was beginning to relax when he asked, "Have you been watching the news lately?"

Charlotte "A few things here and there but I generally don't have time."

Agent Palmer "I can understand. You work 7p.m at night till 7a.m in the morning right?"

Charlotte "Yeah, and then sleep most of the day."

Agent Palmer "And I'm sure an active social life."

Charlotte "I've been very busy lately, but on my nights off... yeah, I like to go out with friends. Is that a crime?"

Agent Palmer "No no no. I just meant that you are a busy woman?"

Charlotte "Life after you move out on your own...bills bills bills, so I like to relax when I can."

Agent Palmer "Tell that to my twenty year old. He still lives at home." They laughed.

Charlotte "Well, I have to go soon. Is there anything else?"

Agent Palmer "I heard you are close to the Reale family."

Charlotte didn't know how to answer. She started to get nervous again. "Well, yes, but things are a little awkward right now."

Agent Palmer "Really, how so?"

Charlotte "A few nights ago, Michael and I.... Michael Reale. Well we are supposed to get engaged, well...more like announce our engagement, on the 4th. We have been planning for months. We picked out a theme and colors and he is getting his invite list together, you know things like that."

Agent Palmer "So he is your fiancé?"

Charlotte "Well, he hasn't actually got down on one knee and given me my ring yet, but yes. Everyone knows. I spend half my time at his house. His sister Rach-El is one of my best friends. She is going to be my maid of honor. We picked out the girls dresses already."

Agent Palmer "So why is it awkward?"

Charlotte "It's nothing really, I mean... (She rolled her eyes) He is just really stressed out right now. His whole family is super stressed about his cousin. I mean... her friends died on that boat. She was the only one that made it into the life boat. I don't know about you, but if that was ME, I would make sure that my friends made it into the lifeboat with me. I'm very loyal that way. It just makes me wonder why she is the only survivor."

Agent Palmer "So his cousin surviving is stressing him out?"

Charlotte "No, that part is great. But she was bad when she came in. She almost died a few times. And then some lunatic comes in and stabs her! I mean that is crazy right."

Agent Palmer "How did that make you feel when you heard about that?"

Charlotte "I freaked out. Michael and I had a very romantic evening, working on our wedding plans, you know... normal young and in love stuff. I woke up and turned on the news and I rush right over to be with him. It's normally a twenty minute drive but it took me hours to get there with all the police cars and stuff."

Agent Palmer "The building was on lock down. How did you get in?"

Charlotte "I work there. So I showed my ID and Mr. Kelly knows that I'm Michael's fiancé, so they let me in."

Agent Palmer "So you rushed to be by his side. Like any loving fiancé would."

Charlotte "Exactly. I love him AND his family. I needed to be there for him."

Agent Palmer "And where did you go once you got into the hospital?"

Charlotte "Well, I went to the ER to see what was going on. Well, some cop 'escorted' me to the ER because that is where I work. I talked to some of my co-workers, I needed to find out that his cousin was ok. Then I went to OR."

Agent Palmer "But you don't work in the OR. How did you get up there?"

Charlotte "All of us nurses know each other. I can't go into a sterile area, but I just went into the nurses' station and asked how she was. Ya know, not to be nosy, I was just concerned."

Agent Palmer "I can understand that. If my wife's cousin was attacked, I would be concerned too. So then what?"

Charlotte "Nothing. I saw everyone was busy. She made it out of surgery, so I thanked God that she was ok, and left."

Agent Palmer "Well, we've taken up enough of your time. Thank you very much and I hope that we didn't make you late for your lunch date."

Charlotte "You are both very welcome. I think I'll make it just in time."

They stood up and walked toward the door. Charlotte opened the door. They said their good-byes and she closed the door. She leaned up against it and brushed the sweat off her forehead and walked back to get her purse and keys. She opened the door and there stood the two men. Charlotte jumped back a half a step. "Oh, you scared me." Agent Palmer smiled. "I'm very sorry Ms Calhoun, I left my pen on your couch. May I come in and get it?" Charlotte stepped aside. "Sure, come on in." He stepped and found his pen quickly and walked out. "I would feel much better if we walked you to your car. The man who did this is still unidentified and walking free." Charlotte "Thank you. Michael is always telling me that after we are married that I'll have one of the security guards around me all the time. I think until then, I'll be checking my doors and windows twice." As they got to Charlotte's car, she thanked them again and was about to get into her car when Agent Palmer said, "Ms Calhoun, may I ask you one more quick question?" Charlotte "A quick one or I'm gonna be late." Agent Palmer "Thank you. What made you leave the hospital again? I mean you raced to get there. Spent hours in traffic, finagled your way into an active crime scene, you were in a highly restricted area talking to your nurse friend, But then you noticed everyone was busy..."

The two agents stood there motionless staring at her. Her mind was racing to come up with an answer. She tried to speak but her voice failed her. "Um...he... I mean, his family is so big and so...and they were all there... I didn't want to be in the way. Yeah, that's it. I know his Grandmother, Ruth, isn't thrilled that he is marring a poor working nurse. So when I saw her, I didn't want to make it weird or anything. So, I just thought that I would be the bigger person and leave. That's all." Agent Palmer smiled, "Hear that Agent J? Now if you had married a thoughtful girl like Ms Calhoun here, you wouldn't have to play referee between your wife and grandmother all the time. One of them should be the bigger person and just leave." Agent Palmer turned to Charlotte. "That is a great suggestion. I'm gonna have to use that line when I'm giving marriage advice." Charlotte smiled nervously. "You can claim it as your own if you like." Agent Palmer "Thank you young lady." Charlotte opened her car door and got in. Agent J closed it for her. Charlotte turned on her car and rolled down the window. Agent Palmer leaned in the window. "Ruth Reale wasn't there." Charlotte sat there feeling the sweat run down her back. The two agents turned and walked away.

Ruth went to the Thinking Room. She knocked and opened the door. She stood there for a moment feeling the warmth of the room. She could smell the saltwater. Ailbe was sitting next to the windows. Ailbe "Listen to the whales singing. They are beautiful creatures. I miss this place when I travel." Ruth walked over to her and stood quietly so she could hear them too. "I hate the thought that my children might have to leave here one day. One family shouldn't carry this entire burden. You should have named Faela'n to be the head of the clann. I'm not cut out for this. Ailbe looked sad and tired. "That is nonsense and you know it, but I think it is time for some changes. If they have declared war after hundreds of years of relative peace, then so be it. I'm tired." Ruth took a deep breath and let it out louder than she wanted. "I have made so many mistakes. I never wanted this. I could never manage this like you." Ailbe never took her eyes off the ocean. "The dolphins are close to the shore line today. They have been good to us…" The women watched for another moment. Ruth finally broke her silence. "We have one question answered. She is the Princess." Ailbe was unphased. "We both knew that before we went to Nepal."

Ailbe felt every bit of her 104 years as she stood up. Ruth followed her out the door and downstairs where Mark was waiting next to a running car. Ruth stopped, she was surprised to see Mark standing next to a Lykan Hypersport. Ruth laughed. "What is this? There are only two seats. Where am I supposed to sit?" Ailbe walked passed her. "In the passenger seat of course. I would never let you drive my car." Ruth shook her head laughing as she got into the car. Mark closed the door just in time for Ailbe to peel down the long driveway.

Michael asked Jonathan to stay with Anastasia while he walked the parameter with some of the protectors that were sent as reinforcements. Then he walked the route that the attacker took. He wanted to get back to Anastasia before Linda came in for a visit. Malachi had also been walking the route over and over again. Something wasn't sitting well with him either. He walked right into Michael as they were both looking down and not paying attention. Malachi quickly caught himself before he hit the floor. "Remember when no one could ever sneak up on us? I miss those days." Michael laughed. "What are you doing here?" Malachi "I was about to ask you the same thing. This has been driving me insane! I can't figure out what is out of place." Michael was excited. "ME TOO! I know there is something I'm missing. Something IS out of place but on my life, I can't find it." The two men walked it together for another hour talking out loud to each other trying to figure it out together.

Michael "Hey listen. Linda is coming over soon. I gotta run." Malachi giggled "Don't let her see that black eye. If she thinks Charlotte hit you… All Hell will break loose." Michael felt ashamed that he hasn't talked to him about the situation with Charlotte. He didn't want to talk about it, but felt that he needed to apologize for his roll. "Yeah about that, I'm really sorry that you got sucked into that. Thank you for being classy about it." Malachi tilted his head a bit. "Sucked into that? I was doing my job. Rach-El and Lindsey are the ones that kept it classy. I wanted to see one of them bap her right in her snot box!

Michael looked confused. "What?" Malachi "Did you link with them and find out what happened?" Michael had linked with them but really didn't want to, so it was like watching a movie that you are bored with so you really don't pay attention. "Yeah I did, but more to say I know what happened. I really didn't absorb it." Malachi wasn't sure he ever remembered Michael not listening to his sister. "Do you want me to link it from my perspective?" Michael shook his head no. "I'm so over it. What would I do with it now? Charlotte is out of my life. I don't want to go backward and get made at her. I'm bonded to Anastasia. I just want you to know that I appreciate your great work."

Malachi shrugged his shoulders, "I get what you're saying, but it's your loss. The faces that Rach-El and Lindsey were making…(Malachi started laughing) it's worth the price of admission." Michael smiled and thought for a second. "You just sold a ticket into your brain. I've gotta see that." Malachi linked the information. Michael was pissed, just like he knew he would be, but he belly laughed when Malachi mocked, "I'm not afraid of you Malachi!" Michael "Boy is she glad she doesn't know how afraid of you she should be." They hugged and Michael went back into the ICU.

Ailbe and Ruth arrived in the ICU. Jonathan was teaching Anastasia a card game. "RUMMY" she yelled as Jonathan protested. They saw the women and both of them busted out laughing. Ruth looked annoyed "A bit rude to point and laugh at someone." Anastasia wasn't holding back her laughter. "What happened to your hair?" Ruth took out a small compact from her purse. "Oh dear Mother! Why didn't you tell me I look horrendous?" Ailbe giggled like a scolded child. "It's very humbling dear." Ruth fixed her hair as best she could. "I wanted this to be a more formal meeting but I'm guessing my mother knew that already." Ailbe just smiled then fumbled with the deck of cards on the bedside table. "Great way to pass the time, but watch Jonathan, he cheats." Jonathan put the cards away. "I was ten years old! And you are a terrible winner." Anastasia was enjoying their interaction. She couldn't wait to leave the hospital and start her life with Michael. She looked at Ailbe. "Can we link and then explain to me what is going on? I don't mean to sound snappy, but you should have seen the look on their faces. (She tried to mimic Michael)... 'That was not English.' What other language can I speak?" Ailbe smiled and walked up to the head of her bed. "Taking charge fits you well Princess."

Anastasia asked. "Can you tell me anything about Princess A'Llwyn? I mean, I can't really be, what 15,000 years old. Even I know that's impossible." Ruth stepped up to stand next to Ailbe. Ailbe quietly said. "The only unaccounted for person in our entire history is you. Your parent's bodies were discovered after the massacre. The search for you was extensive and went on for a millennium. Many in the family are still searching. Some think you stayed on Uanza while others think you tried to get to Atlantis. But without knowing any details about where your parents hid you before they escaped, the search ended assuming you were dead. Then it bacame a matter of finding your remains. And here you are." Anastasia looked at Jonathan and to Ruth and back to Ailbe. "Can someone yell Buzzinga now?"

Ailbe smiled and opened a link. She wanted to focus more on the moment she remembers waking up in the dinghy. They went forwards and backwards several times. Ailbe was disappointed that nothing more was remembered. Then she started to go deeper. She saw flashes of light that were not there before. She went deeper. She felt Anastasia's muscles tense. She saw fog but couldn't see through it. She was not going to risk going any deeper. Michael communicated with her that she was at the veil of the ancestors and he heard them call her Princess A'Llwyn. Ailbe would never go that deep for the proof the elders would demand, but she had everything she needed. She broke the link. Anastasia was excited to know if Ailbe found anything new. "Did you see anything? I keep feeling that it is right there. I can almost touch my memories." Ailbe touched her face. "I agree. There are flashes of light and a deep fog. I don't know if we are trying too hard and forcing memories or if they are a true record. I have my theories, but we will discuss them in private. But for right now... I want to celebrate your bond. This weekend will be in your honor. I'm going to speak to Mr. Kelly straight way. She hugged her and didn't even wait for Ruth to say her good-byes.

Dr. Ziv arrived at the compound. He drove up the long driveway and passed signs that pointed the way to the park, movie theater, grocery store and even a horse stable. He said to himself, "My word! This place is the size of an entire city." He drove up to the main house. He recognized the man that approached his car from one of the Reale security. Dr. Ziv rolled down his window. The man said. "Hello Dr. Ziv. My name is Steven. I will be showing you around." He made a motion to another man that opened his car door. Steven continued. "Leif will park your car and if you would please follow me." Dr. Ziv exited the car, Leif jumped into the driver's seat and left.

Steven started walking toward the front door. Dr. Ziv asked, "How big is this property. It looks enormous driving in here." Steven started giving him a short history lesson as they walked. "There was a time when the Reale family owned this entire island. 42 miles long and 26 miles wide. They refused to allow any cartographer to document it. Most of the family lived here. They were the best seafaring men to ever live. The high points of the island had watchtowers and if anyone came close, they would sail out to meet them. If they were friends, they steered them to safety, if they were foes, they were invited ashore and their ships would be crushed on the rocks. These waters are still known today to be treacherous. The family needed a safe harbor for their own ships, so they hand built the marina. It's in the same place as the original one."

Dr. Ziv "How did they hand build a marina?"

Steven "My ancestors could free dive farther than anyone. They were legendary. Family history tells us that even the Pharaoh Narmer sent some of his men to learn our secrets of diving."

Dr. Ziv "That is impressive. I never heard that in any history book."

Steven "There are a lot of facts that you will never see in history books."

Dr. Ziv "I believe you there, but this is fascinating."

Steven "So as the years went on. My family began to explore the world farther and farther away from home. It was more and more difficult to defend and protect such a large space. So they gave some to indigenous tribes and then civilization arrived on our shores. More land was donated to build churches, schools and the land that we built our hospital on was becoming widely used for the public, so we donated that as well. Our family was widely known know as healers. Did you know that the Mayan King K'inich Popol Hol was even treated here when he broke his leg and the infection was killing him. The very same spot that the hospital sits on today. As a matter of fact, history says that the oldest hospital every discovered is in Sri Lanka, the Mihintale hospital. But under the foundation of the current building, sits the ruins of the original building. Much earlier than the Mihintal."

Dr. Ziv "That is just incredible. You have to be making this up."

Steven laughed, "No. This place has some beautiful and tragic stories. The Smithsonian Institute contacts Great-Grandmother Ailbe every year asking to see our family archives and to hear her stories, but she always refuses. She allows people to see them, but never to record them in any way. Did you know that what you call early man had photography? Granted it was primitive but they had it."

Dr. Ziv stopped abruptly. "Now that is just not true."

Steven stopped with him. "I would never lie, I'm personally into photography. I call myself an artist, but my sister Lindsey calls me more of a paparazzi."

Dr. Ziv laughed. "I have a hundred pictures of my finger. So I gave up trying. But I'm gonna call BS on that one until I see proof. Not that I'm calling you a liar, I just really want to see it so you can prove it."

Steven "Some of our family that left here for Norway were amateur archaeologists. Right in there own back yard in the Aukra region they found an entire city! When they discovered the center of the city, they found a partially burnt library. It was very crude, but it was written language and photographs documenting their history. My family moved a few times and settled in a different area and low and behold the city was 'discovered' about 150 years ago and now everyone wants to know if the rumors are true. The same with Gwendoline cave in Ireland."

Dr. Ziv "So what happened to these books!?"

Steven "We have a few in our archives, but Great-Grandmother said that many of them were taken to Egypt for safe keepings. We have a small tablet here that sparked a rumor that the 'Great Egyptian Library' is under a paw of the Great Sphinx."

Dr. Ziv "Well is it?"

Steven "What the library under a paw?"

Dr. Ziv "Yes."

Steven "Heavens no, it's right under the belly of the beast."

Dr. Ziv "I'm a bit of a history buff, I would love to any proof of any of this."

Steven "I think that can be arranged."

Dr. Ziv was dumbfounded but oddly enough believed every word of what Steven was saying. He wanted to hear more stories but they arrived at the infirmary. Steven opened the door and said, "It is yours to look around. I am needed in the kitchen for a moment. There is pen and paper on the counter. Write down any notes and I will be back in about twenty minutes." He left without another word.

Dr. Ziv was amazed at what he saw. The room was large with four hospital beds along the wall. It had natural lighting from large windows. Everything looked very antiseptic. There was even a small 'nurses' station' with filing cabinets. He opened a draw and saw manila folders with names on them. He took one and opened it. It was a child's immunization records and a list of every time the child had been seen medically, by whom, for what reason, and the outcome. He thought it was very well organized. As he looked around the room he realized that if he or anyone he knows needed medical attention, he would want to bring them here.

Michael walked back into Anastasia's room. He was thankful that he had gotten there before Linda arrived. Jonathan had taken back out the cards after Ruth and Ailbe left. Anastasia announced, "You just missed them but Ailbe saw flashes of light and a deep fog in our link. I'm so excited! My memories are coming back but I shouldn't rush it or push it too hard. Oh, and she confirmed what I already knew... Jonathan cheats at cards."

Linda and her husband Felipe (from Spain) arrived as Jonathan was yelling "I was ten years old!" Linda laughed, "Is he still trying to say he doesn't cheat at cards?" Jonathan threw his hands in the air. "I give up. Main problem living with this family... no one forgets." Felipe laughed and held out a medium size box. It was wrapped with the most beautiful paper and a large bow. Anastasia looked surprised and put her hand to her mouth when Linda said "It's for you. Open it." Anastasia "For ME!?!" Linda put the box in Anastasia's lap. "Yes silly, for you. Don't get overly excited. It's just something I saw and thought you could use it for the party. I heard you are coming home."

Anastasia was meticulous in unwrapping the box. She didn't want to ruin the paper. Michael was excited but sad. He wondered if she had ever received a gift before. "No, you are supposed to rip through the paper to open it." Anastasia looked at him with a serious expression. "Well that just seems rude and uncalled for. Linda took a lot of time on this." Linda laughed. "No, you are supposed to rip it. That's part of the fun." Anastasia was not convinced. "Really?" Linda reassured her. "Yes. I promise. It's fun. Just rip it open." Still hesitant Anastasia ripped the paper off and opened the box. Her eyes were wide open and she hugged the content. Michael asked to see it. Anastasia showed him. "It's my first present but I don't know what it is."

Felipe laughed as he looked at Linda. "I told you. What is a girl with amnesia going to know of American 4th of July clothes?" Linda went into the box and pulled out several items and explained each one. "This is a whistle. You blow into and it makes a loud noise." Anastasia blew into it as Linda had instructing her to do. The sound scared her at first but quickly learned she loved whistles. "This is a hat. We will do your hair in a nice pretty braid like Lucy did and it will keep the sun out of your eyes. These are sunglasses. They protect your eyes from… well, the sun. (The sunglasses had flags for lens) This shirt is the most obnoxious thing I have ever seen, so I thought it was perfect. (It had a waving flag on the front with red, white, and blue fringes along the neck, across the back, down the sides, and down the sleeves.) These are tennis shoes. They protect your feet when you walk. (They formed an American flag when you put them together) These are socks. (They had small waving flags all over them) And this is the best one of all. These are breakaway pants. They have these snaps down the sides so athletes can pull them off quick. But with these, your right leg will still be covered. It is super light weight material so you won't get hot. You are protected from the sun and you can keep your leg open or close it around all that surgical steel Frankenstein looking stuff. It's great right!?"

Michael and Jonathan looked like they were going to burst out laughing, but Anastasia put the whistle around her neck, put the hat on her head, put the sunglasses on her face and hugged the other items. She burst out. "I LOVE THIS!" Jonathan said, "You look ridiculous" Anastasia was far from caring. "Linda, I can't tell you what this means to me. I love every item you chose. This is absolutely perfect. And Jonathan (She looked over at him) I know you are just jealous of my gifts. I will be keeping a close eye on you. If any of my items disappear, I'm coming after you. Like Dr. Ziv said 'I'm like a Wonder Woman'. So watch it mister!"

Charlotte was at a panic level when she arrived to meet the reporter. She was late for their meeting but she didn't care. She went inside and sat at the table. She told the reporter what had happened. The reporter reassured her that he always protects his sources. Charlotte asked, "Can they try to intimidate me like that? They are investigating an attempted murder, not who Charlotte talks to! I have a right mind to call his boss and report him!" The reporter sat there goading her on and agreeing that Michael is a pig for what he has done to her. Before Charlotte knew it, she had told him every detail of their lives together for the past five years. From the day they met, up until the moment she witnessed him confessing his love to his cousin.

She gave the reporter the photos of Anastasia sent to her from her 'anonymous' source at the hospital. When the reporter pressed on who was sending the pictures, Charlotte answered honestly, "I have no idea. The entire staff loves me. Everyone is furious at how I have been treated, not just by Michael, but his entire family. Whoever it is, they send them to me and I give them to you. I didn't take the picture, so I can't get in any trouble." They ended their meeting with Charlotte feeling very gratified that Michael would be just as hurt as she was.

Steven returned to the infirmary with a cake box nicely wrapped and placed in a larger box so it was difficult to knock over.

Steven "Any questions or comments regarding the infirmary?"

Dr. Ziv took a deep breath as Steven walked toward him. "No, the room is perfect. This must have cost a fortune! Do you have the goose that laid the golden egg hidden somewhere in here? And what is that incredible smell!?"

Steven smiled "A little bird told me that your wife Niomi is from Haiti."

Dr. Ziv "Yes she is, but how could have possibly known that?"

Steven "It is my job to know most things about most people who have intimate knowledge of my family. You have taken outstanding care of my family, so hence... I know a lot about you. For example, your wife's family worked with one of my ancestors Dutty Boukman in the late 1700's in an area called Cap Haitian. My ancestor asked for assistance from Mrs. Ziv's family and that assistance was granted. Together they started the Haitian revolution. Dutty Bourkman was forever grateful and bought a large sugar cane field and started a rhum distillery and after it was established, he gifted it to her ancestors. That is where you met her on your first medical missionary trip to Haiti and if my memory serves me right, she offered you a sample of her family's locally famous rhum cake. You fell in love with the cake, the rhum, and with her. So here we are 37 years, 3 kids, countless small pets later... bing-bang-boom... I present to you, her family recipe."

Dr. Ziv stood there in complete shock. "There is NO possible way for you to know any of that! We almost couldn't get married because there is no record of her birth. Birth certificates aren't for the poor in

Haiti. The rich and connected have them, but not for farmers. We had to go through years of red tape to get her out of Haiti and into the United States, and to get her a passport was a bigger nightmare. But how did you know that?"

Steven "When you take care of a Reale, the entire Reale clann takes care of you. Now I have made copies of birth certificates, land deeds, current business proposal, and of course... the locally famous rhum cake recipe. And at her convenience, Great-Grandmother would like you both to come for a private dinner. She can tell her first hand stories of the time she spent in Haiti and the time she spent with her grandparents.

Dr. Ziv "Whoa, wait, what business proposal? Who knew whose grandparents?"

Steven "It is my understanding that your wife has tried to open up a Haitian inspired bakery several times over the 37 years. Am I mistaken?"

Dr. Ziv "No, you are right, but..."

Steven "One of our lawyers is meeting with her as we speak. With her permission of course, we would be honored if she would allow us to serve her cake, in rhum ball form, at our festivities this weekend. We will of course pay her for her time and efforts."

Dr. Ziv "We were planning on spending part of the day here for the parade and BBQ. But are you asking if she will bake for the party? Wait, what lawyer? You need to slow down. I'm not understanding what's happening here."

Steven "Oh look. It seems she agreed to our offer." Dr. Ziv turned around and saw a car pulling up to the main house. The car stopped and his wife jumped out. "Ezriel! Can you believe this!? How did they find that recipe? I have tried for years to remember and they made it perfect. I just can't believe it!" She was at this side hugging and pulling on his arm. "I have SOOOO much work to do. I have to get started." She kissed him on the cheek and was off following her driver into the front door. Dr. Ziv called to her, "Niomi, wait." She yelled over her shoulder, "I'll be home late, don't wait up. They said they will drive me home." And she disappeared into the house.

Dr. Ziv "I'm overwhelmed." He wiped a tear from his eye. "Thank you.

Thank you very much. I just don't know what to say. I haven't seen her this excited in years."

Steven "You have said and done enough. Just promise me that you will stay for as long as you can on the 4th and enjoy the festivities. I trust the location will be acceptable. It is across the street from the diner on Main Street. Let me make this clear, although Great-Grandmother is very excited about this endeavor, we have no hand in this business. Once you have had your lawyer look over the paperwork, and if it is agreeable to you both as a family, then we are out…Well, there is a small fee for the lease of the property of course."

Dr. Ziv thought for a second "There's the catch." Businesses on Main Street were usually very successful. The foot traffic from tourist and locals was high and the shops were high end specialty shops that people came from all over to visit. "I'll look over the offer, but I don't think I could even afford the rent over there."

Steven "I understand. There are other location options I could offer or if you choose to find a location that fits your budget better. We want her to succeed. She seemed to indicate that $1.00 a month would fit into your budget."

Dr. Ziv "A dollar? On Main Street? Across from the diner? One dollar? How can you promise what the rent will be?"

Steven "Great-Grandmother owns the property. Once the paperwork is all signed. Great-Grandmother will add her into her Will as declared owner. My Grandmother will continue the agreement up until you choose to vacate. The current proposal is 99 years. Do you have any questions? I really must run."

Dr. Ziv stood there letting it sink in. This has been his wife's lifelong dream. They tried a few times, but they took some serious financial hits and now he was close to retirement, he didn't want to risk another financial loss. But to see his wife this happy, he would have risked his own life. "How did you…? I mean… why? This must have taken you a lot of time and energy to pull this off."

Steven "I would love to take the credit for days of labor intensive research, but I can't. I just had to go to our library. (He looked at his watch)

Great-Grandmother should be in the kitchen by now talking to her. You see, she didn't just know her grandparents, she was also there for Niomi's birth. She recorded it in her journal and took the information to the officials, but they ignored it saying that farmers did not need to register their births or deaths. Great-Grandmother registered it herself and forgot about the entire incident until our paths crossed again with you caring for my cousin. So consider this a small token of our gratitude for your service to Anastasia. Oh, I tried a bit of that Haitian rhum while our chefs took sixteen tries until they perfected the recipe. I kept a bottle, promise me that you will have a drink with me at the party."

Dr. Ziv smiled. "Make it two and you have a deal."

Steven smiled back, "Fine three drinks it is." as he turned and walked away.

The hospital has been under construction a number of times for upgrades and new units, new wings, and a variety of expansions. When Ailbe's husband Ailill died last year, it was a great opportunity to create the VIP section. Ailbe created a design competition to which anyone could submit a design. No one knew any information regarding who it was for. The emails went out from a third party law firm who specialized in designs for high rise buildings in Dubai.

Open design contest
Looking for security ideas for a VIP room.
Specs: Top floor of 6 story building
Must include: Airtight, Bombproof, extraction
capabilities, and 1 person control
No experience required
No blueprints required for submission
If your idea is selected, you will be hired to
work with a prestigious company.

The ideas came flooding in from all over the world. The email and contest went viral. Everyone with an imagination submitted their ideas. Many people submitted several ideas. Some were of course ridiculous and some were outstanding. Ailbe wanted to see every drawing that was submitted. She could care less about the details, she wanted to SEE what the person was imagining. She spent hours looking at perfect blueprints. Ruth and Se'ighin offered several times to help, but Ailbe kept to herself in the Thinking Room with stacks of papers in front of her and would take a first glance of love it or hate it. The 'hate it' pile was shredded and the 'love it' pile was set aside for a second look. The process was enjoyable for Ailbe, she especially loved the crudely drawn ones. Those where her favorites. She finally narrowed it down to ten designs. She asked Chaya (her grandson Elijah's wife) to compile a team of family members to help narrow the choices. Chaya's family designed and helped build most of the seven wonders of the world, but the Statue of Zeus at Olympia was always her personal favorite. Chaya herself is an engineer. She chose Ace, who is a computer and math genius. He could program a computer to do just about anything. Arden, who is a security expert. He helped Israeli intelligence revamp their entire agency and has Top Secret security clearance in the United States and seven other countries. And Mark, who is a transportation expert. He authored the text books for E.V.O.C Emergency Vehicle Operating Course, The Navy Top Gun program, Helicopter rescue, and High Sea Rescue by the age of twenty. The four family members discussed each drawing for plausibility, reliability, safety, and aesthetically pleasing. Arden's choice was a crudely drawn design by a 9 year old girl confined to a wheelchair. Her facebook submission was titled, **This would be cool to build** and team agreed. But it was a nightmare figuring out HOW to do it.

The ICU nurse Barbara came into Anastasia's room with her arms open. "I have never been so happy to kick someone out in my life! You are an official graduate of the ICU. Gather your things, they are finishing some last minute details upstairs and you are OUT-A-HERE!" Several nurses were behind her clapping. Jonathan was on his feet and bowing to the nurses as if he just won an Academy Award. "Thank you ladies, it has been an honor but we must bid you farewell." Anastasia was thrilled. "Yeah!!" Michael was over the moon with excitement but he couldn't shake that feeling that something was off. Anastasia gripped his hand tighter and linked, "What's wrong?" Michael replied, "I don't know. I can't put my finger on it. It's right in front of me and I can't see it!" Anastasia smiled, "I'm healing very well. I'm leaving the ICU. I can leave the hospital soon. I can go to the party. What feels wrong?" Michael did not respond. He just had a pit in his stomach. He finally stood up. "Jonathan, can you stay here? I'm going to walk around."

Jonathan pulled out his deck of cards. "I told you I'm not leaving. Now who is up for a beat down?" as he looked at Anastasia. Anastasia rolled her eyes, "Please Michael, don't leave me with him again. I can't stand when he cries after I win." Michael smiled at he kissed her on the forehead. Jonathan sat in Michael's chair and started to shuffle the cards on the bedside table. "I didn't cry, I had something in my eye. Now pick your poison. Gin? Rummy? Poker?" Michael left and walked the route that the attacker took over and over and over for two hours until Jonathan linked, "They are ready for her upstairs." Michael looked out the window at the end of the hall. It was dark and the stars were shining so bright. He loved looking up at the stars. Then it hit him.....It's in here!

Michael was frozen. He linked to Arden and Mark a quick message with the information and asked that Arden make calls to the other protectors. Then he called Arden on the phone. "Hey there..Daddy O. I want to have a drill tonight to keep these kids on their tippy-toes. Gotta whip'em into shape. Oh and hey, have you seen Granny around? I'm pissed off that she has been tucked up all day. Have her and the old lady swing by or they ain't invited to the wedding." He hung up the phone and started to walk nervously back to the ICU. He stopped into the bathroom to wash his hands. He turned the water on full force and linked his plan to Jonathan. "We have to be perfect or we all die. Anastasia is to know NOTHING." Jonathan didn't skip a beat. He continued laughing and joking with Anastasia. Michael came back into the room. Anastasia saw the look on his face. She was his bond and trusted him with her life. She tried to communicate in their link, but he just winked at her but said nothing. She felt his tension but knew she had to follow his lead. The nurse Barbara came in, "OK, big move. Let's go." Two hospital employees were standing behind her. Michael said, "Hey honey, we are going to do a drill with our security team. So be a peach and let my guys take her upstairs. I know you're like ok with that. Right babe?" Barbara laughed, "You crack me up. But it's our hospital policy that all patients are to be escorted by hospital staff. There are no exceptions to the rule." Jonathan felt sweat form on his upper lip. "Well... um... Michael. I'm SURE it will be OK if they walk with us. Barbara, how far do they have to come? We need this drill for all these new guys. Help us out... please." Barbara shrugged her shoulders. "Well, if they take a break and you guys move her without my authority, what can I say..." She pretended to pick up a phone "Mr. Kelly, they brought her upstairs before I could stop them." Michael smiled. "Perfect" He took a deep breath and said one word, just one. "Protectors."

With that word, ten men appeared out of nowhere and looked battle ready. Barbara felt a wave of fear as Michael's entire demeanor changed instantly. He unlocked the breaks on the bed and pulled it toward the nurses' station. Ace went to the right side at the head of her bed. Olav stood directly behind him. Hayden went to the left side at the head of her bed. Leif stood directly behind him. Malachi took position on the right side at the foot of her bed. Rolf stood directly in front of him. Benjamin took the position on the left side at the foot of her bed, with Steven directly in front of him. Michael was on the right side of the bed holding her hand and Jonathan took position on the left. Hans stood just behind Michael's right shoulder and Erik stood just behind Jonathan's left shoulder. Anastasia felt the tension in the air and realized the protectors were not only battle ready but they figured something out and they wanted blood.

She tried to relax but it took every ounce of her energy to smile and wave at the nurses. "Thank you all SO much. I hope to see you all at the party." They all waved back as Michael silently gave the order to move. The men were in perfect sync. Michael linked to Arden and Mark "moving". Arden linked back, "We are five minutes out." Mark linked, "We are in the air waiting for your go." They walked to the service elevator which was larger than the regular elevators. Michael felt it was taking too long. 'What if it got to the elevator and sabotaged it?' But that was a risk that he needed to take. Anastasia was terrified to move. She laid there holding Michael's hand. Michael squeezed her hand several times as they waited for the elevator. "So, dudes... Um... this drill will show me who has what it takes to be part of my team. I would hate to have to kick you out. So shape up...or ship out." Michael was desperately trying to sound casual.

The protectors knew exactly what he was doing. They had a job to do and they were going to do it perfectly.

The elevator doors opened and they wheeled the bed in. It was a slow and jerky ride up to the 6th floor. The elevator doors opened and a nurse was standing there waiting to go down. She was not expecting twelve large intensely angry looking men staring at her. She jumped which almost caused a chain reaction of protectors in motion. Jonathan broke the tension. "Can we get out first please?" The nurse nervously stepped aside and the protectors began making their way down the hall to the end corner VIP room. Michael linked to Arden and Mark "Fifty yards." Arden linked, "We are in the parking lot. Three minutes to get into place." Mark linked, "Waiting on you to open this can up."

They slowly and methodically pushed the bed into the room and positioned it directly into the center. The nurse followed them in, "Thank you gentleman but I will take it from here. I need to check her vital signs and…." Michael cut her off. "We are conducting a security drill. I need you to step outside for a few minutes." The nurse did not move. She was about to say something when Jonathan snapped, "NOW!" She was startled and as she was leaving the room she said, "I need to call Mr. Kelly!" Michael looked at Anastasia who was paralyzed with fear. She had an intense desire to run and hide, but she held onto Michael for strength. Michael didn't dare say anything to provoke an attack. He felt that uneasy feeling. It was here, right here listening to every word and watching every move they made.

Just a few minutes ago, Arden had been standing on the second floor balcony overlooking the beach. He was listening to the whales singing and watching the dolphins as they were swimming up toward the marina. The July 4th decorations looked spectacular. He took a deep relaxing cleansing breath. Michael linked to him and Mark, "It's here! It never left. That is what I have been missing. It was an Eile. I'm taking her to the VIP room for extrication immediately." Mark was with Bjorn going over their equipment when he got the link. Mark patted Bjorn on the shoulder, "Well, it looks like you get on the job training from here on out. I fly, you catch." Mark linked the extraction plan to Bjorn. Bjorn grinned, "Got it.

Let's get this done. I have a girl to impress." They started their preflight
check and were in the air in minutes. Arden linked to Ailbe, Ruth and
Se'ighin, "Michael figured it out. It's an Eile, and it's in the hospital. We are
extracting Anastasia now. I'm getting into the car now." Ailbe, Ruth and
Se'ighin stopped what they were doing and headed to meet Arden. They
all got into the car and sped down the driveway. Ailbe shouted. "They want
war. I will give them war. I've been waiting to unleash Hell!" She started
to prepare for what she knew would bring her one step closer to going to
the ancestors. Ruth looked at Se'ighin. "Are we ready my love?" Se'ighin
looked at her and remembered one of the countless reasons that he fell
in love with her, she rose to every occasion. "We are ready for anything."

Once the nurse was safely out of the room, Steven and Rolf stepped
outside the room as Olav and Leif followed them, but stayed just inside
the room. Ace called out, "Protector Ace, A.C.E, command code one."
A computer voice responded, "Confirm Protector Ace. Command code
one." The room sealed with a suction sound. Anastasia felt her ears pop
when the pressure in the room changed. Rolf and Steven turned to face
the hall. The room filled with a screeching scream. Hans and Erik pulled
up carpet squares on both sides of the bed. There were heavy bolts with
large hooks and cables. They attached the two cables on each side to the
matching hooks on the bed. Hayden and Benjamin did the same. Ace
called out, "Command code two" A computer voice responded, "Confirm
command code two." The screams got louder. Anastasia couldn't take it
anymore and cried. "Michael! I'm scared. It's HERE!" Michael jumped
up on the bed and spread across her. The room shook. Hayden pressed
against the head of the bed. Malachi pressed against the foot of the bed,
and Jonathan pressed against the left side of the bed. Hans and Erik took
two steps backward. Four interlocking thick bullet proof Plexiglas walls
came up on all four sides of the bed. Hans and Erik locked them together.
They heard scratching from inside the walls. They heard Rolf and Steven
in a fight for their lives. The sound of muffled gun shots rang throughout
the room. Anastasia screamed. "ROLF! STEVEN! We have to help them!"
Michael put his hands over her ears. "I have you. We have you Princess.
You are safe. We will be out of here any second." Jonathan took her hand

"They are fine. This is what we train for." Ace called out "Command code three." A computer voice responded, "Confirm command code three." A piece of the roof came down and covered the Plexiglas box and clamped down into the two holes on each side. The top of the lid had four thick cables that came together and had a large hook on the top. Ace called out, "Command code four" The computer voice responded, "Confirm command code four" The roof began to open. The gunshots seemed endless. Michael thought "How many Eile have been here?"

Arden slid into the parking lot and drove over the grass until he was close to the building. This was no time for proper manners. He jumped out of the car. He pointed to each person. "You (Ailbe) stay here. You (Ruth) east side. You (Se'ighin) west side. I'm on north." And he took off in a full sprint. Once in place, they linked. Ailbe went deep and called out to the ancestors for help and they were happy to oblige and sent strength.

The link between them was strong and became a visible blue color. Ailbe began to speak the old language. She got louder and louder until the blue became a bright white tangible wall of energy. Inside the hospital, computers were blinking on and off, all the cameras went blank and the electrical system kicked over to a generator.

Mark positioned the helicopter directly over the opening roof. Bjorn was harnessed in and connected to a winch. He jumped out of the helicopter and repelled onto the box. He linked to Mark, "Lower the claw." Bjorn hooked the four cables to a large hook in the center of the claw and guided the claw around and into the holes that the lid also attached to. Hayden, Malachi and Jonathan secured themselves with harnesses that were under the carpet and they strapped Michael down on top of Anastasia with tie downs. Ace called out, "Command code five." The computer voice responded "Confirm command code five." They felt the box shift and heard a slight cracking sound. Bjorn called out, "Heads up." as six ropes with what looked like seats on them lowered into the room. Mark saw the roof access door open and Rolf and Steven stepped out onto the roof. Olav, Leif, Ace, Hans, Erik, and Benjamin each took a seat. "Command code six on my mark" the computer responded, "Confirm command code six on your mark." Mark pressed a button to lift the six men up to roof level.

They stepped out of their seats. Bjorn pressed a button for the winch to lift him back into the helicopter. Ace linked, "Throw me the bags" Bjorn kicked a box out of the helicopter and it hit the roof with a thud. Ace called out, "3-2-1-mark." The box lifted slightly and Mark met the lift so there would not be any slack on the cables and claw. The hydraulic system in the floor lifted the box as the helicopter matched the pressure and it took off for home.

Ailbe was in for a fight and the ancestors were surrounding her. Anyone on the first floor felt a slight breeze as energy moved up to the second floor. The protectors on the roof were armed and ready for one or a hundred. They heard loud screams that sounded like large cats about to fight. The second floor lights went slightly dimmer as the energy rose to the third floor. The protectors felt like they were being surrounded. Benjamin noticed the water cooling tower and shouted, "The tower!!!"

The box was high and away from the hospital. Ace called out, "Command code seven." The computer voice responded, "Confirm command code seven." And the roof began to close. Ailbe moved the energy up to the fourth and fifth floors. She was moving the Eile up floor by floor to the roof where the protectors would do their job and either capture or kill them. The bright white light attracted onlookers who called the police department to report the strange lights. Assistant Police Chief Curtis Cappola instructed the 911 operators to reassure any callers that it was just the Reale family testing lights for the July 4th party.

Benjamin aimed his weapon to the water tower and fired an E.M.P (electromagnetic pulse). It sounded like the tower was writhing in pain. He fired again as Rolf and Steven ran toward the screams. They already killed dozens but they wanted to kill them all.

Ailbe pushed the energy into the 6th floor. Everyone on the 6th floor heard scratching and clawing in the ceiling and walls. The protectors had their eyes on every opening. They knew that the Eile would have to run up and away from the energy or they would die in excruciating pain. The plan worked perfectly. Several Eile slithered out of the air conditioning vents and several more from the cooling tower. They were stunned from the EMP and worse by the ancestors' energy. Ace pulled open the box and took out the contents and quickly handed them out. "One bag, one snot ball. If we run out of bags, FRY the bastards. The bags looked like large black garbage bags but they had thin metal mesh lining them.

Ace linked, "Done." Ailbe smiled and thanked the ancestors but they were already gone. She waited for Ruth, Se'ighin and Arden to return to the car. Arden linked to the cousin in Washington DC the information of what happened and asked if he could run some damage control and clean up, then they headed home.

Agent Kal Palmer was going over the video of the attack on Anastasia. "God this just doesn't add up!" His supervisors had been blowing up his phone for updates. He knew that the Reale family is very connected and he wanted to make a great impression. Solving this case quickly would advance his career. His personal cell phone rang. It was from a restricted number. He wasn't going to answer it, but he is on the highest profile case in the country and he didn't want to miss anything. The voice on the phone was the Director of the FBI. "Good evening Kal. I will make this quick. Earlier today I authorized a risky extraction of the Reale woman. There is no more threat to the public. I have a courier outside your place with the statement you will give the media that will be swarming the hospital soon. I need you over there immediately." Agent Palmer was confused. "Sir, how is there no danger to the public?" Director "Kal, you have solved the case. You had a person of interest, you leaked the information that you were moving her to flush the individual out, your plan worked flawlessly, you have a suspect in custody. It is all in the envelope at your front door. Great work son. There is a promotion in this for you." And the line went dead. Kal opened the front door and there was a large manila envelope. He opened it and read the content.

The phone rang and Piper answered, "Hello." A man with an official sounding deep voice asked, "May I please speak to Mr. James Kelly immediately?" Piper had been very patient with the phone ringing all day and night and her husband sleeping at the hospital, but she was almost at her breaking point. "Sure, why not." She called out. "James, pick up the phone." He quickly picked up the phone, "This is Mr. Kelly, May I help you?" "Well, you already have. This is the Director Torn of the FBI.

I wanted to call you personally to congratulate you and to reassure you that the bureau will have a construction team out there immediately to complete repairs. Do you have any questions?" Mr. Kelly was confused. "I have no idea what you are talking about." Director Torn "Oh, I would have thought that Agent Palmer filled you in by now. He had a person of interest and devised a risky plan to have the Reale woman moved. It was flawless except the concussion grenades made a bit of a mess. I have men on the way there as we speak. We don't want the hospital to be inconvenienced any more than it has already. Oh, and one of your diligent nurses, who was just doing her job, might have gotten a little confused as to what was going on. This was a FBI led mission. I heard there is talk around the White House of a Presidential Medal of Honor for you. Thank you for your time." And the line went dead.

Mark flew to the compound and gently placed the box down ten feet from the front door. Once the claw and hooks were detached, he flew back towards the hospital. Malachi took off his harness and said, "Protector Malachi M.A.L.A.C.H.I." A computer voice responded, "Protector Malachi confirmed."

Malachi "Command code D.U.N done."

A computer voice responded, "Confirm command code D.U.N done." The roof unlatched and slid slightly off to one side. The side locks fell to the ground and the four walls fell open. Hayden and Jonathan removed their harnesses and the tie down straps from Michael and Anastasia. Michael lifted himself up off of her and she opened her eyes. He kissed her quickly. "Was that as good for you and it was for me?" He laughed but she still looked terrified. Her voice was shaking, "Where are we? Are we home? Are we safe? What was that sound!?" Michael nodded yes as Jonathan looked over to see Rach-El and Lindsey putting a ramp down across the stairs and Antonio and Aharon grabbing the head of the bed. Antonio tried to calm her nerves a bit. "You are safe now. The doctor is already inside waiting to for you. Michael will be right behind us." Antonio and Aharon pushed the bed up the ramp and toward the infirmary.

Michael bent over with his hands on his knees, Jonathan reached out his hand to help him up. Michael had waves of emotions. "Why didn't I realize that!? How could I not know that Eile were living in the fucking hospital!?" He looked around at the other protectors. "Did we get the son of a bitch? I want the one that did this. It is MINE to kill!" He stood up and followed his uncles to the infirmary. Jonathan looked at Malachi and Hayden, "Let's promise to never do that again." Malachi smiled, "I thought it was fun." Hayden laughed, "Just like a day at Disney." The three men started to disassemble and remove the remnants of the box.

Director Torn had four teams of FBI contracted construction workers on the 6th floor VIP area beginning repairs by the time Mark and Bjorn flew back to the hospital and picked up the protectors and the bags off the roof. Assistant Police Chief Curtis Cappola arrived just prior to the swarm of news media vans. Then Agent Kat Palmer with Agent J, and then Mr. Kelly arrived. Curtis had been linked all the information, he sat in his car for a second before getting out. "Well, let's get this shit-show behind us so we can get the party started." Agent Palmer had stopped to pick up agent J and was updating him on their statements. Agent Palmer "Shit, I hope we aren't late!" as they pulled in the parking lot just ahead of Mr. Kelly. The men all got out of their cars and walked into the crowd of reporters. Agent Palmer shouted over the rush of questions. "I will be holding a meeting with the staff inside and we will be back out here in ten minutes to answer all of your questions. This has been a good day ladies and gentleman."

The three men walked into the hospital and into Mr. Kelly's office. Mr. Kelly was furious. "So why wasn't I made aware of what was happening? I am responsible for everyone inside this hospital. I would have cooperated fully. I have a very good relationship the Reale family. I know they trust me and would never consider me a suspect." Agents Palmer and J had memorized their statements and scenario that were sent to them by Director Torn. Agent Palmer said, "We needed everyone to be as natural as possible and to go about their daily routine. If the suspect thought we were onto him, then we could have lost him forever. Which brings me to another subject, your nurse upstairs will be commended for her actions. You should be proud of your employee Mr. Kelly. She is an exceptional nurse. I hear was she was pretty shaken up thinking that the Reale family blew up the hospital." Mr. Kelly "Oh...yes, well thank you. We train our staff to look out for the patients, no matter what. But I head she is shaken up a bit. Dr. Besler was here to see Ms Reale when all of this happened. He is talking with her and some of the other staff now. I'm sure she will be fine. So who was it? Who stabbed her?"

Agent J stepped close as to whisper in Mr. Kelly's ear. "This is where I need your help. We have to protect the public. Interpol has been tracking a lone wolf terrorist for several years. A few months ago he fell off their radar and showed up here the day before Anastasia was rescued. He's been seen around the hospital several times at night and early morning. Seems he was jamming locks to some of the service doors. Agent Palmer over here wondered if he was trying to get to the Reale woman, so we contacted her family overseas with our suspicions. Turns out that Anastasia had called the authorities on him years ago to report that he was planning to attack Annapolis." Agent Palmer interrupted, "Agent! That is highly classified information!!! You CANNOT tell him that!" Mr. Kelly quickly said in a whisper, "No, I'm ok. I would never speak a word of this to anyone! Ever! Your director called me at home and said that the President is thinking of giving me a medal for helping you guys out. I'm a steel trap. I know how to keep my mouth shut." Agent Palmer thought for a moment. "Ok, we can trust you, but don't breathe a word to anyone. Do you promise?" Mr. Kelly "I promise." Agent J continued as Agent Palmer turned his back to the men shaking his head. "Well, Anastasia was cleared of any wrong doing, she is a credit to her family. But then she disappeared. Her family didn't know if she ran away with him or if she was kidnapped, but he clearly had something to do with her scars.

What a brave girl, being tortured all this time. Her escape was is a miracle. She was desperate to come here and warn us. But she couldn't remember anything. Her amnesia was his dumb luck and gave him time to plan to kill her. He hacked into the security system, and the rest is history. He was actually hiding right under our noses behind the garbage dumpsters. That's why our dogs couldn't even find him. But Agent Palmer had a plan of flush him out.... And it worked perfect!" Mr. Kelly was hanging on his every word. "So then what happened?" Agent J "Well sir, the rest is

'Top Secret FBI Extraction Protocol.' I'm not even sure of what those guys can do. I'm just an agent. Those guys are the real tough guys, if you know what I mean." Mr. Kelly nodding his head yes. "I do. I mean, I don't know, but I know what you mean. Well, I wish I could shake their hands. Job well done! And I swear on my Grandmother's grave that I will never say a word about this." "Agent Palmer turned back around. "You are a true patriot sir. The President will most defiantly hear of this." Mr. Kelly looked ten feet tall. "After this, the media will be a piece of cake." and walked toward the door with a swagger.

The three men walked out of the hospital and toward the crowd of reporters. Curtis had set up a small podium and the reporters had attached their microphones to it. Mr. Kelly stepped up to the podium and the two agents stood behind him. Curtis joined them smiling and shaking the two agents hands. He introduced himself in his best game show announcer voice. "Good evening friends. I am pleased to announce that the hospital and our community can sleep well tonight. The efforts of the FBI have yielded a great harvest here tonight. I hand over the floor to the very capable Agent Palmer." He clapped as Palmer stepped up. "Thank you Mr. Kelly. This community is lucky to have such strong and capable leadership. My Name is Agent Kal Palmer P.A.L.M.E.R. Agent J, spelled J, and I have completed countless interviews and concluded a person of interest. That person has been under surveillance since those interviews. Due to the close proximity to the victim, we felt that immediate extraction would solve two issues.

1. To get Ms Reale to safety and
2. To flush out the person of interest.

The extraction was a bit more dramatic than we expected but our mission was accomplished. Ms Reale is safe and being attended to by a physician as we speak and we have a person in custody. There is no further threat or risk to the public. You can all relax and enjoy your July 4th weekend. I will not be able to answer all of your questions due to the complexity and ongoing matters, but just department issues...This case is officially solved. I understand that the Reale family is eternally grateful and hopes your bosses will allow you to stay and enjoy the festivities. I hear the rhum balls fantastic. Now I open it up to Assistant Police Chief Curtis Cappola before I take questions."

Curtis wanted nothing to do with smiling for the camera. He wanted to get to the compound, but he had a job to do, and he was going to do it very well. "Ladies and gentleman, Thank you for being here at this late hour. I don't have much to add. I would like to thank the FBI for their outstanding efforts in solving this case in what I consider record breaking time. They have been in constant contact with my office in a coordinated collaboration of agencies to make our city truly the safest in the nation. Thank you all very much. I return you to Agent Palmer." Curtis stepped back and stood next to Agent J and Mr. Kelly. Agent Palmer went back in front of the microphones. "I can only take a few minutes with you all and I want to get to everyone, so one question each and then if we have time, we can circle back around. Any questions?"

Reporter #1 "Who do you have in custody?"

Agent Palmer "We have one person in custody."

Reporter #2 "Can you give us the name?"

Agent Palmer "No I cannot."

Reporter #3 "Is it a man or a woman?"

Agent Palmer "All I can say on the matter is that we have one person in custody and we do not expect any further arrests."

Reporter #5 "From the pictures we saw of Ms Reale, how can she be moved so quickly?"

Agent Palmer "We exaggerated the reports of her injuries and we staged the photos so the attacker would think they had more time to strike again."

Reporter #6 "Wait, YOU staged the photos? YOU fed them to us? That is unethical to use the media like that! Is your agency aware of this? Ms Reale gained a lot of sympathy after viewers saw those. Are you aware that there could be some serious repercussions from this?"

Agent Palmer "That was more than one question, but all good ones. It was my suggestion to stage the photos. The Reale family was against the idea at first, but after reviewing the facts, Ms Reale herself was willing to do anything for public safety and did not concern herself with her own embarrassment. I'm not implying that her injuries were not severe and life threatening, but we just added a touch of Hollywood gore to them solely for the purpose of luring the attacker closer. And then we sent them anonymously to a hospital employee who we knew had a grudge against the family. That employee gave them to you. That is all I will say about the photos. Mr. Kelly will be given all our information and the hospital will address that internally."

Reporter #6 "Is the family in hiding? Can we expect to hear statement from them soon?"

Agent Palmer "Ya know, you guys are pissing me off. I don't care if you splash my face all over the TV or call my boss. I asked the Reale family NOT make any statements, but I was told that Ailbe Reale insisted on saying something at the parade. So I asked her if I could see her statement before she said anything that can't be released yet. So Ailbe Reale gave Agent J a quick blurb of what she wanted to express to the community that she loves. It's for them (He pointed out toward the general community) not for you, but I think you should hear it." He looked back at agent J, who was taking a piece of paper out of his jacket pocket. He went to hand it to Agent Palmer, but he stepped aside, "Can you read it please." Agent J stepped up to the microphone. "Hello, my name is agent J. It is a pleasure to be here. I'm glad this question was asked. Agent Palmer and I think it shows the integrity and decency that this family has for their community. I hope the Reale family understands why we thought you should hear this too." He looked down at the paper and read.

"*Our dearest friends and neighbors. Your outpouring of love and support through this most grueling time is the sole reason that we insisted on pressing forward with our annual July 4th parade and BBQ. Many of you know that we do not have any hired assistance the day of the event. We fail in comparison to the service and friendship that you all provide to us on a regular basis, but we do try. We are blessed to have Anastasia with us. She is looking forward to meeting each of you. Please be careful with her leg and be mindful that she is quick to fatigue, so if Michael yells at you, don't take it personal. Thank you for celebrating life and love with us on this beautiful day. And a huge thank you to Mrs. Ziv for sharing her Haitian rhum balls with us. She just opened a shop on Main Street. I had some and they are impressive."*

Agent J put the paper back into his pocket and Agent Palmer stepped up next to him. "Wow, sounds like the 104 year old matriarch has a lot to hide don't it! No more questions." He turned and walked off, Agent J following quickly behind. They walked to their car, got in and left. Agent J looked at Agent Palmer, "Academy Award winning performance partner." Agent Palmer smiled, I need a beer." Curtis stepped up to the microphone. He looked at the reporter who asked the question. "And that is how you piss off the FBI. Ladies and gentleman, we are done for the night. drive safe."

He turned to Mr. Kelly "I'll talk to you about Charlotte later. I'm exhausted and glad this mess is over." Mr. Kelly "Charlotte!?" He was shocked. "Charlotte is the one who has been talking to reporters and gave them those photos!? I just don't believe it!" Curtis yawned loudly, "Yep, I saw the tapes and heard the recordings myself. I have to go tell Michael and the family now. I don't know how they are going to react. And this is gonna kill Tom. He is sitting with the family during the parade. They are honoring him and Rick for finding Anastasia." Mr. Kelly thought for a moment, "I'll call her and give her a few more days off. I need to see and hear what she said and did for myself. I need to meet with the board about what we are going to do... Charlotte? Really? I just can't wrap my head around that." Curtis shook his head. "Me either. Everyone was getting ready for a big proposal. I guess that ain't happening." They two men shook hands and Curtis left.

Arden, Ruth, Se'ighin, and Ailbe arrived back at the house and went directly into Ruth's office. They held hands and linked to the entire family and updated the information then broke the link. Ailbe linked to the protectors in the helicopter with Mark, to bring the Eile directly to The Shed. Mark responded, "Be on the ground in ten and in the shed in fifteen." Ailbe took a few moments to collect herself and calm her emotions. "Ruth, please give me the update on the party." Ruth understood that her mother needed to relax after connecting to that much energy. "Slightly behind schedule, but no worries." Ailbe "And Lucy?" Ruth smiled, "Everything is arranged, it is up to her if she comes." Ailbe smiled with her most wily smile. "She will." Ruth laughed, "Mother, you look utterly wicked!" Ailbe gave her best evil laugh, "Mwah ha ha" Arden interrupted, "Mark is almost here. Let's get it ready."

They stood up and walked back downstairs and passed the infirmary. Anastasia was in there with Rach-El, Lindsey, and of course Michael looking every bit of the over protective husband. They continued through the house, out the back door, across the deck, onto the beach and to a large concrete shed looking structure with a heavy steal door with three locks. Arden took keys out of his pocket and unlocked and opened the door. The air was thick and stale. Se'ighin turned on the row of switches that were just inside the door. The room came to life. Fans turned on and moved the air around quickly and brought in fresh salt water smelling air.

Ailbe and Ruth stopped for a moment and watched as dolphins swam by. Ruth said, "They are majestic creatures aren't they." Then they heard the whales singing. Ailbe "Yes. They have all been good friends to us." Arden and Se'ighin were already halfway down the hall when Ruth touched Ailbe's shoulder. "Come on Mother, I'm going to need you." Ailbe "You don't need me for this, you just hate this." Ruth chuckled, "You know me so well."

Mark landed on the helipad near the main house. The protectors jumped out and reached back in for the bags containing the Eile they just captured. There were only ten bags in the box and the orders were to put only one Eile per bag, and to kill the rest. Ace took pictures of more than twenty dead Eiles on the roof before he lit them on fire. If a De'nola ever saw a dead Eile at or near a beach, they would think of it as a big weird looking jellyfish and pay little or no attention, but seeing twenty on a roof might raise an eyebrow. Burning them had always made sense. A. Because the protector knows it is dead and B. They look like melted plastic when they are burnt.

Ace looked at the protectors and back at the bags. "Grab some bags and follow me." They followed Ace around the back of the house and into the concrete structure. Steven was the last one in and he closed the door. They walked down a long sloping hallway until they got to an open door and into large round room. The walls at the bottom were lined with a wire mesh that was loosely covered with clear thick plastic. The walls were bent in slightly and covered with what looks like wet oily paint. There were four stainless steel tables with high sides. Ruth, Se'ighin, Arden and Ailbe were each standing in front of one, holding a control panel in their hands. Ruth said, "Give us each one. Put three in the cooler and other three in the hot box." The men did as they were told and all but Ace left the room. They lined the sloping hallway every ten feet.

Ruth took a second to steady her emotions. These creatures are the cause of all Azili pain and suffering. They forced them to abandon their home. They murdered them indiscriminately. They hunted down the royal family and tortured, murdered, and mutilated their bodies. And for what?! The Eile thought the Azili could gift them with the ability to walk on land as well as swim in the sea like they could. The Eile wanted to walk, but they had no legs. The solitary reason for their rage boiled down to jealousy. They wanted what they didn't have.

Ruth remembered the names of everyone they murdered as she looked at Ace. "Pour it onto the table." Ace opened the bag and emptied it onto the table. Ruth turned the table on and slight frost appeared. The Creature reared up and tried to slither over the side. Ruth turned it up and the creature stopped but growled at her. Ruth demanded, "Which one of you is in command?" The creature lifted a tentacle at her and Ace cut it off with lighting speed. All the creatures howled in retaliation.

They had the same ability to link but their link was always open and to all of them. They attacked with pin point precision. They were countless bodies but one mind. When the Azili first encountered them, they were disorganized and considered a lower life form. The Azili took them in and taught them how to focus. Their communities grew as fast as their rage. Ailbe looked at Ace. "Let me see if mine is willing to talk." Ace opened the bag in front of her and poured it on the table. It was much feistier and immediately went for Ailbe's throat. Ace was ready, but Ailbe grabbed the tentacle and stared at the creature. In the old language she said, "You will never be mistaken for a superior. You are a low life form." The creature attempted to grab her other arm with a tentacle, but Ailbe is unnaturally fast, and she thrust her hand into its head, pulled out a small sharp item from her pocket, opened its boneless body, shoved the small item it and held it face down on the table for a second as the small device exploded. The creature instantly turned into the consistency of warm Jell-O. "Sorry, I must be getting slow in my old age." She said to no one in particular as she looked around the room.

The Eile went silent. Ailbe grinned. "I think I have their attention." Se'ighin nodded to Ace. He opened the bag on his table and poured it out. The Eile elongated to over six feet high. Se'ighin just stared at it. "The ladies asked you a question." It looked over at the bag on Arden's table. Arden took a knife he had strapped to his back and opened the bag. "Slither out or I will dump you out." It did. "You have declared war after all this time. Why?" It responded, "You stole from us."

Arden instantly thought of Anastasia. It continued, "We want it back." Arden could barely contain himself. He was thankful that Michael was not here. "The girl!?" With enthusiasm it continued, "She is ours. If you don't give her back, we will hunt you to extinction. She has the power to give us what we want. So the choice is yours. One girl or all of you." Arden looked at Ace and he set it on fire. It screamed and fought to get away. Arden watched it burn to death then he picked up a bag out of the cooler. He cut open the top and poured it out. "Now I will tell you that you will never get the Princess back." This one was more timid, "She is not your Princess." Ailbe went to the table, "Then who is she?" it hissed, "She is none of your concerned. If we are gifted with legs, then we will leave and never ask for anything else." Ailbe raised her voice, "Lie! You will never stop wanting more. You could walk today but want to fly tomorrow and start another war. When is it going to end?!" It leaned toward Ailbe, "Give us the girl and it will end." Ailbe looked at Ace and he torched.

This went on until they had two left. Ace poured them out onto a table. They huddled together saying over and over that they want the girl. Ruth leaned toward them, she was less than an inch from the largest one's face. "I will leave you two for Michael." She smiled and slowly stood up straight. The two Eile screamed as one. "NO!!!!!!!!!!" She broadened her smile. Se'ighin and Arden laughed and walked out. Ruth never broke eye contact. Ailbe said, "Oh dear. How long have one of you survived a protector's questioning? I bet that's going to hurt." She laughed in a vociferous laugh and also left.

Ruth calmly said, "Last opportunity low life. Agree to go back deep into the sea and never rise five hundred feet from the surface or we will destroy your entire species. We are not the pacifist race that you first met. We have been around the De'nola for a very long time and have developed some of their habits, like crushing bugs... Michael will be in later to welcome you to the surface in his own special way." She started walking toward the door. One of them lifted the other up and over the side of the table and it raced for the door. Ruth shut it quickly with herself still inside. It hit the door and touched the wire mesh. It retracted and curled up into a ball. The other one stood up straight and tall. Ruth knew that this is the one that is in command. This is the one who attacked Anastasia. It hissed and jumped for the wall in an effort to escape. It slid down to the floor avoiding the wire mesh. It sprang toward Ruth, she caught it with one hand and grabbed its tentacles with her other hand. Both Eile hissed and growled at Ruth, but she just stood there holding it. "I will not be coerced into killing you. Oh no... I will not deny my grandson the pleasure of doing to you what you did to his bond." The other one stretched tall. "She bonded with the murderer Michael! NOOOO Not him! I will kill them both!" Ruth knew that Michael had killed more Eile than any other family member in their entire history. Ruth laughed as she said, "And I will give him orders not to kill you. He will have years of fun with you two." She threw the one she had in her hands against the wall. She opened the door and walked out.

Michael was thankful that the resident doctor was there. He reassured everyone that there were no injuries from the terrifying helicopter ride, and Anastasia was calming down quickly. Rach-El and Lindsey had her laughing by the time Ailbe and Ruth walked in. On their way to the infirmary, they discussed telling Michael that they have two Eile in the shed, but they decided that everyone needed tomorrow to relax, regroup, and focus on the preparations.

Tomorrow was Friday July 3rd. They only had one full day left before the parade and BBQ. Ruth looked very gratified as she walked straight to Anastasia. "What a day you have had! We must link every detail. I want to feel that exhilaration." Anastasia shook her head. "I wasn't enjoying myself. Well, up until Michael jumped on me. That was nice. A big hot smelly terrified man jumping on a small cold smelly terrified girl. I was surprised there wasn't some kind of chemical reaction and we burst into flames. If it wasn't for Jonathan singing, I would have screamed the entire way." Ailbe and Ruth laughed.

Michael protested. "Hey, I'm not smelly."

Jonathan disagreed. "You know I love you, but you reek of cheap hospital soap and hand sanitizer."

Ailbe "Michael, go shower. We are all here with her. She'll be fine."

Anastasia agreed. "It has been a long day. I feel safe here. I'm home with my family." Michael kissed her but stayed nose to nose. "I love you." Neither one of them moved. Anastasia kissed him slowly, "I love you more."

Michael "Impossible."

Jonathan "Who turned Pinocchio into a real boy? I liked him better as a heartless protector machine."

Anastasia was still nose to nose with Michael when she laughed, "Are you a heartless machine... My protector?"

Michael looked very serious but still nose to nose "Shhh Princess. I may have a hard candy coating, but I have a soft gooey center. That's a secret, so don't tell anyone." Anastasia "All your secrets are safe with me."

Ruth smacked him on his shoulder. "Ugh... Go take a shower." Michael gave her a quick kiss and left the room. Ailbe clapped her hands together and linked to all the women in the compound, "Girl talk, everyone else skedaddle. You have work to do." Jonathan was the only man left in the room. The doctor went back to his room adjacent to the infirmary. Jonathan began to feel out of place. "I'm going to go and raid the kitchen. I heard Mrs. Ziv made some amazing rhum balls." As he was almost out the door, Ailbe yelled out, "Bring me back a few... And DON'T be stingy with that rhum sauce!!!"

The women sat very causally laughing and joking about a wide variety of subjects. Other female family members stopped in. Soon the room was packed with family. Anastasia was enjoying every second of her finally being with family. She was truly safe and accepted. Of all the things in her life that she had missed out on, girl talk was the number one on her list. She asked, "Ok. Please forgive me if I speak out of place... but I want to know everything about you and Bjorn!" as she looked at Rach-El. Lindsey squealed, "Me too!" Ailbe leaned in, "Oh, I do too." Ruth leaned back in her chair. "I'm all in. Every detail!" The women spoke for hours.

Michael had finished his shower and went to the kitchen to bring snacks back for everyone in the infirmary. He saw Jonathan sitting on the counter top, with a bowl of Mrs. Ziv's rhum balls. "Oh my God Michael, you have to try one of these. Where have these been my whole life?" Michael reached in to get one and ate it. "Oh YEA... I'm hooked! She'll be opening a shop on Main Street. I'm officially her best customer. Let's take some for the ladies." He put together a quick tray of cheese, crackers, fruits, and drinks. Jonathan jumped down and the two men headed back to the infirmary. They heard the women laughing. Michael pulled over two chairs. He and Jonathan sat there for hours enjoying every second of it.

Michael felt Anastasia feeling tired. In their link he asked, "How about wrapping it up?" She instantly said, "Noooo" Michael "Tomorrow is another day. Your first full day home. I will not risk you over doing it tonight. We have our entire lives to stay up late. I'm calling it a night for you." Ailbe was also thinking it is getting late. "Ok ladies, I think we have done enough bending poor Anastasia's ear. Tomorrow is a busy day for all of us." Anastasia did not want this night to ever end, but now she felt the fatigue. "Oh nooooo. I don't want any of you to go."

Michael and Jonathan walked into the room. Michael put up his hands, "OK ladies, I'm Jasper the Jerk and this is my partner Box of Rocks. We're the fun Police and I say this room is having way too much fun. Time to go ladies before Hobo the Hellhound gets wind of this." Everyone hugged and kissed Anastasia as they left and gave mean faces to Michael and Jonathan. Rach-El and Lindsey gave them both big hugs and kisses as they left. Ruth stood up and whispered something into Anastasia's ear and as she walked pass Michael, in her best old Chicago gangster voice she said, "So copper… I see you brought your hired gun and the cannolis." She grabbed a rhum ball and left.

Ailbe was the last woman in the room. She stood up slowly. There were SO many questions that needed to be answered and the Eile just added to the list. She looked at Anastasia and said, "You will stay here in the infirmary tonight. The doctor and nurse will have their doors open after we leave. I need you to be well rested. We have some work to do in the morning." Then she turned to Michael. "And I need you to get a good night sleep as well. You have been running on fumes for weeks. Now say good-night and go to your separate beds for tonight."

Anastasia felt her warmth and love. "I wish I could remember my own Great-Grandmother. I'd hope she was just like you." Ailbe was moved. She had every memory of every one of her people. "When you are stronger, I would love to share that with you. She was a strong brave woman." Anastasia asked, "What was her name?" Ailbe "She had many titles, but the one that the world knew her as, was simply *Babe*. The world went dark when she went to dine with the ancestors. I can still feel the sadness in those memories." There was a deep sense of loss in Ailbe's face. Anastasia tried to remember, but it was just a blank. "When I remember her, I will share with you all the happy times." They two woman hugged and Ailbe left.

Michael pulled up a chair and sat next to the bed. "What an intense day. I've trained my entire life to be prepared for anything and I am completely exhausted. But here you are… You look like you could keep going. How are you so amazing?" He leaned in and kissed her. She laughed, "You and the protectors did all the work. All I did was lay there screaming in my head like a frightened child. Have I thanked you yet today for being my protector?" Michael was caught off guard by a wave of failure he suddenly felt. "Good night my love. We all need to get some rest." Anastasia felt his pain. "You need to sleep in your own comfortable bed tonight. I am here and I am safe. I truly insist." Michael's body language was protesting long before she finished her sentence. "ABSOLUTLY NOT! You will not lie here alone." She lowered her voice. "I'm not here alone. I am home where there are a hundred people that I can hear right now. And Jonathan is going to be passed out drunk on rhum balls in the hall. Please… allow me to not worry about you tonight. I feel you wanting to be in your bed every night. I must be a horror of a wife to make you sleep down here. Now I insist." She pulled her shoulders back and lifted up her chin. "Good night. I choose this as a battle. Now if you wish to challenge me further, be prepare to loose." Michael laughed and bowed slightly. "I concede to your will." He could not imagine loving her any more than he did right now. "Keep our link open to everything. Don't toy with me. I want to hear you breathing. If I feel ONE thing, I'm coming back." They were inches from each other. Neither blinked.

The doctor and nurse opened their doors and came into the room. The nurse said, "Ok. Let me help you get ready for bed. I want to elevate that leg." As she started to wash her she said, "You will feel better after a cool bed bath and clean pajamas." Michael kissed her quickly. "Remember our deal. I'm a blink away." She smiled. "I will see you in the morning. I love you." He smiled and left as he heard the doctor ask, "Would you like something mild to help you relax?" Michael turned around, "I would love to see that." The doctor looked at Anastasia, "Not to knock you out, but to help you relax. It might make take the edge off the anxiety." Anastasia shook her head 'No' and suddenly felt scared. Michael quickly went back to her side. "You are 100% in control of your body! No one can 'tell' you what to do anymore. All we are doing is suggesting and offering. Your 'no' is the final word. I need you to really know that." She smiled and lifted her head up to look at him eye to eye. "I'm getting used to it."

Anastasia looked at the doctor. "I appreciate you looking out for my best interest, but I don't want anything in my body that will dull my senses. I find I am more uneasy with medication in my body." Michael was proud, "Spoken like a true Wonder Woman." He kissed her forehead and walked out heading for his room. The doctor said, "I understand how you feel. Michael is right, the more you communicate with us, the better care we can take of you. Dr. Ziv will be coming in the morning to take the subclavian out." Anastasia looked at him confused. The young resident laughed, "I'm sorry, I'm still in doctor language mode. The IV line in your neck." Anastasia was so focused on healing her leg and her chest that she completely forgot about her neck. "Out of sight, out of mind. I forgot about it under that gauze." The doctor nodded, "It was scheduled to come out earlier today, but then all the craziness happened. I'll be glad for you when it's out. One more thing we can check off our list."

Anastasia felt very comfortable with the resident and the nurse. Michel felt her relax. As he got up to his room, he heard Anastasia in their link, "Yep, now I feel every muscle ache and pain. I think I will ask for something mild." Michael responded, "It is your choice." The resident was documenting her vital signs when Anastasia said, "Excuse me, I should have listened to your counsel better. I do feel I would like something mild. My muscles all feel like they are tightening up." The doctor smiled, "I can give you a mild muscle relaxer and check how you feel in an hour. I will be spending the night right in that room." He pointed to an open door. Anastasia could see the bed inside. The nurse spoke up. "And I'm sleeping in the other room. Both of our doors will be open. We will hear you if you need us." Anastasia felt at ease with her choice. The resident doctor "This is a Flexeril 5mg. The dose I would normally give you would be double that, but for your first one, we will start small." Anastasia took the pill. "Please turn out the lights and everyone retire for the evening." She closed her eyes and the doctor and nurse did what she asked.

As Michael walked into his room, and paused for a moment. He felt the wave of failure again. He sat on the edge of his bed and took a few deep breaths. The last few weeks had been life changing several times. He stripped down to take a shower. The water felt good on his sore muscles but FAILURE was all he could think of. He tried to focus on Anastasia. Her breathing was relaxed and deep, she felt calm and safe, and she was finally asleep.

He got out of the shower but didn't dry off. He plopped onto his bed just looking up at the ceiling. "I need to call Charlotte soon. She didn't deserve any of this. She must be hurting and confused. I will make it right for her. I failed to make her feel important." He didn't want to think about Charlotte. He had so many other things to do. "Why does she keep popping into my head?" He stood up and grabbed a pair of lounge pants and was going to go back downstairs, but he could feel Anastasia was still asleep and feeling comfortable with her surroundings. He lay back down on his bed and thought, "Who made my bed? I love the feel of fresh sheets." His mind went blank and quickly fell asleep.

Arden and Bina were lying awake. As Michael's parents, they could easy feel him. Bina "I'm sick to my stomach knowing that he is beating himself up like this. I hate it and I hate her (Charlotte) more for hurting my baby." Arden laughed and hugged his wife close. "Our baby is handling himself brilliantly. I don't think I could handle all this as well as he is. All we can do is be there for him and let him know how proud we are. He will know about the Eile soon. I want everyone to have one more party before we go to war."

Arden kissed Bina on the top of the head. She said, "I want to go talk to Charlotte. I'll take Rach-El with me, that will give him some time." Arden wasn't convinced of his wife's plan but he trusted her. "If you know it to be best, then I'll jump in and help in the kitchen while you and Rach-El take all the time you need. BUT I warn you...if anyone complains about the macaroni salad... I'm throwing you under the bus." The two of them laughed and hugged each other until they fell asleep.

Ruth and Se'ighin were feeling the burden of leadership. They were curled up in bed just listening to the sounds of the ocean. The waves, the wind chimes in the breeze and the distance sounds of the marina. This has been the first home of their people since they escaped. They were refugees here, but with no way of ever going home. Ruth knew, they all knew, that it was their fault that the Eile were even here. They were resolved to make it right and a safe place for both De'nola and Azili. "I hate war." Ruth finally said in a whisper. Se'ighin "This has been a long time coming. We have learned a lot since Atlantis, but I don't think they know that yet. They seemed to only know of Michael and his hatred of them. They think of us as cowards and easily scared." Ruth "I am terrified to meet them in the water." Se'ighin "This is your choice to continue down this path. I want to eradicate them once and for all. Not one more Azili death should be by their species!" Ruth "Why can't they just stay deep in the ocean? That is what they are designed to do. Help me understand." Se'ighin "There will always be creatures who will never be happy with what they are. They are

too busy being angry at what they are not. There is no understanding that."
Ruth "They are in for a very rude and painful lesson. I choose to protect
and defend this family. After the party, we will meet them in the water.
Hug everyone you see the next few days, it might be the last time you see
them." She buried her head into his chest. She made no sounds, she just
let the tears flow.

Rach-El was dreaming of Bjorn. Bjorn was linked to his parents telling
them about Rach-El. Jonathan fell asleep, well…passed out with crumbs
on his face. Linda and Felipe were rubbing Linda's baby bump. Linda said,
"I think Stephanie is going to follow in the footsteps of becoming one of
the strong women in this family." As Felipe drifted off to sleep with his
head on Linda's lap. Ailbe was up in the Thinking Room. She leaned back
in the reclining chair. This was her favorite room in the house. She felt
closest to home.

She opened a link and went deep to the ancestors. "I need a few more
days before I cross this veil. They need me just a little longer. I ask for a
blessing of strength for Michael. He will be first one in the water leading
this charge. I'm just so tired… I have no right to ask anything of you since
you heard my plea. I'm asking more for the Princess. She deserves happiness." She kept the link open but it was a struggle through her quiet crying. The fireplace roared to life. The tree growing straight out of the wall
dropped some of its leaves. The room glowed with warmth and energy.
The ancestors responded, "The Princess with have her bond… But ask no
more…You asked the unthinkable, which was granted after much debate.
We look forward to blending with both of your energies soon." Ailbe was
content, she felt the deep bonds and growing love in the family. She looked
out the windows, out into the ocean. The whales even seemed content. She
thanked the ancestors, "Thank you, we will be there soon."

Michael woke to feeling Anastasia was afraid. He raced out of his
room and down into the infirmary before she realized he felt her. He was
running so fast and barefoot that he couldn't stop quickly enough and
ran right into her bed. His eyes were wide open as he looked around the
room trying to find the Eile that he knew must have been there. Anastasia
chuckled, "What in the world are you doing?" He felt she was calm. He

grabbed his chest and was breathing heavy. "You scared the shit out of me. I felt you, you were afraid." She lifted her eyebrows and was trying not to laugh. "I'm so sorry! I woke up and didn't know where I was for a second. You felt me that strong? It was less than a second. Then I closed my eyes and you flew into me and scared me." The doctor and nurse both came running into the room when they heard voices.

The doctor asked, "Is everything OK?" Anastasia "Yes, thank you. He just came down for one more good night kiss." The doctor and nurse turned to leave. Michael called out to them. "I'm taking her upstairs. I can't be this far away." Before anyone could respond, he scooped her up in his arms and walked out. The nurse and doctor started to follow them, but the nurse put up her hand. "Let me go and get her comfortable. I'll come get you if there is a problem." The doctor nodded and went back into his room.

Anastasia wrapped her arms around his neck and snuggled into him. He was very aware of her leg and carefully brought her into his room and put her on the bed. The nurse walked in behind them. "Hand me all the pillows you have." Michael gathered up several pillows as the nurse propped up her leg and positioned her. The nurse asked, "Are you comfortable?" Anastasia smiled and rubbed her eyes. "Yes, thank you for all your help. I feel like I'm on a cloud. Do they teach this in nursing school or are you just an Angel of Mercy?" The two women laughed. The nurse smiled, "I hope you get a good night sleep. I'll be right outside if you need me." Anastasia "Nonsense! You need some rest. I'm sure you will be notified immediately if I need anything. Now good night." She yawned and closed her eyes.

Michael looked at the nurse and said, "I appreciate your care. I promise I will call you if we need you. Now we are all exhausted and need some sleep." The nurse nodded. "Fine, good night." And she headed back to the infirmary. Michael carefully got into the bed and held Anastasia's hand. "You would tell me if you were uncomfortable, right?" Anastasia still had her eyes closed, "Ailbe instructed us to get some rest and if this is where you need me to be for you to get some sleep, then this is where I am most comfortable."

Michael watched her until she fell asleep. His heart didn't stop racing until he felt her in a deep sleep. He looked around the room and suddenly realized, "That must be why Charlotte keeps popping up in my head, she has a load of stuff here! You idiot. How insensitive to bring Anastasia up here before you cleaned it out." He felt another wave of failure as he slowly got out of bed and began to quietly collect everything of Charlotte's. He went down stairs and grabbed an empty box that read "Flammable" and "Sparklers" and "Caution" all over it. There were going to be enough sparklers that if they were all lit at once, they could probably be seen by the International Space Station.

Michael took the box upstairs and neatly folded and packed all of Charlotte's things and anything else that reminded him of her. He looked around and gasped thinking. "Are those the sheets that Charlotte and I made love on?!" But as he focused on the sheets he didn't recognize them. He thought, "Someone bought me new sheets, came into my room and put them on?" He wasn't alarmed because the house had cleaning people, but he never asked for help in his room before. He knew that both his mother and sister were aware that Charlotte spent the night. Maybe they were being their usual protective selves and wanted to make his life less stressful.

He wasn't as close to his baby sister Amani. His parents were traveling around Africa when she was born and he was focused on training. By the time they came back, he was off training with other clanns for a few years. He loves his baby sister, but Rach-El was the one that knew him best. Half the time, Rach-El didn't even have to link with him to know what he was thinking.

He brought the box containing Charlotte's things and put them in a storage closet at the end of his hallway. He taped it up and wrote "Charlotte" on all sides in big bold black marker. I would be safe until he could return it to her. He went back in his room. He sat next to Anastasia and listened to her breath. He watched her chest rise and fall. He was content. In their link, he knew she was relaxed and felt safe. He laid down on his side and faced her. He whispered so quietly, "I love you my wife." He heard in the link, "I love you more my husband." and he fell asleep.

CHAPTER 5

*F*riday July 3rd. The house was shaking with activity by 6am. It was a perfect morning and it was forecast to be a perfect weekend. Ruth was already awake and standing on her private balcony looking out at the ocean. The sky was bright blue, wispy white clouds were moving slowly across the sky, a cool breeze caused small waves to gently lap onto the beach. She heard the whales singing louder than she had heard in a long time. She noticed a pod of dolphins were jumping out of the water and playing in the distance, her coffee was hot and had a hint of caramel in it. This was a morning that she was going to enjoy and remember as perfect for the rest of her life.

Ailbe woke up in the Thinking Room. She felt renewed, rejuvenated, and ready to dive into the final preparations for tomorrow. Jonathan woke up to loud banging on his door. He knew he was in his room, but couldn't remember how he got there. He muttered, "Whaaaaaaat!?" A very angry chef announced, "Mrs. Ziv is going to wallop you!" Michael and Anastasia woke up but neither wanted to get up yet. Michael loved this moment. His wife next to him on a cool July morning. His windows open with a fan filling the room with the smell of the saltwater. He loved the sounds of the ocean and even more so, the sounds of a busy happy house.

Charlotte was not going to be the scapegoat. She continued her conversation with the reporter well into the night and made her way back home. She was tired and still anxious about what the agents knew and didn't know. She noticed a lot of activity once she got back onto the island. Cars racing down the street, foot traffic, police barricades going up, she chalked it all up to getting ready for what should have been HER big day. She opened the door to her apartment and instantly realized that someone had broken into her apartment. "I bet it was the FBI!" She immediately went into her closet and found her lock box with her jewelry in it. It wasn't damaged and she has the only key. She opened it and nothing was missing. She really couldn't find anything missing except a few refrigerator magnets, wall calendar, mayonnaise out of the fridge and her hairbrush. She started to think it must have been a hungry long haired homeless person. She cleaned up the mess and started calling all of her friends who worked at the hospital. Before anyone could tell her about the events of last night, she gave her version of events and continued to declare very matter of fact, "I have done nothing wrong."

The gossip pool was deep at the hospital. Everyone couldn't wait to talk to her and get the scoop, which she was eager to provide under the pinky swear promises of, "I'll tell you because you're my friend, but you didn't hear this from me." When she was satisfied that her roll as the victim was firmly established, she stepped outside to get her mail. There was a tidal wave of reporters pushing microphones in her face and asking questions at the same time. She went back inside with a crushing feeling that maybe she said too much.

She packed a backpack full of clothes, grabbed her purse, keys, cell phone and charger and a bottle of wine and crawled through her back window. She made her way through the back of her apartment complex and onto the next street. She was careful not to be seen as she walked several block to circle her way back to her apartment complex, got in her car and quietly left. She drove to her parent's house but the media was there too. She tried calling several of her friends but no one picked up their phones. She noticed a voicemail from her friend Emily that simply said. "Hey mate, the hospital and everyone in it has gone bonkers. Stay low for a bit." The only other place Charlotte could think of was her dad's boat. She headed for the marina.

The individual docks were gaited. You have to have a boat to gain access. The marina only gave out two electronic keys per boat, but she had gotten one from Michael because her dad was always afraid of loosing his and his friend Rick had the other one. The Reale Marina was very particular about who they let dock their boat there, and they had a long waiting list. It would be a perfect place for her to go. Security was always very restrictive, and dock master checked everyone who came on and off the property, regardless if he had known someone for years. He made them come into his office and sign in and sign out. If a boat owner had invited guests, they were told in advance to bring photo ID or they would not be allowed on the dock. Charlotte always hated it, but today she was grateful.

She pulled into the marina and parked right next to the office. She went in and was about to sign the book when the Dock Master said, "Well, just maybe for today you can park your car inside the gates over there in the back, and darn it, my pen seems to be all out of ink. I know you're here. You call me if you need anything." She went around the counter and hugged him. "Thank you. I just need to be alone right now." He nodded his head, "And to think about it all… I get that. Now git going. And stay out of the water. I hear there are a bunch of big jellyfish out there." He turned and kept filling out some tide charts.

Charlotte was quick to do what he suggested. She parked as far away from the gate as she could. It was close to the dock that her dad's boat was on, and his was in the last slip. She made her way down to the 42 foot fishing boat. It had a sleeper cabin, bathroom, and a small kitchen. She would tell her dad that she would be here for a few days while things cooled off. She knew the hospital offices would be closed, so she left a message on Mr. Kelly's office voicemail and not her supervisor, to call out sick. Her dad always had food on board and enough liquor to celebrate when he and Rick caught 'big ones'. She took some time to relax before she cleaned the place up a bit and settled in. She looked around, "This will do nicely for a few days." She opened the bottle of wine and sat on the back deck with her feet up and was going to enjoy the beautiful day. "This will all blow over soon and if Michael doesn't come and apologize to me by tonight. I'll have to go to their stupid party tomorrow and fuck one of his cousins. Jonathan… you're up buddy. I'll have to put some meat on his bones, but he will do for now." She took a sip of wine… "Now coming here was a stroke of genius." She finished the first glass and poured another.

Bina was taking Arden up on his offer to help out in the kitchen so she could go and talk to Charlotte. She called down to the kitchen and gave a list of items to have placed in a basket. She wanted to leave soon and get this over with. She talked to Rach-El who was not as enthusiastic about her mother's plan. "She is not my favorite person right now and I'm sure I'm not her's either. But I do honor and respect what you are trying to do. I'll come with you but if she gets snarky with me, she'll figure out real quick that I will shiv a bitch." Bina blinked a few times. "Remind me to have a word with your training instructors." Bina took Rach-El and went into the kitchen, grabbed the waiting basket, and left.

First they drove to Charlotte's apartment but saw a media standing around a food truck. Rach-El said, "Her car isn't here. Don't even stop." They drove by her parent's house and still no sign of Charlotte's car. They drove passed several other places that they thought she could be. Bina "There is no way she would be at the hospital, right?" Rach-El looked at her mother, "After last night? Um… NO." The two women thought for a second and said at the same time, "The marina". Rach-El called the Dock Master's office. "He should be off today. We should just drive over." But the Dock Master answered the phone. Rach-El was caught slightly off guard. "Oh, hey. Good morning. It's Rach-El. Rach-El Reale. Why are you working today?" He knew Rach-El very well. She used to come by and listen to his stories of high sea adventures. He was a dedicated seaman who was hired by Se'ighin Reale after he was injured on a commercial fishing boat and could no longer fish. And without any other skills, he lost his health insurance and almost his home. Se'ighin had heard about him from Curtis and offered him a job. "Charlotte Calhoun came before the crack of dawn this morning. I didn't think it was right to leave her out here by herself." Rach-El said firmly, "You are a good man. My mother and I are going to come by and see her. Can you please have the gates open. I think a few reporters might be following us." He huffed, "Red belly bottom suckers! You ladies come straight in."

Rach-El hung up the phone laughing. She looked at Bina, "Do you ever love a De'nola so much that you wish they were one of us?" Bina laughed in agreement. "Several times dear, several times."

They pulled up to the marina and through the gates. They saw Charlotte's car and parked next to it. Bina looked at Rach-El. "I know this is going to be difficult for both of us, but remember, we are here for Michael. He needs less stress, not more knowing his beloved sister shived this bitch." She grabbed the basket and walked away with Rach-El standing there stunned. Bina had already waved her master key across the sensor pad and was walking down the dock by the time Rach-El thought, "What did she just say?" and ran to catch up.

Mrs. Ziv arrived at the main house by 6:30am. She was tired in the best way possible. Her phone has been ringing off the hook since yesterday asking for the Grand opening date, web site information and when orders could be taken. She finally had to put a message on her phone that the grand opening of her store will be announced soon, the web site is almost complete and thanking them for their interest and to please call back after the date being announced. "So much to do. How do I start a web site? I hope I didn't get in over my head."

Once at the main house she was directed to go straight to the kitchen and there has been an incident. She rushed to the kitchen to find the head chef still scolding Jonathan. "Now you can explain to her how many you ate!" Jonathan looked at Mrs. Ziv. "Good morning and congratulation. I am your new baking assistant for the entire day."

The chef "And why are you her baking assistant?"

Jonathan "I kind of enjoyed your rhum balls."

Mrs. Ziv tried hard to hold back her laughter, but she burst out. Jonathan thought she was crying and grabbed her and hugged her. "No. Please don't cry. I promise I will stay here and do it all. I'm SO sorry." She pulled away and he realized she was laughing. "Child, how many did you eat?"

Jonathan "More than a few, but less than all of them."

Mrs. Ziv "A skinny boy like you must have been three crows flyin backwards in the wind! That is 45% alcohol. The oven burns it off the first time, but then they soak in it. I know grown men who were bottle fed this stuff and they can't eat but a few." Jonathan thought back to last night. "Oooohhhhh, that's why I slept so well."

Mrs. Ziv "How do you feel now?"

Joanthan"Yeah, I'm a little hung over, but I'm here to make this right. I'm ready to bake." Mrs. Ziv clapped her hands together. "You are singing my song." And they got busy baking. Within the hour, the entire house smelled heavenly.

Anastasia tried to get up without disturbing Michael. She knew he was awake but she was enjoying feeling him so relaxed. Michael, without moving a muscle or opening his eyes. "Why don't you ask me for help? I have no evidence that says you are graceful with two working legs. Now you expect me watch this without laughing and hurting your feelings?" Anastasia kissed his cheek. "You would laugh at your injured wife?" Michael "Yes, when my wife does something foolish... Then yes." He opened his eyes and she was nose to nose with him. She kissed him with a slow passionate kiss. Michael had never dated an Azili before. He didn't know if this was an Azili kiss, or if this was a bonded kiss. He didn't think any more about it, he just knew he wanted to kiss her forever.

Anastasia whispered, "I wish we were the only two people on the planet." Michael held her so tenderly. "Focus only on me my love. There is nowhere else I'd rather be than alone with you." They kissed with so much devotion that he felt slightly lightheaded and almost as if he was floating. He smelled Jasmine in the air. His exposed skin got goose bumps from the breeze. He wanted to make love to her, but there was nothing that could compare to this. This was making love with her. He imagined taking her in his arms and pulling her so close that she became him, a part of him. He could keep her from all the bad things that this world had in it.

He wanted to see her face as he kissed her. He started to open his eyes. He saw an amazing flash of light and he felt tiny hot tingles over his entire body. With lightning speed, he pulled her tight and flipped her over with him on top of her. He was careful to move her leg without twisting it. His eyes were darting around the room as if he were expecting an attack. She looked dazed. "What happened?" Michael started to relax when he didn't see any immediate danger. "Did you feel that?" Anastasia nodded, "Yes, but what was it?" He looked at his body as if he were expecting burn marks. "I have no idea. But I think we need to find out." Michael linked to Ailbe the information. "I'll come down." was all she responded.

The two of them were almost scared to move when Ailbe knocked on the door. They called her into the room. Ailbe "Well, I want this to be a lesson to both of you. (They looked at her as if they were going to be told something terrible) I am always right." Michael had never underestimated any family member. He knew that in this family, the older you are, the more you know. Ailbe was grinning. "I recall telling each of you to sleep in your separate beds. My suspicion was that you would not, I was young once too… Princess, your memories are desperate to come back. I believe that when you were being intimate with your bond, that is when you felt more loved than you have felt since we escaped. This is difficult to understand, but it sounds like your link is so well established that now you can pull Michael into a memory or a feeling." Michael looked confused but Anastasia looked like a light bulb went on in her head. "So… I pulled Michael into one of my memories? Like I remember being happy? Arrr! I hate my brain. Why can't I remember?"

Michael pulled her closer. Ailbe smiled softly. Michael said, "It sounds like your memories are coming back. You can't rush this. Those flashes of light that Great-Grandmother saw in the link, and the flash of light that we just saw and felt, it sounds like they are memories. I think I should call the trauma therapist Dr. Besler. I don't want your memories to flood back all at once, especially anything bad." Ailbe spoke up, "Michael, you are wise beyond your years. I called Dr. Besler last night. He will be here by noon. Anastasia, before you reject this, I must insist." She quickly turned and left before Anastasia could say anything, but she called back to Michael, "You are most welcome for the new sheets." Michael let out one chuckle and shook his head.

Anastasia looked at him. "I was going to say I didn't want to talk to him, but she did make it clear, 'I am always right'." Michael was still shaking his head about the sheets. "Yes, she did. Now that she has schooled us both, let's start our day with a good breakfast and a trip to the infirmary. Dr. Ziv is going to take that thing out of your neck." She lifted up her arms so he could scoop her up. Michael opened up his door and there was a motorized wheelchair with the leg extension already in position. There was a note, *Put her down* taped to the seat. Anastasia laughed. "I'm loving this." Michael put her in the wheelchair and she was off like a rocket.

They went down into the kitchen. It was packed with family and hired staff busy with last minute details. Jonathan was smack dab in the middle of it all covered in flour and sugar. Anastasia asked, "How can I get that picture framed in 8 x 10?" Michael laughed "You find a safe place to park this thing and I'll sneak in and rescue some eggs and bacon." She screamed, "BACON! Get lots of bacon!" As she found an opening near the end of the table. Everyone was coming over to say hello and hugging her. She was soaking it all in.

Michael found his way in and out of the kitchen rather easily with two plates full of fun breakfast foods. He stopped and watched the scene at the far end of the table. Things have never been so crystal clear to him before. Being a husband, a father, a family member, this is what makes life worth it all. He made is way down to end of the table. Anastasia looked at him with child-like enthusiasm, "Does everyone really have access to this? You can really just get it anywhere?" She really didn't want an answer, she just wanted to eat.

After breakfast they headed for the infirmary. The residence doctor and nurse had finished their shift and were giving report to the new resident doctor and nurse. They all said their pleasantries and the new resident doctor asked, "May I asked how you slept? You look well rested." Anastasia smiled, "I slept very well, thank you for asking." The nurse started checking her vital signs and the dressing on her leg. The doctor took x-rays of her leg and then examined the incision site on her chest and wound to her leg. Michael asked, "How is she doing doc?" Doctor "Well, her vital signs are perfect. The skin on her chest is healing incredibly fast. Don't be over confident when you see it looks great, the bone underneath is going to take weeks to heal properly. The leg… The stitches can come out next week, but they almost look like they can come out sooner. But again, don't get overconfident." The doctor looked at Anastasia, "Please listen carefully, you can NOT put any weight on it yet. The x-rays are looking very promising.

The bone is remodeling at an incredible rate, but this will take time. Dr. Ziv will be here soon. He is the one who makes the decisions on when the pins and rods come out."

Anastasia smiled, "Call me when he gets here. I have places to go and people to see." She spun the chair around and didn't even wave goodbye as she left. Michael didn't know how to explain her unnaturally quick healing to a De'nola. "She got a really great night's sleep." He shook the doctor's hand and pointed at the door. "Um... I should follow her." And he left.

Bina called out, "May we come aboard?" Rach-El stepped passed her mother and stepped onto the boat. "Hey Charlotte, are you here?" Charlotte had started drinking very early this morning and was half asleep when she heard Rach-El. She yelled out, "I'll be right out." She quickly changed her clothes, combed her hair and brushed her teeth. She wanted to look her best. She thought that Michael had to have sent them. His mother has never come to her apartment or her parent's house. She was positive that her plan had worked. Bina would be telling her that Michael is miserable and wants her forgiveness. She looked in the mirror and opened the door. Bina and Rach-El were standing on the deck. Bina was holding a basket. Charlotte felt she had to play slightly coy. "Hello Rach-El, Mrs. Reale. You both look good. Why aren't you busy with party planning?" Rach-El's blood was about to boil. Bina stepped toward Charlotte with the basket. "I thought you could use some comfort items."

Charlotte "Are they from Michael?"

Bina "No dear, they are from Rach-El and me."

Charlotte "So where is Michael?"

Bina "Michael is very busy at the house. He has responsibilities there."

Charlotte "So he has no feelings of responsibilities here? To me? We have been together for five years. We are supposed to announce our engagement tomorrow. And now he has other responsibilities?"

Rach-El "Charlotte, you know he loved you very much..." Charlotte cut her off

Charlotte "LoveD? That is NOT love. We were together a few nights ago and now he is saying he loveD me.... No, I can't hear this."

Bina "Charlotte, Rach-El and I wanted to come and talk to you. We want you to know that we are here for you. Yes, we know that Michael had planned to propose to you, but things happen."

Charlotte "So are you telling me to wait and he will come to his senses?"

Bina "No, Michael is now committed to Anastasia."

Charlotte "His cousin! How disgusting is that?"

Bina "She is a distant family member, but regardless, neither one of them planned this. It is something that happened naturally."

Charlotte "I don't believe that. I think that you just can't handle him marring a poor working girl. I need to hear this from him. He would never just throw all this away."

Rach-El "We have been good friends for a long time. You know that neither of us would ever want you to feel like he is throwing you away. It would kill Michael if he knew you felt that way."

Charlotte "Well he is killing me. I have never been hurt so bad in my life, I did nothing to deserve this!"

Bina "We all know you didn't. Michael is under a tremendous amount of pressure. The entire family is. I suggest that we all take a deep breath and wait a few days. All of this will settle down and Michael will come and talk to you."

Charlotte "Wait a couple of days? Why not now? Is he that much of a coward that he can't come and apologize in person?"

Rach-El "My brother is not a coward!"

Charlotte "Then where is he? Is he parading around his new girlfriend? Is he telling everyone about their years together and how they met? Oh wait… THEY JUST MET!"

Rach-El "We tried to come here and talk to you. We tried and make it right. But the fact that you are so self-centered and it took Michael five years to see it is beyond me. I was your friend long before you were his girlfriend. I tried to warn him, but he was in love with you so I let a lot of things slide."

Charlotte "What? You tried to warn him about me. What is that supposed to mean? I put up with so much crap from him, I am the best thing that has ever happened to him."

Rach-El "No, his wife is the best thing that ever happened to him." She turned and stepped off of the boat.

Charlotte "WIFE? They got married?"

Bina "Yes. They got married in a small traditional family ceremony. They will have a formal wedding when she is healed." Bina did not have this conversation in mind when she thought of coming to speak to Charlotte. She was hoping to deescalate not inflame the situation. Charlotte stood there in shock. She felt rage boiling up inside of her. "Listen clearly. I want Michael to come down here and talk to me himself or I will tell everyone everything I know about him and his family." Bina lowered her voice, "We came here because we care. Ailbe herself has insisted that you come to the party. We all want to see you happy and successful. And we want you to be happy for Michael. If you like, I can arrange it so you and Michael don't even run into each other. Please come, have a few laughs, a few drinks, and dance with your friends. The entire town is going to be there. Show up with your chin up. We will have a wonderful time. Just think about it. I personally hope you come."

Charlotte lowered her voice to match Bina's. "If Michael comes down here and talks to me like a man, and if he asks me to come with him, then I will come. But until he comes down here... No. Now please leave."

Bina "Well... I truly hope you change your mind because that is not going to happen." She stepped off the boat and left before Charlotte had a chance to say anything more to her face. She was, however, yelling obscenities as Bina walked to the car where Rach-El was already waiting inside. She got in and put her head on the steering wheel. "If you would have kicked her in the throat, I would have given you a million dollars." Rach-El huffed, "I would have done it for a rhum ball." Bina linked the information to Arden but he did not respond.

Dr. Ziv arrived at the main house and was directed into the kitchen. He saw his wife laughing. She was directing kitchen staff while standing in front of a mountain of newly backed rhum balls. He got her attention but she just blew him a kiss and kept working. He headed toward the infirmary saying out loud. "Is that really the woman that I said was too dependent on me to fill her days, and wished she had a hobby. Be carful what you wish for Ezriel." He found his way to the infirmary and walked in. "Hello.... Where is my patient?" The resident peeked out from behind a desk. "Oh Dr. Ziv. Someone got her an electric wheelchair and she has been a social butterfly. The nurse is having a difficult time keeping up with her. I told her I would call her when you got here. I have to thank you, I have really seen that laughter is the best medicine. She looks great." Dr. Ziv "She is an amazing young woman." He said while he was looking around the hall. He had never noticed the stunning architecture of this place.

Within a few minutes Michael and Anastasia arrived with the nurse close behind. Michael lifted Anastasia up out of the wheelchair and into the hospital bed. Dr. Ziv "Let me take a look at you. You are remarkable! I can definitely take this out of your neck and the stitches are almost ready." The nurse prepped Anastasia's neck and Dr. Ziv removed the IV access line. Anastasia "Thank you. How long until you get these things out of my leg?" Dr. Ziv smiled at her, "Soon. Give it all the time it needs. I have never seen anyone heal like you before. My orders going forward are for you to rest for the remainder of the day. Tomorrow you can go to the parade, but then take a nap. Wake up to get some junk food into you, but then take a nap, have a margarita, listen to some music until you need a nap, watch the fireworks, and go to bed." Michael laughed. "I can't get her to slow down. So if you make that an official order, then I am duty bound to follow it to the letter." Dr. Ziv pulled out a prescription pad, "It is an official order." Anastasia "Is it ethical for both of you to gang up on my like that?" Before either one of them could say anything, she jumped off the bed and back into the wheelchair... and she was gone. The two men stood there staring at each other. Dr. Ziv said, "Well, I see you have your hands full. Good luck keeping her well rested. I will see you at the party tomorrow." Michael "I look forward to seeing you there. It's going to be a fantastic day." Michael went to find Anastasia. As he was walking down the hall he felt a sharp quick pain in his back. He thought of Charlotte.

The rest of the day was filled with growing excitement. Anastasia was getting familiar with the inside of the main house. She flew up and down each hallway and in and out of every room. She was venturing out onto the back deck and onto the beach. Michael had been jogging after her for over an hour when stopped to get a bottle of water. She went out onto the beach. She felt it. Michael felt her fear rising and began running to her. "What? What's wrong?" She didn't respond, he just felt her terrified and she lost consciousness.

Michael felt their link break. He linked to the protectors. "Get the doctor!" He got her just as their link broke, he picked her up and started running back into the house. The doctor met them in the hallway and started calling out orders to the nurse. The other nurse was calling Dr. Ziv. Michael got her into the hospital bed in the infirmary. Several of the protectors were at Michael's side. Jonathan was still covered in flour and sugar when he was suddenly at the head of her bed. He was telling her quietly in her ear the entire time that she is home, she is safe, she is loved, and Michael needs her to fight.

Michael kept trying to link with her, but it was like she was gone. Her blood pressure was up but not critical. Her heart rate was pounding but not critical. Her blood sugar level was normal. The resident said, "It appears to be a syncope episode. It just means she passed out. I think she might have over done it today." Michael didn't answer, he continuously tried to link with her. Ailbe and Ruth arrived. Ailbe also tried to link with her with no luck. Michael was clueless. The only time he couldn't link with her before was when she died.

Ruth asked Ailbe, "Why can't you link?" Ailbe was also confused. "I don't know. It's like she's gone." Michael responded, "What do you mean she is gone? She isn't dead!" The doctor was trying to explain, "When people pass out, they are unconscious, not dead." No one was paying any attention to him. Ailbe grabbed Ruth's hand, "We can try together." Michael was going out of his mind waiting. The pain in his back ran through his body again. He thought of how much he had hurt Charlotte and this could be some kind of Karma. Ruth motioned for Michael's hand. He gladly tried to add to the energy to link with her. "THERE!" he yelled. She was very far away. Ailbe tried to stop Michael from going deep after her but his mind was faster than her's. She thought of how much he has grown in these past few weeks. But this was still reckless. Michael didn't care. He could not live without her by his side. He called for her over and over.

Ailbe asked, "Where is she? I still can't find her? Is she close to the veil?" Michael didn't have much strength left. "I can feel but I still can't find her." He continued to call for her.

Fifteen minutes had passes since she went unresponsive. The room got warm, like every piece of equipment was over heating. Michael felt lightheaded and the link was broke. Anastasia opened her eyes screaming and seemed to be in the fight of her life. She was kicking, biting, scratching and punching in every direction. Jonathan never left his position, he never stopped his reassuring her that she was safe. The doctor was filling a syringe with a clear liquid. He pushed one of protectors to the side. "This will help calm her down and he plunged the needle into her hip. She was starting to relax long before the medication took effect. Michael linked with her easily. "We are all here. You are home. You are safe." She looked at him, "Michael!?" He grabbed her face. "I'm right here." She burst into tears as she looked around the room. It was full of protectors and other family members that came to help. "What happened?" Michael "You tell us! We were outside on the sand and you passed out." Anastasia was still shaking. "I don't know. I don't remember much. I felt weird like I had to run. I heard someone telling me to come back, that Michael needs me to fight. So I started to fight. That's when I woke up fighting."

Ailbe looked at Ruth and the two women left abruptly. Michael didn't even question it. He just hugged her tight. She almost couldn't breath. The doctor and nurses went back into their rooms but kept their doors open so they could keep an eye on her. The family members started heading back to what they were doing. The protectors filed out slowly. Everyone wanted to give them time alone. Michael finally let her go. They both noticed that Jonathan was at the sink for a very long time. Anastasia asked very cautiously, "Jonathan?" He hesitated before he turned around. Michael suspected that Jonathan might have had a punch or two thrown his way, but he is a protector and could have dodged them easily. But now he realized if he would have dodged them, then Anastasia might not have found her way back.

Jonathan turned around but did not want to face Michael. Both of his eyes were red and swollen and already turning black and blue, his forehead

had two one inch gashes that needed stitches and his nose might be...
no, it was broken. Dr. Ziv arrived out of breath and looking confused. He
looked at Jonathan, "What the Hell happened to you?" Anastasia could
not have felt worse, but she broke out into a belly laugh that was contagious. Michael and Dr. Ziv started to snicker but joined in with Anastasia.
Jonathan even began laughing so hard that his forehead stared bleeding
worse and he felt lightheaded. The doctor and nurses explained what happened. Dr. Ziv "Ok little missy, you go upstairs and go to bed. I'm not
playing. I agree with my resident that you have pushed yourself too hard.
The nurse will help you upstairs and Michael will be along shortly." He
looked at Michael but waited until he gently lifted her out of the bed and
onto a stretcher. The nurse had taken Anastasia out of the room before he
continued, "You should know better! What are you thinking? She should
still be in the hospital. She is at risk for a dozen life-threatening compli-
cations. Now what is it going to take for you to understand the gravity of
this situation? She died just a few days ago!? I made it very, VERY clear
that she needs rest. Am I making myself clear?" Michael knew he was right
and felt ashamed that he didn't follow his orders. "You are right. I will do
better. I'm going to make sure she is comfortable." Michael left knowing
he failed again. Dr Ziv looked at Jonathan. "You look pitiful. I'm so glad I
asked Se'ighin for an x-ray machine."

The resident doctor helped clean him up as Michael went up to his
room. He helped the nurse get her into their bed and propped her leg up
with pillows then she headed back to the infirmary to help Dr. Ziv. Michael
got into bed and held her hand. "I couldn't find you anywhere. Ailbe said
you were gone. I don't understand. Where did you go?" Anastasia "I don't
know. I just knew I had to run." Michael couldn't shake the pit in his stomach. "Please stop leaving me." Neither wanted to talk anymore.

Jonathan saw the x-ray on the computer screen as soon as Dr. Ziv hit
the button. Lindsey wanted to be with Jonathan as soon as she heard what
happened. She arrived just as Dr. Ziv took the x-ray. Lindsey saw Jonathan
in the bed and laughed. "Wow, she kicked your ass!" Dr. Ziv raised his
eyebrows at her. "Be nice young lady. From what I hear, your brother did
a very nice thing. It's unfortunate that he sacrificed his face to do it, but

I will make him look handsome again soon." The resident had given him a mild pain medication and he was starting to feel woozy. The nurses finished cleaning his face and prepared him for the stitches. Dr. Ziv gave him injections into his nose and the cuts on his forehead to numb the area. The stitches took less than thirty minutes to complete and adjusting to his nose took another twenty minutes. Another x-ray confirmed that nose was set correctly, then Dr. Ziv bandaged his forehead and nose. "We are all done. Now get some rest. You're gonna be light headed for a few hours. So you can stay here, or maybe your sister can stay with you in your room." He looked over at Lindsey who was nodding yes. Se'ighin walked in with Dr. Besler. Dr. Ziv updated Se'ighin on what happened as Lindsey said, "While you gentlemen talk, I'm taking my brother up to his room." She took him by the elbow and they left.

The two doctors discussed Anastasia's updated health and emotional status. Dr. Besler asked Se'ighin if he could either have Michael and Anastasia come down stairs or he would go up to their room. Se'ighin went upstairs and knocked on the door. He could feel them comfortable and resting. Michael felt him and quietly told him to come in. Se'ighin sat on the edge of the bed. Michael asked, "Did you figure out what happened to her today? Can we just leave our minds? It is like when we choose to go to the ancestors? I'm just so confused." Se'ighin "Michael, this is something new to all of us. I'm just as confused as you are. No, we can't leave. Even the ancestors are in the link, they are just on the other side of the veil, but they're still there. I think it would be healthy for her to see Dr. Besler. He can't do any worse than we have done trying to figure this out."

Michael agreed and said he will help her get back to the infirmary in a few minutes. Se'ighin left. Michael gently touched Anastasia's hair. He could feel everything about her. He focused on her hair and how she looked when he first saw her. Her hair was full of sand, seaweed and salt water. He felt every strand between his fingers. He thought in the link, "Where did you go? You said you had to run...Where is your safe place Princess?" She subconsciously whispered, "Home. I ran away back home." Michael whispered in her ear, "Where?" Anastasia slowly opened her eyes. "Maybe that is a good question for the therapist. I have no more room in my brain for more questions. I'm too tired." She looked tired and felt like she had a set back, but she scooted herself to the edge of the bed. Michael picked her up and carried her down stairs and back into the infirmary.

He sat her in a reclining chair. "I will give you your privacy, I need to go find her wheelchair." Dr. Besler thanked him. "We are not going any-where. Feel free to come back whenever you choose." Michael looked at Anastasia. "I'll be close." She tried to smile at him as he left.

Michael retraced their steps and went outside and onto the beach where her wheelchair had been. He was glad no one had moved it. He wanted to know the exact spot where she felt 'weird'. He looked out into the water. The dolphins were very close today. He could see their faces looking at him. He put his hand up as to wave to them. A large one with scars on its face came in closer and just watched him. He could hear the whales singing louder than he had heard them in a long time. He called out, "Thank you," as he turned to look at the flurry of last minute prepa-rations. He felt guilty that he wasn't helping, but he knew that his duties were with Anastasia. His eyes scanned the beach... "The shed!"

Michael knew they must have caught or killed at least one Eile and he knew that his grandmother must not have wanted him to be told any thing until after the party. Could Anastasia have known one must be in there? Could she feel it?

The shed was built exclusively to interrogate Eile. Its round thick walls were electrically charged and blocked all of their communications. The bottom three feet had an electric mess and clear warmed plastic covering it. The walls bent slightly inward and were painted with a mixture of zinc, oil, and acetone. There were no air shafts, nothing to climb onto or into. Four stainless steel tables that could get boiling hot or a block of ice in seconds stood in the center. Two circular areas were enclosed with hot or cold Plexiglas. The entire shed was built so that they could not escape nor could they be rescued. Michael thought it would be impossible for her to sense them. Michael linked his thoughts to Ruth.

Ruth was with Ailbe in the Thinking Room. Ruth "It's worse than we thought. She felt them in the shed. How is that possible?" Ruth had a horrible thought. "Oh my God! Mother, could she be part Eile?" Ailbe put her head into her hands. "What could they have done to that poor girl?"

Charlotte watched Bina and Rach-El drive away. She was almost speechless with rage against them. "I'll show them. I'll show up tomorrow and find Jonathan. I'll flirt with him right in front of the entire family. Michael knows that he has had a crush on me forever." She went into the kitchen and took out a gallon jug of vodka and the orange juice from the refrigerator. She made herself a very strong drink and returned to her seat on the back deck of the boat and drank, cursed out loud and continued to plan her seduction of Jonathan. "OR... ... Maybe Malachi! That would get back at Rach-El and Lindsey too for sic'ing their dog on me. I bet one of them has the hots for him. What a perverted family! Wouldn't that be perfect if I married Malachi." She opened up the basket that Bina had left. It was full of cheese, crackers, fruit, chocolate, pastries, and a small zip lock baggie with a small label.

Haitian Treats

990 Main Street

Ruimte Island, VA

"What the Hell are Haitian treats?" But she was hungry and not drunk enough yet to care. She allowed herself to wonder what was going on back at her apartment. What happened at the hospital? Did the FBI wanted to talk to her? What if any of the news Michael had seen or heard of? She knew that no one in his family are big TV watchers. She always was talking about a TV show that she watched and his family would just stare at her. She brought several DVDs over to watch up in Michael's room, but that was the extent of it.

Michael linked with Ruth and Ailbe, "Can I come up? I want to know what's in the shed." Ruth responded. "Go check on Jonathan and we will be on my private balcony." Michael walked passed the infirmary to check on Anastasia. She was still talking to Dr. Besler and he looked very attentive to her. He felt she was tired, but at ease with him so he continued upstairs to Jonathan's room. He knocked and Lindsey opened the door. He was about to step in when she put a hand on his chest. "You know that

I am the first one to tease him, but even I feel bad for him. Please don't laugh at him again. He looks so pitiful."

Michael saw him right after Anastasia hit him and wondered how bad he could be, but he agreed and walked in. Jonathan was sitting up in bed. Michael was shocked. Both eyes were deep black and purple. The whites of his eyes were red. His nose had long hard material over it to keep its shape with gauze packed in each nostril. His forehead had two areas covered with large bandages, but you could see his entire forehead was one large swollen bruise. Michael had never seen any of the protectors look this bad, not after training, not after wrestling around, not even after the time that Malachi tried riding Lindsey's horse and it bucked him off and he landing flat on his face. Michael "I can't even look at you right now. The photos of tomorrow's party are going to be epic."

Lindsey smacked Michael on the back. Jonathan just looked at him with a pout face and sounding like a child with a stuffy nose. "I was hoping to see Lucy there, but I don't want anyone to see me like this." Michael suddenly felt nauseated. "I need you to know that I truly honor you. Not just as my family, but as my friend. You have stood by me through my worst days, but most importantly, you stood by Anastasia. I can only hope that I am half the man that you are." Lindsey was wiping tears from her face. Jonathan tried to smile, "You both have my loyalty. You know that." Michael smiled. "Yes I do. I just wanted you to hear me say it. And if Lucy is there tomorrow, she will know that you let a girl tap dance on your face for love. That should earn you some brownie points." Jonathan tried to laugh but he grabbed his nose. "Ouch, don't make me laugh. It hurts." Michael turned to Lindsey, "If he needs anything, you let me know first." She hugged him and whispered, "Thank you. He needed that." Michael kissed her on top of her head and went to talk to Ruth and Ailbe.

They were on Ruth's private balcony over looking the ocean. Michael leaned on the railing. "This is my favorite spot in the house." He noticed the pod of dolphins was still circling where he saw them earlier. Michael pointed to them, "The big one was just staring at me." Ailbe "You are still too young to hear him, but he knows you have the Princess. He stayed with her out in the water." Michael shook his head like he was trying to shake something loose. "What? Anastasia said talked about having a friend that helped her, and she thought she heard a large dolphin and a whale talk to her. That was real? Was that THAT dolphin?" Ruth nodded "oh yes, that was real. That is when we first knew she had to be the princess." Michael put his hands on his head. "We will circle back around to that. I want to know what happened back at the hospital." Ailbe "I want you and Anastasia to enjoy tomorrow. I will link you every detail after that. There is nothing good that can come from doing it now. I had Ace move them to the other shed. They are far enough away that she will not sense them."

Michael "THEM? How many of THEM do you have?" Ruth "Two" Ailbe "We had ten, but we left two of them alive so you can express your feeling. Now anything else will have to wait until after everyone has a good time tomorrow. Do you reject my suggestion? Do you have another?" Michael calmed down his rising frustration. "Great-Grandmother, I trust you and I can see the wisdom in your choice, but I would have liked to know, but I see that it was better to wait. Anastasia would have felt my rage toward them and I want nothing more than for her to have a day that she feels nothing but love and amazement." He stood there looking every inch of perfect soldier and a loving husband. Ailbe was proud. Ruth was thinking that he will be a great leader. Michael "I'm going to head back down to Anastasia now. I want to talk to the therapist too." Ruth "Go to her." Michael left knowing that everyone was behind him and his wife.

Dr. Besler and Anastasia seemed to be comfortable talking about her scars together. Michael walked in to hear him say, "I'm glad you feel safe." Michael interrupted. "I will protect her with my life." Dr. Besler turned to him and smiled. "I owe you an apology. I don't know if you remember the day we met? (Michael remembered that day clearly) We were in the interdisciplinary meeting when Anastasia was attached. I saw you as full of rage and prone to violence, but I was wrong. I have heard from several people, who have stopped in here about you. I think this is the perfect environment for her to safely get her memories back." Anastasia was smiling widely. She reminded Michael of a child who got an A+ on a test. He loved when she was proud of herself. She was more secure with herself by the hour. "I didn't think that I could ever love you more than I did this morning watching you eat bacon, but now watching you talk about your scars.... You are my hero." He just kept looking at her. Dr. Besler almost felt like a voyeur. "Well, on that note, I will let myself out. You both are exhausted and need to be left alone the rest of the day. Doctor's orders." Anastasia "When do I get to see you again." Dr. Besler "Our deal was for an evaluation and if you found our conversation helpful, then I would make myself available to you. I'm not going to push you. Our mandatory visit was today and I'm satisfied that this is a healthy environment for you." Anastasia looked at Michael. "I enjoyed it. He gave me some great ideas on how to stay calm when my 'fight or flight' response is triggered, like earlier." Michael smiled. "I would love to be more involved with the next visit, if that's ok." Dr. Besler was impressed with their openness and respect for each other. "Tomorrow is the 4th. I'm actually planning on being here with my family. I won't be able sit down with you for a block of time, but if you have any questions, please feel free to find me. If you want, we can schedule to meet on the 5th. Sound good?" Michael "Sunday the 5th? I'm not going to ask you to work on a holiday weekend. How about Monday the 6th?" Dr. Besler "Mental health should be treated as seriously as a broken bone or a ruptured appendix. I have no problem being here on Sunday. But this is your home and I am just a guest." Michael shook his hand. "Anyone who goes out of their way to genuinely help a Reale, is much more than a guest. We look forward to seeing you Sunday." Dr. Besler "See you then, I think I can find my way out. You all look very busy today." And he left.

Anastasia was excited to share her conversation with Michael. She linked him their entire meeting. She said, "I feel empowered! I will work on looking at these scars and instead of thinking about what happened. I will think, *look what I survived*. Great idea right?" Michael wished he could have given her that gift. He smiled, "I look at you and I know there is nothing that you can't do. Now, we are going upstairs and relaxing the rest of the day. Tomorrow is going to be a very busy day. Remember what Dr. Ziv said.... Do a little and rest, do a little more and rest. I will be following his instructions to the letter. This is a battle that I choose." He picked her up and carried her upstairs.

Ace asked Malachi, "Can I steal you away from setting up your bartending duties? I'm moving the two Eile to the other shed. I don't want to kill them before Michael gets his time with them." Malachi loved bartending. He was perfect at it. He could mix up thousands of drinks in a very dramatic show that only a true mixologist could. "Sure, I'd love to piss off a bucket of snot right about now."

Ace had two bags with him. He unlocked the door and turned on the lights. As they walked down the long hallway they each fantasized about killing them, killing all of them. They got to the door and could hear the beastly sounds of growling. Ace opened one of the bags as Malachi gripped the door handle. "Ready?" he asked as he opened the door. The Eile jumped at Ace's throat. Malachi caught it mid-air. Ace held the bag under it. Malachi tried to drop it in as it spread its tentacles in every direction. Malachi laughed as he pulled out his knife and severed three of its tentacles. All Ace heard was the air being moved with a 'swo' sound and a plop on the floor. It fell into the bag screaming.

Ace latched the bag and they went after the second one. It stretched tall. "I want to talk to the old one Ailbe." Ace laughed. "Naw, you had your chance. She asked you politely, and you said no, so now it is up to Michael to talk to you.... But he is in no mood to talk." Malachi stepped forward and took the bag from Ace and held it open. "Please resist!" It started to move toward the bag. "Tell Ailbe she has one more chance to give us back our dog. We promise to go back into the deep and never come back up." Malachi just stared at it until his eyes seemed to glow a bright blue. It slithered into the bag hissing, "It is one girl or all of you." Malachi kicked the bag. "Shut up before I cut you up too." It started curing at him as he closed and latched the bag. The two men debated with one another about killing them, but decided to let Michael have his fun.

Arden took a golf cart and drove down to the open area park where everyone was meeting in the morning to begin the parade. The road was closed to traffic in preparation. Arden drove the route to make sure everything was in place. Including the grandstand, where the family and honored guests were going to be seated. Each group would stop, perform, have photos taken, and score their performance. Ailbe sent personal invitation to the people she wanted to honor. Most were health care providers. But

Tom and Rick were to be seated with the family in the grandstand. Mr. Kelly and his wife Piper were going to be in the first car leading the entire parade. There were ample bathroom trailers, bleacher seating so everyone could sit and see comfortably, ambulances strategically placed if anyone needed medical attention, thousands of flags that were going to handed out to anyone that wanted one and water stations with large coolers full of ice and water. Arden was satisfied that everything was in place.

He drove the golf cart all the way to the end of the parade route, which was actually inside the compound in a large open play area for the children. At that point it was a moderate walk to the main house where the party was going to be held. They had transportation to and from the end of the route for anyone that did not want to walk. But for those who did, they had loads of activities along the way. Arden continued up to the main house.

All the private doors and elevators would be on bioauthorization access only. The main floor would be open for everyone. Many of the doors were removed so that guests would know they could access that room. Signs were posted on private rooms. But most people were just going to pass through the house anyway to get to the backyard. There were two dance floors. One near the house for the older crowd. The music wouldn't be so loud so people could easily talk, but fast enough that people would be dancing. The second dance floor was closer to the water. It was done with a younger crowd in mind. The music would be all popular club style, and the adjacent bar would have adult and kid friendly drinks. The light show and disco ball were already tested by the time Arden was doing his final inspection.

The beach was lined with large Tiki torches every four feet and a thick red rope connecting them all with large lit signs "No swimming" and "Beach closed". There were four bars in the back yard and beach, two in the front of the main house, and one inside the house. One of the two in front of the house was beer and wine and the other was for Elijah's favorite charity, 'Misty Hills Animal Rescue'. Where you could sample local wines and donate to save a life. The one inside the house was a martini bar. It was near the library for the people that have waited all year long to take a peek into the Reale history books. Two protectors would be watching everyone in that room very carefully. The four bars outside were going to be the fun places to be. Malachi would be front and center. He planned to have several of his well chiseled protector cousins perform some risqué choreographed dances every few hours.

There are four food stations in the front of the main house. Each having a different simple menu. A hotdog and hamburger station. A chicken station. A pizza station and a vegetarian station. And six stations outside. Four are the same as the front stations but the additional two in the back are desert stations. Mrs. Ziv's Haitian treats will have stands next to the grandstand, at the end of the parade route, and just outside the library doors.

The children will be well entertained with a petting zoo, face painting, arts and craft stations, a place to make their own dance and music videos and a playground. Parents can sign their children into the areas and leave to enjoy the more adult portions or can stay with their children. All the children friendly areas are enclosed and any parent who signs their child(ren) in are given matching wrist bands, beepers to contact them with, and their photos are taken. The children are to be supervised by several family members at all times. Arden felt he could finally relax. Everyone in the family felt the same way. They worked very hard for the past few months. Now it was time to relax because tomorrow is going to be fun but busy.

July 4th 5:00am. Ailbe woke up to the sounds of whales singing. She slept in the Thinking Room again. She felt fantastic. She went down stairs and made a large container of coffee. There was no hired staff today. Today the family was to serve the community. Anything that needed to be done by staff or venders was completed yesterday, or it just wasn't going to get done. The parade participants were scheduled to arrive at the starting point by 6am. Ailbe arranged breakfast for everyone marching. She was thinking what would be her favorite group. She always loved the children best, but that would be decided in a few hours. The parade was to start at 9:00a.m. and be finished by 11:30a.m. The BBQ was to begin at 12:00 noon. She had a few last minute details to attend to. The most important one was Jonathan. If Lucy were to come, she would have to meet with him prior to leaving the house.

There were things in Ailbe's past that she did not want to share with anyone. She would put all of her memories in link and share them to Ruth on her final day but not sooner. She was running out of time. She set out the pre-made breakfast for the family and went upstairs to Jonathan's room. Lindsey had stayed the night with him to make sure he was comfortable. Olivia and Antonio were very proud of the strong links that their children had to one another. Ailbe woke Jonathan quietly so she would not disturb Lindsey. His face was sore and his pride hurt, but other than that, he felt great. He was just as excited as she was. They went upstairs to her private wing of the house. Jonathan had never been up there before. There was never a reason to. They walked to the Thinking Room door. Jonathan knew of the Thinking Room and knew that you had to be invited in. He was nervous.

The Thinking Room is where the family is closest to home. He felt intimidated as he stood there and he felt Ailbe feeling conflicted. "Great-Grandmother, whatever you need me for…I'm here for you, but if you're unsure, then you should wait. Nothing takes you this long to decide." She shook her head. "You are right my sweet boy, and that is why I need to share this with you." She opened up the door and the room lit up with a beautiful soft blue light. "The room likes you. Now come, sit by the widow with me. I must share something with you." Ailbe put her hands on both sides of his head and being very gentle, she touched her forehead to his. She linked her most dishonorable memory. She broke the link and left the room looking every minute of 104 years old.

Jonathan felt her pain but he couldn't understand why she shared it with him. He felt a new appreciation of her limitless kindness for the first time. He was too young to absorb much information from an elder. His head was pounding and he didn't know what to do with her memory. He stayed in the Thinking Room for awhile watching the small waves, feeling the ocean breeze, watching the dolphins with new understanding and listening to the whales singing with clarity. He wanted to get back to his room before Lindsey woke up.

Ruth and Se'ighin woke up and wanted to go to the beginning of the parade route. They knew the media would be watching their every move today. Ruth was about to call for Jonathan when she felt Ailbe link to him and thought, "Poor Jonathan, what is my mother's burden that she can't even share it with me yet. If anyone can help her with it, it is clearly sweet Jonathan." Ruth and Se'ighin went down to the kitchen for a quick breakfast and walked out the front door where a fleet of golf carts were already lined up. Se'ighin assisted Ruth into one and they were off. Ruth was giddy and looking forward to the day.

Michael woke up before Anastasia and quietly went downstairs. He was grateful that someone made coffee and put out the pre-made breakfast pastries. He took a tray and made two plates and four cups of coffee. He was heading to Jonathan's room first to drop off a plate. He saw Jonathan coming out of the elevator to Ailbe's private area. "Good morning cuz. Meeting with Ailbe so early? That must be a doozy. She never asks for anything on the 4th." Jonathan nodded his head in agreement. "You brought me a 'I'm sorry my bond messed up your face' coffee!" The two men laughed as Jonathan opened his door.

Lindsey woke up to the sound of the two men laughing in the hallway and was coming out to see them as Jonathan opened his door. Lindsey put her hands out. "COFFEE" She took a cup off the tray. Michael asked, "How did you two sleep?" Lindsey stretched. "My back is screaming at me for sleeping in a chair, but I can't wait to get this party started. Is Anastasia up yet? I'm going to go help her pick out her outfit." Michael laughed. "No. She wants to wear what Linda bought her." Lindsey made an angry face, "No! I won't allow it! That is the most hideous outfit on the planet. I can't. I just can't. I'll go talk to her." She grabbed a plate off the tray and put the other cup of coffee in the center and walked off. Michael said, "Let's go down to the infirmary and have the doctor take a look at you. I need to make sure you're ok." Jonathan took two pastries off the remaining plate, and the two headed downstairs.

The rest of the family was waking up and starting their day. Excitement was in the air. Everyone jumped right in with last minute details. Once everyone was up, Antonio started playing some energetic Latin music. The entire compound has speakers throughout the entire property and they are controlled from the main house. It can be limited to one or all areas. Antonio opened up all the speakers and shouted into the microphone. "This is a party no?!!! So enjoy the sounds of my people." And he turned the music up.

Ruth and Se'ighin could hear the music as they headed to the beginning of the parade route. Se'ighin laughed, "Antonio is up." Ruth followed quickly with, "So everyone else is too." They loved their lives, they loved their children, they loved their children's bonds, and life was good... As they arrived, they both noticed the news vans had parked where the signs all clearly read *No Parking* and *Officials parking only. All others will be towed away.* Se'ighin said, "I dislike them immensely." Ruth smiled and waved at them. "It's only for today. I'm sure they will have something else to sink their fangs into by tomorrow. I just don't do well with being nice to people that are trying to dig up drama and harm my family." Se'ighin loved her diplomacy, but he had to agree that enough is enough. So they both painted on smiles and were going to do their best to truly enjoy their favorite day of the year.

They walked around talking to all the groups. The floats were getting last minute details, the singers were drinking hot tea with honey, the school marching bands were tuning instruments and lining up, the clowns were filling their pockets with beads and small toys, and Mr. and Mrs. Kelly were already proudly sitting in the convertible car ready to start the parade.

Rach-El was up and dressed and running into Michael's room when she saw Lindsey. Lindsey said, "What a perfect morning! Are you coming to help Anastasia pick out an outfit too?" Lindsey knew she was. Rach-El laughed. "She will not wear that hideous outfit!" The women laughed as they heard Anastasia call to them from inside. "Come in...." The two women opened the door smiling. They saw that she was still in bed with her leg safely elevated. The two girls jumped on the bed and snuggled up with her. Rach-El started singing the song that was playing and Lindsey grabbed a brush off the nightstand and used it as a microphone. Rach-El linked Anastasia the words and the three women laid there singing loudly and horribly out of tune. Several family members that passed by came in and joined them on the bed. Bina heard the horrible singing and said out loud, "I love my life." Arden stepped out of the bathroom in his boxer shorts with a pretend microphone and shaking his hips. He made his way over to his beautiful wife… Aharon and Isabelle were in the kitchen listening to the growing concert. Aharon offered his hand to his wife, she took it and they started dancing. Elijah and Chaya were in the shower together. Malachi and Benjamin were sitting on the back deck watching their little sister Amelia doing her best impression of singing and dancing "Like Uncle Antonio." Olivia was looking for Jonathan and danced the entire way to the infirmary. Michael and Jonathan sang the song to each other as they danced in perfect synch. And Ailbe opened a link to everyone in the house to take in every detail.

Once the song was over, Lindsey kissed Anastasia on the cheek. "You fit right in." Rach-El agreed. Anastasia could not imagine her life without them. Rach-El "So, clearly all eyes are going to be on you today. So… we have to introduce you to the world in style, first impressions are the most important. We are officially your glam-squad for the day." Anastasia cut her off. "If Michael sent you to change my mind… NO. I'm wearing what I want to wear. I don't care what anyone thinks of me. If Ailbe herself told me to wear something different, the answer would still be no." Michael and Anastasia's link was almost to the point of being unbreakable and Michael knew every word of what was said. He opened a link to Rach-El "You are going to lose this one. I'm telling you. I feel it to her soul that she is going to wear that outfit." Anastasia smiled at her husband's supportive tone. "You all better bet your sweet cheeks!" Rach-El almost fell off the bed, she laughed so hard. "Where have you been getting all these phrases?" Anastasia looked proud. "Michael calls it my 'bat-like hearing'." Lindsey "Well then…we will have to have perfect hair and makeup."

They helped her into a shower and washed her hair. Lindsey trimmed it slightly and gave it some body, then did a beautiful braid with small white flowers in it. Rach-El did her makeup in neutral tones but bold beautiful deep red lipstick. Jonathan was given the all clear by the doctor and the two of them were told not to come back to the room yet, so they went out and sat on the back deck with Malachi and Benjamin. They invited all of the new protectors to come and join them. Several of them made their way out to join them for a fresh cup of hot coffee and pastries. It soon turned into a perfect time for them to connect on a deeper level, not only as a family, but as a team.

Rach-El and Lindsey helped Anastasia get dressed and announced to her that they were done. They turned her around so she could look in the mirror. Anastasia stared at herself without making a sound. Rach-El "I'm sorry if you hate it. I can change it." Anastasia finally said, "No... I... um...I think I just had a flash of a memory. I like it. I hope Michael likes it too." Lindsey "A memory? Should we call Great-Grandmother?" As Lindsey was about to link with Ailbe. Anastasia lifted up her hand. "No, not a memory, I just felt like I recognized myself for a second." Michael felt it too and was about to bolt back into the house, when he felt her relax again. He was anxious to see her, not for himself, she was perfect just the way she was, but that she **felt** pretty is what he wanted to see. Antonio went to the microphone. "The parade will be starting soon." He turned the music to a variety setting and lowered the volume. Everyone started making their way to where they needed to be.

Michael and Jonathan made their way upstairs and into Michael's room. Anastasia was nervous to see Michael. She hoped he liked her hair and makeup, but when Michael and Jonathan came into the room. All she could see was Jonathan. Her hands covered her mouth. "Oh my God Jonathan!!! I...I am so sorry! Did I do all of that to you?!" Her eyes were locked on Jonathan as she struggled to stand up on her own. She pushed away all the hands that tried to help her. Michael wanted to help her, but she warned him not to. She had tears in her eyes and she hobbled forward. When she put weight on her leg, she felt an intense amount of pain shoot up her leg and she fell hard onto the floor. The four of them instinctively moved to help her. She snapped, "DON'T TOUCH ME!". Lindsey could not watch and closed her eyes and turned her head away. Rach-El stood there motionless as tears welled up in her eyes. Michael watched his wife struggling as tears rolled down his face. His thoughts were of her pain and he could not save her from it. He felt useless.

Jonathan waited for a moment. He watched her as she focused on her excruciating pain. He knew she was willing it away. He bent down to her and extended his open right hand and simply said, "Princess." Anastasia looked up at his hand and locked eyes with him. She slowly put just her fingertips in his hand. She positioned herself and stood up, fighting through searing pain. The room was dead silent. Anastasia looked deeply at Jonathan as she stood there. She was finally about to say something when Jonathan bowed slightly and lifted their hands toward Michael. Michael moved a step toward them and he took both of her hands in his. They didn't speak or communicate in the link. Michael picked her up in his arms and held her tight. He turned toward the door and walked downstairs. Lindsey and Rach-El held hands and watched as Jonathan followed closely behind them. Rach-El finally said, "What just happened?" Lindsey "I have no idea." The two women left to go to the parade.

Michael immediately saw the golf cart that he asked to have a leg rest and the addition on the back, so her wheelchair could easily be driven on and off. He sat her inside and positioned her leg so she would be comfortable. Her wheelchair had already been charged and was on the back. Jonathan, Lindsey and Rach-El got into the back and they drove the scenic route down the beach to the grandstand. Michael said in the link, "You are beautiful." She replied, "I'm a monster."

Michael took Anastasia's hand and squeezed it. She took a deep breath and said out loud, "I'm going to need help with the customs of the day, but I would hate to think that I am keeping any of you from enjoying the day. Rach-El, where is Bjorn? And Lindsey, am I to understand that Erik is an excellent rider? And Jonathan...(She had to pause so her voice wouldn't crack) Any word from Lucy?" Rach-El was relieved that the awkward silence was broken. "Bjorn will be working during the parade, but I'll be meeting him back at the house." Lindsey blushed slightly, "How did you know about Erik? We're going to go riding tomorrow, but for today he asked to meet up with me after the parade." Jonathan didn't respond for a few minutes. Anastasia's heart was almost too heavy for her to bear. He finally said, "I hope Lucy comes, but no one knows for sure."

Mark was downstairs waiting for Ailbe. Ailbe wanted to be early so

she didn't miss a moment. She shook off the feelings about linking with
Jonathan this morning and was now excited to party. Ailbe arrived, and
Mark extended his elbow. "Your chariot awaits milady." Ailbe laughed.
"Is this the fastest golf cart?" Mark was her transporter after all. "I tricked
it out myself." As Ailbe stepped in she said, "Good boy" and they raced
down the scenic route on their way to the grandstand. Ruth and Se'ighin
also made their way to the grandstand.

Every family member greeted everyone they saw with genuine ges-
tures and words of excitement that they could attend. Everything was in
place. Everyone from the Mayor to Tom and Rick, were already in their
seats when Michael arrived at the grandstand. He lifted Anastasia out of
the golf cart and carried her up the stairs. He thought, "Note to self. She
feels much lighter. Check to see if she is eating enough." Anastasia saw
Tom and Rick sitting in the back row. "My saviors!" She struggled out of
Michael's tight grip, put her arms out, and leaned to hug them. The two
men sheepishly stepped toward them and hugged her. Tom said, "It is
so great to see you. The first time we saw you, you didn't look so good."
Rick chimed in, "I didn't think you would know who we were. We tried
a few times to come in and see you, but we couldn't get in." Anastasia
gasped, "That's horrible! I am truly sorry. It would have been my honor
to see you both there, and I recognized you from the photos Michael
showed me in the news papers. I wouldn't have survived without you."
And as if she had a memory, she lifted her arm and said, "Kneel" in
strong sounding regal voice. Michael pulled her in closer to him and
said to the very confused looking men. "She said 'kneale' k.n.e.a.l.e,
In Greek it means I'm forever in your debt." Tom and Rick both said
"Oh..ok." Tom said, "We lean something new every day." She hugged
both men again. "Please sit closer to me. I won't be able to talk to you
much afterwards, so I want to feel you as much as I can." The two men
smiled and sat in the two chairs directly behind her." Michael smiled,
"Gentleman, we will talk more later, but Great-Grandmother is about
to be seated." Michael assisted Anastasia into her seat and positioned
her leg until she was comfortable. He sat next to her and in the link,
"Well that was a little odd." She nodded. "It was like another flash of a

memory." Michael "We will explore that later. Today is for fun and junk food." Anastasia "I could use a lot of that."

The parade was spectacular. Several times, the singers brought Anastasia to her feet (with Michael's assistance) with excitement. Ruth was beaming with pride. Jonathan was seated right behind Michael. He was distracted and hoping to see Lucy. As the parade was nearing the end, he assumed she stayed home to care for her parents. He could have arranged help for them, but maybe it was not meant to be. When the last group of marchers was done, Ruth stood to say a few words of gratitude for the entire community for their continued love and support. She introduced everyone who was seated in the grandstand to cheers after each name, leaving Anastasia for last.

Ruth "And now I want to formally introduce you to Anastasia. Many of you know the tragedy that brought her to us and the struggle to save her life, but that is her story to tell. Without further ado… Anastasia Reale." The crowd erupted in cheers as Anastasia fought to stand up. Michael reached to help her but she clearly needed to do this on her own. She painfully made her way to the microphone which increased the crowd's enthusiastic yells, whistles, clapping, and calling out encouraging words. She looked around at the crowd. A tidal wave of love overwhelmed her. She felt lightheaded and pitched forward slightly but caught herself. Michael thought, "She remembers something!" As she tried to focus on the faces in the crowd, she did.

A few of her memories flashed into her head. She remembered feeling the weight of responsibility. She wanted to run, but she knew she had a duty and she always performed her duties very well. She stood up straight and smiled brightly. "I stand here only because of the compassion and bravery of two men. Tom and Rick are my true heroes. They are not trained professionals, they are just simply kind men. They will forever have my loyalty. To the medical staff, you have my deepest appreciation. And special thank you to my friend Lucy, you have my respect. I love you all very much and I look forward to getting to know each of you better." She waved at the crowd and fell backwards into Michael's arms. Everyone gave a collected gasp. Ruth quickly began speaking as Michael carried her off the grandstand and into the golf cart. Ruth "She is fine everyone, she is a little tired and slipped. The party is in full swing at the compound, so please everyone, Enjoy!" Mark had Ailbe in the golf cart in a second and was heading down the beach path toward the house. Ruth and Se'ighin were a second behind them.

Michael was in full protector mode. He laid her across the front seat of the golf cart and headed full speed toward the house. Michael felt he could have run faster than the golf cart. She had her head in his lap. She was weak but awake. "I'm fine, really. Slow down."

Michael "No, you almost passed out again. We are going home and resting."

Anastasia "No, I just had a memory. Well, memories of back home."

Michael "Home? Where is home? Do you remember where you have been?"

Anastasia "My original home. Where I was born."

Jonathan wanted to go with Michael, but as Mark was getting Ailbe into the golf cart, she linked with him. "No, stay here and look for Lucy." She broke the link and was gone. He wasn't sure if she saw Lucy or not. All the protectors were focused on their jobs, so Jonathan was focused on his, to find Lucy if she was here. He asked himself, "Did Anastasia just mention her in that speech. So many people were involved in her care and she mentioned her???" He was slightly agitated that so many people kept approaching him to talk, but he knew it was a family duty to always be cordial.

Then he heard her familiar voice. His world stopped when he turned around and saw her.

Jonathan "Lucy, I'm so glad you could make it!" he said it with a little more enthusiasm than he wanted.

Lucy "What happened to your face!? Are you ok? Are you in pain?"

Jonathan "Oh, just a little mascara accident. Note to self...Always buy waterproof."

Lucy "Well, if you don't want to talk about it, then I respect that, but as far as me being here, I couldn't say no after you contacted my parents, now could I?"

Jonathan "I didn't contact your parents. I promise. I don't know what you are talking about."

Lucy "Really? Well someone did."

Jonathan "I really don't know what to say. How were your parents contacted?"

Lucy "I'm not really sure I believe you... But I got this letter (She pulled out a bright yellow envelope from her purse.) in the mail. (She took out the letter.) It says that due to my exceptional grades, the Reale scholarship has awarded a full tuition reimbursement and continued scholarship. My parents were speechless, and then...they received this letter. (She pulled out another envelope from her purse and took out a handwritten note.)

Dear Mr. and Mrs. Vans,

It would give me great delight if you would grant me the honor of accepting these 2 paramedics and wheelchairs to assist you during your day with us at the parade and the following party at our home on July 4th.

Sincerely,

Ruth Reale

Jonathan "Um... That is my grandmother. I had nothing to do with that. I swear. That had to come from Anastasia. As far as the scholarship, the family reviews all of the local schools and votes on those. I'm not on that committee. This could have been voted on last year."

Lucy "Very coincidental don't you think?"

Jonathan "Fate is funny that way. Are your parents here? (Trying very hard to change the subject.) I would love to take credit for all of this." They both laughed.

Lucy "They're over there, running people over with the motorized wheelchairs." They walked over and Jonathan extended his hand to her father and introduced himself, then to her mother.

Jonathan "Mr. and Mrs. Vans. Nice to meet you both. I trust you are enjoying this beautiful day."

Mrs. Vans "Nice to meet you too. Lucy said that you set all this up."

Jonathan "No, I wish I could take the credit, but like I explained to Lucy, my family is huge. I have very little to do with party planning or scholarships. My grandmother wanted today to be accessible to everyone, especially now with our new understanding of disabilities. Anastasia gave my grandmother a list of everyone she wanted here the most, and when Grandmother found out how many people could not attend due to certain restrictions, she rented every available wheelchair. She is calling this July 4th Freedom and Independence."

Mr. Vans "Well Mrs. Vans and I are gonna make the most of today. We can't get out much. Lucy tries, but she is only one girl and pretty busy."

Jonathan "I'm thrilled that you both accepted. Can I steal Lucy for the day? We have so many activities planned."

Lucy "No, I really need to stay with my parents."

Mrs. Vans "Ridiculous Lucy! You go and have fun for once. We're fine. We have these two. (She pointed at the paramedics standing less than a foot behind them.) They don't speak English very well, but they are so sweet."

Jonathan looked up and saw them for the first time. They both smiled. One said, "We are new to the area. We are here from Spain to finish school." Jonathan felt the link and said, "Hello cousins. Thank you." They both smiled. The other said in the link, "We will treat them like family. Nothing will go wrong."

Mr. Vans "See Lucy, we are just fine. Now we want you to go and have a good time. You'll just hold us back. Now GO." He turned on the power button on his wheelchair, hit the forward button as Mrs. Vans sped passed him laughing. "Come on. I'll race you." And they were off down the street as the two paramedics (cousins) jogged after them. Lucy was shocked and turned to Jonathan. "Well, I guess you're stuck with me." Jonathan smiled "Aww poor me. This is going to be my worst day ever." Jonathan tried to take her hand to lead her across the street, she looked down and put the two letters back into her purse and said, "Ok, lead the way. I've never been here before." Jonathan crossed the street and headed back to the grandstand. The golf carts were parked behind it. "Good, then I can give you the scenic tour on our way to the main house."

Michael drove to a side door of the main house. He walked around to pick her up. "Please don't argue with me. I want you to rest." Anastasia "I'm fine, really. I was just overwhelmed for a second. I think I need to see Ailbe and Ruth." She linked them in with her and Michael, "I've remembered something." Ailbe "Later Princess. Our duty right now is to make sure that everyone has a great time and forget any troubles for a little while." Ruth "It seems the more you relax, the stronger your memories are. I'm sure there will be several triggers today. We will see you later and in private. I don't want to rush this." Anastasia felt at ease. "You are both right." Michael was still in protector mode. "NO! Anastasia is going back to our room. I want protectors at the door NOW." Ruth "Do not make me angry. You will not like me when I am angry. Everyone here is safe. Anastasia is fine but she does need frequent rests. Now have a drink, relax, and enjoy." Ruth and Ailbe ended their link. Michael "Despite my wanting to shield you from all of this, I have to trust my elders. So instead of pouting, I have to go and have a good time." Anastasia kissed him on the cheek. "Good. Now if this party is really for me, then I'm going to have fun." She motioned for her wheelchair, which he brought to her side and helped her into. Once she was comfortable she said, "Now take me to get the best margarita in town." as she took off at full speed.

Ruth linked to the family Chaplain Peter to pray over the food. Peter turned on his microphone. "May I have your attention please. The food is ready so I'd like to take a moment." Everyone stopped what they were doing and in their own way was open to receive. Peter "Whatever you call your higher power, Let us pray. Dear God, we honor your presence in every person that will cross into our home. Bless the food and drink and keep everyone safe. Oh, and if you have time, come on down and have a rhum ball. Amen." Everyone repeated, "Amen." Peter "Let the party begin."

Jonathan drove the golf cart down the beach road back to the main house. The beach looked inviting and calm. Lucy was mesmerized. "This is just so beautiful. I forget the world is more than studying and work sometimes. Just this alone is all I would need to make today perfect." Jonathan looked at her. There was sadness in her eyes that he wanted to take away, even just for a day. They drove down miles of beach not talking much until they reached the main gates of the compound. Lucy said, "Your family owns all of this? That is crazy." Jonathan drove to the front door. Lucy was amazed at the enormous size of the house but felt it was warm and inviting. Jonathan said, "Let me take you around a bit." Lucy wanted to see more but felt that it was inappropriate for them to be alone for too much longer. Jonathan drove her around, showing her the compound. Lucy said, "It's huge in here. It's an entire city in here." Jonathan laughed, "Yea, kind of. The small houses are for family members that don't want to be so close to everyone. Privacy around here is as much or as little as everyone wants. Any family member is welcome to live here."

Lucy "For Free?"

Jonathan "Family would never pay rent. It's all of ours. We all know that."

Lucy "What happens when someone dies?" Do they have a will? Who gets what?

Jonathan "I guess when you look at it that way, it sounds weird, but the family just absorbs it and goes on. When my great-grandmother Ailbe dies, things she wants people to have will have already been told. Like jewelry for the girls, but the property just goes on."

Lucy "So no fighting about who gets what ring, and who gets what watch?"

Jonathan "No. most of that stuff is just around somewhere. If someone wants to wear a certain piece, they just ask. But I don't think anyone feels it is theirs. I mean a wedding ring or something, but it's just not a big deal around here."

Lucy "Wow. That sounds like Utopia. No fighting. I wish my family was like that. My mom's family is super greedy. They all fight over things. My dad's side is more about people. You couldn't tell from meeting him today, but he is just all about family. After the accident, no one came around to help us. He was really hurt. So we moved away from everyone and just focused on our lives. I had to get back into school and make a better life for us."

Jonathan "That must be hard that it's all on you."

Lucy "I would do anything for my parents. They are amazing people. My dad taught me that things just way you down. So when you don't need much, it's easy to get by on what you have." Jonathan had an overwhelming desire to take care of her.

Lucy "We are the only Hindu in the area, but my dad has always followed his traditions. Once I'm done with school and start working, I want to open a small Hindu temple."

Jonathan "Really? I think that's great. I was just in Nepal. I saw some of the most beautiful temples."

Lucy "Wow. I bet that was amazing. I've always wanted to go to Nepal. My father's side is from there, he still has family there, but he doesn't know anything about them."

Jonathan "Then I will take you."

Lucy laughed. "I bet you say that to all the girls."

Jonathan "No... I don't mean to sound like a crazy guy in a bar giving you a one line type thing. I'm serious. For your graduation. I promise to take you to Nepal. When we go inside, I will set it up. Better yet, you and your parents go. I don't want you to think that I would ever attach strings to it." Lucy looked at him. From the first moment she met him at the hospital she felt something special about him. Not because he was from a rich family, but because he obviously loved and is devoted to his family. Lucy didn't see much of that in this world. And now he seemed to be genuinely interested in what she was saying. She tried to bring some levity back into there conversation. "Stop it. This conversation is getting too heavy for me. I have one day to cut loose and you promised me a party. So take me to the nearest dance floor." Jonathan smiled. "I did promise you a party and I know that Anastasia wanted to say hello." He drove to the main house but up to the side private entrance. They left the cart there and walked through the house to the back yard. Lucy stood there looking around at an enormous amount of people and the huge space, "I've seen pictures of this place before, but geez. I'm standing here and I can't believe how big this place is!"

All of a sudden, Lucy felt herself being swung around out of control. She felt arms around her body like a vice grip. She was about to punch her way out of the hold when she heard a woman's voice. "LUCY? You must be Lucy. It is wonderful that you made it!" Jonathan and several other people who witnessed the event were shocked. Jonathan cleared his throat, "Grandmother. May I introduce you to Lucy. Lucy, this is my grandmother Mrs. Ruth Reale." Lucy knew her by reputation and by the name on the letter. "Oh, Mrs. Reale, I…" Ruth cut her off. "Stop with the formalities. You call me Ruth and here comes my mother." Lucy "I…I…I could never be so disrespectful as to call one of my elders by their first names." Ailbe walked up with her arms wide open. "Oh, this must be Lucy. I have heard so many wonderful things about you dear." She hugged Lucy like she knew her forever. Ailbe's hug was warm and sincere. Lucy never wanted that hug to end. Lucy asked, "You heard about me?" Ailbe was still holding her by the shoulders. "Oh my sweet girl, this family has no secrets. What you did for our Anastasia has made you a bit of a celebrity around here." Lucy stuttered a bit. "It is nice to meet you too Mrs….." Ailbe looked her square in the eyes. "You must call me Ailbe." Jonathan almost fell over. He has never heard someone outside the closest of family and friends call them Ruth or Ailbe and even that was less than a handful of people that he could ever remember. Ruth took Lucy by the hand. "The party has been in full swing for over an hour and you don't have a drink in your hand or food stains on your shirt yet. UNACCEPTABLE!" Ailbe took her by the other hand and they walked her to the closest bar. Ailbe yelled, "SHOTS! Who wants to do shots with us?"

Jonathan was still standing where they left him. Michael stepped up next to him as Anastasia rolled passed them yelling, "I DO! Make way for the injured lady." Michael whispered to Jonathan. "I need to get her a cow bell." As they watched her bump into several people trying to make her way over to the bar shouting. "LUCY!" Lucy turned around and saw Anastasia. Lucy gave her a big hug and kiss on the cheek. "You look fantastic. I was worried about you when I saw you at the parade. I thought you passed out." Anastasia was so excited to see her. "No, just kind of slipped. It was a big crowd and I felt overwhelmed." Malachi was shouting out, "How many for tequila shots?!" About twenty people made their way over to the bar. Malachi set up a line shot glasses each with a mini salt shaker and a lime wedge across the top. He poured Partida Elegante tequila into the glasses. He rang a large brass bell and shouted, "Lucy gets the Partida

Spirit Bird charm!" Ailbe shouted, "On my count salt, shot, lime...1-2-3"
Everyone licked the back of their hand, did the shot and bit the lime wedge.
Ruth was first to slam down her shot glass and yelled, "One more time!"
Malachi started to repeat the routine. Michael and Jonathan both stood
there with their mouths open in disbelief of what they were watching.

Michael "What are we looking at?"

Jonathan "It has to be dream, right? We are sleeping and this is not
real.....is it?"

Michael "We have lost them to Bangkok."

Jonathan "We lost them to tequila."

The two cousins grabbed chairs and sat there watching. Jonathan had
seen Ailbe dancing and drinking in Nepal, but nothing like this. Their
grandmother was the most reserved, proper and respected woman on
the planet and their great-grandmother was a sarcastic second. Michael
suddenly grabbed Jonathan's arm. "Oh My God! Now they are dancing!"
Se'ighin found his way over to his wife as Ailbe grabbed Rick. Lucy took
Anastasia by the hand and the two of them were swinging their arms and
turning Anastasia in circles. Jonathan said, "I need to marry that girl."
Michael nodded in agreement but was too scared to look away for fear that
he would miss every detail of what he was watching.

Rach-El and Lindsey came up behind them and asked, "Wanna
dance?" Jonathan asked, "Are you seeing this too?" Lindsey laughed, "Yes,
and everyone but you two bumps on a log are having a great time." Michael
felt slightly ashamed for staring at them. "Well, I guess if we can't lock
them up and keep them safe. Then we have to join them." Michael jumped
up and took Lindsey by the hand. "Shall we show these fools what real
dancing looks like?" Lindsey smiled. "I thought you would never ask." And
they hit the dance floor. Rach-El looked at Jonathan. "Well cuz, that just
leaves you not having fun. Shall we show them how we do this?" Jonathan
"My face hurts, how about shots first?" Rach-El "And THAT is why you
are my favorite cousin." There were two shots of tequila left on the bar.
They did the shots and walked onto the dance floor. Jonathan totally forgot
about his face.

Half hour later, Jonathan saw Bjorn out of the corner of his eye looking at them. He said to Rach-El, "I think you have an admirer." Rach-El smiled and grabbed his arm. "I have the worst crush! Am I acting like a school girl? I think Great-Grandmother is playing match-maker." Jonathan "I need a break, you young kids have way too much energy for me." She laughed, "I'm two years younger than you old man!" She kissed him on the cheek. "Thank you." And she walked toward Bjorn. "You look bored." Bjorn "No, I could watch you have fun all day." She laughed in her best flirtatious way possible. "Would you like to dance?" Bjorn was suddenly very awkward. "Um… I really never learned how." That was all Rach-El needed to hear. "Then it is your lucky day. I am a great but patient teacher." And the two of them headed for the dance floor. Michael and Lindsey were mid-flip when Erik broke in and asked Lindsey to dance. Michael was thrilled. He made his way back over to Jonathan and they pretended to share oxygen.

Jonathan finally asked, "So let me ask you about Lucy. Did you know about scholarship and the two Azili acting as paramedics?"

Michael "They are paramedics. They came from Spain to help out. Most of their protectors have a medical background if someone gets hurt. I had Malachi do a little bit more digging. She checks out. I mean really clean. She is exactly what she says she is. A hard working girl taking care of her parents. I don't think she's even been on a date since she started school. That car accident was bad. They both have a lot of nerve damage. They can walk but not far and not very well. I linked everything to Great-Grandmother and she just said to leave everything else up to her. I guess she got Grandmother involved and the two of them had some good luck sent their way. Even asked Ace to wire one of the houses on the compound. Great-grandmother insisted that everything be wheelchair accessible and those wheelchairs are a gift from Anastasia."

Jonathan "Wait… Grandmother? Our Grandmother? Ruth Reale is going to offer for them to live here?!? What is happening?"

Michael "You need to talk to Great-Grandmother. She will explain everything."

Jonathan "Wait….." Jonathan started to connect some dots.

Michael "Before your head explodes. Yes, she is related to the old man in Nepal."

Jonathan was trying to figure it all out when Lucy came up to them with a drink in each hand and one she was biting on the rim of the cup. She handed one to Michael and one to Jonathan and she took the one out of her mouth. "Here, you both look like you need these." Lucy was clearly tipsy but having a great time. "I need to check on my parents. Have either of you seen them?" Anastasia wheeled up. She was hot and sweaty and reached for Michael's drink. Michael pulled it away from her hand. "Hey, this one is mine." Lucy "Here you can share mine." Anastasia snapped and pulled up her sunglasses slightly. "Is your's a margarita?" Lucy and Anastasia burst out hysterically laughing. Michael linked to Jonathan. "That must be an inside joke." Lucy took a deep breath." Ok, now I need to go find my parents." Jonathan could see she was getting nervous. "Come on, We'll go find them." They walked through the house. Jonathan linked to the protectors "Anyone seen Lucy's parents?" The response was, "In the parlor for massages." Jonathan suggested, "Let's check the parlor. We turned it into a spa for the day for anyone disabled to get manicure, pedicure, haircuts, and massages." Lucy thought that was the sweetest idea and hoped her mother was up there to enjoy that. They walked in and looked around. They didn't see them. Lucy asked, "Excuse me. Has anyone seen Mr. or Mrs. Vans?" One of his cousins said, "Oh, they are in their room getting a couple's massage." Lucy laughed out loud. "A couple's massage? Never, no way. Not my parents. Wait… their room?" Lucy seemed to want to panic. Jonathan opened a link to whoever he could. "Ok. What room is their room? Lucy is about to panic." Ailbe responded laughing. "My wing." Jonathan's eyes went wide. Lucy asked, "Are you gonna puke" as she tried to relax and take another sip of her drink. Jonathan was still confused when he said, "No, I think they must be in one of the private rooms." Lucy shot back, "They would never!" Jonathan laughed. "I didn't mean like they snuck into a room. I think my great-grandmother must have allowed them to rest in one of her rooms." Lucy felt embarrassed that she snapped at him. "Oh, sorry, but now I really need to find them."

Jonathan and Lucy made the long walk across the house. They came to a private elevator. Jonathan put his hand on a red screen and the door opened. A computer generated voice began, "Jonathan Protector. Please identify your guest." Jonathan "Lucy Vans." The elevator went up to the second floor. The door opened and Lucy was overwhelmed by the opulence. The floors were pink and white marble. Large carved pillars that were twenty feet tall made of white marble. Large veins of clear quartz seemed to create its own light. The ceiling was painted with an entire scene of beautiful greenish orange grass with herds of animals that she had never seen before, running over hills toward a castle. The air was fresh and smelled like tropical plants and jasmine in the breeze. She said, "Wow. This is unreal. This place reminds me of what I would think that Mount Olympus must look like."

Jonathan loved how she was taking it all in. Like she was trying to remember every detail. "This area is strictly off limits. Family doesn't even come up here. This is Great-Grandmother's private part of the house. When she dies, my grandmother will have her office up here." Lucy felt amazingly sober. "My parents have never been in a place like this. They must be so uncomfortable. I should get them home." She walked down the hall to where she saw the two paramedics sitting in chairs eating. "Sorry to interrupt you while you're eating, but could you please tell me where my parents are?" One of the paramedics smiled. "They are in with the massage therapists getting a couple's massage." Lucy felt like something was wrong. She knew her parents would never agree to something like that. She pushed open the door with a loud 'bang'.

Mr. and Mrs. Vans were both laying face down on massage tables with a small table between them with a bottle champagne and strawberries on it. Mrs. Vans popped up her head. "Good God girl! You scared me." Lucy asked, "What are you doing?" Mr. Vans didn't move. "What does it look like we are doing?" Mrs. Vans was still looking at Lucy. "Where are your manners? You don't barge in a room like that." Lucy's face was turning red. "I couldn't find you and then I thought that all of this might be making you uncomfortable. I...I...I'm sorry." Mr. Vans "Ailbe said to come up here for a massage and take a nap if we were tired." Lucy "I just got worried." Mrs. Vans "Worried? About us? We just wanted to stay out of the way so you could have a good time for once. Ailbe said that the family is having a private dinner and invited us to be there." Jonathan "Lucy, they are in good hands here." He turned to her parents, "You guys enjoy the massages and I'm sorry for scaring Lucy. The paramedics have my personal cell number and they will text me every ten minutes to let us know where you guys are. Is everyone ok with that plan?" Lucy, both her parents and the paramedics nodded in agreement.

Jonathan took Lucy by the hand and they walked back to the elevator. Lucy was looking down at her feet. "I'm so embarrassed, I should really just go home." Jonathan "I will arrange a car to take you home if that is what you want, just know that you have nothing to be embarrassed about. My family does not open up very easily and they all seem to feel the same way about you that I do. We're all comfortable around you and your parents. You have impressed the unimpressable." They both laughed. "This is how my family shows true appreciation, by accepting people for who they really are." Lucy tried to smile. "Let's just go back to the party. I really need to get the visual of my naked parent drinking champagne and getting massages out of my head."

Rach-El and Bjorn were inseparable the rest of the night. They were heard laughing and seen dancing and drinking well into the night.

Lindsey and Erik were seen headed down to the stables. Steven stayed his distance, but kept an eye on his little sister. Not that he didn't trust either one of them. He is a protector and regardless of the festivities tonight, he knew that a war was coming.

Michael had gotten very frustrated with Anastasia's wheelchair, so he picked her up to dance and had not set her back down in hours. They laughed and drank and danced as if they were the only two people within a hundred miles. Ruth looked at her love Se'ighin. "This is exactly what everyone needed. We have done a good job with our family. I can't imagine how our lives are going to change soon." She started to tear up. Se'ighin took her hand and put it to his chest. "My heart beats for you and our beautiful family. I will do whatever it takes to keep all of us safe." He kissed her passionately. Ailbe had a list of people that she contacted for the private dinner. She stood behind Ruth and Se'ighin and coughed softly until they noticed her. "What an example you two set for the young people. Get a room will you." She giggled as she sat down and said to Ruth. "Almost time for dinner." Ruth linked to the protectors to gather the guests for the private dinner. As the select group was gathered, Ruth linked to Jonathan to have Lucy stop by and see her parents.

Once the select group was all seated. Ailbe stood and nodded for the champagne to be poured for a toast. Several bottles of Perrier-Jouet Rose Belle Epoque was poured and set in ice buckets around the table. She cleared her throat. "Dear friends. I want to personally thank each of you for your heroism in saving the life of our beloved Anastasia." She went on to thank everyone by name and why she selected this eclectic group and the roll that each person played in her recovery. "Now lift your glass... To Anastasia. May her life be long and happy." Everyone took a sip of champagne.

Dinner was simple but elegant. It was more for intimate conversation than a meal. But as a desert cart went around the table, Arden stood up. All eyes focused on him as he tenderly made his way around the room personally thanking everyone and informed them that a token of gratitude was in an envelope under their charger plate, and then he returned to his seat. Ailbe finished her desert, stood up and announced, "The night is for the young. Please feel free to enjoy the rest of evening. We have plenty more surprises in store for everyone, but these 104 year old bones are feeling the effects of having a very good time. Good night." She turned and left without assistance.

Jonathan arrived with Lucy to see her parents. "Mom, Dad, You guys look great!" Mrs. Vans had a new hairstyle and Mr. Vans had a close shave and hair trim. Ailbe had guessed their sizes for dinner clothes for both of them. "Ailbe said we could spend the night if we wanted. We can relax and let you have the whole weekend off."

Lucy "The whole weekend? We can't impose on them the rest of the weekend."

Ruth cleared her throat. "I will not allow rudeness in my home."

Lucy "See! You guys are being rude!"

Ruth "Not them dear. You."

Lucy "Me?" she was genuinely shocked

Ruth "Yes dear, You. Maybe you don't realize that loyalty in this family is the strongest connection we have. You stepped up and protected my family, regardless of your own position. You did the right thing. We will never forget that. You are now and will always be a proven loyal friend to this family. Any Reale home, is your home." Ruth bowed slightly."

Lucy "I'm sorry if I insulted you. I don't accept that I did anything to deserve that level of gratitude. So I will just say thank you for your kindness towards my parents. They deserve your generosity."

Ruth smiled and kissed her on the cheek. Ruth then spoke to get the attention of the room. Ruth said, "My mother is much more dramatic than I am. I will just quietly say thank you all and good night." Se'ighin took a long stem rose out of the vase in front of him and bit down on the stem and stood next to Ruth. He grabbed his wife by the waist, almost aggressively. Tango Santa Maria blasted out of the speaker and they danced the seductive Argentine Tango for several minutes before they tango-ed out the door. She looked over her shoulder into the dinning room. "Don't wait up...." and they were gone.

As the dining room was empting out, most people were heading back outside to the party firmly grasping their envelope. Lucy asked, "What is it?" Mrs. Vans "I don't know. They gave it to us after desert." Lucy "I want to know, but I'm afraid it's something that we could never accept." Ailbe linked to Jonathan. "I have to explain what I showed you earlier." She added to what she linked him this morning. He could feel his great-grandmother's intense shame that she has refused to discuss with anyone, and the unthinkable blessing that she asked from the ancestors. Jonathan's head was pounding again. There are reasons why elders don't link a lot of information to the younger family members. Their brains can't handle it. But Ailbe had to risk it. Jonathan was the only one who could make them understand. Jonathan stumbled backwards as Lucy caught him. "Paramedic!" She called out as the two paramedics ran to his side. Several family members who were also in the room to serve the guests, rushed to his side. Jonathan began to protest, "I'm fine, just Malachi makes really strong drinks. Dr. McKay was one of the few in the small group and insisted he allow the paramedics to check his vitals. "OK, but I already feel better." He linked to the protectors who were all in a full sprint to get to his side. "I'm fine. Ailbe linked some information. It was like a brain freeze, but I'm good!" They all responded with a laugh and went back to what they were doing. The paramedics reassured Dr. McKay that his vital signs were normal, there were no signs of infection of the two forehead lacerations, but they were not going to touch his nose. Dr. McKay was satisfied for now but added, "I would still like to see you when I see Anastasia tomorrow." Jonathan agreed and Dr. McKay left to go back to the party. Jonathan smiled at Lucy, "See, I knew you cared about me." Lucy laughed, "I just think you need someone to look after you." He pulled her close and kissed her on top of the head. She smiled. She had been developing feelings for him all day long, but her heart had been so guarded for so long... she told herself several times, 'Stop it Lucy! You have too much baggage. He just wants to get in your pants.'

Mr. and Mrs. Vans opened their envelope together. It was a small card that simply read, *"Please follow Jonathan"*. Lucy felt a wave of anger as if she was right. "What the hell is this? Now I follow you to your room? You are really fucked up! And to think that I was this close to falling for your stupid charm!" She ripped off the Partida Spirit Bird charm (From the tequila bottle) and threw it at him. "Take that to your rape room!" She turned toward the paramedics and yelled, "Get us out of here please." She started walking toward the front door wiping away tears as she started to run. The memories of the night she was attacked by a childhood friend came flooding back. Jonathan looked at her parents. "I swear, she's wrong. I didn't plan any of this. I just found out...." Mrs. Vans cut him off. "Why are you explaining it to us? Go, go talk to her." Jonathan starting running after her and Mr. and Mrs. Van slowly followed.

"Lucy! Wait! Please stop!" Jonathan was almost out of breath. He was still lightheaded from his link with Ailbe, and now his face was throbbing again. Lucy ran out the front door and there was Michael and Anastasia in a golf cart. Anastasia looked at her and felt her pain and struggled to stand up. Lucy fell into her arms crying. The two women didn't talk. Anastasia just held Lucy. Both women just felt safe being with each other. Michael watched his wife and felt he could never love her more than he did right now. As he stood there, he became aware that the pain in his back had moved down the back of his legs. He figured that dancing and partying for the past few hours was the cause, and he was gonna be sore tomorrow. The thought of Charlotte missing the party popped into his head. "Why am I thinking of Charlotte? I hope she's ok. I need to talk to her soon." Jonathan came running out of the house. He stopped when he saw Anastasia and Lucy. He sat down on the steps to catch his breath. Michael walked over and sat by his side. Both men wanted to do something, to say something that would make this better. Jonathan linked to Michael. "She thinks I have a rape room! What man would ever… Why would she ever think…" then he understood. Michael responded, "No man ever would… She wasn't hurt by a man, she was hurt by a coward." Jonathan thought of all the times he grabbed for her or touched her without thinking. "What do I do now? Will you assign her a protector for me?" Michael asked, "Aren't you a protector?" Jonathan was in no mood for jokes. He felt he couldn't be happy again after hurting her and he broke the link. Mr. and Mrs. Vans rolled out the front door.

Lucy stopped crying and looked at Anastasia. "I'm sorry." Anastasia "Sorry about what?" Lucy wanted to talk about anything else. "I've been meaning to tell you all night that I think your outfit is brilliantly hideous." The two women started to laugh. Anastasia "Can I tell you a very well known fact? But it hides a tiny little secret." Lucy was wiping her face and trying to look somewhat presentable. She noticed several people walking around and felt embarrassed. "About what?" Anastasia smiled, "The fact that my Jonathan loves to flirt with strong independent women, but has secretly only fallen in love once." Jonathan linked to Michael. "What is she doing!" Michael responded, "I have no idea but I bet it is going to be amazing to watch." Lucy suddenly felt sad for Jonathan. "What happened to her?" Anastasia leaned in and whispered in her ear. "She got scared and ran away from him before she could find out what an amazing man he is, because the last boy she trusted hurt her very badly." Lucy was speechless. She turned around and saw her parents holding hands and Michael and Jonathan sitting on the steps. Anastasia "Did he tell you how he got injured?" Lucy was fighting back tears. "No, he just made a joke about mascara." She laughed remembering it was actually funny. Anastasia said,

"I felt so afraid yesterday that I escaped to my safe place. The doctor said I passed out. But Jonathan knew better. He knew I ran away and I might never find my way back again. So he stood at my head and talked in my ear. He guided me back. As I woke up, I didn't know where I was. I though I was being cut again, I heard him telling me to fight. So...I fought and I fought hard... Jonathan never moved." Anastasia looked over at Jonathan but continued to talk to Lucy. "He never even made a sound. He just... stayed with me. Michael and I didn't even know I hurt him."

Anastasia wanted to tell her more, but that was Jonathan's story to tell. Lucy turned back and looked into her eyes. She saw the way Anastasia was looking at him. "Do you love him?" Anastasia didn't take her eyes off Jonathan as she smiled and answered, "Yes I do. Very much so... not as my bond, but if I had to choose a life to be sent to the ancestors, Michael or Jonathan, I would freely surrender mine. Michael and Jonathan sat there numb and speechless. Mr. and Mrs. Vans silently wept.

Lucy walked to her parents and gave them a quick hug and turned to walk towards Jonathan. Michael stood up and went to Anastasia. He was in awe of his wife. "I don't know what to say." He picked her up and held her head close to his heart. "I could imagine that you would have been the most powerful Queen in all of our history." Anastasia wished she could remember her life, but she loved this life. She kissed him softly but with enough passion to light up a galaxy. "It is the highest honor for me to be your Queen."

Lucy sat down next to Jonathan. "I don't know how to apologize. I had no right... I can stay calm and stick up for everyone else, but not for myself. I go straight to defense and rage." Jonathan was now very aware of where his body was and what he considered a friendly touch could be a trigger for someone else. "I need to work on what I did to trigger your feeling that caused you to be defensive and angry. There is a trauma therapist, Dr. Besler, coming to see Anastasia tomorrow. I'm gonna talk to him about how I can be a better educated man." Lucy threw her arms around his neck.

Mr. Vans watched his daughter and felt for the first time in years that she would be ok. He took a deep breath. "Is this a party or a therapy session?" Everyone was glad that he broke the tension. Jonathan stood up and said, "I have something to show all of you. Lucy you could ride with Anastasia or take your own cart. Mr. and Mrs. Vans, your batteries were charged up while you were getting massages. If everyone would please follow me, we are running a few minutes late. Lucy got into the golf cart with Jonathan and sat close. Jonathan smiled. "I would never hurt you." She kissed his cheek with a quick peck. "I think I knew that... I have walls..." He said, "And I have a lot to learn." And they headed down the street.

Mr. and Mrs. Vans kept close so Jonathan could point out different places that they were passing. Mrs. Vans asked, "Is this all one piece of property? This is an entire city in here." Jonathan laughed. "Yes it is, And it's all family." Mr. Vans "Wait... So everyone who lives in here is all the Reale family? How many people live here?" Michael called out, "We have family all over, but we are the biggest compound. Almost two hundred people live in the main house and well over four-thousand live out here." Mrs. Vans "Are you guys a creepy cult?" Jonathan laughed and swerved the golf cart. "No, nothing that that at all. We're more like a race of people that fled here. Ya know, Safety in numbers." Mr. and Mrs. Vans both laughed harder than they expected to. Jonathan stopped. "And...We are here." Lucy looked around. "Here? Where?"

Ace opened the door and walked out with his arms open. "Mr. and Mrs. Vans, so nice to finally meet you!" He shook both of their hands and turned to Lucy. "And Lucy, I'm Ace Reale. I saw you at the hospital, but you probably don't remember me." He went to hug her, but Jonathan linked, and he put his hands in his pockets and took out two phones. "I will explain everything once, and when we get you all moved in, we can go over it as many times as we need to. Now if you would all please follow me." Lucy put her hands up, "Move???" Mr. Vans pulled up a few feet. "Move what where?" Ace said, "Jonathan, have you told them?" Jonathan looked at Michael for help. Michael linked, "This is all between you and Great-Grandmother."

Jonathan took a deep breath. "My Great-Grandmother has recently discovered that our families have a long deeply rooted connection. She didn't know that you all existed until I told her about Lucy. Once she found out, she offered the compound to all of you. If you accept, you will be the first De'nola who's ever lived here." He looked at Lucy. "NO strings attached. This is a three bedroom home that Ace has been working on to make wheelchair accessible. It can be controlled with those phones. We have every service imaginable here inside the compound. We don't hire much outside the family. Some family members don't need any help, but others do." Lucy just stood there with her mouth open. "You want to give my parents a house?" Jonathan smiled. "None of us own any of these houses as individuals. It all belongs to all of us. If you would feel more comfortable, I can have an agreement written up that you all can stay until your deaths. Or if you like, I'm sure my grandmother will agree for you to have a lawyer of your choosing, write up an agreement of whatever wording you choose for her to sign."

Mr. Vans didn't want to talk any more. He said to Ace, "Show me what to do." Ace smiled. "Great. Follow me and I'll show you around. But I have to get something first. Stay here." Lucy was thinking that she had completely lost her margarita buzz and wished she had a drink. Ace came back out within seconds with a cardboard box top and four red plastic cups in them. Michael and Anastasia each grabbed one. "Thank you!" then he went over to Jonathan and Lucy. Jonathan took his and said, "Thanks cuz. Perfect timing." Lucy put her hands up. "OK!!! So that is the big secret right. You guys are all mind readers or something? I know there is some-thing different about all of you." She looked at Ace waiting for an answer. Jonathan laughed and pulled out his cell phone. "I was thirsty and asked him if he had any water. He said he has a pitcher of margaritas..." Lucy's shoulders dropped, "Ok, now I feel stupid again." Mr. Vans shook his head. "I love you, but sometimes I don't understand you." He zipped passed ev-eryone and up the ramp into the house. Mrs. Vans followed closely behind. Lucy was trying to think of something snarky to say but they were gone before she could think of anything.

Lucy walked up to Michael. "Is this for real?" Michael said, "My grandmother told me about this a few days ago, but she swore me to se-crecy. I just told Jonathan about this. He had nothing to do with it." Lucy "Is this a rich kid's way of getting some new toy to play with, so he can hold this over my head?" Anastasia looked at her. "What does your gut tell you? And I will promise you this. If you or your parents ever want to move from here, then I will have a house built for them anywhere that they choose to go." Lucy felt warm when she spoke to Anastasia. She knew she was telling her the truth. Lucy put up her hands. "I surrender. I will keep our apartment for the next few months. I'll just have to see how this plays out. But what kind of people give people houses?" Jonathan put his head down. "Whoever said we are people?"

Michael linked, "Careful my drunken cuz." Jonathan responded, "I have strict instructions from Great-Grandmother AND Grandmother that when I am alone with Lucy, I have to answer every question honestly. I'm so stressed about this." Michael was trying to understand any logic in that. "Then I suggest you leave for Norway tonight." Jonathan laughed and broke the link. "Lucy, can I show you something? Your parents are going to be here for a while. The paramedics can get them back to the house." Lucy was still very confused but she got into the golf cart. He was hesitant to get in, not because of Lucy, he just wasn't sure how to have a conversation like this without linking. She saw the fear in his eyes. She looked at him. "I don't know why, but I do trust you and that is what scares me. But can we just forget that I lost my mind earlier? Please…" She patted the driver's seat and he got in. Michael held on to Anastasia as he made a quick sharp U-turn. "We are headed back to the party. Link if you need me." Anastasia yelled, "See you back at the party." And they were off.

Lucy looked confused, "Link?" Jonathan "Communicate, but easier." Jonathan drove up to the highest point on the island. On a clear night you could see most of the island, but you could most definitely see the entire compound. They could hear the party echoing all over the mountain. It was dusk and the sunset would be spectacular from here. Jonathan had a bottle of champagne in an ice bucket with some fun snack food waiting. Lucy tilted her head. Jonathan said. "Say the word and we leave, but look at the food first. It's all garlic and stuff. I was worried that you were going to try some moves on me. So I am prepared to fend you off with horrible breath." Lucy laughed so hard that she tripped and he caught her. She looked deep into his eyes and saw a flash of blue light. She turned around

quickly thinking it was a shooting star reflection. "Did you see that?"
Jonathan had no idea what she saw. "See what?" "There was a flash of blue
light. It looked like it was in your eye." He didn't know if he could do this...
"No, I didn't see it, but that was my charge, my ancestors so to speak.
Great-Grandmother and Grandmother told me to never lie to you. So if
I don't do my job, they will know. Angle on my shoulder or a little birdy
type saying in some cultures." Lucy looked at him and started laughing...
"You guys are hysterical." Jonathan opened the champagne and set out a
thick blanket and put the food in between them. He said, "I need to tell
you a story. It will explain the house better." Lucy nodded yes and poured
a glass of champagne. "I am all ears."

Jonathan took a deep breath. "Well, your Great-Grandfather saved my
Great-Grandmother's life when they were kids. Her parents had frequent
business trips to Nepal where her parents would always hire his parents
for certain things. Ailbe's parents were seen as very old school stuffy rich
people that didn't mingle well with outsiders. See, our family has enemies, enemies that want us dead. So Ailbe was only allowed to play with
other family members for safety reasons. But her and this boy became
inseparable friends. She actually had a terrible crush on him, young love
and all. Well, one day she wanted to go out for a hike and he refused. He
didn't want her to get in trouble for being with him. He would risk getting
a beating just to be near her, but he wasn't willing to risk her getting in any
trouble. So she very defiantly left and he followed to keep her safe. She
didn't know the area and ignored his pleas to turn back. After all, she was
a Reale and was being groomed to be the head of the entire family one day.
She felt that she could do anything she wanted and anytime she wanted to
do it. Well, she dredged on through deep snow with the boy close behind,
continuously begging her to turn back. Ailbe fell through the ice and into
a cave. She fell about thirty feet and was knocked unconscious. He yelled
for help, but he knew they were miles away from anyone. He needed to go
for help, but if he left her, she would die. So he jumped in with her so she
would not die alone. He broke both of his legs, but he never complained
of pain. When she woke up, she tried to link with her parents, but snow
and ice blocked it. Then a snowstorm came through that night and they

had another four feet of snow. She was not used to the cold and started shivering. He took off his shoes and socks and put them on her hands to keep them warm. They huddled together like that for two days before they were found. The Nepal government called it a miracle that the Reale child was found alive and well, never mentioning how she really survived. Her friend was not so lucky... He lost all of his fingers and toes and his legs could not be set because it was almost three days by the time he got to a doctor. Ailbe's parents wanted to get him the best care possible but his family felt the shame that their child caused the incident and they refused help. They moved out of the area very quickly and no one seemed to know anything about what happened to them. Ailbe looked for years until she heard he had died. She went on a one woman mission to find his grave. She was haunted by what happened. Then one day, strictly by luck, she saw a man walking a large heavy basket on his head. He was bow legged and shuffled. She looked at his hand that was steadying the basket on his head and he had no fingers. She ran over to him..." Jonathan had to pause. He felt his Great-Grandmother's intense pain. He felt sick to his stomach. Lucy wasn't even trying to hold back her tears. They were silently running down her face. She took Jonathan's hand. He couldn't look her in the face. He just swallowed hard and continued... "They immediately recognized each other. She took the basket off his head and they walked fifteen miles together, mostly in silence. They arrived at the small one room mud-brick hut. She put the basket down and demanded to know every detail of what happened after they were found. He explained that his parents could not take the shame. So they took away his name and abandoned him in the streets. He walked everywhere to find food and work. He would do any-thing for an honest pay. He met a woman and they got married. She was already pregnant when her parents found out that he was the boy that almost killed the rich little girl, her parents took her away. He left the area and found a farmer who would give him the property that they sat on if he promised to work for him for free for five years. He was very excited to announce that he only had four more years to go. Ailbe insisted that he come with her, but he refused. She wanted to find his wife and child, but he wouldn't accept any help. He would only say, 'God shows them to me in my dreams, and that is enough.' He was still loyal to his parent's word that they would never accept help from The Reale family. She begged him for years, but he always refused. She visited him every chance she got. He was her only friend outside the family. They told each other every secret, every dream, everything. Ailbe broke every rule in our family by telling him. But she trusted him. She loved him. Her parents forbid her to ever bond with him, so she complied. She understood her duty to family, but no one could keep them from being friends. Ailbe married my great-grandfather Ailill. They were very happy and they had eight children. The old man found a second wife, a good woman. She was an honest hard working strong woman, and Ailbe loved her very much. They built a small home and had two sons. His wife died when the boys were young. But he did a great job raising them to be honest and hard working. Ailbe tried to help his two sons several times, but they respected their father and refused. Ailbe told him time and time again that he did nothing wrong and he should not feel bound to this parent's word. It was her arrogance. It was her shame. She even tried to give him back his name, but he refused. Everyone calls him 'the old man'. Even his own children, granddaughter, and great-grandson calls him 'Gaya', which means old man. He has never complained, he has never asked for anything, all he wanted from her was her love. So Ailbe decided that if she could not make things right in this life, she was going to request a blessing from our ancestors. A blessing that is forbidden to even ask. So... knowing the risks, she pleaded her case, and after long debates, he was given the blessing of an Azili. He is the only one outside our race to ever receive it. The ancestors went a step further with it. Any of his descendents who know of his loyalty and of his word to his parents would be bound to it. Your father might have heard rumors before his 21st birthday, but never knew the whole truth. You as of your 21st birthday never heard any of this. Your father is partially bound, but you are not."

Lucy had a million questions running through her head, but her thoughts were of the old man. Through tears she asked, "So my great-grandfather and Ailbe know each other? What a beautiful story" Jonathan waited for her to connect the dots. Lucy looked out into the ocean. "My dad left Nepal when he was a baby. He met my mom when he was seventeen and they got married right out of high school. He never really talked about his family much. He just told me last year that he heard stories about his grandmother being taken away from her husband, but I don't think he ever heard any of this. If he did, he never told me. I'm floored! I have to tell him." Jonathan waited a few moments before he said, "Lucy, I met him. I met the old man. Ailbe said that once you take the house, she will take all of you there. Ailbe and the old man are going to the ancestors very soon." Lucy sounded panicked, "What? Like a suicide pack?" Jonathan "No! Not at all. We can choose when we go. It's nothing like suicide. We plan it, like a trip. Then we go. The ancestors come and take us home." Lucy "Um that sounds just like suicide. I need to talk to my dad." Jonathan didn't know how to explain it and she really wasn't understanding what he was saying. "Lucy, I need to explain it better. We live long lives by your standards. The average natural life expectancy here is about 75-80 years. An Azili natural life expectancy here is about 200-250 years, at home, it's much more. That would cause a lot of questions in the modern world. When we feel that we are done. We talk to our ancestors and they agree or disagree. There has never been a suicide in our family."

Lucy said, "I'm on overload. Can we go see my parents? I won't say anything to my dad until he speaks to Ailbe." Jonathan "Thank you. I know she wants to show him some pictures and stuff." He was picking up the blanket when she caught herself watching him. She believed every word of what he was saying. She could feel his pain. He handed her the blanket "It's getting dark, the fireworks start at 9:00. I don't want to miss it." She took the blanket as he fed the rest of the snack food to the birds. He watched them eat for a second and said, "Thank you for watching over us." He put the empty bottle in the back seat and got into the golf cart. He looked at her. "Are you ok? That was a lot of information to process." She smiled and nodded yes and sat closer to him. "Just a little cold." Jonathan drove her back to where they left her parents in total silence with her head on his shoulder.

Michael and Anastasia got back to the house. Anastasia fought to hold back a yawn. Michael "You have had a very long and exhausting day. Why don't we call it a night?" Anastasia "No, please. I want to watch the fireworks." She said through another yawn. He walked around the golf cart and picked her up. "We can watch them through our window. It will be a perfect view. We have time to get you cleaned up and out of this atrocious outfit, and into our nice clean comfortable bed." She yawned again. "Nooooo, lets go down to the fire pit and the other dance floor. I heard Lindsey and Erik are back from the barn and cutting a rug." As she put her head into his neck. Michael felt her drifting off to sleep in his arms. He held her there for a moment... He kissed her forehead and walked into the house.

Linda was yawning as she turned the corner and saw them. Baby Stephanie jumped. Linda "I haven't spent any time with you guys tonight. Why don't you let me help get her cleaned up and into pajamas? And you can go say your good nights. I think Rach-El would like to see you." Michael carried Anastasia up to their room and gently put her down on the bed. She opened her eyes to see Linda. "How is your baby girl today?" The baby was jumping again. Linda "I think if you don't say hi to her soon, she is going to start kicking my liver." The two women laughed. Michael said, "I will be right back. I'm just going to see Rach-El and be right back up." Anastasia nodded sleepily and focused on baby Stephanie. She closed her eyes and put her forehead on Linda's belly. Anastasia started laughing. Linda could feel the love and affection they had for each other. After a few minutes Linda asked, "What could a baby have so much to say?" Anastasia smiled. "Your daughter is a wise one. She is advising me." Linda was laughing "Advising you!? On what? She is months away from being born." Anastasia kissed Linda's belly. "Children are closes to the ancestors. She knows that we would all be happier at home. She is trying to explain to me how to do that." Linda wasn't sure of what Anastasia meant by that, but it was a very long day and both women were half asleep, and now baby Stephanie was happy and relaxed. Michael had called for the nurse to go up and help Linda on his way out to find Rach-El. The nurse arrived and they got Anastasia cleaned up and into a beautiful pink silk camisole. They pushed the bed closer to the window so she could see most of the sky. She was in a deep sleep within seconds. Linda and the nurse walked out quietly.

Jonathan and Lucy arrived back to the house where they left her parents. Lucy yawned and stretched. Jonathan "You have had a long day. I will make sure I have you driven home safely or there is the adjacent room to your parent's if you choose to stay here." He offered her his hand to help her out of the golf cart. She took it and they stood there for a second. He wanted to kiss her so badly but instead he smiled. "You even have the old man's eyes." Lucy slid her hand behind he neck and guided his hand around her waist. He was clueless what to do or say, so he stood there. He didn't move. She said "If we go see the old man, will you come with us?" He tried not to look into her eyes any longer. "If you want me to." She closed her eye "I do." And she kissed him. He felt all of her deep fear melting away. She kissed him until she heard her mother. "Ace just left, but we said yes. We move in this week. Ace thought of everything." Jonathan laughed and Lucy put her head on his chest. "I guess I'm homeless now." Jonathan laughed, "Pick one, any one. I'll have you moved in by Monday." She giggled and looked up at him. "Feel like heading to the fire pit?"

Jonathan looked at his watch. "OH. I have a dreadful thing that I have to do with Malachi like right now. But you can NOT laugh." Lucy "Oh yeah? I have to see this." She jokingly snapped her fingers. "Bring me my chariot good sir." Jonathan bowed. "Right this way Mrs. Realeeee... Ms Vans." He thought, 'Did she just hear that? Did I just say that!?' Lucy stepped into the golf cart. "I am officially in like with you, but if you keep this up, I'll be in love with you soon." She tried to laugh. He said, "That has been my plan from the second I met you." Lucy looked forward "Good plan."

Rach-El and Bjorn were down toward the fire pit on the beach by the other dance floor. Michael linked with her and she excused herself and ran over to him. "I really need to ask you something." He was slightly alarmed. "OK?" She took a deep breath. "When did you know you were in love with Anastasia?" Michael shook his head. "What? I don't know when I fell in love with her. I didn't even know it while I was in love with her. Why? Where is this coming from?" Rach-El "I tried to link with mom but she has her block up. Her and dad got their groove on and poof, they were gone." Michael "Bjorn?" Rach-El jumped up and down for a second. "Yes, he is everything I thought I ever wanted in a bond." Michael "He's a good man. He is lucky to have turned your head once, let alone thinking he could be your bond. Just be honest with yourself." Rach-El "But you wouldn't reject him?" Michael smiled. "No, I would think he is a very lucky man who is in for a life of excitement with you. Then I would have to kick his ass for touching my sister." They laughed and hugged.

Malachi linked, "Almost ready gentlemen?" Michael knew about this earlier, but if Anastasia was sleeping, then he wasn't going to participate. He felt her wake up. She knew he wanted her to see something. She knew it was happening soon. She desperately wanted to get downstairs to watch. She called out to the nurse to come back and help her. Michael kissed Rach-El on the cheek. "I'll be right back, Have Anastasia's wheelchair next to the dance floor for me please." And he took off running. A few moments later, all the lights go off and the music stops. Both dance floors were filled with *BOOOOOs*. Antonio took the microphone. "Ladies and gentleman, this will just take a minute to fix. Everyone grab a fresh drink." Michael wondered if he had enough time? He made it to the back deck in three strides. He ran at a full sprint to the stairs, and took them four at a time. The nurse had already dressed her in a robe and slippers as he grabbed a bag by the door, scooped her up, and ran back down stairs. Rach-El had done what he asked, and he set her down into her wheelchair. He realized he had run faster than he ever had before. "That was weird right?" Anastasia giggled "Looks like the ancestors have given you a blessing." He kissed her quickly and said, "Talk later, this is for you Princess!" and he jumped into the darkness. Antonio was heard through his microphone. "I think we found the problem." Then his tone changed and he continued. "Now, does everyone have a fresh drink?" The crowd cheered and whistled. "Then let's hear it for the boys!!!" He flipped the lights on. Malachi, Jonathan, Steven, Mark, Hayden, Benjamin, Michael, Bjorn, and Erik standing in the middle of the dance floor. They were dressed very provocatively with Cowboy hats pushed down over their eyes, red scarves around their necks, sleeveless plaid shirts, jeans that fit just right, and cowboy boots. They slowly walked around the dance floor. Lucy saw Anastasia and raced over to sit next to her. Rach-El and Lindsey ran over and stood right beside Lucy. Anastasia was front and center for the show. Lucy was smiling ear to ear. "Did you know about this?" Anastasia said, "No, I had no idea. They hid this very well. I didn't even feel this in our link." Lucy still didn't know what a link was but she was watching Jonathan with eagle eyes. The song Moonshine in the Trunk by Brad Paisley started to play. Lindsey looked at Rach-El and shouted, "Shut your face!" Malachi was in the front, the other men formed a diamond shape behind him with Michael in the back. They started to dance with perfect precision. Each man was going up to various women in the crowd that gather around them and pulled red bandanas out of their back pockets and put it around their necks. The crowd was going insane. Michael could feel Anastasia staring at him with desire in her heart. Lucy leaned over to her. "Are these guys for real? I am seriously falling for him." Anastasia smiled. "He has the heart of a knight." Rach-El and Lindsey were screaming so loud that Ailbe could hear them. A few lines into the song they all ripped their shirts open to reveal their chiseled bodies. Each one of them had flawless stomachs. Their jeans rested just below their hips and every woman's eyes were imagining where that 'V' muscle ended up. Half way through the song, the shirts were slowly removed and handed to a screaming woman in the crowd. The music skipped a few notes, the lights went out, and the spotlights turned on a few feet away, with the song Run the World by Beyonce playing. A team of eight female protectors stepped onto the dance floor. The men looked confused, but gave up their space. The crowd was on their feet screaming as the women danced in full black uniforms. After a few minutes, the music changed again to Light 'Em Up by Fall Out Boy. The men walked back out on the dance floor with baseball hats and sneakers on, and acted as if they were pushing the women off the dance floor. Ailbe was watching from her deck and whistled so loud that her own ears were ringing. The woman pretended to fall off the dance floor and changed into black leather pants and high heeled shoes and stormed the dance floor as the music changed to The Champion by Carrie Underwood. The men came back with Woman, Amen by Dierks Bentley. The women came back with a hip hop version of Confident by Demi Lovato. Anastasia didn't notice that Michael wasn't dancing until the music changed again and the spotlight was only on Michael. The song Marry

You by Bruno Mars was playing. The protectors had all partnered up and were dancing around him as he stood in the center singing the song only to Anastasia. When the song was almost over, the other protectors were holding their counterparts. The crowd was almost silent. All the dancers slowly turned around and were focused only on one woman, Anastasia. Michael was singing to her as he danced towards her, making some powerfully suggestive moves. The other dancers were mimicking his moves but on a slightly lesser scale. Every woman wished she was Anastasia and every man wanted to learn those moves. Michael scooped her up in his arms and danced a few of the moves with her. Just before the end of the song, he put her back in the chair. Everyone in the crowd felt like they were witnessing something eternal. The second the music stopped, the men were frozen in a position of a semicircle around Michael and the women were standing behind them smiling. Michael was on one knee with Jonathan boldly standing behind him. No one dared to breathe, the air even stayed still. Jonathan leaned down and handed something to Michael. Michael took a deep breath to talk. The crowd pressed in slightly to hear what he was saying. "My bond, my life could end right now and the ancestors would accuse me of living a thousand lifetimes. You complete me in every way. Please wear this as a physical reminder of my love and devotion to you." He took her hand and put a 2 carat princess cut, deep red perfect ruby with baguette diamonds on each side, on her ring finger. She didn't even look at the ring. She tried to stand up, but he picked her up. They kissed and the crowd cheered so loud that Ruth and Se'ighin could feel the entire house shake. Michael carried her upstairs and into their room.

As the music started to play, Antonio yelled out, "Everyone on the dance floor." The crowd of people wanted to talk to the group of protectors that were now breathing heavy and looking for something to drink. Jonathan looked at Lucy who was hand in hand with Lindsey and Rach-El. Lucy was blinking hard. He made his way over through the crowd. "Well that was mortifying." Lucy blinked and shook her head. "Um... WOW... That was... nice. Very nice. I'm a bit.... Um.... I think I need another drink." Jonathan wasn't sure what that meant. He was a great flirt but he never wanted to be serious with a woman until now. Lucy turned and headed for the bar. Lindsey noticed his confusion as he stood there. She felt bad for him, he was truly lost when it came to matters of the heart. She gently pinched his leg and leaned over to him. "I think you got her motor running. She just needs reassurance that you are not playing with her." Jonathan didn't answer. He was sure his sister was right.

He watched her order from the bar and she turned to made eye contact with him. She held up a glass as to ask him if he wanted a drink too. He smiled and nodded as she turned and held up two fingers to the bartender. Kat, Andi and Emily were standing at the bar drooling over the protectors. Kat noticed Jonathan couldn't take his eyes off of Lucy. Kat asked, "Are you and Jonathan a thing now?" Lucy didn't know how to answer that. She said, "I'm just here for the party."

Bjorn ran up to Rach-El who was staring at his chest. He laughed. "Hey, eyes up here." She put her hands around his waist. "Oh my.... I have to see that dance again one of these days." He leaned down and kissed her. "That will have to wait until after we are bonded." Rach-El melted into his kiss. Erik was being mobbed by several women. He was very polite to everyone but he was embarrassed standing there with no shirt on. Antonio handed Lindsey a t-shirt and she brought it out to him. He put it on and she took him by the hand and they walked off the dance floor.

Charlotte woke up in the cabin of the boat. "Happy July 4th to me." She was hung-over but thinking clearly. She got up, took a shower and ate. She had been thinking about going to the big party all night. Her emotions kept going back and forth from angry to sad as she picked out what to wear. This morning she was stuck on angry. She didn't want to see the parade but she would show up right in front of the grandstand and ruin Michael's day. She planned to flirt with Jonathan or Malachi and kiss either one of them in front of Michael so he could see them. She said out loud to herself. "I'll do it." She finally decided on an outfit and she accessorized it with a hat and large sunglasses.

She arrived just as Anastasia started talking. Charlotte thought, "Put your hands down! We aren't your subjects you dumb bitch." When Anastasia called her dad and Rick her heroes, Charlotte screamed in her head. "Now you're trying to turn my own father against me!" When she

fell backward, Charlotte thought "Dramatic much? She did that on purpose so Michael would have to stay next to her all day. What a fake bitch."
Charlotte saw Jonathan and started making her way over to him when she
saw him turn and start talking to Lucy. She thought, "Oh come on! Not
that skanky volunteer? She can't even make it through nursing school. He
would never be interested in that lying thief." She watched them talk for
a few minutes before walking towards them. She panicked and wanted to
hide. She hid behind a large tree and a line of port-o-potties. She heard
Lucy introduce him to her parents. "You are introducing him to your
parents? How desperate can this girl be!?"

Charlotte was angry beyond her limit. She just wanted to hide back at
the marina. She lowered her head and started to make her way through the
crowd when several people stopped her and invited her to the main house
for the BBQ. She politely declined and kept walking. She was thankful
when she was finally passed the main house and could see the marina.
A long time fishing friend of her father's was walking from the marina
toward the main house. He saw Charlotte. "Hey, I thought you would be
at the party by now." Charlotte smiled. "Not yet, forgot a few things. I'll
be up there later." He smiled. "Ok, see you later." Charlotte waved him off.
"OK." and thought to herself, "How rude. I'm sure everyone has heard that
I broke up with Michael by now... geeze."

She continued walking with her head down until she got back to
the safety of the boat. She poured a glass of vodka with a dash of orange
juice. "No use wasting good orange juice." She sat on the back of the boat
drinking, listening to the music and cheers from the party. Every time she
heard the uproar of cheering, she yelled out, "What is Michael's whore
doing now?" or "What did they catch Jonathan's gold digger stealing now?"
During one of the uproars she screamed out, "What is wrong with both
of you!? Those skanky bitches could never compare to me and what I can
offer you. I'll knock them both off their little pedestals! I'm the one who
saved her life! My dad is the one who found her ass in the first place! I'll
knock both of those bitches out cold!" She was getting angrier by the second and drunker by the minute.

The day went by slowly and by the time it started getting dark, she decided she was going to sneak up to the party for a minute. She walked up the beach and watched the party in full swing. She saw Rach-El with a man that she didn't recognize. She spit at the ground. "You traitor! I hope he is as loyal to you as you were to me." She found a secluded area where she felt she could sit and watch without being seen. Everyone was having a great time, so no one noticed someone sitting on the beach. Then she saw them. Michael was carrying Anastasia in his arms and dancing. She became enraged. She screamed out, "That is it! I want to see that bitch die!" She heard a weak voice. "We can manage that for you." Charlotte whipped around, but no one was there. "Get it together girl. You're hearing things." She turned and headed back to the marina. "I need another drink."

She stumbled back onto the boat and into the kitchen to pour another large glass of vodka. She didn't even bother with the orange juice this time. She grabbed a large knife that was sitting on the counter and sat down on the deck. There was a piece of wood that she had been kicking around earlier that she had named Anastasia and Lucy. She put the piece of wood between her feet and started talking to it as she stabbed it with the knife. She started to cry. She suddenly felt all alone. She heard whales singing. For a split second she felt bad. But then she shouted. "Shut the fuck up!"

She picked up the piece of wood and threw it into the water. She wasn't sure if she was just drunk or if it landed on something because she didn't hear a splash. "Great. I just threw away the only thing that loves me." She stood up and felt the effects of the straight vodka. She stumbled several times yelling out, "Even my own dad was there. How could he be there with them? Them! Not here with me, his own daughter. What a piece of shit." She fell on her butt. "Just stay there with them. Suck up to Michael and his family while your own daughter is alone!" She stood up again and leaned over the back of the boat to retrieve the piece of wood. It was resting on a weird balloon. "Stupid party balloon… Hey assholes! These balloons kill marine life you FUCKERS. The whales are even yelling at you. They hate you too." As she bent over to reach for the wood, she felt a wave of nausea. She started to vomit. Then she was gone.

Lucy brought the drinks back to Jonathan. She leaned over and said in is ear, "I'm almost partied out. Can we just sit and talk? I kind of want to hear more about, well everything." Jonathan was not ready for the conversation he knew he was going to have. He trusted his great-grandmother without hesitation, but talking to a De'nola about family… He had a pit in his stomach. Lucy asked, "What's wrong? You look scared." He nodded. "I am. You are either going to think I'm a lunatic or you are going to think I'm lying." Lucy kissed his cheek. "Well, I think you are a good kind of crazy and I strangely don't think you will ever lie to me." He smiled and put out his hand. "Then we are going to have an amazing conversation." She took his hand and laced her fingers in with his. She felt his grip tighten in a protective gesture. He gently guided her through the crowd and into the house. "I have to stop by the library first." They turned a few corners and Jonathan stopped. "Stay here for one second. I just have to grab something for you." He left before Lucy could say anything, but when she looked inside the room, she probably couldn't have said much.

Two protectors were at the door watching carefully every move everyone in there was making. The room itself was square and four stories high. A glass ceiling allowed for natural lighting. An enormous chandelier hung three stories. It was held in place by six large cables and two decorative ropes running from the corners and center of the room. Track lighting was running the length of each floor. Books were floor to ceiling. Several shelves were labeled for the guests to find the area they were looking for. Photo albums, years, maps, genealogy, A-L and M-Z were clearly visible. Dark wood carved beams seemed to be watching over the treasures. Lucy didn't want to leave. She felt warm and comfortable here. Jonathan returned after about ten minutes. She didn't notice him at first. She was walking in small circles taking it all in. Jonathan stood there watching her. He was amazed at her curiosity and how much she reminded him of how he was trained to focus on every detail. He cleared his throat to get her attention. She didn't look away from the room as she backed out toward him. He whispered in her ear, "If you like this…just wait." She turned and smiled. "This room is what my dream room would look like." She noticed he had two boxes in his arms. "Let me take one." He pulled away. "Not yet, follow me." She did. They walked to the other side of the house. She asked, "Where are we going?'

Jonathan "To a very special place."

Lucy "Like a tree fort?'

Jonathan laughed, "Oddly enough. Similar... We are going to Great-Grandmother's Thinking Room."

Lucy joking said, "Ailbe has a make out room?"

Jonathan laughed. "Nope. Not many of us have even been up there. It's really just for our eldest. There is too much information here and most of us can't absorb it. You are the first person outside the family who has even been invited. It is our most scared space here. I was just here for the first time this morning."

Lucy "What? I don't know what to say."

Jonathan "Well, you might not get in. The room has to kind of invite you... Well, the ancestors have to invite you. It's kind of complicated."

Lucy "I don't understand. Who is up there?"

Jonathan "It's hard to explain in De'nola terms. You'll see."

Lucy "What is a De'nola?"

Jonathan "A human."

They came to the private elevator that they had gone up before, but this time the elevator allowed them in without the prior security clearance. When the elevator doors opened, she fell in love with the marble all over again. "Ok, I lied. This would be my dream interior." Jonathan laughed. "This is some of the oldest parts of the house. It was built to be a bit of an optical illusion from the outside, but where we are going is the original ancient structure." They walked for a few minutes, Lucy stopped to listen. It was completely silent. She could only hear the echo of there foot steps. She didn't even hear the party. "Is it ok that we're here?" Jonathan "Great-Grandmother told me that if we needed a quiet place to talk, to bring you here." Lucy "I feel honored." They walked quietly down the long dark hallway. Jonathan stopped. "This is it." Lucy laughed, "Where?" Jonathan just stood there adjusting the boxes. Lucy said, "You seriously had me going... There is nothing here but a wall." Jonathan said, "You have to wait."

Soon a door came into focus. Jonathan opened the door and walked in and put the boxes down. Lucy felt that she should stand there. Jonathan made no move to invite her in. The room was dark but as she stood there,

there seemed to be light, as if there was a dimly lit fireplace. After a few moments the room became warm and brighter. Jonathan said, "I was getting worried. But you have been invited in." Lucy was very confused but went into the room. She was immediately astounded. Inside the room looked vastly different from the outside looking in. The wall looked like the side of the mountain. The room itself was over a hundred feet long and thirty feet wide, with a twenty foot high ceiling. The length of the ocean side was glass floor to ceiling. On her right, there was a large tree growing out of the mountain wall. There was a fire at the end of the room. She was drawn towards it. She put out her hand to touch everything as she walked. A white peacock was perched in the tree and she realized she heard birds chirping. She took a deep breath and smelled tropical flowers, jasmine, gardenia, and primrose. She could feel and smell the salt water breeze but didn't see a fan or an open window. She walked further and saw brightly colored flowers that she had never seen before. She turned to Jonathan, "What are these flowers? I've never seen them before." Jonathan shrugged his shoulders. "I don't know what they're called. Great-Grandmother has a bit of a green thumb."

She walked further and didn't watch where she was going and bumped into a tree. She put her hand on the tree to steady herself. The tree was warm and seemed to try and bend out of her way. She felt connected and without thinking, she hugged the tree and some leaves fell at her feet. Jonathan "I think he likes you." Lucy responded without thinking. "I love this tree." The white peacock stepped out onto a branch and appeared to be staring at her. She looked over at Jonathan. He said, "That is George. He is a full time resident. He hurt his wing and a snake tried to eat him. Great-Grandmother cut off the snakes head and George has been her faithful companion ever since." Lucy laughed. "Stop it! I can't imagine Ailbe carrying knives around." Jonathan smiled. "There is a lot that you don't know about her. I think her skills with a knife are the mildest thing that will surprise you."

Lucy spent over an hour walking around the room mostly in silence. She touched and smelled every inch of the room when she finally came to the fire place. She bent down to see it better. The flame was a bluish green and it seemed to sparkle when she got closer. She muttered, "You are beautiful." The flame grew warm. She was engrossed and felt like she could step into it. Jonathan called her to the window. She stood up and walked away. The flame softened as she left. Jonathan was looking out the window when she slipped in under his arm and whispered. "This is incredible." She tried to see, what if anything, Jonathan was looking at. She felt the breeze through the glass. "What kind of glass is this? I don't see any holes? Is there a fan in here?" Jonathan had to tell the truth. "No. The glass is permeable, this is some of the last remnants of Atlantis after the attack." Lucy laughed. "You crack me up. You can't tell me you really believe that fairytale."

Lucy took it all in. She noticed a bench under her favorite tree that she hadn't noticed before. She sat down and Jonathan sat next to her. He couldn't take his eyes off of her. He finally said, "I have something for you." He reached under the bench and handed her one of the small boxes. She opened it. It was a framed photo of Ailbe and the old man when they were children before the incident. "I thought you might like it." She had tears in her eyes looking at the old photo. "I love it." Jonathan mumbled, "Do you believe in love at first sight?" She didn't take her eyes off the photo. "No." He asked, "Do you believe in fate?" She looked at her hands for a second. "Yesterday I would have said absolutely not, But today, meeting your family and finding out that your great-grandmother knows my great-grandfather... and you met him on the other side of the planet... I'm kind of open to believing some crazy shit right now." Jonathan said, "I'm sorry." She said, "For what" and he kissed her gently on the cheek. She was suddenly aware that she had fallen madly in love with him. There was no denying her feelings. She turned her face and kissed him.

Michael carried his wife up to their room. She had been exhausted and only took a short nap earlier, but now she was wide awake and feeling sensual. Michael was in no rush to consummate their bond. He was solely focused on her safety and healing. He gently put her on the bed and adjusted her leg so it was comfortable. He noticed it was red and swollen. She saw his face and quickly said, "I might have overdone it today. By tomorrow, it will be fine. I promise." He felt that she wasn't in any pain.

He stood there for a moment watching her as she moved her hair so he could lie next to her. "You are incredibly beautiful." She felt slightly shy. "I don't know about that, but I am glad that you think so." He was at her side before she could finish her sentence. Michael "I..." She kissed him before he could say another word. Michael pulled away from her. "I need a shower. All those De'nola seducing me with their eyes... yuck!" Anastasia laughed. "A hoard of beautiful women just voted all of you guys the sexiest men alive and you feel yuck?" He bent down over the top of her. "The only woman that I care about who thinks I'm sexy is you, and Kate Beckinsale, But mainly you." He rolled off the bed quickly and put his hands near his head. "And what about our amazing class of women protectors? I've never seen them as sexy before. I've been training them to kick ass and kill. Now I know they can do it in six inch heels! I have so much to learn." Anastasia laughed and he started a shower.

Anastasia looked at her ring. She felt like it was her new safe place. She had thought a lot about what Dr. Besler had said, and was eager to meet with him again. Whatever she had been through, she would do it all a thousand times just to be with Michael. He taught her the term Post Traumatic Growth and she was embracing it. She heard the water turn off. She could not wait to be back in his arms. She heard a strange noise coming from the bathroom. "Are you OK?" It took Michael a few seconds to get up off the floor and answer. "All good. Just Malachi trying to kill everyone with his jet fuel laced margaritas." He started to feel better in a matter of seconds.

He loosely placed a towel around his waist and opened the door. She said, "Well hello there. But it's hard to see you from way over there. Could you please come closer?" He walked with his best swagger possible. He climbed on to the bed. They could hear the music and people talking outside. He started to move with the music. She pulled him closer to her. He positioned himself over her but didn't put any weight on her. She felt his chest. She wanted to touch every inch of him. He felt like her touch was draining away all of his energy. He wanted to press himself against her. She moved her warm hands around to his back. He moaned as his skin responded to her. She reached the small of his back and felt the towel. "This has to go." He kissed her, "Then this has to go." As he tenderly guided her out of the camisole. And she pulled off this towel.

They searched each other's eyes for any hesitation but all they saw was their bond's love. He said, "I don't want to hurt you." She kissed him and pulled his weight on top of her. She felt his fear. "Please make love to me." He felt a moment of panic and asked, "Are you ready for this?" She didn't answer him. She just pulled him in closer. They heard a sudden collective "WOO-HOO" as the song "Uptown funk" blasted out of the speakers. Michael laughed and put his head on her chest. "We have a cheering squad." He kissed her as he positioned himself over her. She was pulling him into her. He tried to talk to her, he wanted to make sure she was ok. She pulled on his back until he was about to enter her. She arched back and moaned as he slowly pressed deeper and deeper into her. She felt as if there was no one in the world. She whispered in his ear. "I wish we were all alone." She thought he would be heavy, but instead they were weightless. Her body was responding to his every movement. She felt every muscle in her body was about to…

CHAPTER 6

"What is that sound." She opened her eyes. She watched as Michael moaned and lifted up slightly... He suddenly felt a cool breeze on his back and the strong smell of jasmine. He abruptly opened up his eyes and tried to orient himself to where he was. The two of them didn't move or dare to breathe. Michael's eyes darted around. He sprang off the bed and grabbed at anything to cover himself with. He went into full on protector mode. He was looking for anything that could be used as a weapon. He stood in front of Anastasia as she hopped off the bed and grabbed a robe off a chair. She quickly put it on and opened an armoire next to her. She was calling out to Michael but he had already amassed a significant quantity of items that could be used as weapons to protect themselves. She pulled out a bright blue robe and finally yelled, "MICHAEL!" He turned to her. She looked different and what was she wearing? "Stop! Don't panic. We are in my room. We're fine." She handed him the robe to put on. She looked into his eyes, his pupils were so dilated that his eyes almost looked black. He wildly tried to link to anyone, to everyone. Anastasia ran to him and held him tightly in her arms.

Anastasia "Michael! We're home. We're in my room."

Michael "What room?" He was desperate to link to anyone.

Anastasia "Michael, I remember! I remember everything!"

Michael went to the door and opened it with a quick snap. He was ready to take on the entire Eile race. No one was outside the door. He looked down the hall. Nothing looked familiar. He was trying to figure out where they were and how they got there. He heard Anastasia talking but he had to get her safe first. He looked at her. But couldn't understand why she was smiling. He asked, "Is this real?"

Anastasia "Michael I accidently projected us, well, most of us... We are in my room. On Uanza!"

Michael "What... Uanza? Our home? How the fuck did we get.... What! Great-Grandmother questioned if you could pull me into a memory. Is this one of your memories?"

Anastasia "Yes, well No! But it is real. The Royal family can project. When everyone fled, my parents thought I would be safer here..." She was getting frustrated and said, "Oh...come on. I'll show you."

Michael was still breathing hard, confused, and ready for war. But he put on the robe she gave him. He was about to pick her up. "Your leg?" He walked toward her. "Can I look at you?" She opened up her robe. He put his hand over his mouth. "Your scars?" He turned her around. She only had a few small ones and the one on the back of her left leg.

Anastasia "Because, earlier when they came in for me, I was so scared that I instinctively projected my mind. I came home. Back at the hospital, it stabbed me, but I forgot who I was. I forgot how to leave so they couldn't hurt me."

Michael "I must have hit my head in the bathroom."

Anastasia was irritated. "Just come on!" and she ran out of the room and into the hallway. His protective nature over took his disbelief and he ran after her.

Michael "Wait!!! You don't know who could be in here." Michael caught up to her as she stopped in front of a set of carved wooden double doors. "Wait. Don't run away from me. We are not going in there. I need to check it out first, we don't know who is in there!"

Anastasia "We are the only ones here. I promise. This is my... we are safe." She pulled hard on the double doors and they gave way with the loud eerie sound of thousands of years of neglect. He watched her walk in proudly, as he followed close behind. He looked around. It was spectacular.

Anastasia "The throne room… I was always too scared to come back in here, until now."

Michael was awestruck. "WOW. I'm too young to be able to link to the elders' ancient memories. This is beyond words." The room was expansive. The floor was pink and white marble with large veins of clear quartz running through it. It looked like it gave off its own light. The carved pillars were thirty feet tall. The ceiling was painted with a beautiful mural of bright colors. Children were running and playing, animals were along side them in protective stances. The grass was green and orange with snow capped mountains in the distance. Michael was looking up and walking in circles to take it all in. He wanted to remember every detail. He had forgotten for a moment that this was his wife's home. He looked over to see tears in her eyes. She looked at him with such sadness as she stood next to the Queen's throne. "This is where my parents sat, King Robert and Queen EL-la." She moved to stand in front of them. She bowed respectfully at their empty thrones. "Michael, please come here. I want to reaffirm my bond to you, here, at the sight of the creation of all love."

Michael walked towards her as he continued to try and take it all in. He wanted everyone back home to share in this. He felt her growing stronger and more resolved by the second, but she was reliving the death of her parents and everyone she ever knew. He reached her, took her tightly in his arms, and pulled her close. He never wanted to take all of her pain away as much as he did right now. Michael asked, "My love, Can I give you my bond twice?" He lifted up her left hand and saw the ring he had just given her. She smiled. "It is a symbol of our bond. No time, space, or Eile blade will ever take this from my hand or erase it from my mind. I will go to the ancestors with it." She turned and walked to a smaller throne off to the right side of the Queen's throne. She picked up an elaborately decorated sword. She looked every bit like a Princess as she turned with a purpose. Her voice was strong and projecting. "Michael come forth and speak your intention."

Michael stepped forward and went down on one knee. "My

Princess. I Michael Reale make my intention known to you, your court, and to the ancestors, to give you my bond. With the honor of loving you, protecting you, and making you my Queen for the rest of my life until I come to dine at the table of my ancestors."

Anastasia "Is your intention forced upon you?"

Michael "No"

Anastasia "Is your intention to perverse this court in any way?"

Michael "No"

Anastasia "Is your intention to make false statements?"

Michael "No"

Anastasia "Then I accept your bond. Let this court record his intention. I also make my intention known. I Princess A'Llwyn give you Michael Reale my bond. Are there any rejections of this bond?" There was no response. There was no noise. There was no wind. There was nothing. He watched Anastasia for several minutes. She stood statuesque. She continued, "There is no rejection of this bond. So say the court, so it shall be. May the kingdom be aware and honor our bond." She smiled at him. "Rise my husband." He stood up, but he did not move from where he was standing. He knew something was happening. The air turned electric. His body was tingling. The floor seemed to glow. Anastasia looked as if she was listening to something that he could not hear. She finally spoke as if she was speaking to a considerable crowd. "Uanza needs a King with a strong Queen side by side. (She looked at Michael.) She asks if you are such a man to be this King."

Michael "I am."

Anastasia "Are you such a man that will fight for his people?"

Michael "I am."

Anastasia "Are you such a man that will protect your Queen?"

Michael "I am."

Anastasia "Uanza will decide." She took the sword out of its sheath and held it by the blade. Michael wasn't sure what to do. She stood there not giving him a clue. He followed her lead and grabbed the blade just above her hand so he could take the weight of it off her's. After a few moments she announced, "Uanza has accepted your courage." She pulled a small dagger out of top of the handle and placed it in his hand and pointed it at her heart. She whispered, "Draw my blood to prove your loyalty to

Uanza." Michael "NO! I'm not going to hurt you!" Anastasia clenched her teeth. "Then you will not be king! Uanza demands loyalty." Michael was furious. "Fuck that! My loyalty is to you, my wife, my family, not a planet that wants me to murder you."

Anastasia stood up tall. She didn't even look at him. "Then you forfeit your claim to the throne?"

Michael "Yes, I forfeit any claim to the throne."

Anastasia "Uanza can make you ruler of all. You will be what the elders long to be. You will be greatest among our people. I am prepared to die for Uanza. This is what I choose."

Michael "NO! Anastasia. What are you saying? This is crazy. I'm not going to let anything or anyone hurt you!" He tightened his grip on the dagger and threw it across the room. He didn't hear it hit the floor. He hesitantly turned around and saw the throne room filled to capacity with the ancestors. He turned back to Anastasia. She was smiling like a reserved princess. She released her grip on the blade and Michael did the same. He realized his hand was bleeding. He saw blood on her hand too. The entire blade of the sword had a mixture of their blood all down the shaft and dripped onto the floor. She ceremoniously walked to the space between the king's and queen's thrones. Michael noticed a square stone about two feet tall with about a two inch indentation on the top.

Anastasia turned to face the ancestors and raised the sword above her head. "Blood given freely and without pain. I submit the words, actions, and blood of my bond. I Princess A'Llwyn will consent to the ruling of this court." She turned and placed the tip of the sword into the indentation. The sword slid into the stone without making a sound. The ancestors cheered and disappeared. Michael whispered, "Where did they go? What just happened?" Anastasia still looked every bit of a Princess doing her royal duty. "Uanza has chosen." She held out her hand. He took it. She walked him up the steps to the thrones. "My King" as she bowed. He reached down and guided her chin up until she was standing. He bowed to her deeply. "My Queen." He stayed bowing un-til she turned and sat on the Queen's throne. A crown appeared at her feet. He picked it up and placed it on her head. Her face was streaked with tears. Once he put the crown on her head he turned and faced the empty room.

He felt that the ancestors were still there, but he just couldn't see them. "I accept this honor and your faith in me. I will fulfill my duties as your King, but make no mistakes. I am only the face that stands behind our Queen. (As he was speaking, the ancestors were making themselves known.) What she has endured for her people has no title. (More ancestors filled the room.) She has lead the life of a warrior! None among us could have endured what she has. (The room was packed) She is the greatest among us. (The doors and windows flew open.) And I am honored to protect her and love her forever. (The energy of King Robert and Queen EL-la appeared at Anastasia's side, as animals were walking in and through the ancestors' energy.) We will make our home a place of love, safety and family. I give you my word." The ground shook, the animals reared up, the ancestors were cheering.

A large white four hooved creature with a huge set of antlers walked into the throne room. A hush fell over the crowd. The creature walked up to Michael. Anastasia fell to her knees with her head almost touching the floor. Michael knew it was probably wrong, but he was not going to watch his wife kneel in fear to anything. He bent down and lifted her up by her elbow. Anastasia looked horrified as she took a small step to stand behind him. She whispered in his ear. "Michael kneel!" Michael stood his ground. The creature's voice shook the walls but Michael was not going to be moved. "You disrespect me?" Michael met the creature's stare. "No, I mean no disrespect to any life. I bow only out of respect. I don't know you." The creature walked back and forth. "I am. I have always been. Queen A'Llwyn respects me." Michael felt fear in Anastasia and he gave his word that he would protect her from every feeling afraid again. "No. My Queen has never met you. She clearly knows of you and she fears you. I will no longer allow fear to run my life or my family's lives." Anastasia gasped and whispered, "Michael!" Michael kept his eyes focused on the creature. It reared up slightly and came down hard. "You should listen to the Queen. She is wise beyond her years." Michael was ready for battle. "I will always hold her council in the highest regard, but I will not have her afraid ever again. And it seems that you, my honored guest are scaring her." The two stared each other down. No one and nothing flinched. It was up to the creature to respond.

The standoff was unbearable, until the creature took one step back and bowed his head. "It is difficult to be King. But you, King Michael, are just what we need. I am Abantu. I speak for my kind. I will make it known that we serve King Michael to the death. How may I be of service?"

Anastasia stepped forward. "Abantu, I am the last Azili that can project. I was too young to be properly trained before my parents were murdered. I'm not even sure how I brought Michael with me. The Eile have declared war on us again. We need training and we need to get back to our family."

Abantu "I respect all life and…"

Michael "So do we."

Abantu did like being interrupted and stamped a hoof down hard. "I will not clash over property disputes! Eile stay in deep water. Azili stay on land."

Michael "They have held her captive and tortured her! (He pointed at Anastasia.) She escaped and we were protecting her when they came on our land and tried to kill her." Michael turned her around and exposed the back of her left leg. Abantu gasped and reared up high. Michael continued, "We tried to live in peace with them. We gave them the oceans if they promised to stay deep, but now they are coming on land."

Abantu looked at Anastasia's leg. "They attacked the Queen?! Why?"

Anastasia said quietly. "They wanted me to grant them a blessing." The ancestors and animals all gasped. "They demanded that I bless them with the ability to walk on land."

Abantu snorted. "NEVER! They are what they are. No more and no less." He looked at Anastasia. "I was with your parents when they decided that you stay here. Why did you leave?" Anastasia was reliving her memory. "When I heard Atlantis was under attack, I couldn't stay here while our kind was being slaughter. I was too young and foolish to think I could help. I was in training. I could physically project a short distance but I couldn't hold it for long and was always pulled back. I was told to focus and practice but… I was so arrogant… I thought of my parents and I tried for hours to go to them." Abantu listened closely. "Then… I was just there. I tried to find my parents, and when I did, they were already dead… Everyone was already dead. I couldn't remember how to get back home." Anastasia looked at Michael as if she was ashamed and put her head down. Her voice was broken and slow. "They found me in the water. They knew I was the last of the royal family. When I refused the blessing… they demanded a royal child which I refused. So they cut me…" Abantu saw the suffering in her soul. "A'Llwyn…. You have suffered… I will hear no more. I will speak to my kind." He turned to Michael, "You have my allegiance my King." Michael bowed, "And you have earned my respect." Abantu turned to the room. "My business here is complete. He walked through the energy of the ancestors. The animals turned and followed him with their heads held low. Michael felt numb. But the rage was coming.

Anastasia lifted her voice. "Is there any new business for the court?" There was no response. "This court is concluded." She stepped back and sat down deep into her mother's throne. Michael was at her side when he noticed the energies of King Robert and Queen EL-la standing at her side. Queen EL-la reached out and touched her daughter's cheek. Anastasia looked up and through her tears she cried, "Mom, I'm so sorry. I should have listened to you. I should have listened!" King Robert stood in front of his throne. Michael knew he was speaking with the ancestors, but he couldn't see or hear them. He wanted to take her in his arms, but sometimes a girl just needs her mom.

He stood there watching everything, every detail. He noticed Queen EL-la was becoming more formed. He could hear King Robert's voice in the distant. He watched as they became solid. King Richard ran to his daughter. "We don't have much time." The three hugged and cried together. Anastasia was repeating over and over her love for them. Queen EL-la finally said, "No one could find you. But now I understand that there was no one to link your memories to." The three of them held hands and stood tightly together. The room filled with a bright blue light. The floor was pulsating in a magnificent display of colors. The colors were shining on to the ceiling mural as if they were bringing life back into the artwork.

A flock of white peacocks flew into the room and spread their feathers into beautiful white fans around them. Michael could hear whales singing in the distance. Michael was scared to blink. He didn't want to miss anything. The room started to fade. King Robert looked at Michael and put out his hand. "Quickly!" Michael took it and joined the circle. Within seconds, Michael knew everything.

Jonathan was lost in Lucy's kiss. He felt it… Something changed. He tensed up. The peacock George started squawking loudly and uncontrollably. "Shh George! Knock it off." But the bird only protested louder. Lucy laughed. "Jonathan, don't yell at him." She turned to face the bird. "Hello beautiful. What is it?" She waited for a response. Jonathan heard voices outside the Thinking Room. Lucy giggled. "See, he was just giving us the heads up." George gave a quick chirp, turned on his branch, and walked back into his nest. Jonathan shook his head and walked to the door. He peeked out into the hallway to see the two paramedics assisting her parents into their room. Jonathan linked and asked, "Is everything alright?" They responded, "They are very happy and excited. They just want to relax." Jonathan felt Lucy pushing passed him. "Wait a few minutes. They look fine. Let them get into their room and settled in. Then we can go check on them." Lucy listened at the door. Her parents were laughing loudly and playfully. "I haven't heard them like this in years. I love the sound of them laughing." Lucy got a glimpse of herself in the reflection of the glass. "I look like I just went skydiving!" She straightened up her clothing and hair and attempted to help Jonathan do the same. She laughed. "Your hair is a lost cause and I can barely look at your face now that I know what happened. Can I ask you a personal question?" He was nervous. "You are the only person that can ask me any, including a personal question." She took both of his hands in hers. "Why did you take the blows? I mean Michael was there right?" Jonathan didn't hesitate in his response. "I would die for her."

She heard a door close from the hallway. They listened for voices. Jonathan could hear the paramedics but not her parents. "I guess they are calling it a night." She stood up straight. "That's not right. They were so excited about the fireworks. They talked about it all day yesterday." Jonathan looked at his phone. "They don't start for about another half hour. Maybe they just wanted to rest." Lucy looked nervous. "No, something is wrong." She pushed passed Jonathan and walked out into the hallway. The paramedics were waiting for the elevator. She walked down the hall with heavy steps. Jonathan was at her heels. She opened the door, stepped in and flipped on the lights in one continuous motion. Lucy screamed, Jonathan jumped in but instantly diverted his eyes to the ceiling and the two paramedics were inside the room and at the bedside by the time Lucy stopped screaming. Mrs. Vans yelled out, "LUCY! Knock before you barge in a room!" Mr. Vans "Did we invite the party up here? You all can leave now!" Lucy's face was bright red. She didn't say a word. She turned into Jonathan, pushed him aside, and ran out of the room slamming the door behind her. Jonathan and the paramedics were accidently left in the room. Jonathan was still looking up at the ceiling. The two paramedics didn't seem phased at all. One said, "So sorry. Do you need anything else?" The other didn't wait for an answer and said, "If you need us again, hit the button on the phone that Ace showed you. Good night." And they walked around Jonathan and opened the door. Mr. Vans looked at Jonathan. "Are you taking notes?" Jonathan suddenly realized his feet weren't moving. One of the paramedics took him by the elbow and walked him out of the room. They linked, "Well that was awkward!" They all laughed and he ran to find Lucy.

Lucy was outside the Thinking Room. Jonathan thought she was crying but when he attempted to console her, she looked up giggling. "Did you just see what I saw?"

Jonathan "What? Your parents naked and making out like teenagers?"

Lucy "Yep, now I need to go wash my eyes out."

Jonathan "I need to have George poke my eyes out." Lucy laughed and took his hand. She nodded at the door. "I can't find the door handle." Jonathan "What do you feel in that room?" She looked at him. "That's an odd question. But I feel honored that Ailbe said I could see it. I understand sacred places." Jonathan asked her again, "Not what I meant. Not what you think, I'm asking what do you feel?" She thought for a second. "Ok. I get it... Your Great-Grandmother is a clever girl. You have to be 100% honest with me, so now I have to be 100% honest with you... I think I just put her on my 'admire list'... Ok... when I was a kid, whenever felt alone, afraid, or just couldn't sleep, I would go into my special place. A place I made up in my head. It had everything I ever needed. The ocean, the forest, the mountains, a fire, exotic plants, lots of birds, and a dog to keep me company. I even named the dog. I know it sounds corny. Don't you dare make fun of me." Jonathan smiled. "I would never make fun of you. I mean... Look at my face." She pinched his arm gently and snuggled into his chest. The door opened without a sound.

Jonathan looked like he was thinking. She asked, "Why did you asked how the room made me feel? What are you thinking?" He said, "I was just wondering. If the blessing the ancestors gave to the old man... Oh, it's nothing. My head is just spinning." Lucy pulled him into the room. She was so beautiful. He wanted to tell her everything, and she was waiting for him to finish his thought. "The old man said that he knows all of Ailbe's secrets. So he knows about us... I'm sorry, I'm really not comfortable talking about this. I would prefer if you spoke to my great-grandmother yourself." Lucy looked out the window. She knew the feeling of wanting to change a subject. "I'm getting hungry. Why don't we go back to the party, grab a bite, maybe a drink and watch the fireworks." He nodded. "Great idea. I think having your parents down the hall is freaking me out." She laughed and heard a noise coming from under the bench. "Oh, I almost forgot my picture." She reached under the bench and saw the other box that Jonathan carried into the room. She looked at Jonathan who had the most boyish grin on his face. She looked in his hand and he was holding the photo. She was just about to question it when there was a firm knock on the door. The door opened but she didn't see Jonathan move or say anything. It was Mark. "Oh... am I early?" Jonathan gave him one subtle nod. Lucy felt that they were talking to each other somehow. "What is going on?" Jonathan nodded to the box. She pulled it out. It was loosely closed and it opened as she pulled it out. Inside was a sleeping puppy.

Mark stepped into the room. "I'm sorry to spoil the surprise. I'm here to walk the little fellow." Lucy gently reached into the box and picked him up. He was sleepy but when he saw her, he wagged his tail and started to lick her face. She made a few sounds that neither Jonathan nor Mark could interpret. Mark motioned to take the puppy out of her hands. She turned away. "No... I'm never putting him down." Mark asked, "What are you going to name him." Lucy looked at Jonathan. "What I named him in my secret place, Pec." Mark laughed. "Like Gregory Peck?" Lucy kissed his little nose. "No, P.E.C. When I was little, I couldn't pronounce protector. So he was my little 'Pec'ter." Mark looked at Jonathan and linked "Congratulation." Jonathan smiled. He was most definitely hopelessly in love.

Ailbe was in her room sitting in a reclining comfortable chair on the balcony. Her room is the highest point in the house. She loved looking out into the ocean at night. She was feeling each person. She was satisfied that everyone was exactly where they should be and who they should be with. She was happy. She had waited a very long time for this. The last things she would need to do is to reunite the old man with the lost line of his family, hand down her gifts and memories to Ruth, and the rest is for the next generation. She was fulfilled. As she waited for the fireworks to begin, she felt a change. She sat up and tried to figure out what happened. It was a good feeling, but the shift was palpable. She wondered what changed and she wondered if she was right? She leaned back in her chair and felt for the old man. He was not well. He was only holding on until she got there. She called out, "Soon my friend. I will be there soon." She allowed herself to close her eyes, but sleep would evade her. The fireworks started.

Michael stood there for a few minutes trying to sort it all out. His head was pounding. He opened up his eyes and saw Anastasia looking at him with the same wild look that he must have had. "What... I mean, I understand, but is this the physical link? The link is this place, a living library?" Anastasia was getting her thoughts into focus. "That is why no one ever came for me. No one knew." Michael held her. "Now everyone will know. Now everyone will fight. Your memories are all here now." The Azili castle was the link and it held the energy of all the ancestors. They would train and practice projecting so they could get back home and finish this war once and for all. They both understood that they had time. They could project back to when and where they left. Michael scooped her up in his arms. She said, "You don't have to carry me. I can walk fine here." He smiled. "I know I don't have to, but I want to." She nuzzled her face into his neck. "Let me give you the grand tour of your castle my King." They walked around the entire castle. She showed him every room and even though he now had all of her memories, he loved listening to the excitement in her voice as she relived them. They went outside into the garden. It was gorgeous and coming to life more and more as he carried her through. They went back into the castle and he headed to her room. She pointed down another hall. No, we can't stay in robes forever. My parent's room is down here. They will have clothes. Michael smiled and followed her finger.

She opened the door to her parent's room. She took a deep breath. She loved the smell of jasmine and it was so strong in this room. She saw her father's crown sitting on its ceremonial pillow. Michael put her down knowing she wanted to walk around the room. She walked over to her father's crown and stared at it for a few minutes before she placed her mother's crown next to it. She turned to face Michael, who had already lain down on the bed and was sleeping deeply. She got curled up next to him and pulled a light sheet over them. She didn't feel tired until that second. She looked into their link and felt him content. She drifted off to sleep.

When Michael woke up the next morning, for a second he thought he had the wildest dream. But he quickly remembered. He got up and looked through King Robert's clothes. He clearly was not going to find jeans and t-shirts, but he did manage to fine some comfortable casual clothes. He made his way to the kitchen in hopes of finding anything less than thousands of years old. To his surprise, several chickens had made their presence known and left some eggs on the counter. As he looked around, he started to see fresh fruits and vegetables and water. He looked out the window. He watched as the garden had become bright and full. The trees had fruit, the flowers had bloomed and the bees were already buzzing to make honey. "Thank you all very much." He said to whomever he needed to thank. He made a breakfast fit for a queen and brought it back to the bedroom. He quietly opened the door and he froze in his tracks. He was looking at the most beautiful woman he had ever seen. Anastasia woke up and put on one of her mother's dresses. It was a light colored sage green floor length dress with a slight amount of fullness in the skirt which extended into a small train. The neck was a modest sweetheart shape with pearls lining the shape and extending down between her breasts. The sleeves were fine lace with small beads that reflected the sun. The natural waist had a white belt that tied into a bow in the back and draped down to the floor. Each button down the back had a slight luster to it. Michael stood there speechless. She said, "This was my mother's. I remembered I loved it on her." He couldn't speak. He set down the tray and walked to her. She tried to kiss him but he didn't match her lips and she ended up kissing his chin. "Michael, do you hate it?" She knew he didn't but she needed him to say something. "I...I... Can... I...I need everyone in the world to see you in this. I need to remember every detail. I don't want to be a groomzilla, but this has to be your wedding dress." She laughed, but he was very serious. "I'm glad you love it as much as I do. It could never be the same as this one. I don't know if I will ever be able to physically project, but I agree. Do you think this would be appropriate for a De'nola wedding?" Michael was still taking it all in and just nodded yes. "I personally don't care about their traditions, but our family does love a good reason to party. And I suspect that we will have a few more reason to celebrate soon."

He didn't want to take his eyes off of her but his overwhelming desire to rip that dress off of her and feel her legs wrapped around his body was winning the battle. He slipped his hands around her waist as he kissed her. She motioned to protest. She wanted to see the dress for one more second. He moved his hands up to the small of her back and squeezed her until she knew she could not get away from him. She gave into his kiss. She lifted herself up onto her tip-toes so he could reach the bow easier. He untied it and started working on the buttons. Each button drew him in deeper and deeper into his fervor for her. Her body reacted with every movement of his fingers up her back. The high neck in the back was almost too much for his imagination. He hadn't seen that part of the dress. He HAD to see it. He turned her around without loosing his tight grip on her. Her exposed back was flawless. He now preferred seeing her with her scars, but he hated her pain. He kissed along where he knew her scars were. She moaned with raw pleasure. She wanted to be free from the restrains of the dress. She was relieved when she felt the last button was released from its clasp. She forced herself around to meet his lips again. He pulled his shirt up over his head and was desperate to find her lips again. He felt he was starving without tasting her. He picked her up and she wrapped her legs around his waist. He walked her to the bed. He leaned over and was thankful she met his angle and didn't stop the passionate kiss. He stepped out of his pants and crawled on top of her. She positioned herself to take him. She felt him tense as if he was going to say something. She moved her legs up his thigh and wrapped them around his low back. He moved his left hand up to her neck and his right hand down to her thigh. She tightened her grip and dug her fingers into his shoulders. She felt his heart racing. She moved so he could enter her willing body. He slowly but steadily gave her his entire body. She took every thrust with growing pleasure. She loosed her grip on his shoulders and clutched the bed sheets. She was groaning with sheer pleasure. She felt Michael giving in to ecstasy. After hours of being entwined. Her entire body ached with absolute exhaustion. Michael was drenched in sweat as he had nothing more to give her. He collapsed on top of her. He never wanted to not feel her body touching his. He felt her relaxed and almost weightless underneath him. He held her closer and opened his eyes to watch her. She opened her eyes, smiled, and said, "I love you." He responded, "I love you more." Just as he was about to kiss her, they heard a loud boom.

Michael shot up and instinctively grabbed the large knife out from his headboard and took a defensive position. Anastasia instantly knew they were back in his room. "Michael, it was just the fireworks! But how did we get back here? Did you project us?" He put the knife on his night stand and held her protectively. "I have no idea. I don't feel as connected with the link." He felt like a part of him was missing. He tried to connect. He felt close but not close enough. "We are stronger together." He took her hands and they put their foreheads together. They could just reach it together. She said, "Call Ailbe and Ruth!" As she tried to jump out of the bed. She fell hard onto the floor. The pain was intense. She screamed. Michal was lightning fast and picked her up and put her on the bed. He grabbed her leg with both hands without thinking. She grabbed a pillow and screamed into it as loud as she could. He closed his eyes and saw the bone healing. She took her face out of the pillow and watched as vibrant blue light pulsated out of his hands. "You have my father's gift! When did he grant you a blessing?" She started looking around the bed frantically. She was pulling the sheets up off the bed. "What did you loose?" "The crowns!" She shouted. "The crowns have to be here."

She felt her leg was much better and tried to walk on it. The hardware would have to be removed by the doctor, but for now, she would have to make due with it. "It appeared at my feet right? You put it on my head and announced that I am your Queen. The crowns never leave their rightful bearer! They are connected." He helped her look for a second. "Listen. Get dressed. We need to talk to our elders." She got up carefully this time. Threw on the first thing she could find. Michael did the same. In their link, they called Ailbe and Ruth.

Ailbe responded, "We all meet in the Thinking Room." Michael slipped on a pair of sneakers, scooped Anastasia up and was waiting at the elevator. She asked, "Is this to be our lives? One crisis after another?" He felt anger, fear, and a sudden pain in his leg. The elevator door opened. "No, it won't. I'm going to kill every single one of them." The elevator door closed. Anastasia was becoming fixated on the crowns. She knew they had to be here. When the elevator door opened, he walked straight passed the two paramedics without his usual pleasantries. Mark, Jonathan and Lucy were coming out of the Thinking Room. Michael knew Anastasia would be angry if he was perceived as rude to them. Anastasia saw the puppy. "Awe Jonathan is that the puppy from Misty Hills?" Lucy answered, "Isn't he the cutest!? You knew about this and you didn't tell me?" Anastasia smiled, "Jonathan has been talking to everyone about it." Lucy looked at Jonathan. "You were pretty confident that I would be coming today." Jonathan smiled, "A man can hope." Michael tried to smile, "The first firework just went off. That was your warning shot that you have five minutes till they start." Ailbe came down the hall and was in no mood to talk to anyone. She walked directly into the Thinking Room without a sound. Jonathan and Mark both felt the sense of urgency. Mark said, "You guys go ahead. I'm going to stay back for a moment." Jonathan and Lucy left. Michael and Anastasia went into the room. And were quickly followed by Ruth, Se'ighin, Arden, Olivia, Aharon and Elijah. They found seats and waited.

Michael was suddenly very nervous. Anastasia wiggled out of his arm. She swallowed hard. "I have my memories. All of my memories. For those of you who still need proof of my identity. (She said in the old language) I am A'Llwyn. I will first explain my actions and then I will show you the proof." Arden said, "But there is no proof." Anastasia smiled. "Michael and I just returned from Uanza. (Everyone gasped) I accidently projected." Ailbe stood up. "Ridiculous! I know that you are the Princess but projecting takes decades of training and the power of the ancestors!" Ruth took her hand and guided her back into her chair. Anastasia continued. "We met with Abantu who has pledged his loyalty and service in our war with the Eile." Ruth was shaking her head in disbelief. "I say we all get a good night sleep and ban Malachi from ever making margaritas again." Michael stepped up. He was terrified for a second that he might just be going crazy. He stood next to Anastasia and took her hand. He cleared his throat. "When we accidently projected, we confirmed our bond in the Throne Room. The ancestors witnessed us. There were no rejections. Uanza accepted me as Princess A'Llwyn's bond." Anastasia spoke up, "The sword took our blood and the stone accepted it." Anastasia was speaking directly to Ailbe. "Look at our hands!" Michael opened his hand and noticed it for the first time. There was a large scar. Arden grabbed his son's hand to look at the new scar. "Blood freely given and without pain." The Thinking Room fireplace lit up floor to ceiling with bright green flames. George the white peacock flew down and stood in front of Michael and Anastasia, and fanned out his feathers in a protective gesture. Anastasia stood proud. "I link to you... the coronation of King Michael Reale." They all closed their eye. They stayed in the link for longer than usual. Ailbe, Ruth and Se'ighin were the only ones old enough to link for memories of the Azili castle, and even for them it was a distant memory that was difficult to see. They wanted to see every detail. Anastasia looked at Michael and giggled. "There you are." He didn't know what she was talking about, he was too busy enjoying his memory and enjoying sharing it with his family. When they opened their eyes and looked at Michael and Anastasia, they all quickly lowered their heads. Michael looked at his wife, who was wearing the Queen's crown of Uanza. He touched his head. He felt connected with everything. George lowered his fan and flew back up into his tree.

No one moved. Michael finally said, "Um... so Grandmother. What is our next step?" Ruth looked at her grandson. She was proud of the man that he has become. "You are asking me?" She waited for a moment. "Michael, you're King now. There is no need for me to be head of the clann." Michael responded. "I can't do your job! I'm not ready for this. My job is a protector." Ruth walked to Michael. "Well, Uanza thought you were." Michael felt overwhelmed. "No...I need everyone to stay in their positions. Great-Grandmother, this is not your fight. Go to the old man. Take Jonathan, Lucy and her parents away from here. Once they are gone, (He looked at Ruth and Arden.) we will figure out our next move. The Eile are my main focus. We will never have a moment of peace until we eliminate every last one of them." Ruth said, "We need to update the elders." Michael started to relax. "Not just yet. Once we have a plan." He put his hand around Anastasia's waist. "And on a different note. We have a wedding to plan." Olivia laughed sarcastically. "A wedding? In the middle of all this!" Michael smiled, "What better way to keep everyone busy. We all know that the party is laced with reporters. There'll be video splashed all over the news by 11 o'clock about my very public proposal. We can use that to explain our coming and going and family coming in. We can put up huge tents and arrange for a no fly zone around the entire compound. I am open to hear any and all other suggestions." Ailbe said, "We will do as...." Anastasia cut her off. "Ailbe, with all due respect. I will carry the guilt and consequences of my arrogance for all eternity. Michael and I are begging you, all of you, to help us. Michael is not superior just because he was charged with a difficult duty. Treat us no differently than you did fifteen minutes ago. We don't have the benefit of your experiences." Ailbe stood up and hugged her. "Spoken like a wise Queen. I will start my plans for Nepal. I will say my final good-byes in the morning." Anastasia hugged her with tears in her eyes. "Our time was so short. I feel like I will need you soon." Ailbe smiled. "You have everything you need right here." She nodded toward Michael. "The old man doesn't have much time but

I am at your service. I will not be delighted if you call me back. I have waited long enough." She turned toward the door as it opened. Mark was standing outside the door. Mark didn't need to link with her to know she was going to prepare for a trip. He was her transporter. He knew her body language better than she did. Mark said, "Nepal? I will start..." Ailbe put up her hand. "Yes, but...I need you to share your duties with Jonathan." Mark "Is Grandmother coming with us?" Ailbe "No. Lucy will need to see Jonathan in his duties to the family. She is a very tactile learner. We leave tomorrow." She started walking down the hall. "Oh, and once her parents are done defiling my guest room, (Ailbe smiled) please update them. I have too many things to do."

Ruth, Se'ighin, Arden, Olivia, Aharon and Elijah were waiting for anyone to say something. Michael finally took a long deep breath. "So we all agree that we don't say anything to anyone for now? Business as usual. 1) Anastasia will start planning a De'nola type wedding. 2) Grandmother will start gathering any Azili, of age, that want to train as a protector. 3) Father will start training them. 4) Aunt Olivia will gather the healers and anyone who wants to be trained. 5) Uncle Aharon will build up the beach, we need to be certain that they can't get up here. 6) Uncle Elijah, I will connect you with Abantu. I have no idea how he can use your special skill, but I'm sure he can. Are there any rejections?" There was no response. "Are there any suggestions?" There was no response. "Please...I need my family." Arden stood up and walked to his side. "Just because you are my King, doesn't mean that you are no longer my son." The two men hugged. Anastasia said, "Ok. We have a lot of work to do. Let's try and talk as much as possible. I don't want too much of our plan in the link. The elders will know everything soon enough." Michael felt productive but tired. "We will start tomorrow. Let everyone enjoy the few hours left of the night." Everyone agreed and left.

Anastasia kissed Michael's cheek. "What are we going to do about Lucy? She isn't going to agree to postpone school very easy." Michael's stomach churned. "You deal with her. How am I going to keep Jonathan from joining in this fight?" He scooped her up in his arms. She said, "You are his King, Just command him to." Michael laughed. "Have you seen what he allowed you to do to his face? He would rather die than not stand by your side." As they crossed the Thinking Room threshold, George made a cooing sound and the crowns were gone. Michael laughed, "Do they always do that?" Anastasia said, "I think they like being close to home."

Jonathan and Lucy took the puppy outside. The fireworks were synchronized with the music. Lucy laughed as the puppy seemed to think it was some kind of game. Every time one streaked through the air the puppy wanted to chase it, and when one exploded, he would wag his tail, growl and try to bite at it. Lucy said, "I have so many questions. How can I take care of a dog? I have school, my parents, work, and now house-breaking?" Jonathan said, "My grandmother said that I can keep the dog with me when you are busy. This house needs some pitter patter." Lucy asked. "So there are no dogs or kids allowed to live in the main house?" He thought of how to answer that without lying. "Grandmother loves animals, but not in the house. Most of us would move out into one of the free standing houses on the compound if we wanted a pet. My cousin Linda is pregnant. She and Felipe are moving out once she has the baby. Not because they have to, it's just a privacy thing. And my room isn't that far away. (He made a circle pointing at his face.) And this needs a lot of beauty sleep."

Mark finished some arrangements and linked to Jonathan. "Where are you? Need to meet." Jonathan linked that they were in the front of the main house walking the puppy. "Good. I need her too." Within a few minutes, Mark arrived. Lucy knew he had something on his mind but waited for him to talk. "Lucy, how much has Jonathan filled you in?" Lucy was slightly alarmed. "On what?"

Mark "The old man?"

Lucy looked at Jonathan. "Does everyone around here know about my family but me?" Jonathan could feel the urgency in Mark's voice and asked, "What happened upstairs?" Mark said, "We need to leave tomorrow for Nepal." Lucy "Whoa whoa whoa. I just can't pick up and leave tomorrow. I have responsibilities. I graduate soon, my parents are apparently moving here, and I have a job. I'm not like you. I just can't get a thought and poof. Get on a plane and go." Mark looked at them both. "Why don't I take the pup and you guys need to talk. Jonathan, you need to explain it to her and fast." Now Lucy felt more than alarm, she was getting angry. "What the Hell is going on! Tell me right now." Mark picked up the puppy. "Link to me when you are done." and walked away. Jonathan was struggling to find the right words. "Let's take a drive down the beach. I don't want to talk too loud." Lucy bit her lip slightly and planted her feet. "I'm not moving until you start talking." Jonathan put his head down and started to explain. "I don't know what happened upstairs, but if we are leaving tomorrow then it means the old man is dying soon. Great-Grandmother is desperate to make things right for him here. That and… She is the oldest of our kind, which makes her the most powerful, the safest place for her is as far away from the water as possible." Jonathan waited for her to say something. He saw she was trying to sort it out in her head. "Ok. So Ailbe can take my parents and go. I am not risking my future on a family reunion… No, I'm not going." Jonathan "I can't force you to go, but you will be safer if you go." Lucy "No. I'll tell my parents that they should go, but I'm not going." Jonathan. "Please, I don't have a plan B here." Lucy felt that he was holding something back. She oddly didn't question what he was saying but until she knew everything, she was not getting on a plane. Jonathan knew she was tired and this was a long day. "So you have three options. You could risk going to sleep in the guest room with your patents. (Lucy shuddered at the mention of her parents.) Or you could sleep in your new house here. Or we could go to my room and talk more." He quickly said, "Not a rape room! I'll leave the door open. My sister's room is right next door. I just don't want this night to end with you. I want to know everything about you." Mark walked up with Pec. "For a little pup, he poops like an elephant, and on my shoe!" He set Pec down and watched as he ran to Lucy. Mark had a lot to do, so he walked away. Lucy thought for a second. "I'm sorry about the rape room comment." Jonathan smiled, "I'm really a great guy once you get to know me and I'm good looking too… Once I heal up." Lucy nudged him with her shoulder. "I'm beginning to think you're kinda perfect. Let's go to your room for a little bit. DOOR OPEN." They both laughed. Jonathan picked up Pec and they started walking into the house. Jonathan said to Pec, "Good job boy." Lucy laughed, "Was he your ace in the hole for getting me to fall for you?" Jonathan didn't stop walking, "Nope. For pooping on Mark's shoe."

Michael and Anastasia went back up to their room and watched the fireworks out the window. Michael watched her face light up each time a firework exploded into bright colors and widow shaking booms. Ailbe sat in her chair watching the night sky. Ruth and Se'ighin held each other and fell asleep. Arden and Bina looked over their balcony at Rach-El and Bjorn watching the fireworks. They were in a beach recliner. Bjorn was leaning back and Rach-El was between his legs, resting on his chest. Olivia and Antonio were entwined in passion. Aharon and Isabelle were putting together a crib for Linda. Elijah and Chaya were regretting teaching Malachi how to make an authentic margarita, but happily finishing off the last of the rhum balls. After the fireworks finale, the party started to whine down, the crowd started to head home, the music was off for the night, the lights were dim, the food was separated into doggy bags for anyone to take home, the bottles at the bars were almost empty, and love was in the air.

The next morning was a perfect day. The sun was bright, not a cloud in the sky. The house was filled with excitement. Michael and Anastasia woke up to a knock on their door that Dr. Ziv was in the infirmary waiting for them. Michael said, "I know Dr. Besler wanted to see you today, but I don't remember Dr. Ziv." Anastasia "Me either, but I'm sooo glad he's here. Maybe he can take this off my leg." They quickly dressed and Michael carried her down stairs. Michael put her down on the hospital bed and turned to Dr. Ziv. "Good morning. You are here bright and early." Dr. Ziv looked disheveled and tired. "I don't know if I should thank you or damn you."

Michael "For what?"

Dr. Ziv "My wife, and helping her with her adventure. She already has enough interest to stay in business for a year. She kept me up all night long talking about it."

Michael laughed. "Congratulations. I tried a few myself and they are spectacular. She deserves it."

Anastasia chimed in. "How about my leg? I'm a very quick healer and I'm feeling great."

Dr. Ziv "Like I told you before, this is going to be on there for months. It's only been a few days, but let me take a look at it." To his amazement, "Wow, this looks really good. I'll take an x-ray, but it would be impossible for this to be healed by now." He called the resident doctor and nurse out of their rooms to take the x-ray. Within a few minutes it was up on the computer screen. "That is impossible!" he said as he was scratching his head. "It just can't be."

Michael "What? What's wrong?"

Dr. Ziv "Nothing is wrong. It looks healed. But that is impossible!"

Ailbe walked into the room and looked Dr. Ziv in the eyes. "Nothing is impossible my dear doctor. Can we remove the hardware now?"

Dr. Ziv nodded his head yes. "Of course we can." He turned back to Anastasia. "You seriously need to write down your secret potion." As the resident and nurse assisted him, Dr. Ziv removed the pins and rods holding Anastasia's leg in place. "No walking on that! I will have the physical therapist come later today or tomorrow to start you SLOWLY putting some weight on it. I'm serious young lady. It might look healed, but I don't trust it 100% yet." Dr Ziv looked at Michael. "That is a direct order. Do you understand?"

Michael smiled. "Good. That means that I can carry her around just a little while longer." He kissed her forehead. Ailbe looked at Anastasia. "I need Michael for a moment, and I need you to talk to Lucy. She has refused to come to Nepal. I have already talked to her parents about our trip and they are as anxious as I am to leave as soon as possible." Anastasia went to jump off the bed when Michael stopped her up by the time she finished the thought. He bent down to pick her up and a sudden sharp pain in his back made him flinch. Anastasia looked worried. "What was that?" the pain was gone and he picked her up. "Fuckin Malachi and his choreographed dance routine… The doctor said no walking for you yet." Ailbe tried not to snicker, but she couldn't help herself. "Lucy is up in Jonathan's room, and you should watch where you leave your wheelchair. Ace found it this morning in the children's playground. He will be here any minute." Michael put her back down on the bed, kissed her on the top of the head and followed Ailbe. Ace arrived laughing. "Kids must have had a blast playing with this thing yesterday." Dr. Ziv said, "Anastasia, seriously. You have to take it easy." Ace said, "I'll stay with her until Michael is done. Thanks again doc for everything. You do amazing work." The men shook hands and the doctor left. The resident and the nurse quietly went back into their rooms.

Ace lifted Anastasia up and into the chair. She said, "You know I'm fine, right?" He didn't even look at her. "No offense, but Michael can kick my ass and you saw the class of female protectors that he has been training right? I'm officially terrified of them." He turned and walked to the door. "After you." as he waited for her to start the wheelchair. They took the elevator up to Jonathan's room. The door was partially open. Ace suggested that they barge in but Anastasia through her giggles refused. So Ace knocked on the door gently and opened it fully. Anastasia looked into the room. Lucy was fully dressed on top of the covers, and on the very edge of the king sized bed. Jonathan must have put the light sheet over her. He was fully dressed on the cold floor curled up into a shivering ball as close to the bed, without being under it, as he could. And this tiny puppy spread eagle in the center of the bed. Anastasia thought the pup looked like he was grinning.

Anastasia cleared her throat. Lucy was startled and she jerked, lost her balance and ended up on top of Jonathan. He jumped in pain and Pec was on all fours growling and barking like he was a Rottweiler. Ace laughed so loud that he was doubled over. "Oh my God. I just peed!!!" Anastasia was trying to regain her composure but she failed. She laughed way too hard. "Oh my side hurts!!!" Lucy looked intensely serious as she stayed lying on top of him. "Should we tell them?" Jonathan was trying to think back to last night and what he could have said, "Um… tell them what?" Lucy smiled, "I'm moving in. We got engaged last night." Anastasia jumped out of the wheelchair and onto the floor with them. "Fantastic! I KNEW it! King Michael and I will perform the ceremony tonight. Or do you prefer morning? No… Night is much more romantic! You will be our first order of busness!" Ace reached down and lightly punched him on the shoulder. "It was the dog, right?" Jonathan was so confused. Lucy sat up giggling in a wicked tone. "I got you… and I got you." As she pointed to Anastasia and then Ace. Anastasia asked, "You got me what?" Lucy "I'm joking. Engaged? Pftt no... Did you just say King Michael?" Ace and Jonathan both said at the same time. "King Michael?" Anastasia quickly yelled out. "Don't link!" She motioned for Ace to help her up but Jonathan had her half way in the wheelchair before he could move to help her.

Anastasia sat up straight and looked serious. "Lucy, could you please follow me outside for breakfast?" Lucy looked at Jonathan for any response. Jonathan said, "I'll have breakfast sent out there." Ace was suddenly uncomfortable as he pointed between Lucy and Jonathan. "So are we engaged or not?" Lucy picked up Pec and as she was walking out the door, she gave Jonathan a quick kiss on the cheek. "Well at least I know your family would approve of us." And she followed Anastasia. Jonathan looked at Ace. "What just happened?" Ace watched the two women going down the hall. "I'm not sure. But I think Michael is King? And I know that girl is gonna be a Reale." Ace left the room to follow closely behind them.

By the time Anastasia and Lucy reached the back deck, breakfast was already waiting for them. There was a large hired clean up crew that had already been working for over an hour. Anastasia started to lift herself off the wheelchair and onto a chair when Ace lifted her up instead. Anastasia "Thank you, but really... I'm fine." Ace gave her an exasperated exhale and tried to look busy but stayed close.

Lucy "What is going on? I get the feeling that everyone is in on something except for me."

Anastasia "Lucy, I need to tell you something but I need your word that you will never breath a word of it to anyone outside this family."

Lucy had given her thoughts on this before but this felt personal. "You have my word."

Anastasia "Lucy. My name is A'Llwyn. I am the last of the royal family of Uanza. We are at war with Eile. They murdered my parents and countless of my kind. I need you to willingly take Jonathan and your parents and go with Ailbe to Nepal. You will be safe there." Lucy was expecting her to keep talking but she picked up her coffee and just sat there drinking it. Lucy oddly knew somehow that she was telling the truth. "What is the link?"

Anastasia "The link is difficult to understand it has to be felt. It is a living library, the keeper of all memories and communication."

Lucy "And… if you connect with it…you can…what?"

Anastasia "Mostly we use it to communicate and store every memory of every Azili that has ever been. But like any skill, it is difficult to master. Parents with their children is easy. The protectors practice continuously with each other for obvious reasons. Husbands and wives start working on it when they start dating. Friends can work on it. There are some of us who can do it very easily. But most of the time it comes with lots of practice and experience. For example Ailbe is the oldest. She can link with anyone. Linda's daughter Stephanie can link to her mother." She took another sip of her coffee. Lucy watched for any hint of deception. "So you can link with Michael?" Anastasia was becoming excited. "Yes"

Lucy "Can you link with Jonathan?"

Anastasia "Yes"

Lucy "Why? He isn't your husband."

Anastasia "As the royal family, I can like with anyone. I'm not great at it yet, I'll learn, I'm stronger when I'm with Michael."

Lucy "Say something to Ace."

Anastasia "Lucy, this is not a game. I do not want Jonathan to be here for the next week. He will not go if you don't go."

Lucy thought for a second then shook her head like she was trying to get a thought out of her head. "What am I thinking? I have school. The answer is no. I would love to go, but I can't."

Anastasia "I will supply a tutor."

Lucy "Nursing school doesn't work that way."

Anastasia "Anything works that way. I need you on that plane."

Lucy's head was racing. "You said I'll be safe there. Is Jonathan in danger here?"

Anastasia "Yes"

Lucy "How long will we be gone?"

Anastasia "Hopefully not more that a week."

Lucy looked into her eyes. She was hoping Anastasia would start laughing but she didn't. "Can I take Pec?" Anastasia breathed a sigh of relief. "Yes. Your pint size protector is already cleared for travel." Lucy was about to stand up. "One question. How do you, Ailbe, Ruth... How do you know what I'm going to do before I do it? I mean, can you link with me or read my mind?" Anastasia laughed, "No. That is just pure statistics." Lucy "So you are all just math geniuses?"

Anastasia "Good way to look at it. The older and more experience we have, we can see the big picture and how things are connected. Like you and Jonathan. Every choice you make will either bring you closer or farther from him." Lucy understood that. "And what does this decision do?" Anastasia "It just saved his life."

Mr. and Mrs. Vans were in a whirl wind of emotions as they sat in the guest room and the paramedics were helping them get ready. Mark had been making the arrangements for transportation. Ruth asked Olivia to have clothing packed for Mr. and Mrs. Vans as well as Lucy and Jonathan to be ready within the hour. Olivia was scared for her family but thankful that Jonathan would be safe. Lucy was making phone calls and leaving messages that she has a family emergency and would be back in a week.

Ailbe and Michael went up to the Thinking Room. Ailbe wanted to just sit and talk to him like they used to do when he was a young boy. This will be her last time with him. "You were so young when we started our talk times." The two sat there talking about everything and nothing. Michael said. "I'm going to miss this. But now I have seen it with my own eyes...I'm excited for you. I can't wait to go back."

Ailbe "Have you been training in projecting?"

Michael "Just that one day that we were there. We don't know how she did it and we don't know how we got back. We are going to figure out how to connect with Abantu, he is the only one I know that can project."

Ailbe "I'm sure you will figure it out." The conversation went on until Mark came into the room. "Everything is ready." Michael gave her a strong long hug. She was ready to go. Michael smiled. "I don't know what more to say."

Ailbe "Oh there is plenty more to say later." She slightly lowered her head and turned to leave. Michael stayed in the room alone for a few more minutes. That nagging ache was bothering him, and the rock in his gut that he nick-named 'Fuckin Malachi' was distracting him. He looked towards the marina and said out loud. "I really need to talk to Charlotte. I can't hold that off for much longer." He rubbed his stomach and went to find Anastasia.

Lucy finished her breakfast and phone calls, and went to find Jonathan. She was passing through the great room and saw her parents with Ailbe, Mark and Jonathan standing there. Ailbe said, "We are waiting on you." Lucy "Now?!? I have to pack and get stuff for Pec and…" Mark looked frustrated, "Done. Everything is done. Just get in the car." Lucy started to think of a million things that she still needed to do. "But my pass…." Mark looked at the ceiling. "DONE. Now can we please get in the car?" Lucy looked at her parents who looked excited. Mrs. Vans said, "Come on Lucy, we are going on an adventure." Mr. Vans said, "Come on girl. You can't live your life through books. You have to jump into it." Lucy threw her hands in the air. "Jonathan, I give up. Just hold my hand and point me in the right direction." Pec gave one small bark and wagged his tail. Jonathan took her hand and tried to reassure her. "All the clothes you need are already in the plane. Passports have been prescreened and stamped. Pec has plenty of food, water and warm clothes on plane, all the calls have been made, and all you have to do is relax and enjoy the flight." Lucy felt a wave of panic, "Wait, you said 'you have to do'. Does that mean you are not coming?" Jonathan laughed, "I'm coming, but Mark and I fly the plane." Lucy threw her hands up in the air again. "Why do I ask dumb questions?"

They walked outside and there three large black SUVs and one van. Mark walked to the second car and opened the back door for Ailbe, and then he got into the driver's seat. Jonathan opened the back passenger door for Lucy, and then he got into the front passenger seat. The paramedics ushered Lucy's parents to a van parked behind the second car and lowered the ramp. Mrs. and Mrs. Vans drove up the ramp and into the van. The wheelchairs were locked in place. One paramedic got into the driver's seat and the other into the passenger seat. Leif and Olav got into the lead car and Rolf and Hans into the last car. Lucy suddenly felt like this was now a military operation and not a vacation. She wanted to tell Jonathan about her conversation with Anastasia but she remembered her promise.

Mark and Jonathan just made this same trip not very long ago. Jonathan felt he knew the routine of it, but would explain everything to Lucy along the way. Pec jumped on Ailbe's lap and started playfully barking. Ailbe always loved dogs but her lifestyle would never allow for one. Lucy raised her voice, "Pec! Stop that." Ailbe put up her hand. "It is alright dear. I rather enjoy it."

With the De'nola out of the house, the family was free to talk openly. The general mood was light but busy. Anastasia sat on the back deck with Ace until Michael came down. "Well, they are off to Nepal. How are you feeling?" Anastasia "I feel great. I want to meet with some of the ladies of the house and start planning our wedding. (She reached over and kissed him.) And you can go to the marina and try to talk to Charlotte." Michael sat down and rolled his eyes. "Tomorrow. I just don't have it in me to fight. I'm overwhelmed." Anastasia "It will be worse tomorrow. She didn't deserve any of this." Michael reluctantly stood up. "I haven't even had my coffee yet. You are a mean, mean wife." He leaned over and kissed her. She tried making a mean face but it just made her look more adorable. He started to walk away but turned around quickly. "You are going to have to deprive me of a lot more coffee than that, if you think you are going to sneak a quick walk!" He lifted her back into the wheelchair. She kissed him again. "You can read me like a book."

Michael went and spoke to Bina before going to speak to Charlotte. Bina did not want to link him the information of her visit with Charlotte. She just told him that it didn't go as planned and that a few people had reported to her that they think they saw Charlotte at the parade and on the beach. Michael felt a bit better knowing that Charlotte might have been there. He hated the thought that ran through his head a few times that she might be sitting around angry and drinking all day. He needed to clear his head so he decided to walk to the marina. Once there, he waved his access key and walked onto the dock and down to her father's boat. "Hey Charlotte... it's me, Michael." He waited for a response but was slightly relieved when he didn't get one. He stepped onto the boat and looked in the sleeper cabin. As he looked around the boat, he started to get a picture of the last few days. Someone was clearly living on the boat.

There were empty take out food containers. The refrigerator had fresh milk and orange juice and other essentials. There were clean clothes folded on the bed. There were dirty clothes in a pile. Several pair of women's shoes in the corner. But also some disturbing things that made Michael rub his stomach again. There were three empty bottles of vodka and two empty containers of orange juice. There was a large fishing knife was hundreds of small dents in the wood of the deck. There was vomit on the back railing. Her purse was on the counter and her car was still parked inside the fence.

He called out "CHARLOTTE" but no answer. He sat down where he imagined she must have been sitting. He started to hear a faint sound. It sounded like wood hitting wood. He went to the back of the boat and there was a small piece of wood hitting the side of the boat. He reached over to pick it up. It had hundreds of the same indents as the deck. He knew that Charlotte had a temper, even if he never saw it. He could imagine Charlotte sitting here drinking and stabbing the wood. He said out loud. "But where did you go?" He hoped that she walked up to the party and had a good time and just gone home with some of her friends. He saw Kat, Andi and Emily there. "Maybe I just wasn't looking." He stepped off the boat and was walking down the dock. He looked around to notice every detail. He went through the gate and waved into the marina office at the dock master. Michael stopped and took a few steps back. "Do you happen to have a spare blank sheet of paper and a pen?" The dock master was more than happy to help. "Yes I do. Who do you want to write a note to? Tom's daughter?" Michael laughed. He loved him. He was more aware of his surroundings than most of his own family. "Yes sir. Have you seen her?" The dock master said, "Yup. She is pretty mad at you, your whole family really. Out there drinking and cursing like a sailor. I knew you would want me to keep an eye on her. I let her park way down there so those reporters wouldn't find her. Last time I saw her, she was all dressed up and walking up the beach to the party. I went up there for a bit but then I came right back here. I don't like leaving my post when there is someone out here you know. But I didn't see her come back." Michael understood why his family hired him.

Michael "Sir, I can't thank you enough. You are a credit to your kind."

The dock master was confused but he wasn't going to ask any questions. Michael continued, "I'm upset that you didn't get to enjoy the party. I will make it up to you." The dock master laughed nervously. "Awe you don't have to make nothing up to me. It's my job." Michael pulled back his shoulders "Name three things that you have always wanted to do, places to go, favorite restaurant... just name three things." The dock master wasted no time in responding. "I would love my health back. It gets harder and harder to get up every morning. I would like to see my wife Nogaira one more time. She died when I was out at sea. I didn't know about it until we docked two days later. The doctor met me just as I was getting off the boat. And I guess the third thing would be to apologize to my granny. Ya see, she made a cake for the neighbor and I just couldn't resist. I took a pinch off the back but then I lied about it." Michael just stood there, he was disgusted by his own conceited behavior. Michael finally said, "Sir, I don't think I ever got your name." He smiled and looked at his feet. "My mom named me Ambrose McFall III. But the only ones that ever called me Ambrose were my mom and my wife. Everybody else just calls me Kempy." Michael looked at this man and was humbled. "Thank you Ambrose. You have been immensely helpful." Michael started to walk away when Ambrose asked, "Do you still want to write that note?" Michael "No thank you. I'll come back tomorrow." The two men waved as Michael walked away. He was thankful that he walked down, he need to be alone. He walked down to the shore line and sat there trying to think of nothing. He needed to figure out how to be a better man.

Michael got back to the house still stinging from the lesson he just learned. He wanted to go to the Thinking Room. He made his way through the house and up the elevator. The doors opened and he stepped out. Things were becoming clearer and clearer to him. He compared the space to the castle. The family members that built this were trying to make it look like the throne room. Michael smiled and said out loud. "You did a fine job. It looks very similar." The door to the Thinking Room opened. Michael walked in. He hadn't noticed some of the stunning details of the room before. He sat on the bench under a large tree that looked like it was growing right out of the mountain.

He could smell the jasmine strong in this room. He fell asleep for a few minutes. His dreams jumped from Jonathan and Lucy, to Lucy's parents meeting the old man, to the old man was hanging on until Ailbe got there. Then his mind went to the ancestors and how much they interact with us but we don't see it. He woke up questioning everything. He understood why Ailbe would spend hours in this room thinking. He yelled out loud. "HA! The Thinking Room. DUR!!! Now I get it." He laughed at himself all the way down to the kitchen.

He walked pass the dinning room. Anastasia, Rach-El and Lindsey were in there talking. He went into the kitchen and made a small sandwich and grabbed a soda and went back into the dinning room. Rach-El looked at him. "A green wedding dress? No, I won't have my face plastered all over the cover of every magazine 'Reale wedding disaster'. And she won't even link it to me! Unacceptable." Michael leaned down and kissed Anastasia and laughed as he sat down. "You are a mean, mean wife." Anastasia defended herself. "I have been paying very close attention to De'nola traditions, and the wedding dress is supposed to be a surprise." Lindsey leaned her head back and yelled at the ceiling. "To the groom! Not to your bridesmaids." Michael laughed. "Who have you picked?" Anastasia put her hand up. "Lucy, Linda, Lindsey, and Rach-El as my maid of honor." Michael smiled. "Linda is growing by the second. That might be hard for her." Anastasia "I thought the same thing, but baby Stephanie insisted that she will be on her best behavior. I haven't talked to Lucy yet, so don't say anything." Rach-El was in her element. "I called Randy Fenoli for help. He is coming in a few days with some drawings." Michael raised his eyebrows at Rach-El, "I saw the most beautiful dress already. It was THE gown. I hope you don't push too hard on this." Rach-El said, "I just want her to see what else is out there." Michael pretended like he was whispering. "To quote Mr. Fenoli. It is her day." He stood up to leave. "Team bride!" He left to go find Ruth.

As he was walking around the house, he noticed everyone seemed upbeat. But when he really watched someone or talked to someone. Everyone was tired and stressed. He made his way up to Ruth's office. She was sitting at her desk with Se'ighin standing behind her rubbing her shoulders.

Michael said firmly, "That's it!" Ruth jumped, "You scared me!" Michael looked tired. "We have all been going non-stop for weeks. Today, we rest. Unless it has to be done, it can wait!" He turned on all the speakers and in a jovial voice. "Hellooooo Reale family. Grandmother has agreed that if it isn't of vital importance to be done today, then it can wait till tomorrow. That is all. Have a fun day everyone....Oh, and GGgggoooooo Team bride!" Ruth was irritated, "Michael have you lost your mind? We all have things to do. We can't just take a day off from our responsibilities." Michael "Why?" Ruth looked flustered. "Because... we have things to do." Michael "If it doesn't change the outcome, then it can wait." The rest of the day, everyone did whatever they wanted. It was just the moral boost that everyone needed.

Michael woke up to the sound of Anastasia softly humming and flipping through a pile of bridal magazines. "Well you are in a great mood this morning for being up all night." She laughed, "Rach-El and Lindsey are in their element planning this wedding. I was exhausted when I came to bed, but they were still going strong. I found these outside the door this morning. Rach-El was kind enough to mark some pages for me to look at. Who would have thought that a wedding could be so intense... So much work for two simple sentences. But this is a great distraction for everyone. I think that they are taking notes for their own weddings soon." Michael felt a sudden pit in his stomach. "If we all make it." Anastasia was feeling the same way but didn't want it to show. "We have to stay positive. We will find a way. We have the ancestors and Abantu behind us." She put down the magazines and snuggled up under his arm. "I would die inside if something happened to anyone of us." He looked at the ceiling. "Me too." Michael let his mind drift to thoughts of Jonathan. He could feel they were all doing well on their adventure. Ailbe had linked that they were all doing well several times but nothing more. Michael wondered what reaction the Thinking Room would have when Ailbe and the old man crossed the veil. Michael sat up in bed. "Well, time to start the day. How is your leg feeling?" Anastasia lifted her leg and wiggled her toes. "Feels pretty good this morning." Michael smiled. "Good. Brett the physical therapist is coming today. I want his opinion before you go running around." She kissed him quickly on the cheek. "Then you need to carry me to the shower." Michael was more than willing to assist.

Ruth woke up with a nagging feeling. She hated that she lost an entire day of work yesterday but had to admit that the house was much more relaxed. She looked at Se'ighin and smiled. He was normally a restless sleeper, but last night he slept so soundly that Ruth questioned if she pushes the family too hard. She quietly got up and dressed and went down to the kitchen. She would bring him breakfast in bed. She opened the refrigerator and laughed. Anastasia had made them a beautiful try of fruits, pastries, orange juice and a note that said.

'R, Enjoy your morning, A'

Ruth smiled, took out the tray, poured two cups of coffee and went back upstairs.

Arden and Bina were slow getting out of bed. They heard Rach-El and Lindsey laughing and talking most of the night. Bina laughed, "Wedding fever… The struggle is real…" Arden laughed out loud. "There should be a vaccine. But you know how much Antonio and I love LOVE." Bina said." I have to admit that Olivia and I are thinking… maybe a double wedding. Oh dear Lord. Did I just say that? Please stop me!" She pulled the covers over her head pretending to be embarrassed. Arden pulled her close. "Never. You and Olivia can go crazy with it."

Michael and Anastasia finished there…um…morning deluge. They got dressed and headed downstairs to start their day. Everyone appeared to be well rested and talking about what they did yesterday with their free time. Michael saw Malachi, who was also still feeling the effects of over indulging. Azili have fast metabolisms and can easily out drink any De'nola, but a hangover, is a hangover. And Malachi had a whopper of a hangover. Michael was going to tease him relentlessly, but saw the green look on his face and just pointed and laughed instead. After breakfast and listening to laughter and joking, he knew he had to get back to business. He kissed Anastasia, pointed at the sleepy looking Rach-El and Lindsey "You two take good care of my wife, No walking!" they nodded in agreement and he was off to find Ruth.

Ruth was in the library when Michael walked in. "You look frustrated."

He said as he was walking toward her. She made sort of a growling noise. "How much I love and adore some De'nola, some are assholes! Look at this room." Michael looked around, "Is there anything missing?" She huffed, "No, but what a mess." Michael hugged her tight. "But you have your health, your husband, and no guilt to weigh you down." he kissed her on the cheek and sat down hard on the old world brown leather couch. Ruth sat down next to him. "I need to show you something." Michael leaned his head back. "No more bad things. My heart can't take it. I'm over my head, overwhelmed, and I promise to never drink again! Fuckin Malachi." Ruth pulled his ear. "Watch your mouth." He didn't move. "I'mmmmmm sorrrryyyyyy." Ruth stood up. "This might not be the best time for you, but it is the right time to show you." She turned and walked out the door. Michael stood up and followed her like a two year old throwing a temper tantrum. Ruth linked to Ace to meet them at the shed.

Ace met Ruth and Michael as they were walking out the front door. Ace looked very serious. Michael thought of all the times he thought that he had to be tough, but he was realizing that being the toughest didn't make him the best. He wasn't looking where they were headed until they were there. It suddenly hit him. Ruth looked at Michael. "There are only two. Ace will be with you." Michael saw tears in her eyes as he asked, "From the hospital?" Michael's rage was lit. Ruth put her hand on his shoulder. "The big one is the one in the video." She turned and walked away. Ace stepped in front of him and said, "This time, we kill them all." Michael grabbed the door and pulled it off its hinges. Ace could feel his rage, but the door was probably rusted??? Michael walked down the sloping hallway. He was warning the Eile that he was coming for them.

After a long journey, the line of vehicles stopped in front of the Inn. Ailbe grabbed a small duffle bag, let herself out of the car and struggled to walk inside. Lucy wanted to help her but Jonathan softly said. "Leave her be. We wait here." Lucy had been listening to how everyone spoke to each other, watching their body language, and feeling the inflections in their tones. Lucy had already learned everything she thought she needed to know about Jonathan and his family.

Lucy watched the door for over a half hour before the door opened and

Pia-Jiun placed a crude plywood ramp over the stairs. The two paramedics assisted Mr. and Mrs. Vans out of their vehicle and up the ramp. Lucy and Pec followed them inside. Mark and Jonathan were behind them. Leif and Olav brought in the luggage as Rolf and Hans stayed outside watching until everyone was inside.

Mark was always nervous when he didn't know where Ailbe was and this was no exception. Pia-Jiun whispered into his ear. "She is with the old man. Follow me." Jonathan watched him follow Pia-Jiun through the kitchen and disappeared around the corner. Jonathan nodded to the other protectors and they sat down. Lucy stood there waiting for direction as her parents wheeled around the Inn. Mr. Vans said loudly. "Wow, this place is fantastic. So old and rustic looking?" Lucy said, "Dad, it's not old. The old man built this place with his own hands." Jonathan watched her closely. Mrs. Vans was picking up everything and smelling the air. "I love this place. So secluded. A person could really live off the grid up here." Lucy "Mom, I don't think that's the point."

After a few minutes the old man's son Imay came in with Geetu. Geetu ran for the old man's room screaming "AILBE!" Imay laughed and walked over to Mr. Vans and gave him a burly hug. "So you are my lost nephew? Come! Let me introduce you to your family." Lucy watched how everyone had a job to do and did it very well. No one overstepped their roll, but it flowed like water. The smell from the kitchen was the most wonderful thing she could remember, and she realized she was very hungry, but as she was taking it all in, she realized that they must not have an abundance of food. She reminded herself that she is very fortunate.

The mood quickly became celebratory. The introductions were all made and the villagers began to arrive. Music bagan playing loudly, dances were being taught, but Lucy had still not been introduced to Pia-Jiun or Geetu. Nor had she seen the old man yet. It was almost too much for her to take. She walked into the kitchen and without asking what she could do, she just started to stir the rice, saw an empty bucket and a well handle outside, she filled the bucket and came back and started to wash the dishes. As she was washing the dishes she noticed that the opening to the outside was the size of the ramp. It hit her that the ramp was their door.

She walked around to the front steps, picked up the 'ramp' and returned it to the back. Pia-Jiun started to put meals on the plates and Lucy brought them out and placed them on the tables. The protectors remembered this meal from the last time and they were eager to inhale it down. Jonathan sat and ate but this time he enjoyed every bite. Lucy was in and out serving everyone. Jonathan was fascinated by the ease of her motions. She was smiling and laughing with her family, dancing across the floor, but never seemed to stop.

He wouldn't take watching her multitask while he sat there. He got up took some empty plates and walked into the kitchen. He put the plates in the sink but didn't see Lucy or Pia-Jiun. He walked outside and around the building before he saw them through the widow of the old man's room. Lucy was feeding him, Pia-Jiun was helping him get dressed and Ailbe was on the floor playing with Geetu. Jonathan felt he was not supposed to see this, so he went back inside through the kitchen, washed the dishes and went back into the party.

Mr. and Mrs. Vans were totally unaware of anything going on around them except for the village wild party going on. Ailbe was suddenly on the dance floor with the old man. He was dressed in white sneakers that fit him, a pair of gray sweatpants and a t-shirt that said *X-Files, The truth is out there*. Pia-Jiun had Geetu by the hand and they approached Mr. and Mrs. Vans. She introduced herself and gave them both big hugs, Geetu seemed scared of the wheelchairs but warmed up after awhile.

Mark and Jonathan were feeling the fatigue. Pia-Jiun noticed Mark's eyes looked tired and she motioned for them to follow her. She walked them up to the second floor and pulled back a curtain. It was a small room with two sets of bunk beds, a window with a broken glass pane and a lamp on the floor with an exposed light bulb. Jonathan saw their luggage had already been unpacked and placed neatly on their beds. Mark tried to thank Pia-Jiun but she lowered her head and left. He looked at Jonathan and laughed "I guess someone picked our beds for us. Lucky for you, I was gonna call top." Jonathan jumped onto the top bunk and was asleep within minutes. Mark pulled out a book but when his head hit the pillow, he was sound asleep too.

The party raged on for hours. Lucy finally told her parents she was going to bed. Pia-Jiun motioned for her to follow. They walked through the kitchen and into a room with a full size mattress on the floor and a smaller mattress on the side. Pia-Jiun said. "You can sleep in here with me. Your parents will be down the hall." Lucy felt honored, "Thank you. I'm sorry that I haven't had a chance to talk with you yet. This has been a bit overwhelming, but I'm so glad to meet you all." Pia-Jiun smiled but didn't say anything more, she turned and left. Lucy sat on the bed taking it all in and wondered if she should help clean up. She listened to the party continue for another hour before winding down. She heard her parents' wheelchairs and the two paramedics helping them get into bed. She wondered what their room looked like. The other protectors where shown to their rooms. Lucy didn't hear Ailbe or the old man. She was hoping they were alone somewhere talking. The Inn was silent except for the distant sound of soft music. Almost like a lullaby.

Anastasia felt Michael's rage. She tried to communicate in their link, but he was not responding. She knew it was war related. If he wanted her to know, she would know. Michael stood in front of the second door breathing deeply. He grabbed the door handle and crushed it as he pulled on the heavy door. The Eile were hissing. With a thundering voice Michael said, "Which one?!" They growled. He stared at them both. "Which one? I will not ask a third time." Ace stepped back. He felt heat coming from Michael. Michael turned to Ace. "I need a moment." He closed the door between them.

Ace pounded on the door. "Michael! There are two of them in there! Open the door." Ace heard hissing and howling and unnatural screams. He knew that Michael was not the one screaming. But he stood ready for anything. The screaming continued as Ace began to almost get bored standing and waiting. He sat down and just waited. It was hours until the room was quiet. A few minutes later Michael opened the door. He looked like he had already fought the war single handedly. As he stood there to catch his breath, he finally said. "We come back tomorrow first light." and walked away. Ace looked into the room. Both Eile were stretched very thin with knives holding them in place. Ace thought he saw a pattern and quickly realized that Michael cut each of them in the exact places of Anastasia's scars. As he closed the door, he said. "We will see you tomorrow." They hissed and cursed as Ace closed the door. By the time Ace ran down the hallway, Michael was gone. Ace called for Aharon to have his team come and fix the door immediately.

Michael's rage could be felt by everyone. Anastasia was with the physical therapist when he came out of the shed. Anastasia tried to communicate with him but he didn't respond. He linked with Ruth. "Meeting NOW in the Thinking Room." He went directly there. He wasn't thinking, he could only feel, and he only felt the frenzy of war. The Thinking Room was wide open by the time he reached the floor. He walked in and the room looked angry. There was no breeze, the fire was burning blood red. He began pacing the floor.

It was less than five minutes before Ruth followed by Arden, Olivia, Elijah and Aharon arrived but it felt like days to him. "They did this. They declared war! I will end this NOW!" he yelled so loud that the widows shook. Ruth approached him and started to say something but he snapped, "Where are the Elders? When are reinforcements due to arrive? Why isn't the tent up? Are the healers trained?" Arden put up his hands, "Michael, slow down. The tent is being erected today. Every of man and woman willing and able to fight will be her within two days. I will have them trained in a day. Most of the healers are here. We still haven't been able to reach Abantu. And we can't afford to have the elders here too soon. They will sense it and attack! We can't go off half cocked. We need to be prepared." Michael was trying to calm down. Olivia stepped to him. "We need to get the children away from here soon. Where do you want them to go? I was thinking to separate them into groups and…" Michael put a hand up and didn't hesitate to assert his authority. "No, we are not separating the children. Send them all to Ro'nnad's compound in Mongolia." Olivia gasped, "That will take a week!" Michael was in no mood to have to explain his decision. "The Erdenet mountains are far enough from any ocean and high enough not to matter. I want everyone under the age of sixteen on a plane tonight. Charter as many planes as we need. Get them out of here now. I'm ending this!"

Ruth quietly but firmly said, "I will contact my brother myself and make the arrangements." The tightness in Michael's chest was starting to ease up. He walked to the window and leaned against it. "Please go." No one moved. Arden felt his son's anguish and wanted to take the pain away but all he could do was watch. Michael relived the Eile words over and over in his head. Ruth motioned her head toward the door as if to tell everyone to leave.

Once they left the room, the Thinking Room door shut and was gone. Ruth sat down without a word. She knew that Michael would tell her when he was ready. After an hour of standing there, he could finally feel a breeze on his face. He looked out the window and saw the dolphins jumping. He listened harder and he could hear the whales singing...or were they yelling? He wasn't sure, but either way, he could breathe without wanting to vomit or kill something. He finally responded to Anastasia. "I love you. I will be down soon. I just need to clear my head." He knew she heard him and she respected that he needed space. Ruth said, "Rach-El will stay by her side." Michael felt a wave of gratitude. "I can't do this. I can't send anyone to their deaths. We can run away again." Ruth "We tried that once and they followed us. We tried again and they almost annihilated us. We take a stand here. Michael looked down the beach. It looked so peaceful. "I need to take a walk." He turned around and she could see the despair in his eyes. He didn't say a word as he walked toward the wall where the door used to be. "Please, I promise I won't slam it." The Thinking Room opened its door and let him out.

He walked down the hall toward Ailbe's private room and down the back stairs so no one would see him. He walked down the beach slowly. Before he realized it, he was at the marina. The dock master saw the look on his face and knew he was a man that did not want to talk. But when Michael saw him, he waved and asked, "How are you doing my friend?" The dock master pretended like he was too busy to talk much. "Busy as usual, but I still haven't seen Tom's daughter Charlotte around. Tom came down looking for her this morning. Just thought you might like to know." As he fuddled with something of no importance. Michael tried to smile. "Thank you Ambrose. I have some of her friend's numbers. I'll track her down." The two men didn't need or want pleasant good-byes, they just kept about their business.

Michael walked up to this highest point of the compound and sat down on the sand. He sent text messages to Kat, Andi, and Emily asking them if she was with any of them. He was concerned when each of them texted back 'no'. He called the hospital to see if she was there, also no luck. He tried her parents, a few other work friends, Mr. Kelly, he even called Agent Palmer to see if for some odd reason that he knew anything. No one seemed to know anything about where she could be. He tried to empty his mind of everything and just think, but the thoughts of war, dead family members, Charlotte, getting the children to safety, Anastasia being tortured and countless other horrible thoughts kept eating away at him.

He sat there for almost two hours trying to force good thoughts into his head but it was useless. He needed to get back to Anastasia. He stood up to start heading back to the house when he doubled over in excruciating pain. He felt like had been shot in the stomach. He looked down at his hands convinced that they would be covered in blood. He rolled over to one side trying to scream but no sound came out. He tried to call for Anastasia in the link but couldn't concentrate enough to send anything. He laid there vomiting. He was all alone, scared, and helpless.

Anastasia was almost in a panic. After Michael left the Thinking Room, Ruth went to see her. "Michael needs you now more than ever. You must be strong for him." Anastasia asked, "What happened!" Ruth looked down at her hands, "The night that we moved you here, we captured several Eile. I wanted at least one day that my family could relax and enjoy themselves without looking over their shoulders. This morning I told Michael about them. I have never seen more rage in any one man before. I know now that I was wrong. I should have just killed them." Anastasia took a long deep breath. "I understand and I would have done the same thing. What can I do to help him? I feel his mind being torn apart. I wish they had just killed me when they found me. You didn't need me to warn you. You have been training for this. I don't mean to sound over dramatic, but all of this IS my fault."

Ruth took Anastasia by the hand. "Our family has become a bit over-indulgent lately. If they would have attacked us here and killed me, who knows what would have happened. I don't have the answers, but I know that you saved a lot of lives." Anastasia tried to find something in that to hold on to. "So what is the plan?" Ruth filled her in on family converging here at the compound. The children are being moved by tonight to the mountains in Mongolia and the elders will arrive at the last minute possible. Then we go into the water.

Anastasia shivered. "I wish Ailbe was here. She is so strong." Ruth said, "When she goes to the ancestors, I will have her strength as the oldest of our kind, expect for you." Anastasia tried to smile. "I have no experience, but I will gladly lay down my life for anyone of us." Ruth "I know you would. I just hope that somehow my mother convinces the ancestors to stop this war before it starts." Anastasia was confused. "I thought Ailbe chose this time so she could bring the old man across the veil." Ruth "Oh, she did. But fate is a funny thing. When the ancestors granted him a blessing, he refused at first. They offered again. He refused again. When they offered a third time, he accepted but under one condition. That once he and Ailbe crossed the veil, that the Azili would finally know peace. They accepted." Anastasia "I never knew that! I was always told that the ancestors are forbidden to interfere. Yeah, they could give blessings to help, but they agreed to intervene? That is great! No war! Did you tell Michael? He has to know about this."

Ruth closed her eyes for a moment. "My problem is, that they did not agree to intervene. They just agreed that the Azili would finally know peace. Something that vague scares me terribly. I'm only telling you because I fear that Michael is not thinking rationally right now. You are his wife and our Queen. You are the only one who can help him pause and think." Anastasia "No one wants this war. But do you think it is a necessary evil or should I talk Michael out of it?" Ruth "All the elders agree that they declared this war. I see no other way but to attack them as soon as possible." Anastasia "Please… Tell me what to do." Ruth "We all need Michael to think clearly. I can't tell you what to do, I don't even know what I need to do. I would think keeping his eyes on the prize would benefit him." Anastasia looked and felt so lost. She sat there as Ruth collected her composure and left.

The next morning Lucy woke up to the sound of water and that soft music stuck in her head. She looked around and it was still dark out. She got up and put a robe on, put the leash on Pec and went into the kitchen. Geetu was filling buckets with water from outside. Pia-Jiun was boiling it. Lucy watched as the mother and son worked in sync. Pia-Jiun noticed her and quietly said. "You remind me of Ailbe." Lucy felt honored by the compliment. "Thank you. She is a very beautiful woman." Pia-Jiun laughed. "No, not like that." Lucy said, "I'm sorry, but I don't understand." Geetu laughed and playfully splashed her with water. "No? You don't see it yet?" and he ran off for some more water with Pec on his heels.

Pia-Jiun just laughed and asked Lucy to go into the hen house and gather the eggs. Lucy was happy to help and went outside to look around. She didn't see a hen house. She walked back into the kitchen rather embarrassed and asked "Where is the hen house?" Pia-Jiun laughed and walked out the back door. Lucy followed. They walked about two hundred feet toward what Lucy thought was a parking lot. Pia-Jiun opened a car door to a Mercedes and there were chickens sitting in boxes. Pia-Jiun reached under each hen and handed Lucy the eggs. They went back into the house and started breakfast. Once the eggs were cooked, the oatmeal made and the toast done. Everything went into the oven to keep warm. Pia-Jiun and Geetu grabbed bucket of boiling water and headed up the stairs. Lucy grabbed one and followed. They went up to the roof and poured the boiling water into a large reservoir. They did this countless times until the container was full.

The sun was starting to peek over the mountains. Geetu poured a bowl of oatmeal and headed into the old man's room. Lucy asked, "Pia-Jiun, can I help feed the old man? Geetu can go play." Geetu was more than happy to hand her the bowl and he darted out the door to go chase the rooster around the yard with Pec. Pia-Jiun smiled and went back to cleaning. Lucy took the oatmeal into the old man's room. Ailbe was sitting on the side of his bed singing to him while he slept. She was touching his face as if she needed to feel every crease in his skin. Lucy did not want to seem surprised as she walked over to him. "Good morning. I loved hearing you singing last night, but I can come back when he wakes up." Ailbe "That is fine. Leave it here and I'll help him when he wakes up." Lucy put the bowl on a small table and turned to leave. Ailbe asked, "How are you feeling?" Lucy "Who me? I feel great. Thank you for bringing us here. My father is so happy. He would have never met them if it wasn't for you." Ailbe smiled, "That is wonderful. I'm very happy. But how do you feel here?" Lucy smiled, "I love it." Ailbe turned her attention back to the old man and started singing again.

Geetu's laugh was contagious and the house rang to life. The paramedics helped her parents take a nice long hot shower, then they took nice hot showers, then the other protectors took showers. Somewhere between the protectors laughing and snapping towels and the steam coming out of the bathroom that it hit her. The hours of getting the water, boiling the water, and carrying it upstairs, No one was grateful. She was hopeful that they just didn't know but she was going to give everyone a good piece of her mind. She looked at Pia-Jiun who was looking back at her smiling. Lucy was about to say something and she nodded her head no. Lucy took two small buckets, she put a small amount of dish soap in one and went outside. She filled each one about halfway with water and went into Pia-Jiun's bedroom. She took a clean sock from her bag and washed herself first with the soapy water and then rinsed with the clean water. She got dressed and was excited to start the day.

Michael was doubled over in intense pain for hours. Just as the pain felt like it was starting to ease, another wave of pain would hit. He was at the highest point of the compound and no one could see him. He was hoping he would just pass out but no luck.

Everyone was clean and fresh and hungry after a great night sleep. Jonathan was eager to go into town and purchase food. He still felt guilty about his last visit here and he is still convinced that he may have liver damage, but he learned his lesson and swore that if he saw that jar, he would run out screaming. Pia-Jiun was putting breakfast on plates and Lucy was bringing them out and putting them on the tables. Her parents where sitting next to Imay. They were telling stories about their childhoods and sports. They were excited that Imay was going to take them into the village today to go shopping and sightseeing. Lucy looked at the excitement in the room and thought, "Life is good."

Jonathan noticed she looked distant and deep in thought. "I want to go into the town. Feel like taking a ride or do you want to stay for more stories? He laughed but not because he thought it was funny, he just felt some tension. Lucy smiled, "Let me see if Pia-Jiun needs anything. Hey, can we take Geetu?" his eyes lit up. "Absolutely, I love that kid." Lucy smiled and walked into the kitchen. "Hey, do you need anything? We are going to run into town and poke around for a little bit." Pia-Jiun smiled and nodded no. Before she could say anything, Lucy asked "Can we bring Geetu with us? I can help him later if he has any chores." Pia-Jiun called for Geetu and whispered in his ear. His face lit up and he ran to Lucy. "Good! When we get back, you can kill the goat. I really hate that." and he ran out the front door yelling "Come on. Let's go." Pia-Jiun laughed, "That is his chore..." Lucy looked at Jonathan "Please tell me she is joking." Jonathan grabbed the keys from Mark and they headed for the front door.

Jonathan felt a sharp intense pain in his low abdomen. He felt like he had been shot. He doubled over screaming. Mark pushed Lucy aside and knelt down next to him. By the time Ailbe was at his side, the pain was easing up. Ailbe "What happened!?" Jonathan was slightly embarrassed. "I don't know. Maybe I ate something funky that didn't agree with me. But it's going away. I feel much better." Ailbe became the ultimate great-grandmother. "When was the last time you pooped?" Now Jonathan was completely embarrassed. "Thank you for asking in front of everyone, but if you must know, today."

Ailbe helped him up. She linked with him. "I don't feel anything wrong, but just in case, I will have Imay call the doctor." Lucy tried to help Jonathan out of this. "We are going into town to look around. If it happens again, I'll have him see the doctor then. We are taking Geetu and Pec with us." Ailbe laughed. "Oh good, a boy and a pup will be of great help in an emergency. But you kids run along." Lucy kissed Ailbe on the cheek, grabbed Geetu's hand and they left.

Ruth had nervously walked around the house hugging children

good-bye and trying her best not to melt into a pile of tears. Eighteen school buses were lined up to take them all on an incredible adventure to see Mongolia. Ruth was showing them pictures of the compound there and telling them all about the wonderful things they are going to see. Several of the mother's had decided to go with them, but all of the men volunteered to stay and fight. The children were all excited and yelled and waved at everyone standing outside as the buses left. Ruth could not bear the thought of never seeing them again. She thought that this is what her family must have felt like during the last war that destroyed Atlantis. She was fortunate that they could get some family to safety. The Atlantis attack was a complete surprise.

Now that the children were gone, they could focus on the next thing. "Where is Michael? He should have been here with the children." Ruth walked up to the Thinking Room, the kitchen, dining room, library, infirmary, when she finally linked to Anastasia. "Where are you two?" Anastasia responded. "I'm in our room. I still can't get a response from Michael." Ruth "I'll find him." Ruth found Arden, "He was broken with rage when he left. Can you or Bina find him?" Arden was suddenly very concerned. Bina felt it too. Arden linked to the protectors to come for a meeting at the beach. Malachi was the first one there. "I have not been able to link to Michael all day." as more of the protectors arrived. Arden quickly informed everyone that this was now a search party. They all knew what to do and shot off in every direction.

Ailbe could not shake the feeling that something was wrong, very wrong. She linked to Ruth but all she would respond was, "How is the old man?" Ailbe did not like this. She went back in with the old man and told him about it. With a weak voice he said, "You should not have brought all these fighters here. They should be with the family. Keep Jonathan and Mark, but send the others back." Ailbe thought for a minute. "You are right." She called Mark into the room. "We will have villagers to help with Mr. and Mrs. Vans, I need you, Jonathan, and Lucy to stay. Send everyone else back home immediately. Something is very wrong." Mark "I should go too." Ailbe shot him a reprimanding scowl. "Do as I say." Mark left the room to talk to the other protectors.

Within the hour, they took two cars and headed for the airport. Mark linked to Ailbe. "They are on their way home. The old man feels close. Should I take Pia-Jiun?" Ailbe "Yes, Thank you. Good-bye Mark. I will always watch over you." Mark swallowed hard and approached Imay and Mr. Vans. "Hey, if you guys get busy and want to stay in Katmandu for a day or two, here is a credit card. Stay and enjoy! Mr. Vans took the credit card. "What a great trip this is! I've always wanted to spend some time there." Mark patted him on the back. "This trip is 100% for you. Go do what every your heart desires." He watched as Imay and two villagers got Lucy's parents into the van and drove off to sightsee and shopping.

Pia-Jiun approached Mark, "The old man feels close. I think we should give them privacy. I need a few things. Will you drive me or do you need to stay close to her?" Mark was relieved that he could speak openly with Pia-Jiun and not have to deal with more emotions. He couldn't shake the feeling in his gut that something was very wrong. He wanted to get home soon.

The protectors were trying desperately to link with Michael. Anastasia was with Bina waiting for any word. Michael heard them calling his name. He tried to roll over but all he accomplished was to start vomiting again. Malachi heard a noise and tried to focus on where it was coming from. He shouted, "ON TOP OF THE HILL!!!" Everyone raced to the high point and found him. Malachi bent over and picked him up. Benjamin was on the other side. They were more than a mile from the house. Ace screamed in the link. "Found him! Bringing him to the infirmary. Have the doctor and nurses waiting. He's hurt." The protectors were fast, but they raced him into the infirmary quick even by their standards.

Anastasia was waiting at the bedside when they brought him in. The doctor and nurses were working on him even before they put him on the bed. Michael's heart was racing, his breathing was erratic, he was curled up into a fetal position and couldn't move, the pain was still so intense that he couldn't talk, he couldn't link, all he could do was just lay there paralyzed.

After more than thirty minutes, the doctor looked at Bina. "Does your son every have panic attacks?" Bina felt insulted. "No" Anastasia quickly added. "But he has been under a tremendous amount of stress." The doctor ordered a tranquilizer. After another thirty minutes, Michael could whisper one or two words. Anastasia was constantly trying to communicate in the link, but he couldn't respond. The doctor ordered an extra dose of the tranquilizer and within another thirty minutes Michael felt like he could relax enough to fall asleep. The doctor said, "I think this was a panic attack. I found nothing wrong with him. He is reacting well to the medication but I think it would be best if he went to the hospital for a full work up." Anastasia and Ruth quickly said, "NO" at the same time.

Arden took a deep breath and looked around the room. It was packed with protectors and many more family members were waiting in the hall. "Ok everyone, he is going to be fine. Let's give the doctor room to work. We will update every fifteen minutes and sooner if there is a change. We all have something else to do." The room started to clear out but Malachi stayed. He was not going to move and Arden knew there was no use trying.

Rach-El and Lindsey were pacing the hallway floor. Rach-El could not bear to see her brother like that. The two girls were going over every option of what happened. They were far from accepting of a panic attack theory. Hours went by and there was no change. Anastasia looked around the room. Everyone looked confused and scared. She quietly said, "Please, you all are exhausted. Go to bed and I will stay here. I will call you immediately if there is any change." No one liked it, but they agreed. Rach-El and Lindsey were already asleep leaning on each other on the floor in the hallway. Malachi was leaning up against the wall, but made no motion to move. Anastasia was more concerned with Michael than who was going to stay or go. She stayed at the head of his bed with her hands on both sides of his head and her forehead on his.

Ruth was at the door with Bina holding hands. Ruth had a sudden terrible thought. She linked to Arden. "The Thinking Room" Arden shot back. "I'm NOT leaving my son." Arden felt that Ruth could burn a hole in his head with her glare. Ruth turned and walked toward the elevator Arden followed quickly. Once in the elevator Arden started to protest. "Listen..." Ruth put her hand up. The elevator door opened and they walked right to the Thinking Room. Arden finally said. "What could be so important..." Ruth cut him off. "A royal child! The Eile demanded a royal child!" Arden was not following her train of thought. Ruth paced back and forth as she mumbled. Arden insisted, "Mother, what are you talking about?" Ruth looked out the window towards the marina. "Charlotte is missing... Could Charlotte be pregnant? Could the Eile have Charlotte?"

Arden and Ruth went down to the shed. The new door was in place. Arden unlocked it and they walked down the long sloping hallway. Ruth had hoped that at least one was alive. Arden held the door as Ruth readied herself for an attack. Arden opened the door and Ruth gasped at the sight. The two Eile were alive, but barely. They had hundreds of knives pinning them onto the wall. Ruth quickly noticed that the knives were in the same positions as the cuts on Anastasia. "Get them down." Arden and Ruth took them off the wall and put them back onto the tables. The large one hissed. Ruth looked at it. "Has your kind taken a De'nola?" It looked coy, like a cat playing with a mouse. "Why do you care about someone who hates you as much as we do?" Ruth felt the blood drain from her face as she realized her fears were true. Arden pushed a knife into the other one. "We will never allow you to harm her." Ruth walked out and back towards the house. Arden closed the door and hit a small button which sent a mist of salt acid down into the room. The Eile hissed and cursed, but Arden and Ruth were long gone. They needed to call in the elders immediately.

Sometime around 4am, Michael opened his eyes and looked around. Anastasia was asleep with her head next to his and her arms on his chest. Malachi was asleep on the floor. His mother Bina was in a reclining chair next to his bed. He tried to move, but his stomach felt like he would vomit if he tried any harder. He tried to relax and think of what happened, he still felt confused and scared. He allowed his mind to travel wherever it needed to go. He felt light and cool. Then he felt a sudden chill. He opened his eyes. It was so dark. He wasn't in a bed, but standing in a cold damp hallway. There was a dim light at the other end. He started to walk toward the light.

He heard noises but nothing he could figure out. He stopped and thought, 'Am I dreaming? Did I project? Where am I?' He heard a woman's voice, "Hello? Why are you doing this?" He continued moving towards the voice. He walked into a dimly lit room. His eyes needed to focus for a second. "CHARLOTTE!?" She was strapped down to a table and had a large gapping cut across her abdomen. "Michael! Is that you? Michael help me. Someone grabbed me off the boat!" Michael was horrified.

Anastasia was instantly on her feet. She heard Michael call out Charlotte's name. In their link she called back, "Michael. Where are you?" He responded. "I don't know. I'm here with Charlotte. They, The Eile, they have her." Anastasia was confused. Eile have never cared about a De'nola before. Why would they take Charlotte? "Michael, get out of there!" Michael was still having a difficult time processing everything. "Where are we? Can I project Charlotte out like you projected me to Uanza?" Anastasia wanted to scream, but she needed to stay calm and get him out. "No, she is not Azili. We will get her out, but for right now. You need to focus and get back here."

Charlotte was crying and reaching for Michael. Michael grabbed her hands. "What do they want you for? Did they say anything to you?" Charlotte was terrified. "I don't know. They keep talking about a dog a royal baby." Michael froze. "A what?" Charlotte through tears. "I don't know! Half the time I can't understand them. They just keep talking about they want their dog back and this time they will force her to give them a royal baby." Michael stumbled back against the wall. He looked at her stomach. He focused as hard as he could. He heard a tiny heartbeat. He felt fear....he felt his child.

Anastasia stumbled backwards and fell into Malachi. Malachi was instantly awake and caught her before she hit the floor. "What's wrong? Is Michael ok?" She felt numb. "Michael is fine. I slipped. I need to get some fresh air." She walked out the front door and straight down the driveway. She didn't know where she was going, she was just walking. Her mind couldn't think. She walked for about ten minutes before she felt a wave of panic, her legs were shaking, she felt as if she was going to vomit and or pass out again. She fell down to her knees. "Wait. This is the same feeling I had the other day. This is the same feeling I had when they were coming in to cut me. Is there one here?" She started to look around getting ready to fight. But nothing, no movement. She noticed the shed. She took a few deep breaths and stood up. "Are there Eile in there?"

She wondered as she slowly approached the door. The feeling of utter panic was getting unbearable. She reached for the door but saw all the locks. Now she was turning her panic into anger. She grabbed the door and felt the energy of the ancestors pulse through her veins. She pulled on the door and it came off with the sound of twisting metal. Now her anger was becoming fury. She made her way down the sloping hallway. She willed the door to open, which it gave way. The larger one hissed. "I knew you would come. Now let's go home dog." Anastasia looked at the smaller one and by her sheer will and fury, it was dragged to her feet. "Do you have the De'nola named Charlotte?!" It hissed. "Yes, she is a fragile one. She is almost too easy to kill." Anastasia reached down and grabbed it, it screamed in pain as it burst into flames from the inside. The larger one was scared.

They had kept her drugged and asleep most of the time. When she was close to death they would put her in a cryogenic sleep until she was fully healed. But now she had her memories and the strength of ancestors. She would be untouchable, and now that she has bonded. The two of them could defeat their entire species. The Eile had to get and keep them separated. It stretched to look her in the eyes. "I will make you a deal. The De'nola for you?" Anastasia's head was spinning, she realized that they didn't know that Charlotte is pregnant yet. Anastasia knew that she had to move fast. If they don't know yet, they will figure it out soon. They know who she is, they know that Michael is her bond. They know he has a claim to the throne. They will figure it out any second! She blurted out "Fine. I need to see Charlotte on the beach in ten minutes." It smiled, "Done."

Michael whispered in Charlotte's ear. "Shhh you have to be quiet. I promise I will get you out of here. I need to go and get help. Just do whatever they tell you to do. Just know that I am coming right back." He started to make his way down the hall. Charlotte started yelling. "Don't leave me here. MICHAEL! Don't leave me!" He felt his way back to where he had projected himself in. He sat on the floor trying to relax. He concentrated on the child, his child. He tried to communicate his feelings of love and protection, he left the child relax slightly. He turned his focus back to Anastasia. He could feel her but she wasn't talking. "Anastasia, my love…" Anastasia closed their link. Not because she didn't want to talk to him, but she was terrified that the Eile would somehow hear and figure out that Charlotte was pregnant with a royal child.

Anastasia moved away from the door and turned off the electrical current running through the bottom part of the wall. The Eile slithered out of the room and down the hallway. Once outside, it stretched tall and tried to walk. It was clumsy and awkward, but oddly proud of itself. Its tentacles kept giving way and it was slither back to the ground. They walked to the shoreline. It said "Well! Get in." Anastasia was willing herself to loose all feelings, all of her memories, all of who she is. This is how she survived before, and she will do it again. "Charlotte first." The Eile hissed, "She's coming."

Michael sat in the dark hallway thinking of where he wanted to be most in the world. He needed to get back to Anastasia. They would deal with anything together. He knew his child could not hear him yet, but he said, "I promise, I will get you and your mother out of here safely. I'll be back." He felt a peace. He was starting to feel pulled back when he heard Charlotte screaming. "Where are you taking me? Leave me alone!" He heard the voices becoming more and more distant. He waited for a few more minutes and was going to go towards the sound but then nothing. He felt alone in the hallway. He didn't feel the child. "Where did they go?" He knew he needed to go get help and quick. He sat down and just took long deep controlled breathes.

He was back! He opened his eyes and shot up off the bed. His grandmother, his parents and all of his aunts and uncles where coming into the room. Ruth shouted, "Where is Anastasia?" Michael looked around the room. Malachi popped up and was at Michael's side. "She went for a walk a few minutes go." Michael was jumping off the bed, "Where? Which way? You just let her go?" Malachi was suddenly ashamed, "She said she needed some air. I think she is just outside the front door." Michael was in a full sprint. "Call the protectors!"

Ailbe and the old man were sitting on his bed. Not talking, just enjoying the peace and quiet. Everyone was out of the house and they could finally relax. He looked at her. "Well my old friend. It's time." She helped him lie back on the bed and get comfortable. She lay down next to him and they held hands. They both took a deep breath and exhaled slowly. They felt warm and weightless. The old man felt sunshine on his face and smelled jasmine. He felt a hand touch him. He opened his eyes, Ailill was standing over him smiling and said, "Thank you." Ailill reached down and pulled him up by the hand. He looked over and saw Ailbe standing there smiling. The old man looked around in amazement. The bright colors and warm sunshine. "Are we here?" He was shocked at how strong his voice sounded. He felt no pain. He looked at his hands with all of his fingers. He wiggled his toes and laughed. Ailbe gave him a big hug. "Yes, we are here. Let me introduce you to everyone." He looked at Ailill. "I knew you would be the first one to greet us." Ailill smiled and said, "You are honored amongst our most honored." The old man knew everything about Ailbe, but now he understood everything.

Ailbe knew her work was not done yet. She knew the war was starting soon. She would push all the boundaries of the veil and lead the charge into the water. She heard Ruth calling for her. She asked the old man and Ailill to walk ahead, she was going to tell Ruth that she is with the ancestors. She sat down and felt the grass and the breeze. She thought of Ruth. It was difficult to communicate through the noise and confusion. She thought of Anastasia. But it felt like she was drifting away. She thought of Michael who was in a frenzied panic. Ailbe shot up screaming. "She cannot go back to them!!!"

Anastasia saw a disturbance in the water. She was motionless as she watched two Eile drag Charlotte up onto the beach. One of the Eile slapped her and she coughed and opened her eyes. She saw Anastasia standing over her. Before she could say anything, Anastasia put her finger to her lips. "Shhh. Michael is on his way. Don't make a sound until I am gone." They heard people screaming Anastasia's name. The Eile hissed, "You gave your word dog." Anastasia was silent as she started to walk toward the water.

Michael saw her in the distance. He started screaming. "NOOOO!" As he ran faster and faster. Anastasia didn't turn around. Tears started to flow down her face. She was up to her knees. Ailbe broke all the rules and went to her. Anastasia saw her above the water. Ailbe shouted, "No! Go back to Michael. Fight this." Anastasia lifted her chin. "I gave my word."

Michael was less than a hundred yards away. He saw Charlotte scrambling to get away from the water. Ailbe was begging her, "Please stop!" He ran passed Charlotte and into the water. Ailbe felt the last bit of Anastasia fad away as she said, "Save the last royal child." She was gone.

Mark was loading supplies into the trunk when he felt Ailbe cross. He was sad but knew that this is what she wanted. Pia-Jiun felt light headed and leaned up against the car. Mark caught her by the elbow. "Are you ok? Here, sit down in the car. I'll put the heater on." She smiled and stood up straight. "I'm fine. The old man is gone." Mark watched her as she continued with loading supplies. "We should stay away for a little while longer." And she walked off. Mark quickly followed to catch up to her. "Are you ok?" She said, "I am sad for me, but I'm happy he is with your ancestors." Mark was shocked but Pia-Jiun smiled, "The old man was not the only one that knew Ailbe's secrets. I have been watching all of you since the day I was born." Mark smiled and followed her.

Jonathan was laughing with Geetu as Lucy was trying on funny hats when he felt Ailbe cross. Lucy suddenly looked sad. Geetu was still laughing. She made eye contact with Jonathan and said, "I think we need to get back, right now." Jonathan lowered his head slightly. "Not just yet." Lucy was alarmed, "I just had a bad feeling." Geetu ran to her and hugged her legs. "Don't be sad. This is what they wanted." Lucy bent down and hugged him tight. "Did you feel it too?" Geetu "Isn't that why Ailbe came back so fast? I think she took him to her heaven." Lucy thought for a second. It felt like things made more sense... "I think so."

Jonathan was amazed and understood why Ailbe had such a strong connection with the old man and his family. He wished that all De'nola were like them. Lucy said, "I have a bit of a headache. Can we sit down for a little while?" Geetu said, "You have to be hungry, you don't eat anything." Jonathan thought for a second. "Why haven't you been eating?" Lucy tried to make light of it. "I just haven't been very hungry." Geetu "You lie." He jumped off the bench they were sitting on and called out. "I'll be right back." and he ran down the street. Jonathan looked concerned. "What is going on?" Lucy shrugged her shoulders. "I just wanted to make sure that everyone had enough to eat. It's no big deal. I'm fine."

For a split second, Jonathan felt he could link to her... Jonathan suddenly felt Michael screaming for Anastasia. He jumped up and started yelling for Geetu. "Lucy, we have to go. NOW. Grab your stuff. GEETU!" Geetu came running out of a store with a soda and a plum. He handed it to Lucy as he ran to keep up with Jonathan.

Mark was watching Pia-Jiun as she effortlessly navigated the busy streets and shops. He never had a conversation with her before. He asked, "Can I ask you a personal question?" She giggled, "Personal? Do I reserve the right not to answer if I say yes?" Mark was an expert at reading De'nola, but she was different. He asked, "Where is Geetu's father?" She just nodded her head and said, "No" and continued walking.

Mark felt a wave of grief and terror. He stopped in the middle of the street to try and link with anyone back home. Several people bumped into him. Pia-Jiun saw the look in his eyes and took him by the elbow and started walking back to the car. She finally said, "Something is very wrong. You are all behaving like you have to hide here. What is going on?" Mark felt more comfortable with Pia-Jiun than any other De'nola. "I don't know. We are on the verge of war back home. We have orders to stay here till the end of the week. I should be there with my family, but Ailbe told me to stay here." Pia-Jiun didn't have to think about it. "Then you must stay. We will have the service for the old man and Ailbe, and then you can leave. But for now, we go back to the Inn."

Mark and Pia-Jiun, Jonathan and Lucy with Geetu got back to the Inn within minutes of each other. Mark and Jonathan went upstairs without a word. Lucy and Pia-Jiun unpacked the cars. Mark and Jonathan tried to link to anyone back home. The links were confusing, like everyone was talking and yelling at once.

Michael dove into the water. He couldn't find her. Arden dove in behind him. Then all the protectors arrived and started diving deeper and deeper in the water. She was gone without a trace. Michael was exhausted and had taken in a lot of water but he refused to give up trying. Arden and five other protectors had to grab him and force him back onto the beach. He was screaming and pushing everyone aside to get back into the water.

Rach-El and Lindsey were driving in a golf cart. Malachi picked up

Charlotte and threw her into the back seat and yelled, "Get her back to the house. Call 911 and get her to the hospital." Lindsey was driving and Rach-El jumped into the back seat to keep Charlotte calm. "Charlotte, it's me. We are going to get you to the hospital right away. We have a doctor at the house. You are going to be fine. Just hold on OK." Charlotte was still in shock and just kept crying and holding her stomach.

Lindsey drove to the house where the doctor and nurses were waiting. They put her onto a stretcher and wheeled her into the infirmary. 911 was already called and on the way. The doctor started to clean the wound as one of the nurses called Dr. Ziv. "Dr. Ziv? Sorry to call you on your cell phone, But we found Charlotte Calhoun on the beach with a large gash across her stomach. 911 is almost here. Can you meet us at the hospital?" Dr. Ziv "Absolutely, I'm leaving right now."

Ruth was now the eldest of her kind, she linked to every adult in the entire family. "My dear family. We are officially at war. The Eile abducted Charlotte. Anastasia traded herself for Charlotte's release. Official story is that Charlotte has been distraught, drinking heavily and not thinking clearly. She started the boat engine and fell in the water and apparently hit her head and cut herself on the propeller... She is pregnant with Michael's child." Everyone gasped. Mark and Jonathan stood there unable to move.

Michael saw the ambulance speed down the road. He was on his hands and knees vomiting sea water and coughing it up out of his lungs. He was distraught and closed his link to everyone in an attempt to focus solely on connecting with Anastasia. The protectors were diving deeper than they every have. But every time they came back up, it was more of the same. No sign of Anastasia. Arden motioned for everyone get out of the water. Ruth sat down in the sand next to Michael. "We will find her. The elders will be here in a few hours. Ailbe is with the ancestors. The children are gone. We will fight to the death to get her back." Michael could barely speak. "Why? Why did she go?"

Ruth was holding back her emotions. "Because she is our Queen. She sacrificed herself for your child. She had a small window of opportunity before they figured out that Charlotte is pregnant." Michael "SHE KNEW? How did she know? How did you know?" Ruth lowered her head. "Just as you felt your child, we knew. She broke your link so the Eile wouldn't somehow figure it out or they would never have let Charlotte go. Anastasia had no time to think about it." Michael called out to the ancestors "Take me now! I can't live with this!" Ailbe did not dare break another rule. She just whispered in his ear. "I'll find her."

Jonathan let the wave of shock pass him slowly. Then he started throwing things in bags. He looked over at Mark, "Don't just sit there! Help me get this shit…You know, fuck it, just leave it. Get in the car." Jonathan was halfway down the stairs when Mark called out. "We have to stay here. Well, at least until the end of the week." Jonathan walked back in. "What!? NO, I'm going home. We need to leave NOW!" Mark didn't move. His heart felt like he had abandoned his entire family. He called out to Ailbe, "You have to give me more than this! I need to know WHY I can't go home and fight!" There was no response.

Lucy and Pia-Jiun could hear the men yelling, but neither one of them dared to go upstairs. Geetu was his normal happy sweet self. He bounced upstairs, and started his chore of cleaning the room. Jonathan didn't want to scare him. "Geetu, I'll clean up in here. You can go outside and play." Geetu nodded no. "Ailbe said that you would explain why Lucy smells different." Jonathan tried to laugh, "You never tell a lady that she smells." Geetu shook his head and looked up to the ceiling. "He doesn't understand it yet." and he ran off.

The ambulance pulled into the emergency room. The Assistant Police Chief Curtis Cappola, Dr. Ziv, and Charlotte's dad were already waiting inside. Dr. Scott was on duty in the emergency room but when he saw Dr. Ziv. "Ezriel, Thank God you're here. I've know Charlotte since she was a baby, this is going to be another heart breaker." Dr. Ziv. "This is why we do what we do. The Reale family has been put through too much these past few months." Curtis Cappola leaned in. "I'm here in an official capacity, but I over heard that she might be pregnant." Dr. Scott and Dr. Ziv both called out. "Add a pregnancy test to that blood work. NO X-RAYS until we get those results." Dr. Ziv patted Curtis on the back. "I'm glad you spoke up!" and he walked into the room where they took Charlotte.

Charlotte was mumbling about weird men taking her and one stabbed her. Dr. Ziv started two IV lines before the blood work came back. One of the nurses handed him a piece of paper *'BHCG -----positive'*. Dr. Ziv had to rethink his entire plan of care and quickly. He bent down to Charlotte. "Your blood work says you're pregnant. I can give you a local anesthetic to suture you up, but I can't risk harming the baby" Charlotte "Pregnant? I can't be pregnant…" She started thinking of the last two times she was with Michael was the only two times he had never used a condom. She always told him that she was on the pill, but she wasn't. "No…not now… Why now?"

Ruth stood up. "I need to go to the hospital." No one responded. She linked to Se'ighin who was back at the house keeping the family focused on war preparations, to come down and pick her up. Arden and Bina sat quietly next to their son watching the water. Rach-El and Lindsey had driven back down the beach in the golf cart and just sat a few yards away watching. The protectors started walking back to the house. The sun was starting to come up. Michael saw the dolphins jumping in the water. Two of them kept coming closer and closer. Michael locked eyes with the big one. It just floated in the water. Michael was hoping it would suddenly start speaking English and tell him where Anastasia was, but no luck. Michael sat there with his parents for hours without moving.

Back at the house, the tents arrived and they were being erected in a large square and L-shape. One looked like it was half way into the water. The local government issued a *No Fly Zone* for the next month over the area after a rather large donation was made to each of the board members re-election campaigns. The resident doctors and nurses were told that they were no longer needed but would be paid their entire contracted amount. Family was arriving by the bus loads. Fighters were to go straight to the training gym and healers were to go straight to the infirmary. Supplies for the infirmary were being delivered by the truck loads.

Ruth and Se'ighin arrived at the hospital. Ruth's shoulder felt heavy. Se'ighin put his hand around her waist as they walked in. Mr. Kelly was called as Charlotte was being brought in. The board of directors had already voted to fire her for HIPPA violations. He left her messages, but had not heard back from her yet. He felt it was going to be awkward until Ruth

Reale called him personally to reassure him that the Reale family felt no
ill-will towards her and still consider her a part of the family. He arrived
shortly before Ruth and Se'ighin did.

He was standing just inside the ER as Ruth walked in. "I need an update on Charlotte." Tom saw Ruth walk in and went over to see her. "Tom!"
Ruth gave him a hug and Se'ighin shook his hand. Ruth continued, "I'm
so sorry about everything that has happened. We all care for Charlotte
very deeply. When Michael saw your boat like that, he started a search
party right away." Tom had tears in his eyes. "I knew she was mad at me for
going to the parade. This is all my fault. I should have stayed with her like
she wanted. I don't think I can live with myself." Se'ighin "It isn't anyone's
fault. It was an accident. We are just glad she was found and is going be ok.
Any updates on her condition?" Tom rubbed his eyes. "Not yet. Dr. Ziv
is in there with her now. Dr. Scott said he would be out to talk to us once
they got her stable."

Mr. Kelly was just standing there making sure everyone was friendly.
"I'll go in and see if I can find anything out yet." He disappeared inside.
The waiting room was quiet until Dr. Ziv and Dr. Scott came out with
Curtis looking very official. Dr. Scott was smiling. "Wish we could all stop
seeing each other on professional levels. But Tom, Charlotte is a lucky
girl. That propeller could have done a lot more damage. It didn't cut any
major blood vessels or organs. It's big, but not life threatening. She hit her
head pretty hard. We called in the neurologist Dr. McKay. Ruth, you will
remember her. But she is pretty confused about what happened. So we just
need to reassure her that she is safe."

Tom was getting some color back into his cheeks. "When can I see
her?" Dr. Scott said, "Soon, but I need to tell you folks one more thing.
Charlotte is pregnant." Tom gasped. "What? She and Michael broke up."
Ruth quietly asked, "Is the child ok?" Dr. Ziv said "We have called in an
OB/GYNE. The ultrasound is being done in a few minutes. The injury is
to her abdomen, just below her ribcage. It should not have any effect on
the pregnancy. But this is an early pregnancy and she is traumatised. We
will have to wait and see." Tom looked worried again. Ruth put her hand
on Tom's hand. "Tom, we are family now. We will all be here for her and

the baby. The circumstances with the parents have nothing to do with the child. I give you my word that this child will know nothing but love and security.

And as soon as Charlotte is ready to travel, we will send all of you on a spa week in Colorado. I will make all the arrangements. Dr. Ziv, when can charlotte travel?" Dr. Ziv "Travel? Well, I just put sixty stitches in her belly. She needs to be here for a few days. The stitches come out in about ten days if everything is ok. So maybe a spa vacation in two weeks is more reasonable." Ruth "Two weeks? Unacceptable. I need…" Se'ighin cut her off. "Poor thing… two weeks is a long time for a young vibrant woman to be stuck here. She has been through a terrible trauma. Tom, we will talk and see how she feels. I'll have some family stick around here until she can get home and rest." Tom said "I know she has been wanting to get out of town and clear her head a bit. Maybe when she gets out of the hospital, I'll drive her over to Tennessee and visit some family for a few days."

Ruth added, "Tennessee is perfect. We have a large RV that has very comfortable seats that she would be perfect to travel in. I can even have a driver and a nurse travel with you." Dr. Ziv sensed that Ruth was pushing hard to get Charlotte out of town. He wondered if Michael and Anastasia were getting married soon. But that was none of his business. "It is all up to Charlotte and how she feels. I'm going to go back in and check on her. I'll come and get you in a few minutes." Tom was pacing back and forth. Ruth and Se'ighin wanted to get home as quickly as they could but they sat there as a family.

Every sound Michael heard, he imagined it was Anastasia screaming. Bina could feel Michael's turmoil. "Why don't we go back to the house?" Michael didn't respond. Arden "Michael, you can do more from the house. We will attack as soon as the elders get here." Michael quietly said, "You go." Arden and Bina stood up and brushed the sand off of them. Bina kissed his head. "I'm here if you need me." They started walking back to the house. Lindsey and Rach-El were in a golf cart just a few yards away. Arden just nodded an acknowledgement that he saw them and kept walking. His images of Anastasia's screams were getting louder and louder in his head.

He felt like he was going to go insane. He tried to relax to project. His mind would only replay his last sight of her walking into the water.

Jonathan was pacing the floor as he watched Mark. He finally asked, "What are we waiting for? Ailbe and the old man crossed. We need to get home." Mark took a deep breath. "For some reason we need to stay for the week. I'm not going anywhere." Jonathan "I just don't understand why! Our entire family just imploded and we are told to sit on our hands?! This makes no sense." Mark put his head in his hands. "And that is usually the best time to do exactly what we are told until it does make sense." Jonathan threw his hands up. "Fine!" He looked up towards the ceiling where Geetu was looking and yelled out. "You better explain this quick. I'm really freaking out."

Pec was scratching at the door. Lucy put on her coat and told Pia-Jiun. "I'll be back in a few minutes." Pia-Jiun nodded as she went back to putting the supplies away. Lucy walked out the back door and closed her eyes. For some reason she felt it could help her hear better. There was no sound, it was eerily silent. Pec started barking. Lucy looked but couldn't see anything, but Pec just got louder. Lucy picked him up and put him inside her coat and started walking in the direction that Pec was looking. Lucy noticed how bright the colors looked. She started hearing a faint sound. She stopped to focus on it. It almost sounded like the lullaby Ailbe was singing. It was a beautiful sound and she felt drawn to it. She looked around and couldn't imagine where it was coming from. She thought she would follow it for a few minutes. Pec's barking became louder. His tail was wagging and he was trying to jump out of her coat. So Lucy pressed forward.

The sky started to turn gray, she thought she should head back, but the music must be coming from right over the next small hill. She got to the top of the hill and the music stopped. She saw an old mud-stone structure in ruins. Just two of the walls were still standing. No roof, just piles of stones and a few mud bricks were left. Lucy wanted to explore it further but it started to snow. She turned around and noticed she had walked much farther than she realized. Pec curled up and closed his eyes. Lucy was moving quickly to get back to the Inn. The sky was turning a dark gray and snowing heavier. She started to get worried. Her feet were getting cold and the snow was starting to get into her boots. She stopped to catch her breath. She looked around but couldn't see the Inn, she couldn't see anything. Now the wind had started to blow the snow sideways, Lucy started to panic. She called out in her head. "Jonathan. I'm scared. I need you."

Dr. Ziv and Dr. Scott came out into the ER waiting room. Dr. Scott said. "So far everything with the baby looks normal. She is very early in this pregnancy. We need to keep a close eye on her. The risk for a miscarriage is high because of the emotional trauma. I'm admitting her for a day or two for IV antibiotics and observation. She will be going upstairs in a few minutes. You all can meet her in her room." Tom breathed a sigh of relief. "Thank you. Does she know I'm here?" Dr. Ziv patted him on the shoulder. "Yes, she knows who is here and who is not here." Ruth knew what he meant and didn't respond. She was not going to justify why Michael was not here. "Thank you. We will go upstairs and wait for her." Ruth hugged both doctors. Se'ighin shook their hands and sat back down. Dr. Scott added, "One of the nurses will be right out with the room number." The two doctors walked back into the ER.

Rach-El and Lindsey were sitting in the golf cart. Lindsey said. "Randy! Randi Fenoli is coming in a few hours. It's too late to cancel him." Rach-El didn't take her eyes off of Michael and said, "I'm staying here. You go and talk to your parents. My vote is that we keep up appearances." Lindsey wanted to find something to laugh at but she felt like she would never laugh again. Rach-El got out of the golf cart and walked over to Michael and sat down beside him without saying a word.

Lindsey went back to the house and linked to meet with her mother and hoped that her father would be there too. Olivia linked. "Meet in the library." She got to the house and walked into the library. She was surprised to see Arden, Bina, Aharon, Isabelle, Elijah, Chaya, her parents and Bjorn there. Lindsey looked around,"Um… What did I do now?" Olivia smiled, "You and Rach-El are a team to be reckoned with. I have to assume that the question of a wedding is what you needed to speak to me about." Lindsey was very uncomfortable. "Yeah… um… we have a few appointments today. I can deal with most of them, but we don't know what to do with the wedding dress designer." Bjorn stepped forward. Lindsey looked very confused. Bjorn said. "I have already spoken to your..." Lindsey cut him off. "NO! I'm not going to have a De'nola wedding with you! I just started dating Erik. Rach-El is the one who is already picking out names for your kids!" Bjorn laughed, "No offense to you, but that is not what I was going to say. I was going to say that I have already spoken to your elders here and my clann's elders about Rach-El."

Lindsey tried to laugh but it sounded more like a nervous gurgle. "Oh, so what am I doing here?" Bjorn took her hand. "Out of respect for your relationship with her. I wanted to speak to you. I wanted to know if you would reject me offering my bond to her?" Lindsey smiled, "Phew!" She hugged him. "I'm so happy that you found each other. You are perfect together. I can even feel your connection to her. I hate that it is under these horrible conditions, but I would never reject!"

Everyone in the room erupted in cheers. Bjorn looked at Lindsey. "You were my last conversation before I spoke to her. I don't like the circumstances either and that is not why I want to ask her. I knew from the first day I met her that she was the one for me. War or no war, I have found my one true love." Lindsey's smile was beaming. Olivia stepped up next to Bjorn and looked at Lindsey. "So, to answer your question. We will be planning a wedding. I understand that Mr. Fenoli is Rach-El's favorite designer..." Lindsey smiled, "What can I do?" Bina said, "Continue to do what every cousin/best friend/maid of honors do... Just act natural and be there for her." Lindsey nodded, "I can do that." Bjorn said, "I need to go speak to Rach-El."

Charlotte was brought up into a room and was being settled in by a floor nurse. Tom, Ruth and Se'ighin were waiting outside the door. The floor nurse came out. "She is all ready for visitors." Tom started to walk in but Ruth and Se'ighin stayed outside. Tom "You guys can come in." Ruth responded, "You see your daughter first. I would ask for a few minutes alone with here. I'm sure you understand, a woman to woman conversation." Tom nodded and walked in. After a few minutes Tom came out. He looked at Se'ighin. "She is still pretty mad. I'm gonna go home for a bit and get some rest. I'll be back later today." Se'ighin "She has had a rough few weeks. I might be upset too. I'll walk you down to your car. There are a few things that we need to discuss." Tom and Se'ighin walked down the hall. Ruth watched them for a moment and then she went into Charlotte's room.

Charlotte was in the bed with the head up in a reclining position. She looked at Ruth but didn't say anything. Ruth walked in and pulled a chair closer to the bed. "How are you feeling?" Charlotte "Fine." There was a few second pause before Ruth said, "The doctors say that you will only need to be here for a day or two. Your father has expressed your desire to get out of town for a few days. I have a driver and a lovely RV that will keep you traveling comfortably... To Tennessee I believe." Charlotte stiffened her lip. "Is Michael getting married soon? Is that why you want me out of town so badly?" Ruth wondered how Michael ever thought he loved this woman. "For now, their public wedding ceremony is off." Charlotte wanted to cheer, but wanted to keep Ruth talking. She wanted to know every detail. "Why? I mean, Michael and I have been together five years. She just washed up a few months ago." Ruth felt a wave of anger. She wanted Charlotte to know only what would benefit the family, which now included her child. "They both have a lot to think about." Charlotte "Does Michael know about our baby?"

Ruth "Yes"

Charlotte "Is he even going to come and see us?"

Ruth "Yes."

Charlotte "When?" She knew she had to soften Ruth up a little. "I mean that we have so much to talk about. Michael always said how much he wanted kids. I just want to make sure that his baby has (She started cracking her voice as if she was really crying) a relationship with you all. This child will know that they came into this world because I loved, and was faithful to the dad."

Ruth wanted to storm out, but thought better. "I agree that you and Michael have several issues to discuss. But hear me and hear me very clearly. This child will know many things..." Charlotte cut her off. "Don't threaten me!" Ruth cleared her throat. "My dear, you misunder-stand me. It has been a very long night... with Anastasia leaving and all... I meant to press upon you, that you and the child will be very well cared for." Charlotte thought… 'got ya!' and said, "She left? I wonder why. Well, there are a few things I will need for my trip." Ruth breathed a sigh of relief. "Name it sweetheart." Charlotte "The driver of course, for the RV… What do you want me to tell my family? About the pregnancy?" Ruth "I will speak to Michael today. But tell them the truth. You and Michael will be working out the co-parenting issues. This is defiantly his child and he will take care of you both." Charlotte pushed a little farther. "What does take care of mean?" Ruth "You and I can discuss finances, but you and the child are now and forever a member of the Reale family." Charlotte lifted her chin slightly. "Ruth, you and I are going to become very close. We have a good understanding of each other." She rubbed her belly. "And I have a feeling that this little peanut will have everything they ever want." Ruth "I do believe I understand you very clearly." Charlotte smiled. "I know that you all travel with security. I'm going to need Jonathan as my security." Ruth did not expect that. "Jonathan is out of the country." Charlotte thought for a second, "Well then, Malachi. That is really nonnegotiable. I mean, I was attacked. I didn't imagine it and I didn't hit my head." Ruth was going to have a protector watching her, but not Malachi. He was one of the best divers, she needed him in this war. "Malachi has other responsibilities at the moment. I will assign…" Charlotte put her finger up to her mouth like she was thinking and just started talking over Ruth. "Maybe I don't feel like going to Tennessee right now. Maybe I just want to hang around town for a few weeks." Ruth did not like being manipulated. "On second thought, Malachi would be thrilled to spend some time with you." She got up and walked out. Charlotte said out loud to herself. "I need to make you a list of things that I will need." As she rubbed her belly. She called for the nurse to bring her in paper and a pen.

The Inn was quiet. Mark wondered if Lucy's parents were going to stay in Katmandu for a few days. Jonathan was leaning back in the bed trying to relax. He had an odd feeling. He sat up, "Hey Mark, do you feel ok?" Mark thought for a second. "I feel horrible. I feel like I need to get home. Why?" Jonathan stood up. "Where is Lucy?" He didn't wait for an answer. He walked downstairs calling her name. Pia-Jiun was in the kitchen and stood up as Jonathan came in with Mark rushing to catch up. Pia-Jiun pointed to the door. "She went to walk the dog, but that was some time ago."

Jonathan and Mark grabbed their jackets. Mark took the two large containers of pepper that they had just purchased and shoved them in his pockets. It was snowing pretty heavy. Jonathan yelled. "Which way did she go?" Pia-Jiun felt embarrassed that she didn't know. Mark just started walking straight ahead with Jonathan close behind him. Both men started calling out her name. Jonathan was looking for tracks in the snow, but didn't know how long it had been snowing. The wind was getting stronger by the minute, he could barely hear when Mark was talking to him. Mark turned to face him. "We need to go back and get help. She could be anywhere out here." Jonathan said, "You go back. I'll keep a link open with you." Mark handed him the two containers of pepper. "Give me a trail to follow." and he turned around to go back as Jonathan continued walking. Every few feet he would sprinkle some of the pepper in the snow and thought, "He is brilliant."

Jonathan walked and yelled out her name for what seemed like miles. He stopped and tried to listen. He heard… a heartbeat? He saw a faint blue light. He tried to run, but the snow was piling up quick. "LUCY!" She was lying down in the snow shivering. He picked her up and started to carry her back. "I've got you. You're ok." She wasn't talking but she was looking at him. He heard a noise and looking inside her jacket. Pec was curled up around her neck and wagging his tail. "Good boy Pec!" He called to Mark in their link. "I found her. She's alive but so cold." Mark replied, "I'm on my way back to you with blankets." A strong gust of wind knocked him off his feet onto his back. He struggled to get up. The wind kept pushing him back down. He felt her heart slowing down. He knew he had to get her warm or she could die. The only thing he could do was lay on top of her and hope Mark got there soon.

As he felt her life starting to drift away. Pec started barking and wagging his tail. Jonathan tried to smile, "You really are a protector, but if she dies, she won't be alone. (He leaned forward to Lucy's ear.) I'm here with you. I promise I won't leave you. I'll never leave you. I do truly love you. From the first day I met you, I couldn't stop thinking about you. I never thought of you as a conquest, I only thought of you as my future. Please don't leave me. Mark is on his way. Just fight a little more." Jonathan felt warmth around them. He looked up expecting to see Mark with blankets, but instead he saw the ancestors. Ailbe and the old man were standing in front of them smiling. Some of the other ancestors were circling them, they were glowing a warm blue. It seemed like an eternity, but Mark followed by a few villagers, finally arrived. As they approached, the ancestors left. Jonathan stood up as Mark covered Lucy with blankets. Jonathan tried to take Pec out of her coat but he backed up as if he was refusing to leave. Jonathan looked at the pup. "I don't want you freezing either." The pup jumped into his hands as the villagers gently picked Lucy up and carried her back to the Inn.

Pia-Jiun saw them coming and put several more logs on the fire. Geetu was getting more water and putting in on the stove to boil. The villagers carried her straight into the dining room and laid her down in front of the fire. Pia-Jiun yelled for everyone to get out as she started to undress her. She needed to get out of the wet frozen clothes as quickly as she could. Jonathan felt helpless as he kept reassuring Pec that she was going to be ok. Mark was pacing. "What was she thinking? She could have gotten herself killed out there!" Jonathan looked at Mark. "Did you see the ancestors? The blue light?" Mark said, "No. I saw the pepper. The ancestors came to you?" Jonathan nodded. "The old man and Great-Grandmother, they surrounded us."

Mark was trying to connect everything together. "Why? You could have easily made it back." Jonathan "You knew everything about Great-Grandmother except one thing." He linked the information to him. Mark's eyes opened wide. "What!" Mark was starting to connect the dots. He looked at Jonathan. "Hear me out. I'm thinking out loud... the old man saves Ailbe. Ailbe offers the old man a life of leisure... the old man refuses AND his family refuses... Ailbe asks for a blessing knowing that what she asked for is impossible...the ancestors grant the blessing to the old man...but the old man had a condition!.. All the old man wanted was peace... not peace for his species, but for her species...What am I missing here!?!" Geetu was bringing in more hot water from the kitchen. "Did you ever listen to Ailbe?" as he kept walking and dropped off the water to his mother, then he ran passed to get more water. Mark and Jonathan suddenly felt very foolish. They linked with her countless times, but they didn't ever remember listening to any of her stories. They just had the information.

Jonathan felt Lucy was improving quickly. Her heart was beating stronger, her breathing was deeper and she was awake and starting to talk. Jonathan yelled into the room. "Is she dressed yet? Can we come in?" Pia-Jiun "Yes, you can come in." Mark stood there mumbling to himself. Jonathan walked into the room and straight to Lucy's side. "How are you feeling?" before she could answer, Pec jumped out of his arms and onto Lucy's chest and started licking her face. Lucy moved slightly to hold Pec. "Good boy, I told you Jonathan would find us."

She looked up at Jonathan. "I'm so sorry. I didn't mean to walk off. I didn't know I had gone that far and then it started to snow." Jonathan "Shhh don't be sorry about anything." Lucy blinked a few times. "It was the weirdest thing. I must have been hypothermic and hallucinating. I felt like we were on a phone call but we both were on mute. I could almost talk to you. Then I knew you were coming. Then I must have passed out, I thought I saw Ailbe and the old man. Crazy right?" Jonathan looked over at Mark who was standing there with his mouth open. "Could you see our ancestors?" Pia-Jiun stood up and collected Lucy's wet clothes to dry them. "Keep her by the fire." She was walking back into the kitchen. Mark stopped her. "Wait, you know more than you are saying. I think we all need to talk and figure a few things out." Geetu walked into the room to bring in more blankets. "Ailbe said that you have to figure it out on your own." Pia-Jiun smiled and she continued walking into the kitchen. Jonathan looked at Geetu. "What else did Ailbe tell you?" Geetu giggled.

Michael and Rach-El sat on the beach staring into the water. Bjorn drove up in a golf cart and walked over to sit next to them. Bjorn finally said, "What can I do?" Michael didn't move, he kept looking into the water and said, "Keep her safe." Bjorn buried his feet in the sand. "I intend to." The three of them sat there for awhile. Michael rarely even blinked. He was scanning the water for any break in the surface tension. He was ready to dive back into the water in an instant. Rach-El "You need to eat something." Michael "I can't feel her" There was silence. "I think she's dead." Rach-El shot back. "Don't say that! They need her alive." Michael allowed the tears to run down his face. "Then why can't I feel her?" Rach-El could feel the empty void. She knew he was right. She was just gone. "Try the Thinking Room. If she is dead, she will be with the ancestors." Michael "I hope she's dead." Rach-El wondered why he would want her dead. Then he said, "If she is alive, they are cutting her right now." Rach-El wanted to vomit. She stood up and ran toward the house.

Bjorn scanned the water for a moment and said, "We will find her. I'll give my life to find her." Michael didn't move. "I would rather you live a very long happy life... She loves you too you know." Bjorn "She loves all of us, that's why she went back to them." Michael picked up some sand and watched it fall through his fingers. "Not Anastasia, I meant Rach-El." Michael patted Bjorn on the leg. "Please go and protect my sister, I'm fine." Bjorn stood up, "I'm planning on giving her my bond." Michael smiled "I know." Bjorn asked, "Would you reject?" Michael looked at him genuinely confused. "Reject what? My sister being happy? You as her bond? NO! This actually gives me a moment of peace. Now please go to her, she needs you." Michael looked back at the water irritated that he could have missed something. Bjorn walked away without responding.

Rach-El ran all the way back to the house and into the arms of her mother. Bina just held her until Bjorn came in and walked up to them. Rach-El felt him as he was walking toward them. She turned around and crumpled into his arms. He held her close as she cried. Bina walked away to give them privacy. Lindsey saw what happened and sat down. She would talk to them when the time was right. She looked at her watch. Randy was scheduled to arrive within the hour. So the time unfortunately was now. She walked up, "Rach-El, I'm so sorry to bring this up now. But Bjorn needs to talk to you." Rach-El sniffled and wiped her face. "I'm sorry. His pain was too much to take. I need to be stronger than that." She shook her head and hands, she took a deep breath, lifted her chin and pulled back her shoulders. "Protector, do you need healing?" She was training as a healer. Bjorn laughed. "Only if you break my heart?" Lindsey smiled but Rach-El was confused. Bjorn felt her deep pain for Michael. "My love, I know this is the worst time for us to bond. This war is going to be hell for all of us. But I was thinking we need to keep up the appearance of a wedding and with… well, you know. But I know it might be too quick for you, but I was planning on offering you my bond when the timing was better… I was hoping I could plan on what to say… I… but, when I heard… I mean…" Rach-El was trying to follow his cluttered thinking. "Yes, I accept your bond and I offer you mine."

Lindsey jumped up and down. "YEAH!! Congratulations." The two cousins hugged. Then Lindsey looked serious and got down to business. "Ok, Mr. Fenoli is going to be here soon to design your dress. He is bringing several seamstresses to work on it immediately. The caterer is going to be here this afternoon for a tasting. The florist is on their way. The decorators will start tomorrow morning about 9:00 - 9:30…" Rach-El held up both hands. "Stop! I know the schedule that we had for Anastasia… I'm going to do the De'nola wedding instead?" Bina had been standing around the corner, she was not going to leave her daughter crying hysterically nor was she going to miss Bjorn offering his bond. She walked to her daughter's side. "Bjorn spoke to us prior to this morning. If you agree…yes, we need to keep up the appearance of a wedding to explain all of the activity." Rach-El "But we both have training to do. We need Bjorn in the fight and I need to get much better. I can't risk our family like that." Bjorn smiled, "We all need this. This will explain everything to the De'nola. It will free up everyone except you and Lindsey to train. I would never have agreed to this if I thought it wasn't for the best." Lindsey was nodding in agreement. Bina smiled. Rach-El thought for a moment. "Ok, but just remember. You all have created this bridezilla, so you all are going to have to deal with me." Bjorn laughed and picked her up and was about to kiss her. "Wait. We need to have a proper recording of our bond." Bina smiled, "Tonight at dinner. We will all be together." Rach-El kissed him. "So much for a long courtship, but now I get to see those dance moves again." She looked at Lindsey. "Will you be my maid of honor?" Lindsey "Pfft, I'm way ahead of you."

Ruth walked down stairs. Se'ighin was in the car waiting. Ruth got in and slammed the door. "Bitch" Then she linked to Malachi. "I need you at the hospital to protect the child." Malachi responded, "Charlotte?" Ruth "I know, I don't like it either, but only until we can get her out of town." Malachi broke the link. The drive home was quiet except for Ruth's outbursts of, "She has some nerve!" and "What did Michael ever see in that wretched girl?" As they drove up the through the gates into the compound, Ruth saw Michael sitting in the same spot as he had been when she left. She tried thinking of something wise and timeless to say, but there were no words to ease his pain. They drove up to the main house to the sounds of cheering. Ruth looked at Se'ighin. "A moment of peace…We all need this." They got out of the car and walked into the house. Several family members were gathering around Bjorn and Rach-El.

Rach-El saw Ruth coming in. She ran and hugged her. "Grandmother. Bjorn and I have bonded!" Se'ighin reached out to shake Bjorn's hand. "Congratulations. We are over the moon for you both." Ruth looked proud. "Well done. We have a reason to celebrate." Ruth lifted up her hands and shouted. "Where is Antonio? We need some music in here." She linked to Antonio, who quickly responded, "On it." And the music started. As the family felt a renewed sense of energy, the appointments started to arrive and just like that Rach-El put on a brave face and was in full wedding mode.

Michael could hear the music. He stood up and walked closer to the water. He now hated the water. As each small wave touched his foot, he cursed it. He fell to his knees. "Why? We could have done anything together. Why won't you tell me where you are?" Michael noticed the large dolphin, with the scars, was back. It was just feet away from him, just staring. Michael asked, "Can you find her?" The dolphin raised himself up out of the water. Michael asked, "Can you understand me?" The dolphin splashed water at him. Michael was confused but had a flash of excitement. "Do you know where they went?!" The dolphin disappeared. Michael's hopes felt dashed.

He turned and walked back toward the house. He went in through a side door and up to the Thinking Room. As he walked in, the room looked dull. The door closed behind him. George flew out of the tree and as he landed, he just laid down. Michael noticed he had lost a lot of feathers. His beautiful fan was gone. He sat under the tree for awhile before he asked. "Is she with you?" There was no response. Michael was deep in thought. "I will catch one. I will make a deal with them. Me for her." The room went dark. Michael shouted out, "I don't care what you think. I can't bear the thought of them touching her!" The room stayed dark.

The ancestors gathered in the throne room. Everyone had something to say. Ailbe was the newest to cross the veil and she had already broken the rules. She sat and listened until she couldn't take it any longer. "My honored ancestors. We are at war with a species that has hunted us down to near extinction. Our commitment to benevolence has been authenticated. Our oath to protect all life is legendary. Our decree for pacifism has been emulated by countless of worlds. But I would argue that our extreme views have been our greatest failure." There was a collected gasp. She allowed a moment for the chatter to calm down and then she continued. "Yes, we have failed. We are hailed as the greatest, but I look around and see millions of lives wasted. I see an entire world of cowards. We ran away, they followed us, we ran away again, and they followed us again. When do we stop running?" Several of the ancestors left the meeting, others demanded that Ailbe be removed from the meeting.

The old man stood up. Ailbe was shocked, he didn't know their customs and she motioned for him to sit down. He raised his hands and spoke softly. "Thank you all for honoring me with this blessing. (Several of the ancestors who left turned to come back.) I have loved your culture of peace and I have lived my life in that peaceful image. I taught my children your ways. (The chatter in the room died down so they could listen.) I lead by example in my village and in turn, they lived peaceful lives. My own son gave his life so another man could live. (The wind came into the room to listen.) I thought I was learning from an evolved race with higher knowledge. But as I sit here and listen, I realize how wrong I was. (Time seemed to stop.) You're not to be admired! (The double doors flew open with an ear piercing boom.) You are to be pitied. (Abantu walked in.) Now if it is all the same with you, I ask that you send me back." The room erupted with angry chatter and shouting.

Abantu walked up to the old man. The room went quiet again. "Why do you choose to leave paradise?" The old man "This is not my idea of paradise." Abantu "We have no pain, no disease, we have large harvests and true equality. What more could anyone ask for?" The old man "I asked for peace. You all promised me peace. All I see here is fear. I will not spend eternity in fear." Abantu reared up and came down so hard that the marble cracked. His voice was shaking the walls. "What are you suggesting?" The old man was far from intimidated. "I have a great-grandchild named Geetu, he is a beautiful old soul. He has never known fear, he has been afraid. He knows I would meet any menace with greater force." Abantu "So your suggestion is that we scare our enemy?" The old man "No, I would kill them."

The throne room erupted again in shouts to have him removed from the throne room and others wanted him off of Uanza altogether. Abantu lifted his head high and snorted. "That is against everything we stand for!" The old man asked, "What do you stand for?" Abantu snapped back, "LIFE!" The old man scratched his head, "Who's?" Abantu shouted "QUIET!" The throne room was silent again. "ALL" The old man meet the tone but not the volume, of Abantu's voice. "ALL of theirs, but none of your own. If someone came into my home, I would offer them food and shelter. If they demanded my wife, I would force them to leave. If they came to caused any harm, I would cause their death." The room was eager to erupt again, but no one dared make a sound. Abantu paced back and forth for a few minutes. The old man waited for him to stop and then continued. "That is what a respecter of life does. I have lived and taught through love. What greater example of love than to show I am willing to do anything to bring peace and safety into the lives of those I love. I sit here and listen to debates, when the last outpost of your kind is tired of running, tired of living in fear, tired of watching their family being mutilated and on the verge of annihilation. If you were true to your own laws, you would be banning together to fight with them. This is not paradise, this is Hell." Abantu paced and snorted. "Ailbe" Ailbe stood up. Abantu asked "Do you agree with his statement?" Ailbe looked around the room. "Yes" The throne room burst into loud debates again. Abantu shouted, "I SAID SILENCE! Old man, walk with me."

Lucy was feeling better quickly. She was mortified that she put other people in danger. Jonathan was by her side. Mark and Pia-Jiun were making arrangements for a sky burial. The word was getting out to the villagers that the old man and Ailbe were dead and the sky burial was scheduled for the morning. Imay felt it when the old man died, but he had been given instruction to keep Mr. and Mrs. Vans in upbeat moods. The old man did not want his lost grandson to mourn his death but to enjoy Nepal. Jonathan didn't want to burden Lucy with conversation. He just wanted to enjoy that she was alive. He kept recalling what happened over and over in his head. Then he thought of what she said about it felt like being on a phone call, but on mute. He tried to link with Lucy… He felt it. He could link with her!?

Jonathan "MAAARRRRRK. I need you in here!" Mark came running in ready for a fight.

Mark "What!" Jonathan was wiggling to stand up.

Jonathan "I can link with her!"

Lucy sat up. "What? Is there a spider on me?" She started brushing imaginary things off her. Pec woke up and started barking.

Pia-Jiun came running in. "What happened?"

Geetu was coloring in a book and laughing. "You guys are funny."

Jonathan was breathing hard. "I was thinking of what she said. About a phone call. So I tried to link with her." Lucy was still looking for a spider.

Mark said, "Impossible. You can't link with De'nola!"

Lucy said, "What is a Nonna? Are they poisonous? Get it off me!"

Geetu called out shaking his head. "De'nola"

Pia-Jiun put her hands up. "Everyone stop. One at a time… Jonathan, what happened?" Jonathan "I tried to open a link."

Pia-Jiun put her hands up. "Ok, stop there. Mark, your response."

Mark loved that Pia-Jiun was taking control. "Lucy is human, she can't link."

Pia-Jiun put her hands up. "Stop. Now Geetu, do you have anything to add?"

Geetu put his crayons down and went over to Lucy and sat in her lap. He put his hands on both sides of her face. "You are changing."

Pia-Jiun yelled, "Lucy stop! You do not have a spider on you. I need you to relax. Take Jonathan by the hands and put your foreheads together. Think of a connection, a link between you and tell me how you feel." Lucy wanted to run out the door. But she felt that she should do what Pia-Jiun asked. Jonathan walked over to her. Geetu picked up Pec and stood next to Lucy. Jonathan smiled at her, "I'm right here. I know you can do it."

Everyone in the room was holding their breaths. Jonathan looked terrified. Lucy was curious. They held hands and touched foreheads. Lucy saw a few flashes of blue light and pulled away. Jonathan looked at Mark. "She can link!" Mark stepped forward "No freakin way. Move, let me try." Lucy now looked terrified. "What the hell was that?" Geetu said, "Don't be scared. Try it again." Lucy held her hands out and Mark took them. They touched foreheads. There was a slight warm sensation and some dull distant lights but nothing as vibrant as with Jonathan. Lucy pulled away. "What's happening?" Geetu looked at Pia-Jiun. "Mother, can I tell them yet. I don't think they can figure it out." Lucy looked at Pia-Jiun. "You know something? You're not telling me? I have a right to know." Pia-Jiun looked at Jonathan. "I really don't know anything. I suspect a few things. Ailbe spoke to Geetu about her own suspicion of a side effect of the blessing that the ancestors gave to the old man." Lucy said, "This affects me, not him. Please talk to me." Pia-Jiun turned to Lucy. "Hear me out. The only way that the old man could cross the Azili veil was to become Azili, to be Azili when he died. The question is, would that make his blood line Azili. If Azili and De'nola have children, the children are still 100% Azili. Do you follow?"

Jonathan and Mark sat down hard in chairs. Jonathan "Is that possible?" Mark "No, it's not. I've never heard of anything like this in our entire history." Lucy looked at Geetu, "So you think I'm changing?" Geetu smiled, "Me too!" Lucy tried to smile. "What do you feel" Geetu was very proud of himself. "Since they left, the colors look brighter and I think I can hear better." Pia-Jiun smiled. Lucy wanted him to keep talking. "Ailbe said I was going to be a great protector, but she has Mark now." Pia-Jiun stuttered for a moment. "Geetu! Mark is not charged as our protector." Geetu whispered at Lucy, "She really likes him." He turned to Mark. "I think you really like her too." Pia-Jiun shot a look. Geetu turned around "Sorry, was that a secret? Ailbe said our family doesn't have any secrets." Mark stood up desperately trying to change the subject. "I am on complete overload. So what we do know?

1) Ailbe and the old man crossed the veil. Jonathan, you saw them. So we know the old man is with her.

2) For the old man to cross the veil he had to be Azili. To become Azili.

3) If he was blessed with Azili blood, then from his bloodline down... is too.

4) We are in the middle of nowhere in what is now looking like it's turning into a blizzard. We can't get out if we wanted to and no one can get in. So it's us five alone.

5) It seems that we can't link to anyone because of a) the storm b) there is a whole lot of confusing chatter and c) Jonathan and I are too young to talk over everyone, and you guys are well...are infants. Am I missing any facts as we know them?... Anyone? Now is the time to speak up." Jonathan slowly said, "This has been Ailbe's plan along. She wanted us to... to... to what? Teach them what we are? What they have become? I have to trust she knew what she was doing. So I guess Azili class 101 is now in session."

Michael did not leave the Thinking Room all day. Bina had sent up food, but it was never touched. Arden knocked on the door several times, but Michael would never respond, nor would the room open its door. On the second day, Ruth went up to the room. The door did not open. Ruth demanded that the room open. The door reluctantly opened slowly. Ruth saw Michael sitting under the tree staring out the window toward the ocean. "Michael, you have to eat." He didn't move. "Is she eating?" Ruth sat down next to him. "The elders are all here. The Eile have to feel it. If we don't attack them, they will attack us. They don't know you are King yet. It's time!" Michael "I abdicate." Ruth "I doesn't work that way. Uanza chooses. Now if you refuse, that is on you. I'm going to lead this family regardless." She turned and walked out. Michael knew she was right. He stood up and followed her.

They walked down stairs. Everyone was shocked at how gaunt Michael looked. Ruth said, "All the elders and their children, we meet in the library immediately. Everyone else, prepare yourselves." Everyone scattered to get prepared. The library filled up quickly and all eyes were on Ruth. Ruth "I need you all to save your questions till after we link." She stood in the center of the room as everyone formed a circle around her. Everyone held hands and moved in as if they were trying to touch her. Michael stepped into the center of the circle and took Ruth's hands and they touched foreheads. Michael linked all the information. He could hear the gasps. He felt them all receive the link. They all stayed in the link walking through every detail.

Abantu and the old man walked out of the throne room and into the garden. Abantu was expecting the old man to do the De'nola thing and start arguing his position. But the old man stayed quiet. He stopped and smelled the flowers. He raised his face to the warm sun. He listened to the birds singing. He touched everything within his reach.

Abantu "If you still want to leave, I will grant you a new life, from the beginning."

The old man kept walking. "I wish to go back as a young able body man. Not a new infant."

Abantu was shocked. "Why?"

The old man looked confused. "I need to go and fight with my family."

Abantu laughed. "You want to go back just to die again?"

The old man wasn't laughing. "I want to go back and fight with my family, not to die, but so they know I love them."

Abantu "I understand everything, and yet… I don't understand you. I have so many questions for you. But that will have to wait until I get back."

The old man "Are you going to fight?"

Abantu "I am going to get the King."

The old man "What can I do while you're gone? I'm not going to follow your rules. I plan on fighting."

Abantu smiled, "I thought long and hard about Ailbe's request. It was unimaginable then, but now I can't imagine not having your council." Abantu was gone.

CHAPTER 7

*M*ichael broke the link and stood there. No one said anything at first. "I feel you all have questions, but tonight we make our final preparations, try to get some sleep and at 5a.m, we get in the water." With that, Abantu was in the library. "King Michael." He bowed slowly and deeply. The crown appeared on Michael's head. Abantu lifted his head and Michael tried to smile, "Abantu, my friend, it is an honor to welcome you into our home." Michael bowed slowly and deeply. The elders all bowed. Michael "Abantu, we are in desperate need of your help. The Eile have taken the Queen. I can't feel her or find her." Abantu reared up and snorted. "They have Queen A'Llwyn!?" He slammed his hooves down hard. The entire house shook. "The old man was right!" He looked at Ruth, "Delay your plans until we return." Abantu and Michael were gone.

The children had made it to China. Their mothers and chaperones were keeping their sprits up. But several of the older ones were starting to feel that something was wrong. Linda was one of the chaperones. She felt baby Stephanie scared and restless. She did everything she could to keep her mind only on positive things, but baby Stephanie questioned everything. The past few hours she was looking for her auntie Anastasia. Linda was wondering where she was too.

Malachi arrived at the hospital and quickly found Charlotte's room. He pulled a chair to the outside of her door and he sat down. Charlotte saw him as soon as he walked onto the floor. She called out, "Malachi, could you please come in here?" Malachi walked into the room. "What do you want?" Charlotte had been making her list of things she would need for the trip. "Could you please make sure that Ruth gets this list?" Malachi took the piece of paper. "What is all this?" Charlotte "Oh, just a few things for the baby." Malachi started to read from the list. "A chef? A stylist? What is this?" Charlotte looked upset. "I need to eat properly for our expected bundle of joy, and I can't be seen as the newest Reale looking frumpy. Right?" Malachi now officially hated her. But she was his charge for now. "I'll make sure she gets the list." He turned to go sit back in the chair. Charlotte said, "Why are you sitting out there? Come in here and keep me company." Malachi kept his back turned to her as he answered. "I'll be more comfortable out here." Charlotte "No, I want you in here with me so we can talk." Malachi turned to face her. "I am here to make sure that you and the baby are safe and well taken care of. I am not your entertainment." He turned and walked out of the room and sat down. She kept talking to him but he refused to listen.

Pia-Jiun was getting nervous about the storm. The wind was howling and the snow was already up to the top of the steps. Lucy and Jonathan were practicing linking. Geetu was happily playing with Pec. Pia-Jiun started cooking dinner. Mark came into the kitchen. "Can I help?" Pia-Jiun nodded no and kept busy. Mark tried to break the tension. "Crazy the things kids say... Right?... I mean... You're married or something... I mean, you must be. You have a child... Um... he is a great kid...I'm going to go check where he is." Pia-Jiun didn't even look up. "He is where he was. I can hear him playing with Pec." Mark looked over his shoulder. "Oh, you're right. There he is. Well. I'm gonna go upstairs and rest." Pia-Jiun "No, with this storm, we all need to stay together. Help me put some mattresses on the floor. It is going to be a long night."

Mark was eager to do something to help. He followed her up the stairs. She took out all of their loose fitting clothes and pulled all the mattresses out of every room, she grabbed all the pillows and linens and dragged everything downstairs. She stuffed linens and pillows in every crack and around every area that could cause a draft. Mark helped her put extra boards across all the doors and windows. She brought all of the water from the kitchen in to the dining room. She told Mark to stack the chairs into a semi-circle around the fireplace and put all the mattresses in the center. She told everyone to layer up their clothing. She put several layers on Geetu. Mark laughed. "You look like the Michelin tire baby." Geetu looked at him. "I'm not a baby! What is a Michelin tire?" Mark laughed.

Once Pia-Jiun felt comfortable that she has done everything she could do, she started to serve dinner. Lucy jumped up to help. Pia-Jiun nodded no and continued to serve everyone. Lucy could not take another minute of watching Pia-Jiun do all the work. "Please let me help you." Pia-Jiun didn't look at her but said, "You have a lot to learn and not a lot of time to learn it." She told everyone to sit on the mattress, which everyone did, and they ate their dinner. Lucy had only been eating small bites here and there. This was her first full meal. "This is fantastic!" Geetu pointed at Jonathan. "See! I told you she lied." Mark said, "Well, it is clear that we are all family now. I say we finish eating and we tell you all about our history." Pia-Jiun giggled. "It would be nice to understand a few things."

Lucy was feeding Pec and suddenly thought of her parents. Jonathan felt her concerns and said, "They are in Katmandu. It is a big safe city with lots of Western type hotels for tourists. They would have heard about this storm and stayed put." Lucy "Can you feel them?" Mark's laugh was louder than he expected. "No, it doesn't work that way. We make plans for just about any situation. But when things happen unexpectedly, we adjust. Ailbe must have known something. She wanted them out of the house by a certain time." Pia-Jiun asked, "How would Ailbe have known but not you?" Jonathan answered, "The older we get, the more we can see how things work together and sense our surroundings. Ailbe was the oldest of us, so she could comprehend every detail of everything. When I was a kid, I used to hold up fingers behind my back. She guessed right every time. When I asked her how she did it, she said it was easy. She heard the wind move around my fingers." Geetu snapped in the air. "So that's how she did that." They all laughed and talked for awhile.

Pia-Jiun yawned, "It is getting late and we all have a lot of snow to shovel in the morning. I suggest we all get some sleep." Mark agreed. "I'll take first watch." Lucy was confused. "Do you think we are in any danger?

No one could get in here." Jonathan looked at Lucy. "Once a protector, always a protector." Mark nodded and put his head on a pillow. Pia-Jiun laid down and hugged Geetu tight. She tried to pull up the covers. That was the first time Mark felt fear in her. Mark covered them up and watched Geetu smile as he fell asleep. Pia-Jiun half giggled. "We are in a blizzard with no electricity. I can't be ashamed when it comes to body heat or blankets." Now it was Mark's turn to be embarrassed. Pia-Jiun lifted up the covers and Mark positioned Geetu between them. Jonathan felt Mark relaxed and becoming very protective. Within minutes, all three of them were fast asleep.

Jonathan put his head down on a pillow facing Lucy. Lucy was still nervous about her parents but she curled up facing Jonathan and whispered. "When I was out there. I called for you." Jonathan shuddered at the thought of her being out there in this storm. "I thought I heard you… Did you know that when two Azili are in love, they can link very easily? Kind of how Michael could link with Anastasia. Even when she was in a coma and couldn't communicate with anyone else." Lucy's eyes shot wide open. "Wait…what? I need to hear every detail. She has or had amnesia, right?" Jonathan smiled. "I will explain all of that tomorrow. But it turns out that Anastasia is our Princess A'Llwyn." Lucy wanted every detail. "I can't wait till tomorrow. Wait…a real Princess? A royal Princess?" Jonathan "Yep. She is the daughter of our last King and Queen." Lucy sat up. "I don't know much about how it works in England, let alone how it would work anywhere else, but wouldn't she have become Queen when her parents died? And if she is with Michael, would that make him King once they are married? And… didn't she say something about King Michael?" Jonathan thought for a few minutes. "Um… There is a process, but yeah, Michael would have a claim to the throne…But Uanza chooses, he would have to project there… only the royal family can project…It is SO complicated and hard to explain. I really need to get home and find out what is going on." He kissed Lucy on the forehead. "You are already thinking like an Azili." Lucy laughed, "Somehow I feel like my life is just now starting to make sense."

The wind sounded like a train as it started to rip into the roof on the second floor. Jonathan and Mark jumped up. Pia-Jiun was covering Geetu with her body. Mark asked her what to do. She pointed toward the kitchen and tried to sound calm. "Take the doors off the back rooms and nail them to the second floor doorway." Mark and Jonathan felt a surge of strength as they tore doors off hinges and secured the stairwell. Jonathan and Mark worked fast and in synch. Lucy was getting scared and practiced linking to Jonathan. Jonathan looked at her "You are a quick learner. I can feel you trying." Lucy smiled as Geetu stirred and called out for Mark. "Mark, I'm scared. What's that noise?" Mark bent down and whispered in his ear. "It was just the wind." Geetu held out his hand. "Hold my hand so I don't blow away." Mark took his hand and kissed his head. "I'm never going to let that happen. I promise to protect you. (He looked at Pia-Jiun) Both of you." Pia-Jiun felt ashamed but smiled as Geetu closed his eyes and fell back to sleep. Jonathan put more wood into the fire. "It is going to be a very long night."

Imay drove the van with Mr. and Mrs. Vans and two villagers into Kathmandu. They drove directly to the Hotel Shambala and booked three rooms. One for Imay and two adjoining rooms. Imay took their bags inside their rooms as the two villagers assisted Lucy's parents and their wheelchairs out of the van. Imay turned on the weather forecast. "Ailbe, you are a brilliant woman." He turned off the TV and went back down stairs and said to Mr. Vans. "Ok nephew. We are in the famous Kathmandu, you are both fully charged up, we have extra batteries and no time limit. It is going to be a great day." Mrs. Vans said, "I wish Lucy could see all of this." Imay laughed. "I assure you both, they are going to have a marvelous day back at the Inn. Ailbe has a few surprises waiting for them. This is our time, and I'm going to show you every inch of the city." Imay being a man of his word, they went up and down every street, in and out of every shop, tasted something in every restaurant, drank something in every bar and had the greatest day of their lives.

Michael looked around. "Where are we?" Abantu was walking fast. "We are in my forest. I don't have much time to train you." Michael ran up to walk beside him. "Can you train me in a few hours? I'm going into the water at 5a.m." Abantu didn't stop or look at him. "Time doesn't work like that here. That is how the Queen doesn't seem to have aged very much. Between the cryogenic sleep and her projecting her mind, she has defied time. It takes decades and the blood of a King to learn to project. We don't have the luxury of time, but you are the King." Michael "This doesn't feel like Uanza." Abantu laughed. "I didn't say it was."

Michael didn't want to have to pull answers out of him, he just wanted to learn anything that would help him defeat the Eile, he wanted to kill them all. "Is the Queen still alive?" Michael was terrified to hear to answer. Either way he was going to be devastated. Abantu stopped for a moment and put his nose in the air. "Yes" as he continued walking. Michael "Stop! Talk to me. Where is she? Why can't I feel her? How can I get her back?" Abantu stopped and turned around to face him. "The old man has been here one day and has taught me a great deal. Let me ask you a question. Do you love your Queen?" Michael shot out, "YES!" before he finished his questions. Abantu looked at him. "Good. And would you die for her?" Michael said, "Please, just get to the point. My heart can't take this feeling of hopelessness… (He put his head in his hands) I wish she was dead. I can't bear the thought of her with them and what they could be doing to her. Can you take her life? Even if she doesn't want to? Can you exchange my life for hers?" The weight of his pain made his knees buckle. Abantu was moved. "I am humbled by your love for our Queen. Yesterday I knew everything, today I know I have a lot to learn." He knelt down besides Michael. "The Queen is not here, she is not on Uanza. I don't know where she is… I have to conclude that she is where she was. I trust she is still alive. The Eile are very intelligent but they are scavengers. They have never created anything, they only take and use what they scavenge to advance themselves… They were unaware that the De'nola was carrying your child, a royal child. Our Queen had two choices. 1) Take her kind and run, leaving the Eile to fulfill their plan. That would be the end of the human race as you call it. Or 2) Sacrifice herself, get your child to safety, and start the war that would cost countless lives but allow the Azili and the De'nola to live without fear of the Eile ever again." Abantu stood up and started to walk. "We need to start your training." Michael just wanted to stop existing.

The large Eile and several other smaller ones were screaming so loud that the whales around them started to surface in fear. The oldest of the great white sharks dove deep and circled the foreign structure. The large Eile hissed at Anastasia. "You will pay for your deception! You will give us a royal child!" Anastasia was pinned onto the table with steel rods piercing her legs. The pain was intense but she refused to make a sound. She was taking every memory and erasing if from her mind. She recalled every emotion and expunged it. She was trying to will her mind to stop excepting pain. She wanted to give them nothing but an empty shell. The large Eile threw itself onto the floor. "We had a royal child in our hands! How could we have let it go!" Anastasia allowed herself to feel proud one last time. The Eile stood up and was nose to nose with her. "I will send everyone after the one called Charlotte. We will find her and bring her back here." When Anastasia did not respond, it became enraged and picked up a rod and plunged it into her shoulder. Tears slowly rolled down her cheek, but she did not flinch or make a sound. The Eile slid down to the floor and left the room cursing. "Bring me Charlotte!" Anastasia felt the ring on her finger and smiled.

Jonathan and Mark could only lay there as the wind whipped through the upstairs. Jonathan and Mark linked and had formed a plan for the next few days. They knew they were snowed in. They would have to start burning furniture by morning. Mark "We need to do the sky burial tomorrow." Jonathan "Not to sound disgusting, but that back room is -10 degrees… IF there is a room there at all." Mark "This is what nightmares are made of… Do you think that Ailbe and the old man planned it this way? For us to get stuck here. For the storm to take their bodies… I'm just curious on how much of this is by design." Jonathan laughed, "Would you have spent any time with Pia-Jiun? With Geetu? Could I have had more than five minutes with Lucy? WOW, I just blew my own mind." Mark laughed out loud. "Here is another thought… What if this place is ruined? What if they can't live here? They are Azili… Do we bring them home?" Jonathan "What if they want to stay? Can we abandon them here? Without any family?" Mark sat up. His head was spinning. "I guess we… We would have to… I have no idea." He grabbed some more wood and put it on the dying fire. The two men watched the flames flicker in the fireplace the rest of the night as they worked out a plan.

The next morning was bright and sunny. Geetu was the first one awake, quickly followed by Pec. Geetu walked into the kitchen and tried to start breakfast but the room was in shambles. He was scared to walk down the hall towards the old man's room. He grabbed what supplies he could and returned to the dining room. Mark and Jonathan were watching him closely. Geetu smiled and whispered. "I thought you were asleep. I was quiet, right?" Mark smiled and whispered. "You were like an elephant." Geetu ran and jumped in his arms. "If we can't live here, then I want us to go with you." Mark looked at Jonathan and in their link. "Could he have learned to link that fast?" Geetu shook his head. "Did you ever listen to Ailbe?" Mark smiled, "I thought I did until I got to know you better. What did she tell you about linking?" Geetu was proud of himself. He puffed out his chest and lifted up his chin. "When you love someone it's easy. Kind of like a leaf floating on water. But then a bug lands on it and it sinks a little. But then a big toad jumps on it and it sinks." Jonathan thought for a minute. "So linking should be easy but we weigh it down and make it hard…" Geetu laughed. Pia-Jiun stirred. Mark put his finger to his lips. "Shh, let her sleep. I'll make breakfast." Geetu "I'll help." And he happily jumped up and started his day. Jonathan said in the link. "To be so young and innocent, everything just IS." Mark nodded yes and started breakfast.

Jonathan put more wood on the fire and thought the chairs will be next to burn. They had plenty of supplies, now it was just waiting things out. Lucy stretched and yawned. Pia-Jiun woke up quietly and began to fold up the bedding. She saw Mark with Geetu and Pec running around. She went into the kitchen and tried to salvage what she could. She removed a pillow from a crack in the wood and saw the snow up to the windows. She thought of how white everything looked. She listened for any sounds from outside. The silence was eerie. She came back into the dinning room. "Can someone help me look upstairs?" Mark quickly said, "No, leave it for now. It sounded like the roof collapsed. I'm afraid if there is snow up there and we open it up, we are in a bit of trouble." Pia-Jiun agreed and sat back down. Jonathan saw her sadness. "I promise that we are going to be ok.

Whatever is damaged, it can be fixed." Pia-Jiun nodded but Lucy felt she wasn't feeling sad about the Inn, she was sad because she had nothing to do. She wasn't sure how to say something without making her feel bad, so she asked "Pia-Jiun, by any chance did you grab my overnight bag?" Pia-Jiun's face lit up. "Yes I did. I put it with the rest of the bags in the corner." Lucy reached over and gave her a big hug. "Thank you for taking care of me." Pia-Jiun felt a wave of comfort. "I want my lost cousin to have a nice time." Lucy responded, "I believe you." Then she lowered her voice and whispered. "I also believe that you have a right to be happy too." Lucy didn't wait for a response. She stood up and started helping with what ever she could find to do. Pia-Jiun felt uncharacteristically validated.

Mr. and Mrs. Vans and Imay were in a restaurant having dinner when they heard about the storm that was hitting. Mrs. Vans "We need to get back to Lucy!" Imay lifted his hand. "Pia-Jiun has been through hundreds of these storms. She knows what to do. This is normal for us. I'm glad we got the rooms. Looks like we are spending the night." Imay stood up and shouted. "Round for the house!" The restaurant came alive with cheering. The music was turned on and the party started. Mrs. Vans could not shake the feeling that Lucy might be in trouble, but she saw her husband glowing with excitement. She joined in and the night turned quickly into morning. Imay sat down after hours of vigorous singing and dancing. "Phew. I'm exhausted! I need to sleep." Mr. Vans looked at his watch. "6AM! How can we be up all night? I'm normally in bed by 8 o'clock. Should we head back to the Inn?" Imay hugged his nephew. "The roads are probably closed. I will have one of the villagers see if we can get through. But have no worries. Lucy is fine. Pia-Jiun went shopping for supplies. If they are snowed in, they have enough food for days. You worry too much. Nepal is a place to enjoy life." Mr. Vans "I'm sure you're right. Lucy is a smart girl, your Pia-Jiun knows what to do, and they have two strong men with them. Now let's stop for breakfast before we go to bed. I'm starving." Imay laughed, "Don't forget about Geetu. He is craftier than all of them put together." They all laughed.

Michael mustered up enough energy to stand up and follow Abantu deep into the forest. After about an hour of walking, they came to a beautiful clearing. Michael was awe struck. The grass was just tall enough to blow slightly in the wind. It seemed rhythmic. Several hooved animals were there. Most Michael had never seen before. There was a large furry animal that Michael thought looked like a large rabbit, but it had long sharp claws and six inch fangs. Abantu reared up and all the animals turned towards him and quickly bowed. Abantu walked into the clearing with Michael following close behind. "My friends, I present to you King Michael of Uanza." Abantu turned toward Michael and bowed deeply as to show the others he deeply respected Michael. "As I told you before, I called you all here to assist in training him. His war with the Eile is also our war." Several of the animals protested. Michael wanted to start training immediately and did not want to debate this again. He spoke up. "Please, I'm not asking any of you to risk your lives for me or the Azili. I just need training." The rabbit stood on its hind legs. "But if we train you and you use that training to kill. Then covertly, we have killed." Michael was tired and didn't have much fight left in him. He would save it for the Eile. "Then send me home. My fight is with the ones who have hunted and killed my kind to near extinction and now they have my wife." He bowed softly to the crowd. "I leave you in peace." He turned around and began walking away. The animals felt no animosity, no fear and no anger from Michael, just his personal torment. The rabbit thought for a moment. "So you would take on this fight single handedly? With no training?" Michael stopped but didn't turn around. "It's not my first choice, but if it is my only choice, then absolutely." and he kept walking.

Abantu snorted at the rabbit and ran in front of Michael. "I brought you here on my word that I would assist you. Your training starts now." Abantu reared up, came down hard and raced towards Michael with his head down. Michael was not prepared and was thrown thirty feet into the air. He landed hard. He laid there for a second. The animals were all laughing. Michael sat up and opened the door to his rage. "I accept your lesson and give you one of my own." Michael lunged at Abantu and caught him off guard. Michael grabbed his legs and flipped him onto his side, jumped on his neck and held onto his antlers. Abantu gave a loud squeal and the fight was on. The two rolled around pinning each other to the ground and throwing each other off balance. The other animals had never seen anyone surprise Abantu before. They circled the two titans and took notes on Michael's weaknesses.

After hours of bone crushing blows, Michael put his hands up. Abantu lower his shoulder. Michael fell to one knee, breathing heavy, battered and bruised. "Let me catch my breath." He fell backwards in exhaustion. Abantu failed at trying to remain the proper authoritarian. He too, fell onto his knees. He was snorting heavily, and was missing large tufts of hair. One of the points on his enormous antlers was broken, one eye was swollen shut, and a small cut on his cheek. "I understand if you need to rest." He fell onto his side in exhaustion. The other animals did not know what to do. One ran off and returned with a large bucket of water and set it down between them. Neither one of them had the energy to drink. After a few minutes, Michael started laughing. Abantu couldn't move. If Michael chose to kill him, he would be at his mercy. Abantu started laughing, not because he knew what was so funny, but because his laughter was contagious.

The rabbit moved closer. "If you two are done. I have a few observations I would like to share." The rabbit went on with his assessment of what Michael needs to focus on in his training. Michael agreed and forced his feet to move. Abantu just laid there. "I believe you have had enough for today. We start at sunrise. Sleep well King Michael." Abantu was gone. Michael looked around. "Where can I sleep? Is there a cabin or something?" All he heard was laughing as he was suddenly alone. "Ok... camping it is." He gathered some leaves, dry wood, and found some fruit trees. He ate, built a fire, put the leaves in a circle, laid down and fell asleep.

Michael felt the warm morning sun on his face. For a split second he forgot where he was, but it was just long enough for him to feel a blunt blow to his abdomen. He rolled over in pain. "Hey! Let a guy wake up first." He opened his eyes and looked around. He didn't see anyone. He stood up confused. He started thinking he dreamt the punch when another blow landed in his low back. He swung around to see who punched him, when another blow hit his chest, then hip, then across his chin which sent him to the ground. He put his hands up. "Ok. You win. Where are you?" A small voice said, "Down here." Michael looked down to see a small newborn kitten, about the size of a mouse. Michael leaned forward. "You?"

The sweet looking kitten sprang up and twisted in mid-air and hit him with his tail in the chest. Michael had his breath knocked out of him, as he grabbed his chest and rolled onto his side. The three inch beast scampered up his leg and onto his arm. "You let your guard down because I'm small. That will get you killed." Michael was genuinely scared. "I let my guard down because you were cute. I don't think you are cute anymore." Michael quickly snatched the brutalizing beast but didn't know what to do with it.

Abantu came out of the bushes laughing. "I don't think a month is going to be long enough." Michael looked at the small kitten like creature. It smiled at him. Michael loosened his grip and it bit his hand and ran off. Abantu doubled over in laughter. "A month is defiantly not long enough. Michael was rubbing the spots that were now throbbing with pain. "Is kicking my ass your idea of training? You are only succeeding in making me rethink the run away plan." Abantu finally stopped laughing. "This was not my plan for this morning, but it turned out fantastic." Michael looked confused. "I don't get it. What was your plan?" Abantu "I went to the house to pick you up and you weren't there. So the tiny one offered to go look for you... Why are you sleeping out here?" Michael "House? What house?" Abantu started laughing again, "Right through those trees. No one told you to go take a hot shower, eat the dinner in the refrigerator, and get a good night sleep?" Michael sucked his teeth, "They hate me." Abantu fell onto his side laughing. "Yes... it seems that way." Michael was getting angry. "Would you stop laughing? I'm not having fun." Abantu wiped the tears of laugher from his eyes but started laughing again. "I'm having a ball!" Michael walked off towards the house in a huff. "I'm taking a shower. I'll be back in an hour." Michael could still hear his thunderous laughter as a twelve foot bear jumped out of the woods and starting mauling him. Michael was startled and screamed in a high pitch. He could hear Abantu's laugher start all over again.

After another two hour fight, this time with a bear. Michael crawled out of the woods to the same audience as yesterday. The rabbit stepped forward. "Do you see why you loose a lot?" Michael gave him an angry look. "Because I'm here for training but all you do is jump me!?" The rabbit "Or you could think of it as you are here for training against an enemy who doesn't fight fair." Michael sat up, "Ok...Good point, I get that." Then the bear bit into his shoulder and drug him back into the woods. The rabbit yelled out. "Break time is over." Michael still screaming like a teenage girl, yelled back. "That was break time?"

Ruth, the elders, and the elder's children were all still standing in the library after Abantu took Michael. Ruth finally said, "Any questions?" Everyone collected their thoughts and started to rapid fire questions at Ruth. She heard them all and responded. "I can tell you this. Michael is struggling to be King to his kind and husband to his wife. He will stop at nothing to get our Queen back. Yes, he is willing to go to war and quite frankly, SO AM I! Who here is in favor of running?" She was glad when no one responded. "Good, then we all agree. The Eile will all die today by our hands. We will wait until Michael returns before we attack." Someone asked, "Won't the Eile attack us now that all the elders are in one place? Remember the slaughter at Atlantis." Ruth felt her anger boiling. "Let them try. We are not the same race as when we first arrived here. I honor my ancestors but it was their submissive behavior that made us victims. NO MORE!" The elders linked her speech to every family member on the planet. The family was cheering. Even baby Stephanie was jumping. Se'ighin said, "We all need to be ready in a split second. Be rested, be healthy and be ready for anything. We all have something to do." The elders dispersed with a rejuvenated determination to finish this war once and for all.

After breakfast, Mark and Jonathan cleaned up as Pia-Jiun and Lucy removed the extra supports to the doors and windows. They looked outside. Pia-Jiun "Wow, I can't even see the cars. I've never seen this much snow at one time before." Lucy "Are we going to be ok?" Pia-Jiun smiled, "Of course. I am more and more convinced that Ailbe had this all planned out. I just don't know what she was expecting us to do?" Lucy "I wish I knew her like you all did. I just met her. But if she is half of what you all say she was, then my guess is that we will know by the end of the week." Pia-Jiun smiled, "Smart girl." Mark came out of the kitchen saying, "In the mean time, we need to figure out what to burn next… aaannnnddd, we need to talk about the safety of this place. (He looked at Pia-Jiun.) I'm sorry to say but I don't think this place will be habitable when this is over. There is a lot of debris all over the place. The whole side of the Inn is gone. I can only guess about the second floor." Pia-Jiun looked at Geetu who was playing with the puppy and an old tennis ball. "We will be fine." Mark knew she was lying but he would address that at the right time. Mark took a deep breath. "I am certain of that." Pia-Jiun did not look him in the eyes but walked to the chairs and started breaking them apart. "First the chairs, then the tables, then the bar. That will keep the fire for three, maybe four days. We decide after that." Her eyes filled with tears as she broke apart each chair. She knew the old man had made every piece of furniture, and now she was destroying them. There would be nothing left of him soon. She wondered if that was part of the plan.

After a few hours of work, they were just staring at each other. Lucy finally said, "Well this is just slightly awkward." Everyone agreed but no one said anything. Jonathan sat down on the mattress. "Anyone have cards?" There was a collective 'no'. So they all sat down to rest. The only sound was Geetu and Pec. Pia-Jiun started laughing, "Those two have endless energy." Everyone laughed and then quiet again. Finally Geetu said. "I could teach you some songs?" Pia-Jiun popped up. "Wait right here." She disappeared into the kitchen. They heard her moving things around and banging into things. "HA HA yes!" Mark wondered what she could have been looking for. She came out with her hands behind her back and said. "Good news, bad news. Which do you want to hear first?" Mark said, "I could use some good news." Pia-Jiun said, "The sky burial is completed. Next." Lucy said, "I'll take the burden of the bad news." Pia-Jiun said, "Pec pooped in the pile of peppers." Geetu jumped into the game. "I want good news." Pia-Jiun handed him a wooden flute and a small drum that Ailbe had given to him last year. Jonathan said, "Oh no… I hate bad news." Pia-Jiun pulled out from behind her back the jar with the last of the brown fluid in it. She laughed so hard she almost dropped it as she extended the jar towards Jonathan. "Ailbe said to save the last bit of it for you." Mark laughed so hard he grabbed onto Geetu and they both fell over. Jonathan's stomach turned. "No, I'm not drinking that. I couldn't feel my face for days!" Lucy snuggled up to him and kissed his cheek and she looked at Pia-Jiun. "I need to hear every detail of their last trip. Don't skip the embarrassing parts either."

Pia-Jiun took four shot glasses from behind the bar. Jonathan was still protesting as Pia-Jiun poured the liquid into the glasses and handed them out. "Who is going to make the first toast?" Everyone looked at Jonathan. He raised his shot glass. "To the old man. Thank you. You are responsible for bringing Lucy into this world. Now I am complete with her by my side." Everyone shouted, "here here", and they drank. Lucy tried to link with Jonathan. He could feel her. He said, "Ok, I serve the next one." Pia-Jiun said, "But that is my job." In a serious tone. Jonathan looked at her as he took both of her hands in his. "You are an Azili woman. You are equal in every way. We all have a job to do within this family. You are my cousin, not my servant. It is my turn to serve you." Pia-Jiun stood up to run away, but there was no place to run and hide. She looked like a deer in headlights. Lucy looked away. Mark stood up and hugged her. She tried to pull away but Mark could feel that she needed someplace to feel safe. "I got you."

Pia-Jiun stood crying in his arms for awhile. Lucy was watching Geetu. She thought he would be upset that his mother was crying, but he just kept playing. After a few minutes. He called out to the room. "Ok ok ok. One down, three more to go." Pia-Jiun pulled away from Mark. "I am so ashamed. I think between the storm, and my house about to fall down just got to me. Please accept me apologies." Lucy snapped her fingers. "We have a saying back in America. 'gurl pleeze'." Pia-Jiun laughed. "What does that mean?" Lucy explained, "It's not so much what the words mean. It's all about the attitude. Here, let me show you. Snap your fingers, chicken move your neck, suck your teeth, think It don't bother me, and belt out gurl pleeze." Pia-Jiun tried it as everyone rolled on the floor laughing. She proudly announced "By the end of the day, I will have it down pat."

Jonathan poured the next shot. "Ok, who is next?" Mark "I'm going to regret this aren't I? But here we go. To you great-grandmother Ailbe. You asked a dumb kid to be your transporter. I had never been so honored. I watched every move you made. You were genuinely the most loving and caring woman on the planet. I learned to walk by your side and to navigate you safely through some terrifying situations. I was trained to be fearless. And now you're gone, and I'm terrified to be here without you. No one could ever measure up to the amount of love and trust you gave me." Everyone raised their glass, "here here" and they drank.

Suddenly everyone was aware of the pain they were all feeling. They sat quietly looking down at their hands. A light blue mist circled them but they didn't notice. Geetu's voice broke the silence. "Two down and two to go." Mark laughed, "That kid is more John Edwards than Azili." Thankfully, that seemed to break the tension. Mark cleared his throat. "Glasses in, I pour. Who is next on this crazy train?" Lucy nodded and said. "Ok... Ailbe wants honesty... here we go. Get ready boys and girls, the freak show is up to bat... To the old man. Now I understand it was you that has been coming to visit me in my dreams for as long as I can remember. You told me things, and you showed me things that I thought were all my vivid imagination. You even told me about a boy named Jonathan... So here is to my Great-Grandfather, Ashis. It means the one who blesses others." She lifted her glass but no one moved for a few minutes.

Lucy put down her glass and went into the corner where Pia-Jiun had put her overnight bag. She rifled through it for a few seconds and pulled something out. She came back to the group and sat down. She handed Pia-Jiun a journal. "My parents thought I was going crazy, they took me to a therapist who suggested that I keep a journal of those dreams. I carried that journal in my purse for years." Pia-Jiun opened the journal slowly as if it was going to fall apart in her hands and the information would be lost forever. The first line read, *He says his name is Ashis and that he is my Great-Grandfather...'* Pia-Jiun closed the journal and hugged it. Tears poured down her face. She picked up her glass and everyone said, "here here" and drank.

Mark had never wanted to take away someone's pain like he did right now. Lucy looked at Jonathan. He tried to think of something funny to say, but he knew they all needed to let that one soak in. Pia-Jiun finally said, "We have a lot to discuss, but for now, you pour. I guess it is my turn. I have a confession... I am a man." Mark "WHAT?" Pia-Jiun laughed. Geetu laughed and walked over to Mark and pretended like he was knocking on his head. "Hello. Is anyone home in there?" Geetu walked between Mark and Pia-Jiun and laid down with his head in Mark's lap and his feet on Pia-Jiun. "It's past my nap time." He closed his eyes. Mark looked at Pia-Jiun. "How do you handle a kid this small with such a huge personality?"

Pia-Jiun took a deep breath. "Here is to my friend Ailbe. Having a child and no husband has been shameful for my family. Geetu has more love than any child could ask for. Ailbe had said from even before he was born that he was an exceptional child and wanted him to have a proper education. I refused her offer to pay, but I knew I needed to make money for his school. So I sold myself to a man who would send me to parties for his friends. I was not ashamed until the old man found out. He offered the man any amount of money to buy me back. The man got angry and threatened to kill me and take Geetu as his own. He was desperate, it was the only time he ever called Ailbe for help…

Two days later Ailill arrived with Aharon. They went to talk to the man. He demanded money and Geetu in exchange for my freedom. Ailill and the man sat down for a meal, Aharon refused to eat with him, but Ailill was always the gentleman. By the time they got back here, it was clear that the man poisoned him. Aharon took him to the nearest hospital but the poison had already affected his heart. The doctors told Aharon to take him home. There was nothing that could be done. The next day Isabelle showed up at the man's house. I heard a terrible argument, and then everything was silent. She found me and told me to take Geetu and go home. (She took a deep breath and held back tears) The man was never seen again. So here is to my friend Ailbe." She lifted her glass and drank. The others lifted their glasses, "here here" and they drank too."

Over the next month, Michael was jumped by lions, tigers, bears, rabbits, kittens, fish, birds, and centaurs. He was black and blue from head to toe. At the end of each day, the hot showers seem to have a healing property. Michael always felt better. But he missed home. His only comfort was that time would not be affected there. He was starting to get the better of the smaller creatures. Today he was going to start training how to project. He was excited but getting irritated that Abantu was late.

So he walked around outside. He saw Abantu speaking to one of the fish and the fish swam through the air very quickly. Michael shouted, "Hey, what are you planning for me today?" Abantu ran up to him. "Listen, I need you to think of Uanza and the throne room. I don't have time to explain. The ancestors need you immediately and I can't get you there in time. It's about Anastasia!" Michael's panic level went from calm to insane just at the sound of her name. Abantu screamed, "GOOOOOooooo" and Michael was gone.

Michael was running when he ran straight into the large wooden double doors of the throne room. He tasted blood filling his mouth. He was not going to spit in the throne room, so he wiped it onto his already filthy shirt. Michael felt a wave of warmth and love. He was about to start calling for Anastasia when Abantu was standing next to him. "You did it." Michael was livid if there was no information about Anastasia. "Did what? Where is my wife!?" Abantu backed up as Michael stepped towards him. "I needed to get you motivated to get someplace. To project. The only extreme emotion I could think of was the love you have for her. Michael stop. KING MICHAEL STOP! I don't want to hurt you!" It was too late. Michael sprang onto his back with unimaginable speed. He pulled his antlers to the side, slid off his shoulder, and jerked him onto his back. His legs were flailing as he screamed. "Stop! It was the only way!" Michael screamed. "Beg for mercy!" Abantu cried out, "Mercy! I beg for mercy." Michael let him go and walked out.

He walked into the King and Queen's bedroom. It was exactly how they had left it. The sage dress was still on the floor. The bed sheets were askew and he could smell jasmine in the air. He walked over to the dress and picked it up. He held it tight for awhile before he put it on the hanger that Anastasia took it off of. He sat on the bed and relived every second of her. He took the covers and imagined her body touching them just a few days ago. He looked back at the dress. He wanted every thread to be burned into his memory. He had no idea how much time had passed, but it was getting dark. He needed to find Abantu and apologize for his outrageous behavior. He still didn't know how to really project. All Abantu said was to think of the throne room and go.

He took a shower and changed into the King's clothes that he wore before. He took the dress and started talking out loud. He was missing something. "When Anastasia projected us here, we were naked there and naked here. When I project to where Charlotte was, I was dressed at home, but ended up naked there. When Abantu protected me from home into the forest, I was dressed at home and dressed in the forest. When I just projected from the forest to here. I was dressed in the forest and dressed here... So the first two times, my body must have stayed where it was and my energy was projected. These last two times, I must be completely here." He folded and held the dress with all of his strength. He needed to find Abantu, he needed it almost as much as he needed to find her. He felt his emotions drawing him to where he needed to be. He heard snorting and opened his eyes.

Abantu was clearly in a meeting. Michael projected himself right in front of him. Michael gently bowed and stayed vulnerable. "I am truly sorry. My behavior only matches my ignorance. I hope you can forgive me." Abantu snorted again and Michael stood up. He noticed two black eyes, a fat lip, a chipped tooth, and a fist size bruise on his cheek. Michael knew he was going to burst out laughing if he didn't look away. Abantu paced with a limp. He finally said. "It was wrong of me to use your love for the Queen in such a manner. My apologizes to you. I have never known the love you feel. The old man is teaching me that love is the highest and purest motivator. I should have listened better. The meeting that you have interrupted has just concluded. We are all going to accompany you back. And I see you have even managed to collect a souvenir." Michael looked into his arms. He had the dress. "I'm ready when you are." And the room was empty.

Ruth and several of the elders were in the Thinking Room. The room suddenly turned bright blue. The flames shot straight up to the ceiling. George started flapping his wings. Se'ighin said, "I think Michael is home." Everyone ran for the elevator. As the doors open, in the middle of the great room stood Michael and Abantu with a large array of animals. Bina ran to Michael and hugged him. "What happened? You have only been gone a few hours? (She looked at Abantu and continued) We will have more room if we go outside under the tents on the beach." Abantu could not fit through the hallways so he projected out to the beach. Michael linked to Rach-El to come down immediately. As the reinforcement all made their way out to the beach, Rach-El ran up behind him. "Michael!" He turned around and she hugged him. "We will catch up soon. This is for you to hold until we bring Anastasia home." He handed her the folded up dress and he walked out onto the beach. As he looked around his home, he felt proud. He started to speak but he noticed everyone was bowing. He felt a warm sensation around his head. He could feel the connection between every grain of sand.

Things made sense when he was wearing the crown and when he was with Anastasia in the throne room, he understood everything. He needed to regain that. "Our honored guests, Welcome to our home. We have a common enemy that has taunted all of our kind throughout history. No one here is looking for violence, but today, we match aggression with overwhelming love for our family. I give the floor to my friend, Abantu." No one moved and Michael stepped back and Abantu stepped forward. "I have known countless rulers, but none that I would die for before King Michael. He has shattered my horizon and forced me to look farther than I ever knew existed. Our love of life, all life, is duplicated in every faith on every plant in every solar system in all 82 galaxies that I have visited. But it took an old man, a De'nola and a young Azili man to show me what true love is. I now fight for love. We will search every inch of this planet until we find Queen A'Llwyn." Everyone stood there motionless and taking in every detail of him. No one dared ask what happened to his face. Michael walked back up and stood next to him. "None of us will ever live in fear from this or any other threat. Let's make sure that the Eile know we are all here together and we are coming for them. They have one and only one chance to surrender. Bring Queen A'Llwyn here immediately or be annihilated." Everyone opened a link to everyone. The entire De'nola world felt an energy surge. The ancestors were hovering over the waters. Some De'nola even reported seeing strange blue lights flying over the water all night. Some of the creatures walked into the water and spoke in their languages. Michael was sure that the Eile knew they were banded together and coming.

The Eile did feel it. With the countless opened links and all the links directed at them, it was easy for them to intercept them. The largest Eile was furious. He was ordering all the Eile to fan out and kill everything that moved. They would start by starving all the land walkers. Just like they did with Atlantis. He moved the vessel farther under the sand. The Eile felt they were impossible to locate. A few Eile stayed by the large one's side, but all the others left to follow their orders. He went in and said to Anastasia, "Your kind will all die today. They are foolish enough to think they can threaten us? Maybe I will send them one of your fingers or maybe a toe perhaps." What was left of Anastasia's mind was fading. She wondered if she died being disconnected, would she still go to the ancestors. She was hoping that the Eile would not understand that the steel rods had caused an infection in her blood. She would be dead in less than forty-eight hours anyway. Maybe she could hold onto one memory of Michael. Then she could die happy.

With everyone focused on Anastasia, Michael had a flash of her. He screamed out "I FOUND HER!" with that, a flash of light shot passed his head. He felt his crown react. He wondered if the Queen's crown had been looking for her. Abantu shouted. "My generals! In the water now." The elders formed a line at the shore line and started the same chant as Ailbe did at the hospital. A bright blue light shot into the water. Within seconds, a few Eile broke the surface and where captured and brought ashore. The protectors were just a few minutes behind the creatures. The protectors dove deep. Deeper than they every have. The whales joined the search. Michael could not stay on land. He dove into the water as he heard Arden yelling for him to stop. He was a fast swimmer, and he was on a mission. He dove to every rock and ripped it apart. He drove to every hole and ripped it open. He was staying down much too long, but he had hope. He had felt her, even if it was for just a second. He could hear in the link that they captured dozens of Eile, but he knew that there had to be thousands or hundreds of thousands. So he kept diving. He must have been over a hundred miles out at sea. The sun was coming up. He was running on empty. He dove again, but this time a pod of dolphins were joining him. He noticed a large one with scars on his face. He made it up to the surface but with some effort. "Hey, I know you. You are the big guy who hangs around our beach. I have no idea if you can hear me, but I enjoy seeing you around. I have to go now." Michael took a few deep breaths and just before he was going to dive, He heard his name being called over and over. He waited until he heard if they had any information about Anastasia. He listened in the link. More Eile were captured but still no sign of his wife. He heard a boat and helicopter speeding in his direction. He looked back at the large dolphin. "I need to find her." And he dove.

He saw sharks circling something so he went to look. He felt for Anastasia but felt nothing, he wanted to go just a little deeper, but he was already down for too long. He started ascending but felt like he was being pulled down. He kicked hard to free himself but instead, he felt a sharp pain across the back of his ankle. His foot wasn't working. He couldn't make it to the surface. The deep water didn't get much light but the bright morning sun had given him enough that he could see the water turning red. He kicked at whatever he was caught on, and struggling to get up to the surface. His energy was failing him. His lungs were begging to expand. He couldn't see the surface. The sharks noticed the blood too. It was difficult to link underwater but he tried. He opened a link to everyone and anyone who could hear him. "I love all of you. When you fine Anastasia, tell her I will see her on the other side of the veil."

Lucy, Jonathan and Mark sat there not knowing what to do or say. Pia-Jiun had her head down. If she could have turned herself into a rock she would have. Mark gently picked up Geetu's head and put it on a pillow. He leaned over and kissed her cheek. What a fantastic mother you are. He is so lucky to have you." Pia-Jiun's hands and sleeves were soaking wet from tears. Jonathan leaned forward and lifted up her chin so he could see her eyes. "I could never have been that brave. I promise you and Geetu, that you will never be without anything every again." Pia-Jiun picked up Lucy's journal. "Did the old man every say anything about me in your dreams?" Lucy smiled, "I think you have an interesting read ahead of you. He told me you were like a daughter to him. He felt like a failure when he saw you working so hard. I never understood any of it until I got here." Pia-Jiun hugged her. "I'm so glad that you are my family." Lucy laughed, "Gurl pleeze… read the second page." Pia-Jiun laughed and started reading out loud.

"When you come, burn everything. Let the earth reclaim it all. The world never thought me worthy of even a name. Let my body fly into an open field so I don't go to waste. Tell them that I don't want them to ever feel worthless or useless. My son, granddaughter, and great-grandson will never agree to the blessing, but I was wrong. Take them with you when you go. I tried to be all the family that they needed, but what I failed at in life, I will make up for in my death. We are on the other side of the veil watching over you. We were with you in the snow. We will be with you when you bond. And we will be with you when you have your children. My son is grown by now and has lived a full life, but my granddaughter is suffering. Tell her that I was never ashamed of her, I was ashamed of myself. Tell her we were there when she felt the change. We were there when she fell in love. We know she is scared, but I promise her that he will never lie or harm her. We were there at her wedding and we were there at the birth of her daughter Lesa, the one who will never walk the Earth. I love you all more than you will ever know. Tell my great-grandson that I know he ate my chocolate, but that is ok. I left it there for him and tell him that we do not reject his bond with Stephanie. We are honored by his mention of us. Be well. Stay safe, warm and dry. You have three of the best protectors on the planet there with you. Hello Jonathan. Hello Marcus. We promise you… This will all be ok. It is through your love that all Azili will know peace now."

Lucy said, "I wrote that when I was twelve. Look at the date."

Mark jumped to his feet. "There is NO way any Azili could come visit a De'nola child half way around the world and tell them about today! He wasn't even an Azili then. That is not how this works. That is not how any world works! Lucy, I love you like a sister, but there are three people that know that my birth name is Marcus. My parents and Ailbe. You tell me right now how you knew that." He was pacing back and fourth trying to figure out when and how Lucy could have written that down from last night to today.

Pia-Jiun stood up. "Your birth name is Marcus?" He stopped to look at her. Her eyes felt like they pierced his soul. She said, "Geetu dreams of a sign that says 'Marcus' with an arrow pointing." Mark felt weak in his knees. He pulled out his wallet and took out a photo of him and Jonathan when they were kids. "Our dads would take all the boys out camping all the time. Once, when I was about twelve, we were on one of our trips, Michael saw the sign and wanted to take a picture. Jonathan and I jumped out of the car. I always loved this picture, but I had to fold it to fit in my wallet." Jonathan stood behind him. "Hey I remember that." Pia-Jiun's hands were shaking as she reached for the photo. Mark's hands were shaking giving in to her. Lucy couldn't take the suspense so she ran behind Pia-Jiun to look. It was a photo of Jonathan and Mark standing next to a sign that said 'Marcus' and an arrow pointing to him. Jonathan was on the other side, but when you fold it in half, Jonathan is out of the picture.

Pia-Jiun bent down and gently tapped on Geetu to wake him up. That was the first time they saw him cranky. Pia-Jiun said, "Geetu, do you remember telling me about your dream with the sign that says 'Marcus' and the arrow on it?" Geetu was rubbing his eyes. "Yes, I remember." Pia-Jiun "Would you look at this picture for me?" Geetu yawned and sat up. "Listen you guys. Do they have to make it SO obvious to you?" Pia-Jiun snapped back. "Young man, you will not be disrespectful!" Geetu put his head down. "I'm sorry mom." Mark handing him the photo. Geetu's eyes lit up. "Hey, I know this photo. Ailbe showed it to me." Mark said, "That's impossible. It was on and old 35mm camera, when I got the roll developed. Jonathan hated his knobby knees, he tore up the copy and threw the negatives off a scenic view stand in the Grand Canyon. I have had this photo in my wallet and in by back pocket. I can guarantee that she has never shown you this photo.

Geetu handed it back and shrugged his shoulders. "It looks just like it, but Ailbe's has some writing on the back. Something about a hot stone and a cowboy." Jonathan asked, "Rhinestone Cowboy?" Geetu smiled, "Maybe." Jonathan shook his head, "I'm going to freak everyone out. My wallet got wet at the party, I took everything out to dry it out, but we left so quick that it was still wet. So I asked my dad if he had a wallet I could borrow until we got back. He said he just came across an old wallet of mine. I shoved my stuff in and left. This is what I pulled out last night." He opened his wallet and there was the torn piece of the photo of just Jonathan. Mark said. "You said you hated this picture because of your knees." Jonathan "I did, but when I saw that I was adorable without you, I took my side out of the trash. But look on the back." Mark pulled it out and turned it over. 'Hotter than the Rhinestone Cowboy.' Geetu said, "You have the same front photo and you have the same back writing. Ha ha. That is funny."

Mark looked around. "I am officially freaked out." Jonathan sat down. "So am I." Lucy said, "It's gonna get worse. Look at the inside cover of my journal." Jonathan grabbed it and opened it to the inside cover. There was a newspaper cartoon of Glen Campbell in his rhinestone cowboy outfit riding a horse. Lucy had written, 'If I find a man hotter than this, I'll marry him'. Everyone was looking at Lucy with wide eyes. She shrugged her shoulders. "What? He was hot back in the day." Geetu rolled over, "Mom, can I say something, but you can't get mad?" Pia-Jiun said, "I will not tolerate rudeness." Geetu looked at her and made a funny face. "Why are you all so scared? Why can't you just tell each other how you really feel? Lucy, I see you make googly eyes and Jonathan. And when you were out in the snow, he would have never stopped looking for you. Mom, when Mark was here before, you wanted to talk to him. Mark, Ailbe told me that you aren't afraid of anything, and you would fight the devil himself to protect her, but now you're scared of how you feel about my mom? I thought our family has no secrets."

Lucy motioned for him to come over. "Here, Pec needs his snuggle buddy." He put his head on the pillow next to Pec and fell back to sleep. No one spoke for a few minutes. Mark took a deep breath. "Ok... Why do I feel like we are all on the island of misfit toys? But I'm going just take a leap of faith here. Pia-Jiun, I would love for you and Geetu to come back with me... um, with us. You will have your own home and a private school on the compound." He took out his phone and started to show her pictures of the compound. She said. "You all live there? That is bigger than our entire village." Lucy started to explain the compound and that she and her parents are moving in when they get back.

Mark and Jonathan put their hands up at the same time. "Shhh" Jonathan said. "Michael is linking to the entire family." Mark was recapping every few seconds. Lucy moved over to be near Jonathan. She could hear the link but like an old radio between stations. Pia-Jiun could just make out what was going on. Jonathan was back in caged tiger mode. Mark was desperate to get back home. "Abantu is at the house! His generals have been training King Michael...Michael is in the water!" Jonathan and Mark looked at each other. "King Michael?"

Jonathan stood up and started pacing and rubbing his hands. I can't sit here while our family is being killed." Pia-Jiun had a whirlwind of emotions and blurted out, "Mark, Geetu and I will come back with you." Mark smiled and gently guided her up by her shoulders. "May I kiss you?" Pia-Jiun didn't answer, she kissed him. A soft blue light surrounded them. Geetu opened his eyes and saw them kissing. "Geeze. Its' about time." He looked at the blue light. "Are you proud of me Gaya? I did what you told me." Pia-Jiun was looking at Mark but spoke to Geetu. "Is that the old man?" The blue light enveloped her, and held her tight. She felt loved and safe. She spoke to the blue light. "Where is Ailbe?" The blue light separated into two trails. "Ailbe, thank you for loving me when I was unlovable." Mark held her so gently and kissed her again as the blue light moved to Lucy.

Jonathan was watching as the blue light danced around her hands. Lucy asked, "What they are doing?" Jonathan sat down in front of her and put his hands straight out so she could hold her hands just above his. The blue light changed to green. Jonathan laughed, "They are giving you the blessing of healing. We have healers in the family, but the blessing of being a healer is much different. You are now one of the most powerful of our kind." Lucy laughed, "And to think that a few weeks ago I was resolved to spending my life alone and caring for my parents. I had no true friends that I could trust and no family to depend on, and now I have all of you." She looked at the light. "I accept your blessing." The light became dense and heavy, she couldn't hold the weight and she put her hands into Jonathan's.

The light wrapped around their hands firmly for a few minutes and then went to Geetu. The light fully engulfed him.

Geetu giggled and squirmed as if he was being tickled and then it was gone. Mark walked Pia-Jiun back over to the mattress and then put some wood into the fire and sat next to Pia-Jiun. He held her tight. He mumbled, "Burn everything, Let the earth reclaim it all." They all watched the fire dance around the wood and consume it. Lucy had tears in her eyes as she stared at it. "Jonathan… Do you promise to love me for the rest of our lives?" Jonathan didn't move either. "I do… and I offer you my bond. If you accept, I will be yours forever. No amount of time. No amount of distance. Nothing could keep me from you. On my life, I promise to love and protect you and our family." Lucy "I accept your bond and give you mine."

Dr. Ziv walked into Charlotte's room. "Good morning. Let me take a look at you." He took off the sterile gauze pads on her abdomen. "The wound is looking good. I'm going to discharge you today. I just spoke to your father and he said that the RV is ready to pick you up straight from here and take you on a well deserved vacation away from all the stress." Charlotte "No offense, but I can't wait to get out of here. I'm looking forward to a nice long drama free vacation." Dr. Ziv "Well, the paperwork is all done. Your father will be here any minute. And I can only hope that I only see you under happy circumstances from now on." They hugged and he left. The nurse came in to help her get dressed and sign some papers. The nurse asked, "Hey, do you know what is going on with your security guard? He is out there freaking out." Charlotte shrugged her shoulders, "He's a drama queen, just ignore him. I'll get him out of your hair."

Charlotte called out for Malachi. Malachi walked into the room. "What?!" Charlotte pointed at him, "What is wrong with you today? You should be in a great mood. We are off to Tennessee in a few minutes." Malachi was holding back is anger towards her. "I'm not going. Leif will be your driver. He will be here soon." Charlotte was furious. "No. Ruth told me that you were my body guard. Call her right now." Malachi "She is a bit busy right now." Charlotte "Well then, I'm not going unless you come with me." Malachi "I cannot stress to you enough how important it is for you to be in that RV and on the road right now." Charlotte "Well, if it that important, then Ruth will make time in her busy schedule to tell you that you are my body guard." Malachi stormed out. He linked the information to Ruth. Ruth responded, "Oh dear God! Just get her out of my sight! And get back here as soon as you can. Michael went into the water." and she broke the link.

Malachi walked back into the room. "Where is your bag?" Charlotte giggled, "Right there. Daddy is downstairs. Let's go." Malachi picked up her bag and they walked out the door of the hospital. Charlotte's dad Tom opened the door to the large RV. "You gotta see it in here. This is great." He helped her into the RV. Leif was driving. Malachi stepped in and looked at Leif. "Don't say a word. Just drive." He sat down in the passenger seat and linked the information to Leif. Leif responded in the link. "What did our King ever see in this girl?" Malachi laughed, "I used to think she was kinda cool, but ya can't hide crazy for too long." Both men laughed. Charlotte yelled out. "Hey, what is so funny? Can you please just watch the road. Pregnant lady back here!"

Michael tried to open his eyes, he heard voices and felt movement but he couldn't move. His mind went to Anastasia. He felt her close to the veil. He called out to her but the only response was from some familiar voices. "Hold on Michael. We're almost there. Just hold on." Michael had no idea what they were talking about. A male voice started yelling. "We don't have time! Get the healers to the house. Get Arden there too. He is going to need blood." He allowed himself to drift into the link. He needed to feel her. Wherever she was, that is where he wanted to be. He drifted closer and closer to the veil until he could see the ancestors. He remembered the throne room and how beautiful it was. He was almost at the veil looking for Anastasia, but he couldn't see her. Then he thought of his child. He felt the small fast heartbeat. He could feel their connection. The child would need him. His child is heir to the throne now. He could abandon his entire race, abandon his wife, or abandon his child. It was too much for one man. His first priority must be the innocent child. He looked into the faces of his ancestors and waved good-bye for now. He focused on his child and made his way back to the loud voices.

Once voice yelled, "He's back!" Michael heard crying. He heard Jonathan bond to Lucy. He was happy for a second. He reached out to him in a link. "Jonathan. I am proud to be your friend. You have chosen very wisely." He was too weak to hold the link open. Jonathan sprang up and screamed out "Michael! Michael is dying! Lucy, you are a blessed healer now. We have to try." Lucy said, "Ok, but I have absolutely no idea what I'm doing!"

Mark "Quick, everyone stand up in a circle. Hold hands. Now lean in so we are as close to each other as possible!" Everyone was moving quickly. "Now everyone think of Michael and only Michael. (They all felt a link) Good. Now Lucy, you are the healer. See his body, see what you need to focus on."

Lucy cried out, "I can't see him clearly. Everything is all fuzzy. Oh my God, I feel him dying. I can't do this!"

Jonathan squeezed her hand. "I know you can. Ailbe already saw you do it."

Lucy took a deep slow cleansing breath. She focused solely on Michael. "I got him!" Mark "Good. Now look at his entire body. What do you see?"

Lucy "His leg. His leg is cut."

Mark "Great job. Now focus only on his leg."

Lucy "Got it!"

Mark "excellent! Now close the wound."

Lucy "HOW? I'm loosing him!"

Mark "Send your energy to it."

Jonathan yelled, "That size wound could kill her!"

Mark stayed calm, "Her yes, all of us, NO. Everyone, give Lucy what she needs. Don't think of anything else." The room swirled with a warm blue breeze. It became bigger and brighter like a tornado.

Lucy yelled, "I almost got it closed. Just a little more."

Pia-Jiun felt weak, "I can't hold on!"

Lucy yelled, "Please, I just need a little more!"

Pia-Jiun fell to the floor. The blue light started to fade, but it grew larger quickly. The energy burst through the window letting in freezing cold temperature and a ton of snow. Lucy yelled, "DONE!" as she fell forward into Mark's arms. Mark put Lucy's head on a pillow and joined Jonathan in boarding up the window.

Michael felt their energy. He felt his leg muscles, tendons, and ligament reconnecting. He opened his eyes to see his farther Arden with a tube in his arm attached to his own arm with blood flowing through it. "Father, you look horrible." Arden laughed with a sigh of relief. "Because you keep insisting on putting me through Hell! We thought we lost you. Don't move, you need blood." Michael closed his eye and listened to all the voices around him. He asked, "Where's Charlotte?" Ruth answered, "She is safe. She is on her way to Tennessee in the RV with Leif and Malachi." Michael tried to sit up. "Malachi? Of all the protectors, why him?" Ruth rolled her eyes. "Because dear, you chose poorly. Charlotte has now decided that since she can't marry one of my grandchildren, she is just going to piss them all off." Michael huffed. "I will put an end to that practice very soon." Ruth smiled, "On a positive note. The family has been given a new blessed healer." Aharon asked, "Who?" Ruth chuckled, "I'm so glad that you asked. Your new daughter-in-law." Aharon was very confused. "What. Who? He has fallen in love with Lucy. But she is a De'nola." The room was buzzing with chatter. Michael and Ruth laughed.

Abantu appeared in the room. He looked down at Michael's leg. "You take a lot of risks. I'm glad to see that my blessings are put to good use. Now we have our Queen to find. Get up." Michael clamped off the tube that was giving him blood from Arden. He pulled it out of his arm and jumped off the table. Bina tried to protest. "He needs rest! We thought he was dead a minute ago!" Abantu turned towards her. "You are to be known as the mother of the greatest king in your history. Your fear is recorded. But for now, there is work to be done." Abantu and Michael were gone... Again.

Mark and Jonathan got the window boarded up. They stood there for a moment looking at their handy work. They were weak but Michael was alive. They could finally sit down and relax to regain their strength. Mark turned around and felt the blood drain out of his face. Geetu was laying over Pia-Jiun. He was pale and lifeless. Mark grabbed him and felt for a pulse... nothing. He started CPR. Jonathan tried to help but Mark barked at him to get away. Lucy was weak, "What happened?" Jonathan bent down next to her to hold her as they watched. "He must have linked in with us when Pia-Jiun passed out. Children can't do that!" Lucy asked through her tears, "Why?" Jonathan "They are too young to handle all that energy. It kills them." Lucy started screaming. "Take me! Bring him back. Take me!"

Michael and Abantu appeared in the corner of the room. No one noticed. Abantu asked, "You would give your life for a peasant child you just met? Your life is destined for greatness and his is not." Lucy was furious. She stood up and walked directly to the creature with her finger pointed right into one of his black eyes. "Listen you piece of shit. This kid has a right to live. He didn't know what he was doing, he jumped in to help, not to die! I knew the risk. I made my choice. Now bring him back right this second and take me instead!" Mark was still doing CPR. Geetu took a deep breath and started coughing. Mark was drenched in sweat and hugged him tight. Geetu "Mark, you're hurting me." Mark laughed and cried at the same time. "I don't care. I'm not letting you go."

Jonathan smiled and walked to Michael. "Great timing. What is up with the King Michael title?" The two men hugged. Michael looked at Lucy, "Lucy, Thank you for saving my life. All of you have done a tremendous job. I promise to explain it all later. Congratulation. True love always wins." Abantu "Lucy, I have accepted your offer." Lucy pulled back her shoulders. "I'm ready."

Abantu saw no fear in her eyes. He was impressed that she didn't even try to renegotiate the deal. "Are you? You just bonded. Isn't that what have always wanted? To find the one true love that you were so convinced does not exist. How easily you would just throw it away. Maybe it's not what you really wanted after all…" Lucy just stood there looking like a Viking warrior ready for Valhalla. Abantu said, "Ok then. I was right all along." He lifted his head as Lucy said, "Never question the love I have for my husband again." She turned to Jonathan, "I understand it now. I am a peace. I will see you on the other side. I love you." She turned to face Abantu. The two of them stood there for a few minutes. Jonathan had his eyes on Michael. He knew what every flinch meant and Michael was not going to allow Lucy to be taken anywhere.

Mark was holding Geetu. Geetu was giving Michael and Abantu thumbs up and Pia-Jiun was still unconscious. Abantu finally abandoned his staring contest with Lucy and turned his attention to Geetu. "The old man boasts of your bravado. I was in disbelief and had to witness it for myself." Geetu wiggled out of Mark's arms and run to Abantu and hugged his leg. Abantu raised his head laughing. Geetu said "Thank you for letting Ailbe take my Gaya with her." Abantu looked straight ahead. Michael teasingly asked, "Is that a tear in your eye?" Abantu snorted, "Never!" Geetu eyed Michael. Michael readied himself for a child's attack. Boom, Geetu ran full force into Michael. He scooped him up and swung him around. "I am SO proud of you. You have done everything we needed. What can I do for you in return?" Geetu answered quickly, "Can you take my mom's sadness away?" Michael hugged him. "That is something that brought her and Mark together. If I take it away, she will never know what true love feels like. Your mom is going to be a champion for other women." Geetu simply said, "ok." Michael kissed his cheek and set him down. He quickly ran back to Mark.

Michael looked at the two men and put his hand over his heart. "This is all worth it just to see you two happy. I have to go now. We have lots to do." Lucy was exhausted and confused. "Wait, aren't I going with you?" Michael laughed, "Not even close to coming with us." Abantu whispered in her direction. "That was a test. I do that sometimes." And they were gone... again.

Michael and Abantu projected back to the forest. The generals followed a few minutes behind. There was a very large table in the middle of the clearing. Everyone found their seats. Abantu "I need a report. Why can't we find our Queen?" The rabbit stood up. "We all know the Eile are scavengers, they pick up and use anything they can. So my questions are. Who has a way to cloak? Who has cryogenic abilities? And who live a very long time? The common denominator is Azili." Michael stood up. "You better not be suggesting that the Azili have her! We know the Eile do." The rabbit looked nervous. "I'm not suggesting that the Azili have her, but do the Eile have Azili technology?"

Michael sat back. He thought for a moment. Abantu said, "I can smell your wheels turning. Think out loud. This is a round table meeting." Michael leaned forward. "I'm sorry my friends… When we fled, we were chased by Eile. They fired on us and we crashed. We didn't land and disassemble our craft." The kitten stood up. "Where did you crash?" Michael started speaking slowly as if a light were coming on. "You were there this morning, the crater. That's why we stayed there, on the island. We would never allow the De'nola to explore that crater. It is too deep for us to dive… but it wouldn't be too deep for the Eile!" The bear stood up. "But you were attacked more than a hundred miles from there." Michael was on his feet feeling a renewed sense of hope. "There was a huge debris field. It spread over a thousand miles. We spent decades collecting what we could find. Think about it. It all makes sense! If the Eile are using our technology, they can hear our links, because we have antennas to boost our links! They can cloak from us because to us, it's normal! We would never see it. You guys might, but we can't! We have pods for shorter transports, and cryogenic sleep tanks for long travels. That's how they could keep her alive indefinitely. She could only project her mind back to Uanza, but when they woke her up, she was snapped back. She thinks she escaped during one of the transfers… There has to be a part of the ship where I was attacked. Rabbit, you are a genius!" Michael ran over and kissed him on the mouth. "I love this guy!"

Abantu thought for a moment. We need a plan to dive that deep. Azili are the best divers in all the galaxies. If you can't get there…We are closer to her, but still far away." Michael "I can project there!" The rabbit laughed, "No you can't. If it is cloaked, you could end up anywhere." Michael "No, when they had Charlotte in there, the child, my child was scared and I accidently projected there. If I was there once, I should be able to do it again, right?" Abantu thought hard. "It is very risky, almost too risky. The Queen would have to call you to her, like your child did, and she has been conditioned to think it is impossible." Michael felt a rush of adrenaline. "I'll figure that part out." Michael looked around the table, "My friends, except you kitten, I really hate you, but the rest of you. Please help me. Please meet me back at the beach in one of our hours. We can save her." and he was gone. Abantu stood up. "It has been a very long time since I have been amazed. I don't particularly like this type of amazement, but I do like him. I will see you all in one Earth hour." The forest was quiet.

Michael was back in the infirmary. Many of the family members that were there when he left were still there. Arden was shocked to see him back so quickly. Michael said, "Please everyone, I need all the clann elders and all my elders to go to the Thinking Room. Don't link, just go. Where is Uncle Antonio?" Arden said, "In the kitchen. Why?" And Michael was off and running. Ruth and Arden were on his heels. He found Antonio. "Your very special skill set is needed." He told Antonio what to do and ran for the elevator. Ruth and Arden were grinning from ear to ear. When they got to the Thinking Room, the door was wide open.

The fire consumed the entire mountain wall. Michael caught his breath. "Anastasia is here! She is in the crater. The Eile have been using our own technology to hide her. If she calls for me I can project in to her, but it's too deep to dive to, but I can get her out. We can't see it because they are using OUR cloaking. And ready for this! We have been scared for thousands of years that they can somehow hijack our links... Because they can! They are using our equipment, our antennas. The only thing that makes sense is that they have her in OUR ship. Right there!" He pointed out the window. Ruth said. "But you were attacked miles off shore." Michael "I thought I saw something odd, but it was deep, really deep and almost covered in the sand. It must be part of the debris field and the cloak is damaged. That must be how they get around without us ever detecting them."

Everyone started putting the pieces together. Arden asked, "It's hard to link through water and if they do have her down there, the ship can be sealed against any links getting out. Those bastards!" Michael was feeling his excitement overflow. "This is what we are going to do. It will work. First, everyone use your phones and call everyone who stayed behind. Start the phone tree. Tell everyone that at exactly 8:05p.m our time. Every Azili along with Abantu and his generals and all of the general's kind. We will all link together and call for Anastasia. We will tell her to call for me. Once I feel her, I will project to her and get her out. Once I'm in, every second counts. They will know something is up. They know we are coming. They know Charlotte is pregnant, they will keep half of their kind near

Anastasia and they will send the other half to find Charlotte. They will be prepared for all of us, and when they figure out it is just me… Well, let's just say that I'm terrified! But once we reach the surface, I need the ancestors and all the healers to blast the fuck out of them." Aharon asked, "But if they can hear our links, won't they just turn up the cloak?"

Antonio stepped in the room. "That is where I come in. (He turned to Michael) Ace is working on it now. He says it will work. (He turned back to the room) We are going to put all the speakers into the water and I get to play my special Latino party playlist. It will be so loud and confusing to them. Their brains can't separate multiple sounds at the same time. Our technology was not created to cloak music. So they can't block it. We will blast them with music and when we all link, they won't have time to stop us. Anastasia will hear us. This will work." Elijah asked, "What about the marine life? Will it harm them?" Michael quickly agreed. "You are right. I need to get into the water. Somehow we have lost our understanding of some creatures. One of Abantu's generals is a marine creature. He looks just like the Halibut here. He gave me a few suggestions and if I fail, then he will warn them when he gets here. I would hate to think that any innocent creature would be harmed. I will do everything in my power to prevent that. I'm going into the water right after this meeting." Olivia asked, "How do you know that they have split? Half here and half to find Charlotte?" Michael smiled, "Because that is what I would do… But thank you Aunt Olivia, that brings me to another point. Charlotte."

Everyone in the room groaned. Michael continued, "Every elder here, I need you to pick your two best protectors. Then separate your protectors into 2 groups, Expert and Novice. The two best will each choose one from each group until I end up with two groups of equal expert and novice. Is everyone clear on that?" Everyone agree. "Good, once I have each group equal, I need one group from each family here and the other to get to Tennessee. Charlotte is with Leif and Malachi. I was agitated at first, but she doesn't know how lucky she is to have Malachi with her. Once in Tennessee, they need to fan out. Use phones only. NO linking about this. We now KNOW for a fact that they can, have been, and are intercepting out links. Here in the Thinking Room is the only safe place to link. I'm going to have the girls link like it is their job all about this wedding, boys, makeup and clothes. If any of your boys are chatty-katties, I need them too. We have a job for everyone. So many links will keep them busy.

The Tennessee protectors are to be very covert. Their orders will be to kill NOT capture. I don't want to scare Charlotte or her father. Tom is a good man and Charlotte is carrying my child, the last royal child. The Eile are desperate and that makes them unpredictable, and that is the most dangerous enemy to have." Se'ighin asked, "Then why don't we just storm the water with everyone we have? We can just overpower them." Michael bit his lip, "Because if I saw that coming, I would blow up the ship. That would only kill half of their kind, and a nuclear explosion of that magnitude would kill most of the ocean creatures and more than half the De'nola population. They don't care about life the way we do. They would go deep, repopulate, and take over this world too. I won't allow that. Now, everyone has a phone tree to start. Is everyone clear? Are they any questions? Good, I'll be down at the beach if anyone needs me." Michael turned and left the room. It took a few seconds for everything to sink in before the elders jumped into action.

The ancestors were listening with heightened enthusiasm. Ailbe promised she would find Anastasia and now that she knew where she was at, she needed to go to her. She looked around the room for a few moments. For the first time in their timeless history, every ancestor was in agreement. Ailbe slipped into the Thinking Room and followed Michael to the beach. Michael had become keenly aware of his surrounding, mainly due to Abantu's generals jumping him every chance they got, but he was glad that it helped his awareness level. He could feel the warm loving feeling that he always got when his Great-Grandmother was watching him. He didn't stop walking, he just said, "Hello Great-Grandmother. I know you are with me." She was shocked, but very proud. She whispered. "I'll go to her." Michael smiled. "She did say that she had a feeling she will need you soon. This does seem to fit. Tell her I love her and I'm coming." Ailbe was gone.

Michael walked into the water. He remembered the pain in his leg, there was a moment of hesitation and then...bloop... in the water. He swam along the parameter of the entire island. Every living creature he encountered he told to get out of the area. He didn't know if anything understood him but he had to try. This is what the halibut told him to do. After a few minutes of him being in the water, the large gray dolphin with scars on its face swam up and just looked at him. Michael waited for any sign that the dolphin would understand, but nothing. So Michael started talking. "Hello again... My name is King Michael, my wife is Queen A'Llwyn..." At the sound of her name the dolphin swam in circles and made clicking and chirp sounds. Michael continued. "Well, she has been taken again, by a jellyfish that my kind call the Eile." The dolphin jumped and turned and dove down and sprang up out of the water. Michael now understood that he did understand at least some of what he was saying, but he didn't know if this was a friend or foe. But either way, they all needed to be warned. "I need to warn all of the sea creatures to get out of this area, and quick. To rescue my wife, I need to send electricity through the water. It won't cause any damage, but it will kill the smaller life." The dolphin was gone. "Well, I did all I can do." and he swam back to the beach. He heard the whales signing. He knew they would not be affected by the energy.

Ailbe went into the water. This was always a banned place for the Azili. When they crashed here, it triggered an early ice age. In the past 75 years many scientist have asked to explore the crater. The family had adamantly refused all requests. The crater is deep. Deeper than any Azili diver has been able to get to. The Azili were easily diving the Titanic wreck for years to remove proof of their existence long before R.O.Vs could get there. So Ailbe was cautious, even though she had no reason to be. No Eile could ever detect her, not many Azili could either, but in De'nola terms, she was a ghost. Ailbe reached the ship. She wondered how far down it is. There is nothing in the link about the ship in this condition. She looked it over carefully, Michael would link the plans of the ship, but Ailbe wanted to see if there where holes or other ways out. She found a few possibilities but she was anxious to get to Anastasia. She thought to try the infirmary first.

They had a cryogenic tank used for healing in there. She was right, but she wished she had never seen it. Anastasia was lying on a stainless steel table. There was a pile of steel rods on a table next to her, with one end sharpened. There were rods through both of her legs that had her pinned to the table and one through her right shoulder. She had bruises on her face and arms. One eye was swollen shut. Ailbe whispered in her ear. "I will stay with you until Michael comes. He is coming soon. Remember Michael. Remember your husband." Anastasia's left thumb rubbed on her ring. Ailbe was filled with hope. "Please remember Michael" Anastasia cried, "Michael, I'm sorry. I can't do this. I'm erasing everything." Ailbe felt panic stricken. "No! Michael is coming. Hold on!!!" She kept crying, "It hurts, I can't hold on anymore. I warned you that they were coming. I held on as long as I could."

Ailbe gave her some of her energy. Anastasia took a deep breath and coughed up blood. Ailbe didn't know how much energy she could give, but she gave a little more. Anastasia opened her eyes as much as she could. "Ailbe? Where are you?" Ailbe stood in front of her. "I'm here. We didn't know where you were, but now Michael knows! He's coming. Right now. He is on his way." Anastasia was slipping away again. Her voice was weak and every time she coughed, the pain was intense. Ailbe circled the steel rod in her shoulder. Anastasia felt a wave of relief and moaned. "Thank you. Now please escort me to the ancestors." Ailbe screamed out hoping other ancestors would hear her. Several blue flashes shot out of the fireplace, out the window and straight into the water. Ailbe was repeating over and over that Michael is coming, but Anastasia had erased so many memories that she wasn't sure if she could even call for Michael when it was time.

Ailbe felt the presence of other ancestors. She turned around, King Robert and Queen EL-la and several members of their court were standing there. Ailbe moved aside. Queen EL-la moved so close to Anastasia that Ailbe though she was going to try and give all of her energy to her. She whispered. "My brave daughter." Anastasia opened her eyes. The tears rolled down her face. "Mommy, I'm so sorry I failed you." Anastasia coughed and a large amount of blood was flowing down her chin. Queen EL-la said, "I have never had a prouder moment. But hear me child. When I tell you to, you need to call for Michael. Do you hear me?" Anastasia "Michael who?" Queen EL-la gasped and moved back. "She erased him!"

King Robert moved forward and gave his daughter some energy. Anastasia took a painful breath and opened her eyes again. "Daddy!" King Robert motioned the members of his court to surround the rods and when Michael arrived to use everything they have to pull the rods out. Ailbe said, "That could drain you. You would be nothing. I will not allow that." and Ailbe was gone. King Robert firmly said, "You MUST remember. Dig deep and remember your husband, remember your coronation as Queen. Who is your King?!" She was trying. Something sounded so familiar about that name, but it was far away. "My dad is King Robert." King Robert rarely raised his voice and never to his beloved Princess. But this was the exception to the rule. "I am your father, but who is your KING?!" Anastasia dug deep.

Ailbe shot up from the water and into the fireplace. She had no time for debates. She shouted out. "King Robert and Queen EL-la and a few members of the court are planning on sacrificing all of their energy to save their daughter. Whoever is with me, let's go." She didn't even wait for any response and she had no idea who, if any, was with her. She shot back through the fireplace and into the water.

Michael was on the beach waiting for 8:05p.m when Abantu and his generals were asked to arrive. He nodded to Antonio to start the music. The ground was shaking it was so loud. They saw several small Eile come out of the water holding their heads in pain. The protectors quickly killed them. The elders were lined up. The protectors were armed and ready for battle. Every member of the house that did not have a specific job was to link a ridiculous amount of mindless material, were all lined up and ready. The healers were feeling nervous, but they would rather die than live another second under the fear of an Eile attack. The air was sparking with energy. Ruth called out. "The ancestors are here and ready." Abantu and his generals appeared on the beach. Michael was about to give the order. Abantu shouted, "Wait! I have one more thing to do." And he was gone.

Pia-Jiun woke up about an hour later. Her head was on Mark's lap and Geetu was curled up with Pec. Lucy was listening to Mark and Jonathan talking. No one had heard anything since Michael and Abantu left. It was stone cold silent. Jonathan said to Mark. "Not one link, in the entire world? I can't take just sitting here waiting. I have a billion questions. How are you not freaking out?" Mark smiled. "Isn't that kind of the point for me? I've been trained my entire life to control every single detail of my environment, to be perfect at my job. Pia-Jiun and Geetu don't need perfection. They need love." Pia-Jiun sat up. "Lucy how do you feel?" Lucy said. "Actually I feel great. Like I have a new toy and want to play with it." Abantu appeared and said. "Good to know." and they were gone. Jonathan looked at Pia-Jiun very wide eye and sat down in front of her. "Ok... teach me some of that Zen mediation shit right now, or my head is going to explode."

Leif and Malachi also felt very uneasy that the links had all stopped. Malachi could feel his parents and his siblings, but couldn't understand the silence. If there was an order to stop linking, they would have heard it. Malachi finally said. "I wish I knew what was going on. No link. No phone call. I know the party starts today, but I would hate to miss it." Leif laughed. "You know how we love a good old fashion party. I feel it in the air, even all the way out here. Feels like all of them, all the ancestors are showing up. Did the veil come down?"

Charlotte and Tom were watching TV. Tom said, "This is a great way to travel. I could get used to this." Charlotte rubbed her still flat belly. "We are going to get used to a lot of nice thing." Tom said, "No Charlotte, don't go taking advantage of this. I know the Reale family is going to accept this child and care for it. You don't need to go getting fancy stuff just because you can. That is not how you were raised." Charlotte laughed, "The only thing I'm going to ask for is what Michael promised me. He will marry me and we will raise this child together. What's wrong with that? That is what we have been talking about for years. You know I'm not a liar. He even asked you for my hand. Remember? That was what... 2 months ago?" Tom started to say something but she "Shhh" him. She wanted to listen to more of Malachi and Leif's conversation.

Charlotte shouted, "Hey what are you guys talking about? Is there a party this weekend at the house? What's the party for?" Malachi laughed, "Not that kind of party. We are planning a surprise for some vermin in the back yard." Charlotte said, "Well, I know it's not a wedding. I heard that Anastasia found out that Michael has been with me planning our engagement announcement, our wedding, oh and making our bundle of joy. Maybe it is for the best that she skipped town. Or did Michael send her back to where she came from?" Malachi had flashes of duct taping her mouth shut, but just smiled. Leif was openly laughing.

There was a loud pop sound and the RV fishtailed until Leif got it back under control. Charlotte was cursing and yelling until Leif pulled over and stopped. "Geeze! Who taught you how to drive? Michael will hear about this. From now on, Malachi drives!" Malachi looked at Leif. Even though they weren't told not to link, seeing that there was not one single link on the planet, they were not going to mess that up. Malachi stood up and opened the door and stepped out quickly. Leif went and sat by Charlotte. "I'm not one for gossip, but while Malachi is fixing the tire... Tell me what you heard about Anastasia leaving. I heard it was nasty." Charlotte just found her new ally. "Ya know, I always liked you." Leif kept her talking but could tune her out and focus on Malachi. Leif always joked that "Tuning people out is my superpower."

Malachi walked to the back of the RV. There was a flat tire with a steel rod sticking out of. Malachi pulled it out to look at it. It was sharpened on one end. Malachi took a defensive position on top of the RV. He pulled out his phone and called for roadside assistance. The operator said. "Absolutely Mr. Reale, air and road side will be there in 3-2-1. Have a pleasant day." and the phone disconnected. Two Chinook helicopters landed about a hundred yards away as two Pave Hawk helicopters circled. Twenty protectors jumped out of each Chinook and swept the area. The protectors flushed out twenty full grown Eile and found an additional ten spikes on trip wires. Malachi stayed on the roof watching every blade of grass move. The protectors changed the tire and gave the *all clear* hand sign. The protectors returned to the helicopter and were gone all within fifteen minutes.

Malachi's phone rang. The woman on the other end said. "Mr. Reale, this is a courtesy call. Would you be able to answer a few questions for our quality control?" Malachi responded. "Protector Malachi. M.A.L.A.C.H.I 3-2-1." The female "Thank you Mr. Reale, was your assistance sufficient?" Malachi "Yes" The female "Your next service call is scheduled in ten minutes. Good-bye" Malachi jumped off the roof and back into the RV. Leif said, "SHH, we can talk more later." Charlotte asked, "What was wrong?" Malachi answered, "Nothing, just a flat tire. We probably just ran over some road kill. I'll make sure Leif is more careful." Charlotte snapped, "Hey, don't yell at him about his driving." and she went back to watching TV with Tom. Malachi sent Leif a text. "Glad I was here. 20 snot boxes in woods. Pull over in 10." Leif nodded and called to the back. "The fun train is leaving the station." Charlotte yelled back, "Woo-woo." Malachi almost fell out of his chair with laughter.

Abantu was back on the beach with Lucy. Michael snapped. "No! Absolutely not! Lucy and Jonathan are NOT to be here." Lucy put her hand on Michael's shoulder. "I want to be here. I love Anastasia too. Just give me a gun and show me what to shoot." Abantu laughed. "I am enjoying this tribe." Michael scowled at him and looked at Lucy. "You are not a fighter you are a blessed healer. I don't have time to get you back, so what every you do, Don't die!" Ruth grabbed her by the hand. "Quickly, go stand in the water. When it's time, clear you mind of everything except your energy flowing into the water. It is going to feel like…" Lucy cut her off. "I got it" and she ran to where other people were standing in the water. She heard Michael yell. "Remember not to die."

Abantu reared up and snorted. His generals burst into thunderous howls, growls, screams, and grunts. Michael yelled, "Everyone ready!?" There was an earth moving response in unison. "Ready!" Michael "ON MY MARK…3…2….1" and he was gone.

Ailbe returned just as the music started. King Robert begged his daughter again. "Please. Michael is coming, but he needs you to call for him. He needs you NOW." Anastasia shook her head no. "Daddy please make it stop. Just take me to the ancestors." Ailbe still was not aware of how much energy she had at her disposal, but she was ready to give everything she had. "Everyone, grab these rods and pull!" To Ailbe's amazement there were untold amount of ancestors in the room. The Eile would defiantly know they were here. The steel rods melted with so much energy. King Robert bellowed, "Call for your husband now or die!" Ailbe screamed. "The ring!" Queen EL-la grabbed her daughter's hand and said, "Open

your eyes, please daughter open them now and call for your husband!"
Anastasia opened her eyes and saw the ring. "Michael? (Her memories
started to flood back) Michael. Michael! MICHAEL HELP ME!"

Michael was at her side. He had no time to acknowledge the ancestors. He scooped her up off the table as a horde of Eile came screaming
down the hallway. He refused to set her back on the table so he set her
on the floor. His rage was on full display. He dove into the Eile front line
and started ripping them apart with his bare hands. Anastasia started
moaning. The infection was reaching her heart. He saw the ancestors
and screamed, "Take her and get out of here!" King Robert "He is right.
There are enough of us to get her out." The ancestors were watching in
horror as Michael was pushing them farther back into the dark hallway. He
screamed, "Now! Get her out of here!" Until they could no longer see him.
The hallway was clear. Ailbe jumped in. "How did any of you get anything
done?" She grabbed her arm as everyone watched. Ailbe's face was turning
into steam she was so angry. "Just grab a body part and lift you pompous
pricks!" They all snapped into action. They lifted her up. Ailbe said. "Your
majesty, on my mark, you project us out. 3..2..1" and they were gone.

Lucy was the first to notice a bright blue bubble in the water. "There!
In the water!" Abantu and the bear jumped in. The bear grabbed Anastasia
and started pulling her out as a dozen Eile flew out of the water and started
stabbing him. Lucy put both hands in the water and instead of healing,
she started taking their energy. All the healers put their hands in the water
and the Eile screamed in pain. Most died but some slithered back into the
water. The bear stumbled out of the water and collapsed. The sand was
turning red with his blood.

Several protectors dove into the water in pursuit of the escaping Eile
and others picked up Anastasia and carried her onto the beach. Lucy followed the protectors carrying Anastasia's limp body. Lucy yelled. "Put her
down!" Which they uncharacteristically did. Protectors only took orders
from their chain of command or their mothers. Lucy knelt down besides
Anastasia and on instincts alone, put her hands on her chest. A faint blue
light slowly began to appear from Lucy's hands. Lucy had a difficult time
focusing. She called out. "I need help over here!" The scene was chaotic.

All the elders were keeping the veil open so they could channel the ancestor's energy, the healers were either in the water or with the bear, Abantu, or one of his generals, and the protectors were either fighting an Eile or diving to peruse one. The ancestors were already giving all the energy that they could. Lucy suddenly felt very much alone. She wished that Jonathan was here, she thought of Pia-Jiun and Mark, she thought of Geetu playing with Pec. She begged herself to be able to link with them. She cried to Anastasia. "Please don't give up. I know I can do this."

Jonathan felt Lucy's desperation. "Come on, we need to try and link with Lucy. She needs us." Geetu jumped in. "I'm ready!" Mark and Jonathan yelled, "NO!" Mark tussled his hair. "Keep Pec busy." Jonathan, Mark and Pia-Jiun tried over and over to link, but Lucy was confused and overwhelmed. Just as Jonathan felt he could almost reach her, Lucy heard a loud scream. She turned to see Ruth being swarmed by a group of Eile that had somehow gotten behind her. Se'ighin ran to help her. Aengus yelled, "Don't break the line!" Deaglan was on the far end of the elder line and he was distracted for a fraction of a second. He felt an intense pain and he fell grabbing his ankle. He was cut. He tried to call for help as he felt the knife slice through his throat.

Amani was watching in horror. She was paralyzed with terror. The Eile were all over the beach. One hissed at her but when she didn't move it turned toward Deaglan and piled onto the attacking group. Amani wanted to run, but she ran to help the elders. She pulled a knife out of her leg holster and killed two before she realized the elder was dead. She ran to help Se'ighin. He had gotten the swarm off of Ruth, but they had turned on him and attacked with ferocity. He was stabbed several times but still fighting. He saw Amani and yelled. "Get her off the beach." as they pulled him into the water. She starting pulling Ruth away from the beach as she was screaming. "Se'ighin!" Amani fought to get her closer to the house, she was injured and out of the fight.

Amani turned back to the fighting. She didn't know where to help. She saw Lucy leaning over Anastasia and ran to them. "What can I do to help?" Lucy looked up with tears in her eyes. "I don't know." Amani put her hands over Lucy's hands and said. "Try now, and what every you do, don't stop!" Lucy closed her eyes and tried to ignore the screams around her. The light around her hands began to get brighter. Anastasia's shoulder wound began to close. Debbie had been helping the other healers with the bear.

The bear could stand and they helped him off the beach, but they all found someone else to help. Debbie headed to Lucy and put her hands on top of Amani's. Lucy could feel more energy. Abantu noticed the glow of the now bright blue light. He struggled to reach them. He yelled to Lucy. "A life for a life, but this is no test." Lucy yelled back, "I never felt like I had much of a life to begin with, so take it." She opened herself up to give everything she had. Abantu called back but this time his voice cracked. "It's not your life." Lucy's eyes shot open. Amani was pale and barley had her eyes open. Amani looked at Lucy and tried to smile. Lucy cried, "No!" Abantu "It's not your decision to make."

Michael's rage knew no end. Just as he was starting to feel fatigued, he remembered Anastasia and his rage filled his veins again. He had killed dozens, but more and more where coming. He was injured, but he didn't feel any pain until a sharp pain in his calf brought him to his knees. He didn't care he just wanted to keep pushing them back away from Anastasia. But he couldn't move. He turned to look at his leg and there was a steel rod through his calf and into the floor. He tried to grab it and pull it out but the second his hands were on the rod, they grabbed him from every angle. His scream shook the entire island. The Eile plunged another rod onto the other leg and into each shoulder. They laughed at him as he struggled and vowed to rip each one of them apart. The Large one said, "Go kill the rest of them. We will leave this one here until we kill his entire family." They all abandoned him there. Ailbe was the only one that stayed behind. She sat down next to Michael. "I'm here." He knew it. He smiled. "I saw you. How is Anastasia?" Ailbe nodded. "Everything is, as it is. Anastasia is weak, but will be getting stronger soon." Michael smiled. "Good." He closed his eyes. Ailbe gave him a little of her energy and he relaxed slightly.

Anastasia started to become aware of the sounds of horror and the feelings of terror that surrounded her. She opened her eyes hoping to see Michael. "Lucy? No, you can't be here! Get out of here now! Is Jonathan here too?" Lucy had tears streaming down her face but tried to calm

Anastasia down. "Shh. Just relax. You are out now." Anastasia struggled to get up. She looked around and saw death and blood everywhere. Her friends and family were dying because of her. She grabbed at Amani's hand. "I'm so glad you are ok." But Amani's hand was cold and lifeless. She looked at her face and knew she was dead.

Anastasia screamed and struggled to stand up. The flood of emotions and memories of the death and destruction on Atlantis overtook her. She remembered her feelings of fear before, but this time all she felt was fury. She took a deep breath and invited the wrath engulf her. The Queen's crown of Uanza appeared on her head. The bright blue glow of collective ancestors became each individual ancestor. The dead Azili bodies became blinding white as their energies emerged from their bodies. Lucy sat there trying to remember every detail for Jonathan as a single Eile slithered up behind her, pulled out a large knife and plunged it through her chest and into her heart. Debbie tried to scream but it happened so fast. Anastasia turned as Lucy fell. Anastasia bellowed. "Not one more death at the hands of these monsters!" She grabbed the knife from Lucy's chest, pulled it out and sliced the Eile open with it. She looked at Lucy and commanded in a booming voice, "Blessed healer. Heal thy self." and Lucy was gone.

Anastasia walked towards the water. The intense blue light had turned into almost a flame. Millions of ancestors had solid blue forms and quickly overtook the Eile. She started giving orders. "Hunt down every last one. Kill them. ALL of them. Heal the wounded, honor our dead, And BRING ME MY HUSBAND!" Michael felt a surge of energy. He tried to reach a rod in his shoulder, but he couldn't move his arms. Ailbe grabbed onto one of the rods in his leg as he tried lifting his leg, and the rod gave way. They tried the other with the same results. He was feeling stronger by the second, so was Ailbe, she had become solid. She gripped a rod in his shoulder and it seemed to come out with ease. He pulled out the rod from his other shoulder. He needed a moment to catch his breath. "Go check on the family, they need you. I'll be right there." She refused to leave him and helped him stand up. He started laughing as he felt Anastasia's intense power. Ailbe asked, "What could possibly be so funny?" He stood up straight, still laughing. "Let's get out of here so you can see this for yourself." He took

Ailbe by the hand, he thought of his only desire and that was to be next to his wife. So... he was.

Lucy was back at the Inn. She was in the center of the mattresses. She was holding her bleeding chest and shaking with terror. Mark jumped to her side and put his hands over her hands. Jonathan was instantly there with Mark. Pia-Jiun yelled to Geetu. "Boil some water." as she put her hands in the pile on Lucy's chest. Geetu quickly did what his mother told him to do. Jonathan was desperate, "Lucy, look at me. Don't stop looking at me. We are here for you. Take whatever you need." Lucy nodded (More like shaking) that she understood. She kept her eyes on Jonathan. Mark leaned close to her. "Do exactly what I tell you to do. Focus on closing the hole." She felt her own hands were getting weak, but she did what Mark told her to do. She could imagine the hole in her heart weaving back together. She felt her blood flowing through her body and not out through the hole in her chest. She wanted to close her eyes, but Jonathan kept her focused on him. Mark yelled, "What the hell is happening back home!?" They could all feel the chaos, and that no one was communicating very well. But right now, all they wanted to do was to concentrate on Lucy.

Leif and Malachi went another ten minutes down the road and Malachi said. "We need to pull over for a minute." Charlotte and Tom were still watching TV, and didn't seem to notice that Leif was pulling into a large crowded truck stop. Malachi stepped out of the RV and his phone rang. The female voice on the other end said, "Mr. Reale, this is a courtesy call. Are they any further issues?" Malachi answered, "No, how are the roads ahead?" The female voice cracked. "Please hold Mr. Reale, There seems to be some heavy construction back in Virginia." The voice was silent for a few minutes. Leif stepped out of the RV and stood next to him. The female voice came back on the line. "Mr. Reale, the road ahead has been cleared of some debris. Please proceed with extreme caution." And the line went dead. Leif and Malachi tried to sort out the clatter and confusion, but it was too chaotic. Malachi put his head against the RV. "What the hell is going on back there!? We need to be with them!"

Leif stood there with him trying to figure it out. Leif finally said. "The sooner we can get her to Tennessee, the better. But we should stop soon and get some rest." Malachi laughed, "You go tell her, she will love to bend your ear with more gossip." Leif smiled, "Now she feels she has a sympathetic Reale." Malachi shook his head, "Better you than me." Leif got back in the RV and went to the kitchen. "Who is up for a virgin Cosmo?" Charlotte raised her hand. "Oh… me me me. But what is a virgin Cosmo?" Leif pulled out a bottle of vodka and shook it. "I boiled the shit out of it… NO alcohol left!" Charlotte clapped her hands. "Yeah, you are so much fun." Leif made the drinks and sat down next to her. "I wish we met before our little peanut arrived. I bet we would have been besties." Charlotte said, "Well, we still can be. Do you do Karaoke?" Leif laughed, "I have the voice of an angel. But what about you? How are you feeling?" Charlotte slapped his leg. "I can sit on a chair." Leif said, "Perfect, BUT… Only for one hour. Then you rest. Deal or no deal?" Charlotte shouted, "Deal!" Leif kissed her cheek. "Great. I'll have Malachi look for a hotel with a karaoke bar in it." He walked back outside. Malachi scratched his chin. "You are one brilliant mother fucker."

Anastasia walked to the waters edge. She touched her foot into the water and calmly said, "King Michael" and he was by her side. He wanted to hold her, but they had work to do. They held hands, the King's crown appeared on his head. The two crowns radiated blue light in every direction. All of the prior Kings and Queens were lined up behind them, and one by one, it appeared as if they walked into them. All the Kings and Queens in their entire history were now one. All their strengths, all their power, all their blessings were now inside them. Their chests began to glow almost translucent. Everyone could see that their hearts were beating in synch. With each beat, a pulse of light circled them and spread out. Each pulse sent ripples through the sand pushing the Azili and their allies back onto the beach and up towards the safety of the house. When the pulses hit the water, it caused waves to form, which sent the Eile racing to get back into the water. As the blue waves hit them, they died painfully.

The generals could only stand out of the way as they watched the Eile being defeated. Anastasia and Michael were exhausted but exhilarated. The pulses stopped and they held each other tight. Michael finally had a moment to look at Anastasia. "I'm so sorry it took me so long to find you."

She didn't allow him to finish his thought. She kissed him as he picked her up. Their happiness was short lived though. Michael heard his mother scream. His rage instantly returned, as he blindly ran toward the sound his mother's agony. His body was primed for another round of battle, but when he saw his little sister Amani's body, his heart felt defeated. He ran and held her. Anastasia fell to her knees and watched as Arden took her body from Michael's arms. He cried out to Abantu. "Please! She is just a child. Not her, Take me instead." Abantu lowered his head. "She told me to refuse any offers to exchange for her life. This was her choice. She sacrificed her life for her Queen's life." Anastasia "I didn't want anyone to die for me. Please, bring her back!" Abantu still had his head down as Bina started yelling at him. "I am her elder. She can't make deals without me." Abantu just kept his head down. "It has already been done." and he was gone. Michael was about to plead to the generals, but with their heads held low, they left too. Anastasia looked at Michael. "Will we ever have a moment of happiness?" Michael turned toward the family, "No one goes back into the water. I will find the Eile that have gone deep. Get the injured to the infirmary. Take the dead to the Thinking Room. We'll be back." He reached for Anastasia's hand and they were gone.

Lucy was healing when Michael and Anastasia arrived. Geetu was bringing over hot water when he saw them and spilled it. "You must be the Queen that everyone keeps talking about. You're pretty." Anastasia looked at him and smiled. "I have heard many many many great things about you too. Now, we need to go." He said, "Not before Lucy is better." Anastasia walked over to Lucy and extended her hand. Jonathan and Mark felt her trying to get up, so they moved out of her way. Lucy took Anastasia's hand and the entire Inn shook. Geetu grabbed Pec, Pia-Jiun held onto the journal. Jonathan and Mark looked at each other and they were all gone.

The Inn collapsed in on itself as an earthquake split the ground open. In an instant, there was nothing left. Mr. and Mrs. Vans were at the hotel listening to the news when they heard breaking reports out of Virginia about several small earthquakes that had caused small tsunamis. There was no damage, but an island was being evacuated for precautions. They were eager to get back to the Inn when they felt an earthquake themselves.

Then more breaking news that a magnitude 4.0 earthquake hit a small village in Nepal but caused minimal damage. Imay felt that his job was almost done. Just a few more hours and he could relax.

Ruth had a difficult time walking but she helped as many Azili back up to the house as she could. The infirmary was packed and the healers were busy with the most severely injured first. The room became silent as the bodies of the dead, including Se'ighin, Deaglan, and Amani were carried pass the doorway heading up to the Thinking Room. After a few moments everyone continued what they were doing but no one spoke. Debbie stayed by Amani's body. Ruth refused any healing until everyone else was safe. Several of Deaglan's clann were by his side. They were victorious, but they suffered many losses, no one felt like celebrating.

Mark could smell jasmine as he opened his eyes. "Where are we?" Anastasia smiled but the suffering she was feeling was unbearable. "All bonds must be recorded in the throne room. We have decided that we have lost some of our old ways and some of our old ways need to be lost." Anastasia turned to Lucy. "Wait here until your petition is called." Mark looked at Jonathan and asked, "Uanza? Are we home?" Jonathan couldn't think of anything to say.

Michael and Anastasia walked down the hall and into Anastasia's parent's room. They quickly changed into more royal looking attire and went back into the throne room. Most of the ancestors were still on the beach making sure that the Eile were not going to double back and start another attack. But Michael wanted Lucy and Jonathan to be the first official business of his reign. They sat on their thrones and the doors opened. Lucy still felt weak, but as the doors opened, she was awestruck. It was the most stunning sight she had ever seen. Jonathan looked around the room and was mesmerized. Mark and Pia-Jiun looked into the room and both were amazed.

Abantu walked into the throne room and passed Geetu. Geetu patted him on the hind leg. Abantu turned around with a huff at the indignant action. Geetu just smiled and gave him two thumbs up. Pec barked playfully, almost as if he were laughing. Abantu could not hold back his own laughter as he continued into the throne room. He bowed. "King Michael.

I'm surprised to see you here and not hunting down the last handful of the Eile." Michael "They are gathering to regroup. I will deal with them at the right time. But this is much more important. This court was founded on love. The Queen and I thought it would be best to record a new bond first." Abantu laughed, "I am going to enjoy your reign. Please proceed. But may I confess something first?" Michael smiled warmly, "I think you should." Abantu turned to Lucy. "May I present to you my son, Alexander. The first, and greatest of the protectors." Pec jumped out of Geetu's hands and ran to Abantu's side. Jonathan and Lucy looked at each other hoping the other wasn't as confused as they were. Pec stood up and looked almost identical to Abantu.

Alexander looked at Lucy. "I have been your protector since you were an infant. Now you have Jonathan." Lucy was speechless as he continued. "Your life has never been useless, but you kept me busy trying to keep you from throwing it away." Geetu ran pass everyone to stand next to Alexander. "But where is my Pec?" His eyes were sad. Abantu laughed loudly, "He is right here." Geetu held out his hands to the towering Alexander. "I can't walk you, you're too big." Alexander knelt down. "You would prefer me to still fit in your hands?" Geetu nodded as he started to cry. Alexander looked at Michael. "Your Uncle Elijah has been looking after my kind for decades. I have sent many of my children to be place as protectors all over the planet. De'nola children need protectors too."

Michael laughed at himself. "So much I never saw, even though it was right in front of me. Misty Hills Animal Rescue…" Alexander smiled as he turned back to Geetu. "I have been keeping your Pec right here, safe and sound until you got here to pick him up." A small puppy that looked exactly like Pec came running out from underneath the King's throne. It ran right into Geetu's arms. Geetu looked at Lucy. I know he is your puppy, but can I walk him when ever I want?" Lucy looked at Jonathan. "I have my protector. If your mom says it's ok, then you can have him." Pia-Jiun smiled and looked at Mark. "I don't know where we are going to live. Can we have a pet there?" Mark loved everything about that question. "Yes, we can have a dog there."

Michael cleared his throat. "I do have a few things that I have to get back to… Ya know a war is going on. Can I record the bond and instate my chief advisor and the advisor to the Queen?" Jonathan pointed at himself. "Me?" Anastasia stood up and in her royal voice. "The first new business of the court is a bond." Michael stood up. "I witness this bond as pure, honest, and exchanged freely in love. This court will not reject this union." Anastasia continued. "The second business of this court is the appointment of advisors. Are there any who would reject?" Michael "There are no rejections. The appointments of advisor Jonathan to the King, and Lucy to the Queen is now recorded." Michael was about to project back to the beach when Lucy asked. "Is it against any rules if I heal my husband's face? I don't mind the stitches, but the black eyes…" Abantu belly laughed and Jonathan's face was completely healed. Michael and Anastasia were gone.

Abantu was walking out of the throne room with Alexander following him. Geetu was playing on the floor with the original Pec. Pia-Jiun asked. "What do we do? How do we get home?" Abantu stopped and looked at her for a moment. He walked around her and sniffed the air. He began to approach her and she wanted to melt into the floor. He finally said. "Much of my time is spent teaching humility. Most beings lack in that skill, but you have an over abundance. The King and Queen will be back for you in time. Until then, get to know each other better, enjoy life on Uanza, and most importantly, learn to trust. I will be watching you closely and when the time is right, I will come and personally train you for your adventure." Without another word, Abantu and his son were gone.

Michael and Anastasia projected about a hundred miles off the beach. They hovered above the water for a moment. Michael said. "I know this will be hard for you. Do you want me to do it?" She smiled with an air of confidence. "I'm fine. Nothing can hurt us when we're together." The whales were singing. Michael loved that sound. They dove deep. Michael found the debris field and the part of the ship that they would transport Anastasia in when they needed to put her into cryostasis.

They no longer needed to swim down or hold their breath. They easily located the ship, Michael pulled the door open and they went inside. Michael's rage was coming back quickly. They had several De'nola bodies that they had dissected in an effort to learn about the Azili body. Michael heard them coming, they were all coming. The last of the Eile. Anastasia was looking for the leader, the big one. As Michael grabbed each one, he asked. "Where is your eldest? Where is he?!" They would laugh as they died, until the last one said. "He left to search for more of our kind." Anastasia and Michael both knew that it was telling the truth. They put it in a bag, and then projected the piece of the ship back to Uanza.

Next, they projected to Egypt. Anastasia asked, "What are we doing here?" Michael "This is the Siwa Oasis. They won't discover The Great Monolith of Dunning for another three thousand years. This will be perfect to keep this Eile here until we find their eldest. It's hot, dry, and cramped in there. It won't be able to reproduce or escape." The Eile hissed and cursed. Michael asked, "Last chance, where did your eldest go?" It refused to answer. Michael laughed as he projected it deep into the ancient structure. Anastasia took a deep breath. "Almost done my love." She grabbed his hand and projected them back to the compound.

Michael and Anastasia were exhausted. They had nothing left to give. They needed rest. They walked into the infirmary and with bitter sweet hugs and kisses, Michael said, "We will honor and bury our dead on Uanza. Their sacrifice has bought our freedom. Come to the Thinking Room and let the ancestors take their bodies." Olivia and Aharon looked unsettled. Olivia tearfully said. "I can't feel Jonathan. Do you know if he is ok?" Michael looked at everyone, "Jonathan and Mark fine. They are on Uanza. They need some peace and quiet with Lucy, Pia-Jiun and Geetu. We will bring them back in a few days our time. We will have so many things to celebrate by then." Rach-El stepped out of the crowd and almost knocked him over with a huge hug. She didn't say anything, she just needed to see for herself that he was really ok. Michael smiled at her. "We have so much to do for your wedding." She smiled and cried at the same time. He took Anastasia by the hand as they started to walk upstairs. Anastasia stopped. "One more thing before. What about Charlotte?" and they were gone....again

Michael and Anastasia projected into a hotel bar. Malachi and Tom were eating chicken wings and drinking beer. Leif and Charlotte were singing Bitch by Meredith Brooks on the karaoke machine. Michael

approached Tom. "There you guys are. We have been looking for you."
Malachi jumped at them and hugged them. "What the hell is going on?!"
Michael said, "I will link everything to you and Leif. Se'ighin, Deaglan,
and Amani, just to name a few, are with the ancestors. They sacrificed so
we were victorious."

Malachi felt a wave of horror, sadness, and then his anger began to
well up. "No! I need to get home." Michael shook his head, "No, Finish
here. Get her to see her family. You and Leif have done an amazing job."
He turned toward Tom. "Tom, I'm very sorry about hurting your family. I
will make sure that our families are united. I need to speak to Charlotte."
Tom gave him a big hug. "I have no doubt that you will do the right thing.
But you have a right to be happy too." Michael patted his shoulders. Leif
noticed Michael talking to Malachi. Once they finished the song. He said
to Charlotte. "Is that Michael?"

Charlotte pretended to look at her watch. "It's about time." She walked
over and was about to say hello to him when she saw Anastasia. Michael
motioned to touch her arm when Anastasia said. "Charlotte, may I please
have a word with you, in private?" Charlotte was angry, but she wanted
to show Michael that she was not going to run from any conversation.
"Sure. We either have a room upstairs or the RV." Anastasia said. "The
RV might give us more privacy, but which ever you are more comfortable
with." Charlotte looked in her eyes, but didn't see any anger or resentment.
"And how rude of me not to ask how you are feeling." Charlotte said, "WE
are just fine." as she walked toward the RV. Malachi asked, "Should I be
following them?" Michael laughed, "No, but I could use a beer." Tom lifted
up his hand to the bartender. "We need another round please."

Charlotte and Anastasia sat inside the RV. Neither spoke for a few
minutes. Anastasia finally said, "I'm very sorry that you were hurt in all of
this, it was never his plan. We both want to you be happy, and your child is
a wonderful addition to the family. Complicated, but wonderful. I want us
all to be very close. You and Michael are now and forever connected, and
I respect that unique relationship, but I am his wife…" Charlotte cut her
off. "I heard that you cancelled your wedding. How dare you call yourself
his wife, ha! Wishful thinking, you're not even married yet. I know more

about Michael than you ever will. He will always choose his child over you or any other chicky that tries to turn his head. You are nothing but a fling and I forgive him."

Anastasia "We have done the traditional family bonding ceremony. But as you pointed out, we have not done a traditional wedding ceremony."

Charlotte "Listen, I don't know what you want me to say. You are just a stress-fling. Michael is a man of his word, and family is everything to him. He will want to be with me because he loves our family, our child, our home. There is no room in our marriage for you... so ba-bye."

Anastasia "You have known Michael for a very long time, and you are right, he loves his family. That includes you, and the special place you will always have in his heart. That is why I am suggesting that you come and live on the compound. You will have anything you have ever wanted or needed."

Charlotte "Oh, I'm going to live there alright, but we will need our space. We will have our own house as far away from his family as possible."

Anastasia "That will never happen. We need you both to stay close to the family. Michael and I will be traveling for...work."

Charlotte "We? You aren't going to live with us."

Anastasia "You are the mother of Michael's child. You will be looked after for the rest of your life, and Michael will be a devoted father. But the fact that Michael and I are bonded will not change. I am dedicated to make this work between us. Please keep your child's best interest at heart."

Charlotte "I am. And what is best for my child is to have Michael and I married and you out of our lives."

Anastasia "You do understand that Michael is willing to give you everything you are asking for right? Money, houses, jewelry, cars, whatever you want... or... you can threaten his wife, piss him off, and he will fight you with a team of lawyers until he has full custody. He will of course grant you visitation rights, but with thousands of family members all over the world, would you ever feel like you had true privacy with your child?

Charlotte "Are you threatening me?"

Anastasia "Absolutely not! I'm giving you two scenarios. One that you have everything you ever wanted from Michael and the other where Michael turns his anger toward you."

Charlotte "You just proved my point. He has never been mad at be before. (She rubbed her belly.) As a matter of fact, I was just making him happy, very... very happy, a few nights ago. If he is angry, it's at you, not me."

Anastasia "I'm not here to fight with you. I had high hopes that we could find a common ground. I'm exhausted..." before she could finish her thought, Charlotte interrupted her. Charlotte "Exhausted!? Doing what? You've been..."

Anastasia was loosing her patience and put up her hand. "You bore me and I'm done here. Michael's little sister Amani died tonight on the beach. We are heading back right after I speak to you. He is either going to give you everything or take everything. Your choice."

Charlotte was shocked. "I don't know what to say. Did she drown? This is one of the reasons that I told Michael we should move off the island. I don't want our child to live there."

Anastasia felt her face turning red with anger. "So your thoughts are not of anyone but yourself?!?" Anastasia stood up and walked toward the RV door. My offer remains on the table, but my feelings for you have changed dramatically. You are thoroughly the most despicable human I have ever met. Would you like to speak to Michael now?"

Charlotte lifted her chin. "Yes, send him out. I'm feeling tired and I don't want to walk back and forth."

Anastasia walked out of the RV and back into the hotel bar. Tom was the first one to notice her come back in. "Anastasia, are you ok? Charlotte can be kinda mean sounding sometimes. I'm sorry if she hurt your feelings." Anastasia smiled, "You are a good man Tom. But no, she was fine. She just wants to speak to Michael for a minute and then we have to go." Michael asked, "She wants to talk to me?" Anastasia nodded. "Good luck. I was almost tempted to send in the kitten." Michael and Anastasia laughed, Leif and Malachi were confused and Tom thought it was a joke.

Michael walked out to the RV. He knocked on the door. Charlotte called for him to come in. As soon as he walked in she buried herself into his chest and through hysterical crying said, "Anastasia threatened me! She said she would take our baby and run. She has thousands of family members all over the world and if I don't agree to move into the big house... How can you let her talk to me that way?" Michael pulled her away. "Anastasia and I are not going to kidnap our child. We want all of us to behave like adults and think of this child. Yes, we want you to come and live on the compound so we can all be close. This child will have security and the best of everything. What more could you possibly want?"

Charlotte "I only want what you promised me. For us to get married, I want to be a Reale. I just don't want you to buy me whatever I want. I want access to it all."

Michael was truly shocked. He stumbled back and sat down on the couch. "You planned this?! You knew I had hesitations about us... that my family had hesitations about you. You told me you were on the pill. I had a gut feeling about it. You wanted to get pregnant so I would have to go through with marring you. How could I have been so stupid?"

Charlotte "I love you. I gave up five years for you. I deserve to be a Reale. Everything was fine until you said that you could never leave your family. So that is the deal. You give me what I want or you might never see this baby again."

Michael focused on his child. Michael would never allow any harm to come to either of them. Michael knew that every child needs the love and support of their parents, Azili or De'nola. Michael felt his child. He felt a strong connection already. He blurted out. "So you would marry any Reale, Right?"

Charlotte "Jonathan was my next choice, but he was all over that thief Lucy. Malachi would be my third choice, he is the best looking out of all of you."

Michael burst out laughing, "Malachi? Malachi hates you. I mean, he really hates you. Ever since that night in the hospital, he has been fantasizing of ways to make you miserable, but then he found out you're pregnant. He still hates you, but he loves my child." Michael was still laughing.

Charlotte "Don't laugh at me! Your girlfriend made it very clear that you will never give me a moment of peace." Michael had a flash of irritation. "My wife."

Charlotte "Whatever you call her. I don't care. But she didn't go far enough. I want to be married to a Reale. Period. I'll even go so far as to agree to live on the compound, but I want to build my own house."

Michael "Done. Go to Tennessee and have a great time. Continue to heal. By the time you get back, We will have another wedding to celebrate."

Charlotte "Really? A big one? Not just a courthouse paper. I want a big fancy wedding."

Michael "You got it. But there will be conditions. You and our child will stay close for security reasons. My family will have full access to the child. I will have full access to our child. You, me, and Anastasia, we will all co-parent together"

Charlotte "If I can marry a Reale and have full access to anything I want…then yes. But if you want it written up, then you better pay for my lawyer."

Michael smiled, "The only thing of importance to me, is you and our child. You can have anything." He stood up and gave her a big hug. "I'll see you when you get back." She tried to reach up and kiss him, but he walked out the door and was gone.

Michael walked back into the hotel bar smiling. Anastasia said, "I'm glad your conversation went better than mine." He kissed her. "How would you like to eat chicken wings, drink beer and sing some karaoke?" Anastasia laughed, "Just a few hours ago we fought a war. We almost died…again. I'm exhausted. But maybe one song, But then I'm going to bed, right after that beer." The rest of the night was spent eating, drinking, and singing. Around 5a.m, Anastasia finally asked if they had a room for them for the night. Neither one of them had the energy project home.

Lucy and Jonathan had been exploring the castle the rest of the day. Mark and Pia-Jiun picked a bedroom that had two beds and a small bedroom off the side of it for Geetu. They didn't know how long they would be there, so they relaxed and enjoyed their days with swimming and hiking and getting to know each other. Lucy and Jonathan were very much the newlywed couple. They held hands and worked on linking and rarely left

a room without first giving the other a quick kiss. Pia-Jiun and Mark were
growing closer by the second. Pia-Jiun was in the library most of the day
reading everything she could get her hands on. Mark watched her very
closely and was getting comfortable with his new found role as jungle-gym
for Geetu. They were all very much at peace.

The family was trying to get back to some a semblance of normalcy.
They healed their injured and mourned their dead. Arden and Bina spent
hours in the Thinking Room, Ruth felt they were coming to peace after
Michael ordered that the veil be thinned so any Azili could speak to their
ancestor and they spoke to Amani several times through the flame. Ruth
herself spoke to Se'ighin every chance she could. She had chosen to cross
the veil to be with him, but he convinced her to stay and enjoy her life.
There were many happy surprises coming soon very soon. Everyone could
feel that Michael and Anastasia were content and needed some time alone.
The elders and their families were starting to feel strong enough to start
traveling home. Imay explained to Mr. and Mrs. Vans that the Inn was
destroyed but that Lucy, Jonathan, Mark, Pia-Jiun, and Geetu were all
safe, but had to travel north to get out of the country and would all meet
back at the compound in a few days. The children were all heading back.
Linda felt the intense pull to be reunited with Felipe, and baby Stephanie
was anxious to feel Anastasia again.

The only loose end was who Michael was going to have to order to
marry Charlotte. He linked with Ruth and updated her. Ruth had laughed
so hard that she almost choked on a Haitian treat rhum ball and responded.
"Poor Charlotte. She will never understand. But if it isn't for love, ask Leif."
Michael was confused. He knew that Leif could tolerate her very easily,
but he would never ask someone to risk finding love. "Why would you
think of Leif? What if he finds his bond? That would never be fair for
him." Ruth said, "He already has a bond." Michael asked, "Who?" Ruth
"Christensen dear, From Australia. They have been a family unit for years
and both adore children. They would be brilliant co-parents." Anastasia
communicated into their link. "Perfect!" Anastasia and Michael linked to
Leif all the information. Leif asked that they all meet in Tennessee to talk.

Michael and Anastasia had stayed in the hotel for a few days relaxing and feeling that everything was as it should be. They projected to Christensen and explained everything to him, and then they projected to the RV in Tennessee. Leif and Christensen spoke and agreed with several non-negotiable conditions. Charlotte would have her big wedding and big house and a friend to gossip and shop with, Christensen and Leif would continue to live openly and freely as bonds, and they would be known as equal co-parents. Michael and Anastasia loved the thought that this child would be loved beyond measure. Michael smiled at Leif, "Three loving fathers and two amazing mothers. I could not wish for anything better." Life was almost perfect...

Michael and Anastasia projected back to Uanza. The castle was buzzing with news of the King and Queen returning. Lucy felt how warm the castle was when they were there. Pia-Jiun was ready to see her father again. Abantu arrived. "Well, What a pleasant surprise. Everyone here has settled in nicely." Michael reached over and hugged him. "Thank you my friend. We would have all died without you. How can I ever truly gift you a proper thank you." Abantu thought for a second. "I think having a child conceived here after all this time, is all the gift I need. I'm looking forward to having Azili back home. Uanza has missed you."

Anastasia looked at Lucy and screamed and hugged her tight. "Are you? Congratulations!" Lucy said, "No, I don't think so. How long have we been here?" Jonathan said, "It has been about a month I guess?" Abantu smiled. "Not Lucy. Well, not yet anyways. I heard the wind whispering that the King and Queen had consummated their bond and their coronation here." Michael started to think back. They had started to make love in Anastasia's parent's room, but they projected themselves back. Anastasia yelled. "Me! How? Well, I know how, but how? We started to um...You know...but then we were back at the compound. I never imagined... I mean, after everything that has happened? Can I get pregnant?"

Abantu was laughing, "Oh this is wonderful! This child has duel citizenship so to speak. She is the first child of Uanza in thousands of years. Anastasia broke down in happy tears. "ME!" She grabbed Abantu's neck and squeezed so tight he thought he would loose consciousness. "Thank you! Thank you! Michael, we have been blessed with a girl." Michael smiled, "Any rejection to the name Alexandrea. The defender of all mankind?" Anastasia took a deep breath and sung "Alexandrea... what a perfect name. Our own beautiful Wonder Woman. I do no reject it." Lucy and Pia-Jiun grabbed Anastasia's hands and they danced around the throne room laughing and calling out to the ancestors. The room filled with a light blue mist. The room was warm and loving. Michael now had everything he every wanted in his life. Jonathan would be his rock and Mark would be starting a wonderful adventure as the first family living full time on Uanza soon. He promised Abantu that they would project back daily and eventually make it their full time home and visit Earth often. Any Azili that wanted to come home, they would make it happen soon. They projected Lucy, Jonathan, Pia-Jiun, Mark, Geetu and Pec back to the compound. Ruth explained that Imay was on his way back with Lucy's parents. She introduced Pia-Jiun and Geetu to the family. Geetu had an endless list of questions, and Ruth loved every second. And all was exactly how it was meant to be...again.

Printed in the United States
By Bookmasters

Printed in the United States
By Bookmasters